LEE HUNT

DYNAMICIST

THE DYNAMICIST TRILOGY
BOOK ONE

FIRST EDITION
Dynamicist © 2019 Lee Hunt
Cover art by Jeff Brown
Interior design & typesetting © 2019 Jared Shapiro

Distributed by
Ingram Spark, and IslandBlue Book Printing
P.O.D.

Library and Archives Canada Cataloguing in Publication

Title: Dynamicist / Lee Hunt.
Names: Hunt, Lee, 1968- author.
Description: First Edition. 2019
ISBN 978-1-9990935-0-1 (soft cover); 978-1-9990935-1-8 (Ebook/PDF)

Edited by: John McAllister

eDYNAMICIST

For WSK and the Duke

Chapter One

The Lonely Wizard

When an event of an undeniably quantitative nature occurs, most of the survivors hide from it. I have learned not to.

Of all there was or would be, the calculable was my favorite. I reveled in the clarity of the unequivocal, whatever it might reveal, no matter how far it might take me. Even on the battlefield, I loved to make the quantitative manifest.

My love may seem rather broadly defined, but consider that ideas like good, evil, rage, or melancholy are not a part of what I love, for they are the products of childish simplification and defy uniform definition. Most people shy away from the world of the quantitative and prefer instead to sully events with narratives, coloring the real facts with interpretation and the prejudicial labels of a secretly flexible ethic.

The objective certainty that I love is a thing of true rarity.

The latest period of absolute objectivity ended with the final staccato sheets of lightning and their sequel of sharp convulsions. Armor scored, melted, or pulverized, testifying along with limbs separated, burned, ruined, to what had happened.

What *I* had made happen.

The release of energy could be quantified, the dead could be counted, the damage could be categorized and logged. Although most would react with horror if I tried to explain my reaction, these moments of objective truth, however destructive, were beautiful to me. They taught a clear lesson about the physics of the world and about measurable consequences. These lessons were rare, coldly simple, and uniformly knowable.

I deeply appreciated these incontrovertible things because they coexisted in the world with another reality that was anything but simple, objective, or uniform. The other side of the extremity that had been visited upon the battlefield was how it was *perceived* by human beings, how they felt about it.

For feelings are subjective in every way.

Feelings are affected by experience, by training, by unpredictable unconscious impulse, and by individual nature. They are the inscrutable translation of the objective through the unknowable human mind. What I had done was inarguably measurable, but what it *meant* was uniquely different for each of us left alive.

The dust hung still in the air, in an infinite deadpoint into which no one moved or spoke. I imagined that perhaps the survivors did not want to spoil the perfection of the moment, the absolute unction that had been brought to them all. But it was probably just shock from blood loss, exhaustion from already spent screams or perhaps blown ears that simply couldn't hear the whimpers and sounds of the injured.

Or perhaps the stillness was born of fear that more was coming and the realization that nothing could be done about it.

My stillness was one of satisfaction. I respected what I had done, how effective it had been. I was pleased that my calculation and my instincts had both been correct and that I had reached with effortless efficiency into the empyreal sky, pulling from Elysium exactly what was required. I reveled, still and silently, in being right.

Again.

I noticed that someone had come to stand beside me, and I looked sideways to her. Sir Ameleyn Forteys was breathing hard, sweat and dust streaking her face, her armor dented and grimed. Her eyes, however, were bright with tears or excitement. Her helmet was gone, and her braided hair hung over her near shoulder, clumped with debris. I thoughtlessly reached to pull a clod of dirt out of the braided tangle, but she caught my hand with her supernal reflexes, held it for a moment, and gave my fingers a light squeeze.

Beyond the thoughtless moment, I was not comfortable with the contact, and so I gently removed my hand. Hers had been warm. It was time to return to business.

"Form the lines!" I bellowed, although not to her. I heard scrambling from behind me and, shortly afterward, my orders being repeated up and down across the ragged, chaotic pitch.

I turned back to Sir Forteys. I could not see into her and know how she felt, even though she was the most transparent, direct, and moral person I knew. Her heart was not measurable by acts of heraldry or appeals to the empyreal sky. I could imagine what she felt, I could guess what was in her soul, but I could never know it. There was none of the objectivity or the rationally communicable quantitativeness of physics in the feeling and perception at the heart of the person that she was.

Her experience was hers alone.

I thought that her eyes were bright with excitement, but I did not know. So I had to ask her. "What needs doing, Ameleyn?"

"Sir. The Knights of the First *demand* that they give you their surrender personally."

⓪

In the center of a camp filled with tents, my pavilion stood alone.

I stood alone.

I always had.

I have had few hesitations, regrets, or personal inconsistencies in my life. Most things, whether physical or mental, had come easily to me, and I had almost never second-guessed myself. The only chasm I could not cross was the one separating me from the people around me. And so, unknown to my comrades, friends, and even my enemies, I stood alone. There were others in the huge tent behind me, and still more were arranged just outside the tent's entrance around the fire, around *me*, but in the true sense of experience, I was alone.

In the loneliest sense, my fire burned only for me.

I did not begrudge anyone my fire, tent, or company, but none among them knew what I thought, felt, or would do. Those things were mine. They were separated from the sea of others around me as if they existed in another, incomprehensible dimension, as far removed as the worlds of Elysium beyond the empyreal sky. What gulf is an ocean compared to the unknowable experience of another mind?

Thunder rumbled dully in the dark middle distance beyond our lines, a reminder of the energies unleashed in the preceding battle. I may have been the only one who genuinely enjoyed the sound. Certainly the five prisoners in my pavilion were unlikely to appreciate its portent. The glare of lightning barely reached us through the low, thick clouds, and even when it did survive to us, it was quickly absorbed by the brooding gray veil. And so we sat around our fires, or around the lamps in the tents and pavilions of the war camp, each of us floating alone with our tiny lights in a vast, dark sea. Some there are who say that firelight is comforting because it allows our imagination greater rein. They say that, in the glow of the fire, we see a romanticized version of the world and are reminded of old associations, thoughts from childhood, memories of food, friends, and family. We fill the darkness with what we want or what we fear; it is open to, and draws upon, our unconscious needs and biases.

Tonight the fire was comforting.

We had prevailed decisively in a battle that at first it had seemed we must lose. But now, even in the few moments since the slaughter had ended, time had acted upon the facts to soften some details and present a simpler narrative of events. The terror of battle and possible defeat was receding, and the sense of relief was swelling. I suppose the fire light was comforting, with each of us enjoying its dim, soft shading of the world, content in our ignorance of the desolation or beauty that might exist just outside its limited radius.

I did not feel relief, but I did have feelings.

Did I love the men and women who fought with me?

I did, some of them at least, some of the time.

One, all the time.

I thought that what kept me from them, from her, was an inability to articulate my feelings and an intellectual honesty, a stubborn integrity, that doubted love was possible and therefore could not speak a thing that might be a lie. I hated the dissonance of thinking about it. Uniformity of purpose and action, of thought and feeling, were a huge part of what gave me my power. It was the bulk of me, but this aloneness, or at least my regretful recognition of it, was a weakness that I did not care for. It only came upon me in rare moments of triumph or despair. Such as this one.

I stood to go back into the tent, waving my squire Feydleyn to stay and relax. The others around the fire all granted me a momentary recognition: a nod, a smile. A few of them even stood up. I nodded back as if I was one of them and left.

The maps needed attention, and I needed the comforts of the fire not at all. The table was exactly as I had left it. Sir Forteys, who had been poring over the maps, stood up, her eyebrows raised. The five Knights of Armadale, who had been sitting on benches at the rear of the pavilion, also sprang up despite their injuries. I waved them all down.

"They're divided and pushed against their own mountains." Forteys pointed at the biggest map without regard for the defeated knights within earshot. To her they were out of the war and on their honor. She had found her helmet somewhere and scraped off most of the dirt and debris that had covered her. She didn't look new or shiny, but she had her own upright sparkle. "Another few days like this and the war will be over."

"We can only start wars, Ameleyn." I said softly. If I could not look into her eyes and see what she thought and felt—and I knew her well—how could we know what Armadale would do? I only knew what *I* would do.

She looked up at me, laughing softly. "Well, we can ask." She stared right at me. "Just ask."

I didn't say anything, not sure exactly what she meant and troubled by her direct gaze.

"We can ask for their surrender," she added, still smiling. "We could even take these prisoners on parole to talk to them." Her expression grew more serious. "It could prevent more suffering and needless death."

"Where are they?" barked Marshall Aungr, storming through the entry flap, leaving a smear of dark blood where his stump had soaked through its bandages. Aungr was never an icon of etiquette, but he usually said hello before giving orders or asking questions. He was not at his best.

Aungr had been injured in the morning, and I had taken field command in his absence. And had broken the enemy. But here he was, absent a limb but on his feet, back to take command. His reappearance was abrupt and viscerally disturbing. He brought with him the anger of emotional inertia, an inertia of injury and acute pain.

Were we on the edge of total victory or in the grip of murderous rage? A ridiculous question, as out of place as the Marshall's startling reappearance. But it was less ridiculous than sad. The firelight could not have been comforting to Aungr. For him there would be no muted and softened remembrances of the day, no illusory, happy, relieved world. Just anger, pain, and loss. His pain was real, his experiences were real. But his anger was backward looking, seeking retrograde justice as if present action could erase past injury.

A moment passed while I considered where Aungr's unexpected return would take us. The pavilion was becoming crowded as men from around my fire, including Feydleyn, entered. Several members of Aungr's staff, as well as five other members of his command guard, also entered. Other words must have been spoken outside, other actions must have taken place before Aungr appeared so unexpectedly and suddenly. His righteous indignation had been in full flight before he crossed the threshold of my pavilion.

"To whom do you refer, Lord Aungr?"

The marshal spun, looking beyond me to the five surviving, uninjured Knights of Armadale. His eyes were red and narrowed from pain, his skin a weird and unwholesome marbling of sickly gray and puffy red. Every seething breath he took was evidence of his pain and anger. "Them! Why are *they* still in armor? You wiped out the better part of an army, but you left these few in better shape than most of ours? Why are *they* not hanged?"

One does not kick every dog that barks. It would be a waste of time, and this dog had already been kicked. Yet the truth could not be changed for the sake of his feelings.

"They surrendered."

My calm response seemed to incite him to greater rage. Most of the others in the tent winced at the slowly unfolding argument, guessing that worse was to come. The mood had become ugly. I alone was pleased. Authenticity was to be desired.

"To Hati's Hell with you, wizard, and your fucking cold pronouncements!"

Perhaps not totally desired.

I had always disliked certain curses. "Wizard" was particularly insulting to me. But he was in pain, so I overlooked it. Sir Forteys took a step around the table, moving to come between us. Her face was suddenly red, her expression determined. In contrast, though Feydleyn's hand was on the hilt of his sword, his hair looked wet. A bead of sweat ran down his face, starting from his left temple. The Knights of Armadale were on their feet, watching with alarm.

"Those fuckers" he pointed at the knights, "They stole my arm! Just like they tried to steal this county. Surrender? Honor? You think they have honor? If they had it, we wouldn't have been fighting in the first place, let alone mourning all our lost men." But he looked at his stump as he spoke the last word.

I took another moment to consider where this confrontation might be going and what should be done. He was the marshal and deserved a certain respect. Should I try to defuse the situation? Could it be defused? Unfortunately, it was obvious where this maniac was going. Careful words and diplomacy might soothe him, but it might also conceal his true intentions, might make space for the soothing lies that would allow injustice to be done.

I looked the marshal in the eye, stepped closer to him, and spoke softly. "Your arm is irrelevant."

Despite my soft tone, most of the room heard me. Feydleyn released his sword and hid his face in both hands. Gasps broke out all round. Only Sir Forteys kept silent. She simply looked sad. She always saw to the heart of things, and she knew that what I had said was correct. Whether it was cruel depended on perspective. Better a cruel-seeming truth than comforting lies and an issue obscured.

"Irrelevant! To. Hell. With. You. Wizard." He seemed to reach for his sword, twisting, but the stump could produce no grasping hand.

"You said that already. And yes, your injury is not relevant to the law or justice, or the rules and code of war that we all swore to."

Aungr's body stiffened, veins standing out on his forehead. Two drops of blood fell from the bandages of his stump. He whispered, almost groaning. "Hati take you and your cold heart. Let Skoll feast upon it. Codes? Rules? Thousands of our men lie dead out there. Thousands. You talk like a child who hasn't seen the real world. That's what you are: a child! Look out there! Look here!" He pushed his stump and its blood-soaked bandages at me. His words were starting to slur. "It's easy to talk so high and mighty when you haven't paid. When have you ever paid? I wish Nimrheal were not gone."

There was nothing to say to this, but he was right about one thing; I did feel cold. The gulf between us could never be crossed. But I would change nothing, for I was righteous. I let him play himself out.

It took Aungr a few awkward moments to realize that no rejoinder was forthcoming. Off put, he gestured sharply to the soldiers behind him. "Take the prisoners. Find the injured ones as well." He had to pause, gasping for breath. Two of his soldiers left the tent. "They will be hanged in the morning for their crimes. And you, wizard! *I* will see that you pay! You will find yourself under arrest for insubordination and up on ch—"

I held my hand up to the soldiers and broke into the marshal's rant. "These men have surrendered, along with the other knights at the surgery. Their surrender was to me personally, and their safety is on the honor of this army as a whole, on the honor of each and every soldier of the army as individuals, and lastly, directly on my word. You aren't taking them anywhere. They are not to be subjected to rough justice and execution."

The soldiers hesitated. Sir Forteys, however, did not. She rushed through the tent flap in a blur, gone before I had finished speaking my first sentence. One of Aungr's staff officers was knocked off his feet, brushed aside by her passing. She would look to the injured prisoners.

Aungr turned on his men in a continuation of his apoplexy. "*I am in command here, and I said take the prisoners!*" Blood was streaming from his stump now. "Fubhuck you, flibbert!" He screamed something else, stumbling and spitting, but I couldn't make it out. He had passed beyond making sense.

"That is an illegal order. You are relieved of command."

⫯⫯

Of course I prevailed. The soldiers were afraid of me, were almost as afraid of Sir Forteys. And I was in the right, transparently and objectively. So they did what I said and put Aungr back with the surgeon, under guard, until he recovered his senses. The whole episode had been a farce.

"That was tragic. Heartbreaking. There was nothing left of him by the end. Did you have to break him like that?" Feydleyn was always so earnest. His hair was still soaked from the sweat that had poured out of him during the confrontation.

"He was broken when he walked in."

Feydleyn stared at me like an imploring hound, mute, sad.

I sighed, not enjoying long explanations. "His unfitness had to be made clear." Still, Feydleyn stared at me. "We had to protect the prisoners."

No one breaks *my* word.

"You couldn't have just . . ." Feydleyn gestured with both hands. "Pulled him aside and made him slow down until his reason came back to him?"

"The law, my friend, the law. He had rank. I don't pull *him* aside. It wouldn't be right."

Feydleyn broke his gaze, moving on to some new thought. "The surgeon should never have allowed him out. That didn't need to happen."

Sir Forteys entered the tent, strangely hesitant. This caught my attention, for Ameleyn rarely hesitated about anything. She did, when appropriate, exercise a very wise use of timing that might masquerade as hesitation, but that is not what I saw now. She was troubled.

Seeing her like that even made *me* feel fearful. "What is it, Ameleyn?"

Her hands were clenched around a folded piece of paper. She passed it to me. I did not read it, still looking at her.

A tear rolled down her face. "Your mother is dying." I stared upon that tear for a long moment. It was strange to me that she would cry so. Ameleyn had never met my mother.

Feelings are subjective. Aungr, back with the surgeon, had his rage and pain and probably now his shame. Feydleyn had his regret and his sympathy for almost everyone. The Knights of Armadale had relief. Ameleyn's tears told me she felt sorrow. I imagined that her sorrow was as pure and clear as everything else about her. I wished I could feel what any of them felt, that I could cross the distance between us. But I couldn't measure someone else's feelings. They couldn't be weighed or parsed or experienced. I had only my own immeasurable melancholy.

Alone.

Walk It Down

"**W**HAT WAS THE NAME OF THE LONELY WIZARD'S DOG?"

Hervor's Horn! No! No swearing. Lord Latimer's interest in dogs, fictional or otherwise, seemed ridiculous. But perhaps the question was not silly. The incongruity of it coded a warning that Robert Endicott deciphered quickly. Latimer was not a silly man. The question could simply be oblique to his real purposes. *Slow. Be slow.*

"The Lonely Wizard didn't have a dog." Robert Endicott bore a hole into Latimer's gray eyes, looking for some reaction before continuing. He could not read anything in the man. Not yet. *A patient interviewer. Dog!*

"Not really." Endicott paused. "He was the Lonely Wizard. Lonely and alone. *Made* alone by himself. If he had a dog, he would have killed it too. Adding a dog in the children's version was damaging to the integrity of the story."

"So you value integrity." Latimer did not say it as a challenge. He spoke congenially, without rush or pause, and not as if he lacked interest. No, he spoke like a man who cared, but whose cares were opaque.

Another trick? Should I talk about how honest I am? Too obvious, and not … interesting.

Still, Endicott could not leave it alone. "Without integrity, how do we know what's real? Why tell a story if we compromise the telling of it?"

Latimer did smile this time. Just a little. He leaned back, his richly embroidered cuffs coming off the table with a soft swish as he reached into his satchel and pulled out the knife. He placed it carefully on the table and spun it slowly, exhibiting its long, sharp blade. The clear morning light reflected off the weirdly glass-like metal surface, illuminating the circle of its spinning. A stylized E was embossed on the guard between the quillions.

He has my knife.

"Did you make this, Robert?"

"My grandpa helped me." Endicott spoke carefully, fighting adrenaline. *The real interrogation begins now. Slow. Be slow.*

"It is a very good knife, Robert. It was exceedingly expensive. It is hard and sharp, but even better and more important, it isn't brittle."

"Yes."

"Do you know why it has these properties?"

"Yes."

Lord Latimer paused for a moment, his eyes never leaving Endicott's. He returned his attention to the knife and tapped his right index finger a few times on the hilt, then put it back in his satchel. "How did you like Statics?"

The School of Statics? The school everyone goes to? It was boring!

Endicott knew he could not say that. As he searched for a more politic response, Lord Latimer smiled. "Did it seem a little unexciting? Like the books for it were written a thousand years ago."

Some of them were *written a thousand years ago!*

Making an effort not to blurt out that thought, Endicott instead replied, "Perhaps the program was . . . incurious." He added a smile, pleased with Lord Latimer's apparent attitude and his own success at diplomacy.

"Beaten, I think," the lord said thoughtfully. "Not the sort of thinking that makes shiny, sharp daggers or tall, mechanical grain elevators."

The young man froze, wrongfooted once more. Latimer stared over Endicott's shoulder.

He's looking at the elevator.

"Do you want to wear the blue and yellow of the New School in Vercors? Will your grandpa allow it?"

Dogs and Knives!

Endicott fairly floated down the road to home, the weight of thinking quickly but acting slowly was behind him, and the natural exuberance of youth lent him stride and amplitude. The whole interview process was outside Endicott's experience. At eighteen years of age, most things were outside his experience.

The body was mostly there, but the mind was still far from its final form, and he had dug deep and against the grain in his interview with the duchess's man. Not only had it been demanding work being careful, but it also bothered him more than he expected.

Am I a liar? Is being careful, acting slowly and against instinct, also disingenuous? Does it lack integrity?

He leapt over a mud puddle and laughed at his introspection. He knew he was more than one thing, and not the same thing every day.

How is it a lie if I am not certain who I am yet?

Who knew what he could be tomorrow? Something different. Something better maybe. Probably.

How is it a lie to reach for something better?

"Heydron herself!" he swore as he stepped in another puddle.

I wasn't the only careful one in the interview. Why didn't he ask more questions?

A little anxiety had been evaded or, more realistically, deferred. All in all, Endicott preferred that he be the mysterious one if someone was to play discretion so heavily. The special program was more than a little under-described and over-vague, but Endicott was not complaining. The New School was expensive, and tuition was more than daunting even with the money he had acquired from the sale of his knife. The knife Lord Latimer had somehow bought secondhand. It also puzzled him that he was even among the few selected to interview for the Duchess's Program. Although he knew that no one in his class was definitively more intelligent, Endicott did not always test as well as some. It was so very hard to sit still and patient in statics. It was so very difficult to sit still for all the old knowledge, the old unchallengeable stories, being told by old, slow people, too slowly.

A lot of the girls were frankly better at being in the classroom than him and were easier with the teachers too. But only two other students had been invited for an interview from the surrounding communities, and of them, it looked like only Endicott had received the duchess's special invitation to the New School. It was not that Endicott disliked statics; he enjoyed it much of the time, when he could manage to keep his seat and his patience. The New School would, however, be different. Everything new carried at least some sense of excitement. New knowledge was as unknown, as unstoppable, and as effortlessly elevating as a rising tide. New knowledge even changed. Sometimes the old truths were reevaluated, morphing into something else. New knowledge was a gift, and no one knew what it was until it arrived or what it could mean until sometimes much later. Sure, no one died for the new anymore. Nimrheal would not come for them, riding a bolt of lightning or sliding down a cyclone, but it would still be . . . new. Yes, his acceptance was still a puzzle, but a welcome one. With it would come other changes, new discoveries, new life.

The yard appeared with a jarring, surprising immediacy. The mile and a half had gone by so very quickly. The familiarity of the place abruptly seized him as the coin turned on his buoyant fantasies of the New School and the other side showed him leaving his home behind. The hurt mixed heavily with the excitement of the moment, of the larger world opening so hopefully for him. All the way along the road from town, the mix had been more euphoric than sad, but now, seeing his home, it turned to elegy. These shifting feelings were a familiar kind of fickleness for Endicott, a young man full of contradictions and contrary passions. He knew he had to leave the familiarity of his childhood, but no amount of excitement at future possibility could sublimate the sharp, sad, soulful feeling of leaving home. A tear coursed its way down his face, but he could not tell if it was because he was happy or sad. The feeling was like the adrenaline of fight or flight, so different and yet so much the same. His headlong rush paused, he gazed upon his present and passing world and drank in the sights.

Behind the stone house and green surround sat the workshop, the carriage house, and the smithy. This well-kept world was made of stone, steel, pulleys, wheelbarrows, tools, and several rather large, somewhat decorative, instruments of measurement. The totality of it was more pleasing than messy given the generous, orderly layout and neatly trimmed grass. Endicott weaved a long, slow, sinuous, indulgent route between the prized objects of his home.

He crouched beside the stylized Hati-versus-Heydron bronze weathervane. Heydron was a shield-bearing woman in this incarnation. She was usually female, and always shield-bearing, but woman or not, fierce or not, stood a whole lot shorter than Hati. Endicott worried for Heydron as he always did when passing by. Behind her, a group of children sheltered, turning away from the confrontation that was in the wind. The last lines of Heydron's poem rose unbidden:

"If you mean harm to those I champion

Beware my wrath, for I am Sir Heydron."

The rain gauge had a half inch of water in it, which was no surprise to Endicott's boots, or shock to anyone; it was spring, and rain happened. He ran a finger over Heydron's shield, wishing her success against weather and demons both. She was his favorite.

The last notable object was the prized six-foot, polished stone and copper sundial. The dial's gnomon was a copper rendition of Sir Urieyn crouching with a sword held low and Nimrheal falling upon him from on high, his spear the highest point. The Methueyn Knights seemed to be uniformly overmatched by their demonic adversaries in the battle of the yard. Grandpa's rendering of the demons always looked like men; he eschewed the horns the Steel Castle would have added. It had been so long since anyone had seen Skoll, Hati, or Nimrheal that Endicott supposed his grandpa might well be right and the Steel Castle wrong about what they looked like. Either that or Grandpa was being subtle about some point regarding the real nature of evil. The young man ran his thumb over the sharp edge of Nimrheal's spear before sighing and finally turning towards the workshop where he could see the back end of a carriage suspended and his grandpa taking a long look at some part of the rear axle.

"Back already?" Grandpa asked, still looking at the rear axle. He was the same size and build as Endicott, which was undistinguished at first glance. Both men were of medium height, with a spare, wiry build and longish arms. It was a set of traits common to the Endicotts. Everyone said so. They said that Grandpa looked like Robert's long-dead father, less his beard. It made verifiable sense, for Grandpa also looked a lot like Robert. The resemblance between them was very strong, the only difference being the lack of lines and wrinkles on young Robert Endicott's smooth face.

"What's wrong with it?" Endicott sidled over to get a look at the old carriage. He saw right away that the wheels had no suspension. This one would give a rough ride.

"Shaft's cracked."

"Are we going to tear it out or fix it as it sits?"

Grandpa's eyes narrowed a little. "Might be a little talk over that. Lunch is ready."

No one said anything as they washed up. This stoicism was not unusual but got Endicott thinking.

The house was modest when compared to the yard, the workshop, and the smithy, but it also had its treasures, most notably an always stocked kitchen and ready table. Grandma waddled over and gave Endicott an uncomfortably long hug as soon as they made their way into the house. "You just sit down and eat" she said unnecessarily, oddly teary.

"How did you know I would be accepted?" Endicott hazarded while taking a chair.

Grandma passed the carrots with one hand, wiping an eye with the other. "Finlay dreamed it every night for the last week, just about."

"You heralded it?" Endicott said, turning to Grandpa, who was arranging his plate. The old man's hands were still strong. Endicott could see all the veins jumping out as he separated his peas carefully from his carrots and potatoes. The little bit of ham was distinctly separated from the rest, just the way Grandpa liked it.

"I suppose."

"Did you herald anything else?"

"The elevator might fail sometime soon. The bucket assembly might fall and hurt Ernie or Paul."

Endicott jumped straight up from his chair, jarring the table and making a pea fly off his plate into the centerpiece. "Let's go fix it!"

Grandma laughed. "The elevator can wait until you finish eating. I went to the trouble of making you lunch, and whatever is going to happen can just hold off for a few minutes. *You* can hold off for a few minutes for once." She sighed. "You don't even know what's going to break. Or *if* it's going to break."

"Or who is going to get hurt?" Endicott quipped.

"If," from Grandpa, calmly.

"But you dreamed it every night for a week!"

"Once."

"Okay. But I wish I knew what probabilities that *once* portends," Endicott said, "because Ernie or Paul don't need to get hurt at all."

"*Slow* down, boy. Slow. If you can't properly chew your food, you probably can't help anyone." Grandma was up and pacing between the table and the stove, checking the pots still there. "And don't go talking with your mouth full here or in Vercors. It's the capitol. Those fancy people don't like getting spewed by peas."

I wasn't spewing peas!

Endicott was hunched over his plate, fairly shoveling his lunch down. Whenever Grandma looked at him, he pretended he was not eating so fast. He convinced no one.

"I don't think the duke or duchess are going to be eating with my class, grandma."

"That's too much lip from you, boy! For the sake of whoever it is you're eating with, their opinions of you, this family, and humanity in general, learn to settle down while you eat."

"When do you need to be there, Robert?" Grandpa's question cut across Grandma's harangue.

"Ten days. There's some flexibility."

Grandma jumped back in, still glowering at the young man. "Well, your Uncle Arrayn's going to Nyhmes next week. He can take you and your luggage that far and see you to a carriage. So enjoy what little time you still have to eat with us."

Endicott had just about finished, and mopping up with a crust of bread, he looked at grandma. "Sorry. It was good, Grandma." He sat still for three breaths, a long, meditative time to him, and then turned to Grandpa. "So what exactly did you herald failing?"

"The heraldry isn't what is important here, Robert."

For some reason the ground-down grumble of his grandpa made Endicott pay better attention than a louder, clearer voice would have. "How so?"

"You have to slow down and pay attention. Elevator's new. Lots can go against intention. No heraldry sees everything. Promise me something." His eyes were wide and focused.

"Okay."

"When you think you're done, and you've figured it all out, look at it again. *Stop* and *look*. Nothing new comes without a price or a problem."

∇

Every step made the elevator look higher. Every step brought its shadow closer. At a good four and a half stories, it was the tallest building in the town of Bron and one of the newest as well. Its whitewash was still fresh. Endicott did not float his way back to town like he had seemed to float out that morning after seeing Lord Latimer, but his excitement moved him along at a trot. It was not a pace his grandpa would have called slow, but then again no one needed to get hurt in a building that his family had helped design and build, especially one that had so quickly become so important. It was an imposing structure, too, not just tall, but also wide, taking up a quarter block by itself.

Closest to Endicott was the outgoing loading bay with the overhead shoot for the grain and the carriage pad with an eight-foot clearance underneath. The other side of the building had a raised pad with big sliding side doors for the incoming loads. Line of shuttered windows rose four stories up the sides, with a single lonely window on the final half story. The office shutters were open, and Endicott could see people moving about inside.

Ernie must have seen him coming, because he came limping out of the building to chat, his sagging green cap in his hands. "Hey there, young Robert Endicott, what's the doings this afternoon? I thought you were in to see the duchess's fellow today."

Endicott cooled his heels, smiling at the old man. "I already saw Lord Latimer this morning, Ernie. And guess what? I'm going to the New School! I'm going on a special invitation too, with no fees at all. Who would have thought that?"

Ernie pulled the cap onto his head, its visor protecting his eyes as he looked up at the sky. "I might've thought it, boy. If they'd a had that kind of program ten years ago, I'd a bet your uncle Deryn would have gone too. I would have thought that indeed. Want you some tea? I just brewed up some of the good stuff. Three scoops."

"That sounds pretty good, Ernie."

That sounds like sucking on a copper knight. Three scoops. Heydron herself! Bleck.

"But I need to inspect the elevator chain and assembly before we lose the light."

"The whole leg? Well, we can have some after, I guess. Best not to lose the light when there's doings to be done. Indeed. Glad you came. Your uncles all busy today? Starting to sow the fields?" Ernie turned, his long limp making him slow.

Endicott was conflicted, caught between being polite to old Ernie, whom he couldn't help but like, and running past him—possibly brushing him aside in his hurry—and racing into the elevator. But he had known Ernie from his earliest memories, and natural affection won out over his enthusiasm to charge after the problem at hand. He also knew, and respected, his grandpa's insight that this job should not be done quickly. "I guess so, Ernie. I didn't even see any of them at lunch."

Ernie paused on the first of the steps up to the elevator. "Missing lunch. That doesn't sound like yer uncles at all. Must be busy. Well, let's go inside."

Endicott followed him into the office, from where he could see a few of the locals talking on the main floor. There were no incoming loads or carriages, but the elevator was busy. Endicott could just see past the big cycle and its elevator belt into the loading area where two strapping young women were bagging sacks of grain out of the hopper scale, while Paul stood by on one of the small auger cycles.

"Paul!" Ernie called, "Let Glynis and Mair alone and come on over here and help us for a minute."

Paul got out of the pedal baskets, and after saying something to the girls, made his way over, twisting around the big, belted elevator assembly. Behind Paul, Endicott could just see the taller of the two girls, Glynis, taking over on the cycle. Mair's bright eyes caught his sharply as she bent forward to fill one of the grain sacks. Their locked eyes held each other for an instantaneous eternity before Paul's voice pulled Endicott away. "Hey Robert, I thought you were meeting that fellow from the duchess today." Paul had prominent ears, thin, flat hair, and the lean, lanky build and mischievous eyes of youth.

"Been and done, Paul. I am off to the New School in a week." It was hard to keep the pride out of his voice, so Endicott kept it short. "But my grandpa wanted me to take a look at a few things here, starting with the elevator leg."

"Something wrong, you think?" Paul looked back and up at the buckets and the belt system.

"Nope. Probably not, Paul," Endicott said quickly, thinking he was probably lying, "but you know how he is, cautious and careful, explicit and exact."

"All that in just a few words too." Paul rubbed his hands on his dusty pants. "Right then. What do you want me to do?"

Endicott rubbed his hands together, looking things over. "Jump on the pedals for the leg and start peddling nice and slow. Don't work too hard. In fact slower is better. This will take a while, so don't blow yourself."

"Have you never seen these mighty trunks, Endicott?" Paul patted his skinny legs.

"Ahhh . . . right. As improbably massive as they are, I'm going to inspect the chains, gears, buckets, and well, the whole leg. So go easy and let me look close without whipping everything past me." He glanced back at Ernie, who was still beside him. "Maybe Ernie could grab us a lantern and help out."

Ernie went limping back to the office, calling over his shoulder, "Should we open the upper shutters too?"

"Best do, Ernie."

Paul got himself into the pedal baskets and started pedaling smooth and easy. The chain came off the rounded, many-toothed cassette that his cranks turned and disappeared down out of sight into the pit. Endicott knew that in the pit the chain turned a much, much bigger gear that made up the lower housing for the bucket and chain assembly, which formed the elevator leg. The leg itself was comprised of a belt and chain with four-foot-wide buckets set every three feet all the way to the top and around the top gear four stories up, and then back down. The whole thing weighed tons, and no human legs, be they mighty or skinny like Paul's, could have lifted or rotated the elevator leg without the mechanical advantage from the gearing. As it was, Paul's efforts moved the chain and buckets past Endicott at a nice slow pace for inspecting the assembly as it went by.

The elevator was lightening up, which told Endicott someone was opening the other shutters. But he was barely paying attention. All his focus was on the belt and chain. *What could break the chain?* What indeed? The leg chain was heavy-gauge steel, rounded and well-cast. Still, Paul's cycle was only offset a couple of feet from the leg, and if something failed, the whole thing would come down, and he would probably never come out of the baskets alive.

Better look closer.

Endicott breathed slowly and opened himself to the empyreal sky. He focused intently on the chain. He could see the heat on it and all the tiny irregularities of each link. What had looked perfectly smooth before now showed little breaks, planes, and faults. The links went by more and more slowly, as he bored closer and closer, trying to observe the small signs of metal fatigue that would have to be there if his grandpa's heraldry was true. At some point in the exercise, Ernie showed up with the lantern and held it over Endicott's head, but the extra light did not matter now. Endicott could see the chain down to a microscopic level with or without the external source. All the coarse details of the up-close spoke to him, and in those slow moments in the empyreal sky, his anxiety and need to rush fell away. Looking through that domain changed him, at least for a time, from his youthful, perhaps too changeable, too quick self. In the empyreal sky, he experienced a new depth of objective reality, was immersed in a knowledge that he felt *must* be a piece of the divine. While there, focusing on the reality-within-the-reality of the chain, Endicott was perfectly at peace.

For the chronically too quick young man, time at last fell away and was meaningless.

"You cold, Robert? You should try working the leg." Endicott could just hear Paul's comment, and he let go of the sky and settled back from the leg.

"Can I get that tea now, Ernie?" Endicott was shivering. He felt he should have been sweating from the effort, but it always made him feel cold instead. A few of the hands were looking his way, including the two girls and Paul, but nobody seemed especially intent. An Endicott staring nose to the gears was not unusual to anyone there.

He heard Ernie's shuffle and looked up to reach for the proffered tea. Shlerp. "Thank you, Sir Ernie." He could feel it warming him. The tea was good, better than he thought it would be given Ernie's tendency to over-brew everything, although some of the good taste might have arisen from the calmness Endicott took with him whenever he looked upon the empyreal sky.

"That's the good stuff." Ernie bobbed his head, cap in hands again. "So, see you anything?"

Endicott shook his head, blowing out a big, cool breath. "That chain is never going to break. It is sooo overbuilt." Laughably overbuilt, in fact.

There is no way on the knight's earth that this leg is coming down. Not unless the whole building was burned down.

"That's what we told the duchess's man," Paul quipped, resting on his cycle.

Really? "When was he here?"

"Yesterday." Ernie puffed out his chest. "He was mighty impressed, I can tell you, Robert. Told us this would change the town, and he's right. There's talk that because of this here elevator, we're going to get our own grain exchange office too. Right next door. We can sell that big new grain. Good for the town. Lots of jobs. Paul here won't even have to work the big cycle if all that happens. Or he'll be working it more. One of the two." Ernie hesitated. "So, we done here?"

If. Endicott thought about what Grandpa had said.

Slow. Be slow. I better look at it again. And differently.

"No, gentlemen, we need to look just a little bit more. Paul, would you mind cycling again just like before? That was perfectly done."

Before long, Endicott was covered in wheat dust and coughing from it. He explored the pit, inspecting the big teeth and the ratchet assembly there, and began to work his way up the crawlway beside the leg, following the buckets all the way up. Ernie couldn't follow him up the crawlway, but he kept up his chatter from below.

"That Lord Laughimer fella, he was asking after you and your family. We told him how helpful the Endicotts were and what you all done to help build this elevator. We said how your grandpa makes the best steel hereabouts, even if he doesn't make it too often. How some of it was in this very elevator. I even put in a good word for you, Robert. You think about me at that there New School, because I think I helped make up his mind for him."

That certainly explains a few things. Why bother interviewing when we have Ernie here to spill all the grain?

"Well, thanks Ernie. I'll remember it. Can you come around the back stairs to the top of the big storage bins?"

Endicott stepped out of the crawlway and on to the deck overlooking the four enormous three-story grain bins. The upper gear assembly had been in decent shape. There was even room to bring a twin cycle and perch it up top to drive the leg instead of the current setup down below. Nothing could fall on Paul if that was done. And maybe the girls would be more inclined to run the big cycle if it was set there, especially if the ventilation was opened. A vent with a whirlybird could draw out some of the grain dust and make breathing easier up there. A few things could even be done about the leg itself, mainly by adding a set of additional redundant ratchet mechanisms and a bucket bar. Despite coming up with these ideas, Endicott had yet to find anything that truly bothered him about the elevator, but those bins . . . they were disconcerting. They were worth thinking more about.

At some point during Endicott's inspection of the leg, Mair had come up the back stairs and was in one of the big bins, up to her knees in the grain.

"What are you doing in there, Mair?" Endicott called down.

"Well, it's hello now is it, Mister Endicott? Coming on over to elevator, telling everyone what to do and not even a hello? It's even worse now you're leaving and probably feeling all jumped up. That's right, we all heard already." She had a satisfied look on her face as she tromped around in the grain. "You know what I'm doing here, Mister Fancy School. I'm walking it down. If you weren't so busy, you could come down here and join me."

Endicott's face colored. "That . . . ahh, sounds good, Mair, it does look a little lonely in there, but you know I have my orders from Grandpa. Best stick to task."

"Everyone has a boss. Best you remember that."

It does look a little lonely in there with all that grain. What could go against intention here? The young man let himself think about it.

Mair was right, I did know *what she was doing in the bin.*

Walking down the grain was not uncommon and would be happening in earnest here as spring wore on and they sold out grain for seed. When the sleeve opened to call for grain and the small cycle turned the corresponding augers, grain would come down from whichever bin matched the open sleeve and auger. Sometimes the grain would clump or otherwise jam up, depending on humidity and temperature. Whenever that happened, someone would have to climb into the bin and stomp around to get the grain moving again. It was a new practice that they had to learn for the big new elevator.

Ernie had finally made his way up and followed Endicott's eyes into the bins. "Ernie, do you always send the hands up here by themselves to walk the grain down?"

"I don't just send the girls, Robert." Ernie looked embarrassed. "Usually it's me that comes up here."

"I don't mean it that way, Ernie."

Mair was spry enough that it was difficult to think of her having trouble, but Endicott winced when he imagined old Ernie limping clumsily around one of those bins, knee deep in grain. By itself that image was alarming enough, but it was not nearly as dark a picture as the one he came up with next. Endicott didn't need heraldry to imagine Ernie tripping in the grain, suddenly sinking chest deep in it. He did not want to see Ernie's cap on the top of that bed of grain, but no Ernie. Or worse, maybe just a stiff, straining hand sticking out of the sea of seeds. He returned to Mair, tromping aggressively around the bin in a tight little circle, her blues eyes coming up and occasionally catching his. It suddenly was not so hard to imagine her in trouble too, no matter how young and strong she was. She would not need to trip. All that would be required would be time, chance, and the unsmooth operation of the real world.

Maybe Grandpa heralded something he feared and could imagine from home. Fears found it. Or maybe it was just a dream, and not heraldry at all. But this, this could happen. This will happen, eventually.

"Ernie, we aren't going to walk the grain down by ourselves anymore. Not you, and not the girls either."

Chapter Three

Advice

ROBERT ENDICOTT STOOD ALONE IN A GREEN PASTURE, ON THE EDGE OF A SLOUGH. As he gazed over the still waters, his mind rested upon the boundary between his childhood and the adult he was becoming. As changeable, excitable, and brimming with energy as he was, Endicott took a paradoxical joy in this kind of quiet. He had always felt at peace in such places. He had made some effort to come this way. The location reminded him of something from his childhood, a forgotten moment that he knew was important though he was not sure why. He wondered if he would ever stand by a slough like this again. Would he ever revisit this world that was at once so tranquil and empty seeming, yet so full of small, subtle, varied life? Would he still appreciate it if he returned? Would he notice the low background hum of insects and the shy, intermittent chirps of gophers? There was nothing bigger or noisier in the pasture: no cows, no people today except for him. Endicott breathed it in: openness, the subtle sounds, and the calm. Then his mind moved on. And his feet.

This is like so much of The Lonely Wizard: *crossing an empty landscape on a long journey. Only I had more an image of dull browns from that story.*

Leaving the slough behind, he took a cattle path through a thick section of brush and, coming out of it, started up a rise. The gently bending road was not far beyond.

In two sure steps Endicott was over the wooden fence despite his backpack, then a bound across the grass shoulder and onto the road. It had dried out in the week since he had met Lord Latimer, and the road was puddle-free. There was no incentive or excuse to jump or skip, but there was no one to see, so Endicott took what leaps came to mind.

Ha!

The miles went by quickly, and the road got even better, though no more populated, as he made his way towards the large town of Nyhmes, beyond which lay the capital, Vercors itself. A quick snack of cheese, fresh buns from Grandma, and water kept the young man in good spirits, and soon the verge was marked by thick, untrimmed, old hedges with an occasional rock wall marking the turnoff to some of the farms.

A good week behind, a great week ahead.

Both girls had indeed liked the new cycle setup at the top of the leg assembly and had told Endicott so when he had finished it the day before. Thinking of that, and how clever he was, Endicott failed to register the sound of the big horse-drawn cart coming up fast behind him.

"Get out of the way, you little fucker!"

A quick look over his left shoulder put the charging horses and wagon into perspective, along with the scowling, bearded giant furiously lashing the reins. It was an extra-long six-wheeler with six horses, and from the sound of it, a suspension system partly damping out the bumps in the road. The team was bearing straight for Endicott. He took to his heels with an unmanly yelp, adrenaline fueling an almost instant sprint, but the horses were faster, and the gap was closing quickly. Endicott did not need to look over his shoulder to know they were catching up to him. He could hear the horses breathing, the wagon bouncing, and the laughter of the big bastard driving it.

Quick! Be quick! I must be quick!

He expected to feel hot horse saliva on his head at any moment, then being trampled and run over, probably by all six horses and each of the six wheels, his legs all smashed and twisted at wrong angles, and his head almost detached, tongue sticking out sideways, eyes bulging. Then he saw a chance ahead.

A large oval rock sat next to the hedge. If he could only reach it, he could jump the whole thing. He put his head down and poured it on, willing himself to the rock, his heaving, gasping breaths drowned out by the puffing of the horses.

Endicott bounded once to the rock, once to the top, and once more right over the hedge. He stumbled on landing and bounced and rolled in the field, scratched, dirty, but not dead. He pulled off his backpack and inspected the meagre contents for damage. The remaining piece of bread was reduced to crumbs, but nothing else looked too badly out of order.

By the time he negotiated a less acrobatic second crossing of the hedge, the cart and its murderous driver were gone down the road, around a turn, and out of sight. His first few steps dragged a little, but after a few more, Endicott's bounce came back and down the road he went.

Lucky I'm so quick.

A stand of trees shaded the turn of the road, and Endicott was feeling refreshed and pleased with himself when he saw the carriage pulled over, horses facing out to the road on one of the farm approaches.

That skolve! Does he think he can surprise me twice?

He squared his shoulders and marched right up to the cart and the big bearded fellow in it. "Hi, Uncle Arrayn."

"What took you so long?" Arrayn said, almost angry sounding, lacking any trace of either guilt or humour.

"I was stuck in a hedge. Some reckless bastard tried to run me over with his cart!" Endicott walked around the cart and climbed onto the bench beside his uncle. He set his backpack down by his feet. He was not angry. He did not understand and had never even considered why he failed to get angry over any assault on his person. The emotion just seemed to bypass him.

"Well, it's a good thing I'm here now." His uncle smiled this time. "You should pay attention to what's going on around you. You never know where those reckless types could be."

Endicott wondered, not for the first time, what strange hereditary permutation had led to a man like Arrayn being related to him. He had none of the rawboned look of the rest of the Endicotts. Arrayn was much, much bigger, heavier, more hirsute.

He's more like a big black-haired bear.

"I thought you wouldn't catch up to me in Nyhmes until this evening."

"I thought you knew better than walking when you could ride the whole way," Arrayn growled.

"Apparently . . . not."

"Right. Still too wet to even think about planting in the old east quarter, so I got away early. You can come with me to the grain exchange and get a look at the new triticale. Here. Take the reins." Arrayn pulled out a cigar, a taper, and his spring-loaded flint striker. The flint striker was just a spring and a metal hood with steel and flint built into the hood. He squeezed the spring sharply while holding the taper to it. Once the taper was lit, he juggled the apparatus, managed to get the cigar in his mouth, and used the taper to light the cigar. He took two big puffs, put the striker away, and then blew a big cloud of the cigar smoke directly into Endicott's face.

"Phahh. Always nice travelling with you, Uncle." Endicott coughed, throwing back the reins and waving his hands at the smoke.

"I'm always helpful. Brought your luggage, didn't I? And rode the horses hard to catch up to you so you wouldn't have to worry about it." He blew another cloud of smoke towards Endicott, who shuffled down the bench to the right, putting himself as far out of range as he could.

"Yup. You've always been my hero and guardian. What am I going to do at the New School without you to look after me?"

"Start by not getting into any fights."

"I don't fight with people."

"How about that time with the Heights?" Arrayn pointed his cigar at Endicott balefully.

Endicott's heart pumped harder at the mention of the Heights. That fight was in the past, but an echo of his temper that day still found its way to the present. "I did the right thing."

"The right thing? You think you're righteous? Hervor's horns on your righteous, boy! Empyrean protect us from the righteous. No wonder you're always fighting. Fighting is for stupid people, which you aren't. Remember to use that brain of yours; it works. Try to get along with people and forget about being righteous. Be a little more congenial." Arrayn glowered a moment, looking anything but congenial.

"They were picking on Mair, you know." Endicott said angrily, clenching a fist. *And I'm not always fighting!*

"Mair don't need your help. And she didn't ask for your help. If *you* could make the Heights think twice, Mair wouldn't a had problems whipping them."

Endicott had to laugh at the thought, unclenching his fist. *Maybe she would have whipped them.* "I did make a friend."

Arrayn smiled. "Yes, you did. Eventually. But don't let that be an excuse for borrowing other people's troubles, Robert. No one knows you in the big city. We aren't old blood, old money, or even new money, and not everyone is going to give us the same fair chance they give the nobility. Try walking softly and keeping to your own business."

"That's good advice, Uncle." The cadence of talk with his uncle always seemed to follow a predictable set of steps and cycles, with all-too-familiar family stories, pronouncements, and advice. Endicott would have hated its predictability and intractability except that there was always a safety net. What was that net exactly? Was it love? Acceptance? Or was it just that because there was always another argument around the corner, you knew this person would never leave you?

That's family, all right.

"I know it. Might not be a poem in it, but it's good." They came to a bridge and slowed, taking the crossing at an easy gate. "You're the first Endicott to go to the New School, so we expect you'll do us proud." Arrayn took a big puff of his cigar and neglected to blow it out in Endicott's direction, even though he was looking that way. "Finlay probably didn't say it because he's man of few words, but he *is* proud."

"Grandma isn't a woman of few words, and she told me at breakfast. Grandpa was there, and he didn't deny it, so I think you're both right." Endicott wiped at his eyes. "There's a lot to look forward to at the New School, and I plan to make the most of it."

"You better!" His voice was pretty much always gruff and loud, but he lowered it a little as he continued. "Do you have any idea of what you'll learn?"

There's a question.

"That's really hard to say, Uncle. Glynis' older sister went there, for agriculture, and she loved it. She came back with that new fertilizer idea, which turned out to be worth the tuition and then some. That was before the new grains came out, but she said they had quite a number of programs that are like schools-within-the-school there, all different and specialized. Ernie's son went to the Steel Castle, but that isn't where I'm going. I have no real idea what's with the duchess's special invitation class." He had never even heard of the Duchess's Program before about a year ago.

"Huh. What did that Lord Latimer fellow say about it?"

"Not much. He did say that it was a very small group, and that it would be mostly mathematical."

"Math." Arrayn spit over the left side of the wagon. "What good ever came out of math except more math? Maybe we should have dug deep and paid the tuition so we could send you to one of the useful programs."

"There must be something special about this one. You can't even get in just by paying."

"I didn't know that. Enough money will usually get a person anywhere."

"Yes, so they say." As Endicott thought about it, he felt a rising, almost drunken excitement. "It must be something different, I think."

He gazed down the road, then looked back at his uncle. "We've always done pretty well figuring things out on our own or after getting a hint about how to do them. That stitching engine Uncle Deryn built hardly needed more than just a look at the store model. Deryn didn't even have to go to the school to figure it out. Hardly need a New School for that kind of thing. Once a thing is invented, it's easy to reproduce."

Uncle Arrayn chewed his cigar and said nothing. After a moment, the younger man continued. "We could argue down the value of the New School even further by saying that we already knew how to sew by hand. How important is sewing anyway? Who cares, right?" Endicott gestured grandly, then continued without waiting for a response. "Wrong. Because actually making the invention that first time, that initial act of creation, that's special. It's a gift to everyone who comes after. We've done pretty well borrowing off the inventors. Maybe now we get to learn how to become inventors ourselves. That's what I hope happens at the New School. I bet the duchess's invitation is going to be beyond even that. It is going to be a doorway to the new of the new. Unboundedly new. Unheralded. Maybe we're going to invent something no one can even imagine right now. Maybe we will solve a problem we don't even know we have today."

"No limits, eh, boy?" Arrayn had a cool look on his face.

"Oh, I think we could change the world, uncle."

"Change the world?" He ground out his cigar and fixed Robert with a baleful eye. "For the love of Leylah, leave the whole wide world be." He chuckled gruffly and spat. "There's lots of talk about changing the world, Robert. I'm okay with the world changing. I'm even okay with being a part of that, but good changes don't happen because we're trying to change the world. It takes a special kind of arrogance to say, 'I'm going to change the world.' Who knows enough about the whole wide world that they should take it upon themselves to change the whole thing? Not me and not you. For a person to think they know how the world should be changed . . . No, for a person to think they know *how* to change the world, they have to know a whole lot of other things." He gazed off into the distance as if seeking something far away.

"Things that have nothing to do with them, things that are far away. They have to know about need and cost and sentiment, about unintended consequences, and a whole load of things beyond their control. They even have to know the future. They need to know what's good for other people. What's good for all of 'em. Each of 'em. Trying to change the world is either comprehensively borrowing other people's troubles or universally inflicting your own on them."

By now Endicott's excitement was thoroughly deflated. A little of his temper was coming back too, but he tried to hold this in check. "So why did we build the elevator? Or the stitching engine? Or the sword Grandpa made and the knife I sold? You're saying we shouldn't try to make anything better at all!" He glared at his uncle. "There's probably some things not invented yet that would have kept my mom and dad alive."

Arrayn didn't respond for a long time, and Endicott kept quiet after his outburst. They rode on until the bumps in the road seemed a little smoother. "I don't know what could have been different with your parents, Robert. That's past now and best looked to coolly." He watched Endicott, who watched the road.

"It's terrible they're gone. For you, for all of us." Arrayn tried to catch the younger man's eyes, but Endicott kept his gaze fixed on the road. "Do you want to talk about them?"

Endicott did not answer for a long while. Eventually, he just shook his head, and Arrayn sighed.

"That's okay. Let me try to put it differently. Making something better is good, but try to make *your* world better. Change *your* world, not *the* world. Make things that give the *opportunity* for the world to be better, to be enriched. Just don't set out with the goal of controlling the outcome for everyone, because you can't. No one heralds universally or exhaustively. Keep your ambitions down to earth, boy, that's all I'm saying."

Endicott took a deep breath, settling himself down. The hedges had been replaced by short stone walls now, the farms clustering together as they got closer to Nyhmes. "I just don't think it's wrong to dream about a better world, Uncle."

"Dream of the *opportunity* for a better world, Robert. The *opportunity*. Sorry I pissed on your fire, boy. Keep the fire, just keep it under control. Be cool and calm."

Why does everyone keep saying that to me? "Even when I'm being baited like now?"

Arrayn chuckled. "Especially then. This won't be the last time."

Endicott shook himself. He could see the town of Nyhmes not far off. "Well, why don't I start with this opportunity to learn a little new mathematics, and then we'll see what can be done with it."

Arrayn gave the reins a little flick and moved the horse team along. "You'll do something good there, I don't doubt it. I wish I could go too, Robert. But you've got something I don't have."

"Good sense, meticulous hygiene, a calm nature, and a love for all living things?"

Arrayn cuffed Endicott upside the head, nearly knocking him off the wagon.

Chapter Four.

Futures

R OBERT ENDICOTT AND HIS UNCLE ROLLED INTO NYHMES ON A SMOOTH, NEWLY regraded section of road. The younger man's head swiveled this way and that as he took in how different a real city was from the small, quiet town of Bron he had grown up so close to. An old sign indicated that the stockyards were a half mile north of town, but Endicott could see that the heavy wooden fences were much closer than that and could even hear the lowing of the cows as they rode by.

The town was growing.

Spring was a busy time. A steady stream of traffic on foot, on horseback, and by buggy congested the roads. Arrayn spotted a hitching post and pulled the wagon over to rest and take in the sights for a while. Every kind of dress was on display. Cotton or wool, fancy or plain, fine leather jackets and tooled boots, ladies dressed in either gown and shawl or pants and shirt. A lot of things were similar to what Endicott was used to, but more were different. A lot more of the men and women wore swords in Nyhmes, a few even wore armor, and there were certainly more merchants mixed in with the farmers. The most noticeable difference, Endicott decided, was the grander character of the public buildings.

Nyhmes' Steel Castle was much bigger than Bron's and immediately recognizable by its faux eight-sided geometry, rich detailing, military appearance, and the iconography of the lost Methueyn Knights. Attending church services had never really interested the young man. He preferred his churches empty. All the better to explore them alone, when his fascination with the architecture and symbolism was unaffected by the cant of priests or the uncritical chattering of the congregation.

"Be right back," Endicott said impulsively. He hopped lightly off the wagon and jogged down the wooden sidewalk to take a closer look at the building. Arrayn tied the horses and followed in his own time.

In Endicott's limited experience, a town's Steel Castle was always the most ornate and expensive of the public structures. Nyhmes' church certainly exemplified this. Despite its eight distinct apses, it still required an entrance. The entrance was situated between apses and resembled something like a sword, with the hilt as the door. Despite its name, this Steel Castle was predominantly sandstone, but it had a burnished copper roof, and there were twin ten-foot alcoves with inset steel instead of glass on either side of the second-story level of the hilt's cross-piece. Each steel window had a single sword etched deeply into it, with fine writing on the blades. Around and above the double-arched entrance, the sigils of the eight Methueyn Knights glinted in the sunlight. At the base of the entrance was a motto carved into the stone. It said:

"ALL CHANGE IS EQUALLY DEADLY."

Endicott ignored that pessimism. He was more interested in the aspirational sigils of the knights. Each sigil was etched on a two-foot steel plate of its own. Endicott spotted Heydron's shield first. Writing was etched inside it, saying:

"I heard faint words I could not fully understand.
I crossed the bridge to a place that did not exist.
I cannot ken her face, yet her image persists.
I hoist the aegis but with more than just my hand."

I don't believe in angels. Despite this thought, a rash of goose bumps spread like a wave down Endicott's arms. He blinked wet eyes and moved on to the other plates.

Next to Heydron's shield shone, in order, the blazing sun of Urien, the broken sandal of Sendeyl, the massive sword of Michael, the scroll-on-maul of Darday'l, the dread axe of Volsang, the bursting horn of Hervor, and the crescent moon of Laylah. All the angels-cum-knights of the Methueyn order and the singular ideas their sigils represented. Of all the ways to think of the dead order of Methueyn Knights, as angels, knights, or ideas, the last interpretation resonated most with Endicott. It alone seemed truly beautiful.

Ideas. He sighed, doubting that was what the priests emphasized.

Endicott marveled at the thought of what this church must have cost to build, let alone what it would cost to maintain. *And for what?* Yet his skepticism over the cost of a building to absent angels was belied by his visceral reaction to Heydron, not to mention the observable fact that a great many people were coming and going from the structure. The steady stream of folks seemed to span the whole spectrum of the population, young and old, rich and shabby, strong and infirm.

It must have a use or least satisfy some widely perceived need.

A man in gleaming armor walked out of the church, and Endicott's interest spiked. His contradictory attitude to faith, his internal pose of being above it all, were instantly forgotten by the possibility of actually seeing a knight. "Is that a Deladieyr Knight?"

"Could be," Arrayn grunted. "Why don't you throw a rock at him and find out?"

Finding it difficult to resist the old pattern of their relationship and his own enthusiasm for the subject, Endicott went along with his uncle's game. "Why? Because it'll bounce off him harmlessly if he's a Deladieyr Knight?"

"No," Arrayn's big voice boomed. "You might be able to hurt a Deladieyr, but a Deladieyr won't hurt you just for a rock. Course, it's more likely that instead of being a Deladieyr, he's from some secular order of knights. Then you might have a problem. Or we could go on about our business and leave well enough alone. Stop throwing rocks at every person who catches your eye. I told you not to pick fights, didn't I?"

You're not as funny as you think you are.

Refusing to be baited further, and feeling a little flattened by his uncle's indifference, Endicott returned to the wagon. Arrayn untied the horses, and with a small lurch, they moved carefully back into the stream of traffic. Endicott still watched the sites as they drove slowly along. None of them contained mysterious figures in gleaming armor, but there was certainly more of a cosmopolitan feeling to Nyhmes, largely coming from its people, or rather from the fact that that the people came from everywhere. Here and there in the crowd, Endicott spotted the black wool and leather of Novgoreyl, the iron armor of Armadale, the dark skin and upright, orderly demeanor of what remained of Engevelen.

Why are they all here?

"There it is," Arrayn said, interrupting Endicott's reverie. "We'll go drop off our luggage first, so we can back in the wagon."

The Nyhmes Road Way Inn was a three-story, wooden building with a sitting room on the main floor, a kitchen, and an enormous stable out back. Arrayn had chosen it for the stable, which could easily house his big six-wheel rig. The clientele was usually made up of ranchers and farmers, but this time a road crew was there together with all their wagons and heavy equipment. Endicott smiled at the crowd in the tap room, breathed in the smell of oiled wood, and followed Arrayn up the polished stairs.

Their room was on the top floor, with two decent beds, cool water from the town's aqueduct, a basin and drain, and a fireplace. Once their luggage was all settled, Arrayn was keen to get to the grain exchange, so he and Endicott set off on foot without eating or drinking. Traffic was still busy on the sidewalks as well as on the road, even though the afternoon was wearing down.

The exchange was an enormous square building with walls of gray, fossiliferous limestone inset by lighter sandstone borders at the rounded rectangular entry and the windows. The sidewalk around the building was made of the same limestone as the walls rather than the wood that was common in the rest of the town. A man in expensive blue livery hurried another shabbily dressed man off the sidewalk and away from the exchange. Endicott could see that the shabby man's boots were parting and ragged. A sad, stringy bit of dirty sock showed through the parting of one boot.

Shoes not good enough for the sidewalk?

He looked down at his own dusty but otherwise well-repaired boots. The brief scene made Endicott feel sad and even a little lost. He did not like either feeling but could not think what to do with them, so he returned to his examination of the building itself. At five stories high, it towered over Nyhmes and had been easily visible from the Inn. The limestone walls were sealed with some sort of hardened lacquer, which made even the gray matrix seem bright. The fossils in particular seemed to shine. He stopped along the wall near the entrance and traced a long, remarkable nautiloid fossil with his hand. Endicott had often heard about the magnificence of the Nyhmes Grain Exchange, but he found he was still surprised by its size and design.

It's even more impressive than the Steel Castle.

"What are you doing, Robert?" Arrayn looked up at the sky. "Daylight's burning and we have rows to hoe. Let's go." Despite his impatience, Arrayn paused before the double-wide entrance, fishing around in his jacket pockets. "Watch and learn, boy. Everything that happens here is for a reason." Arrayn went through the process of lighting up another of his big cigars and led the way into the building.

Arrayn was not the only smoker. A thick blue haze of tobacco hung about eight feet above the floor of the enormous marble-floored room. Work tables, desks, and wicket counters clustered around chalkboards displaying prices for wheat, barley, oats, and canola. The counters were grouped in sets of three to five. These, Arrayn told him, belonged to the big purchasing conglomerates. Each conglomerate displayed its own prices on its own boards. Twenty-foot-wide, blue-carpeted stairs led from near the front of the room to offices on the second floor, but few people seemed to be moving between floors. The hubbub from a hundred conversations echoed off the walls. The crowds lined up at the wickets, or milling around nearby, looked to Endicott like small-time farmers with perhaps a few traders of a humbler standing than the more affluent merchants manning the wickets.

A smaller group of what had to be wealthier farmers lounged in high-backed chairs near the back of the room, sipping tea from a table near them. Even from a distance Endicott could see that the tea cups were finely decorated Eschle porcelain, but the farmers were not particularly dressed up. Most were in sturdy leather work boots and jackets. He looked down at his clothes, dusty from the journey and still flecked with bits of grass and hedge bramble from the wagon incident. As discreetly as he could, he picked off the largest bits he could see on himself. He had not forgotten the reception shown to the shabby man on the sidewalk. "It seems a bit . . . fancy here, Uncle."

"It's outright opulent, Robert." Arrayn said, puffing out a big smoke ring and leading them over to the tea. He poured Endicott a cup and picked up a chilled carafe of cream. "Can you believe this?" he said as he poured some of the chilled cream into his own tea.

"How do they keep it so cold?" Endicott traced a line of sweat running down the outside of the carafe.

"Cold room or wizard, either would cost if they put cream out every day. And they've been doing that for more than this past year."

Endicott poured some cream into his own tea and tasted it. *Delicious.* "I'm not denying it's good or that I like it. I would drink it every day if I could. But who pays for it? How is it economic?"

"The grain, Robert. Dress it up all you want, the business is the business, and right now it's the new grain."

The business is grain, and the farmers produce it. "I'm having a little trouble with that, Uncle. The farmers may be the producers, but they aren't rich."

"No?" asked Arrayn with knowing gleam in his eyes, obviously disagreeing.

Endicott's few dim memories of his father told him he was right. "Farmers farm and work and get so dirty sometimes you can't see their skin through the black, and they have sore backs and knees and breathe in grain dust, and cough and cough and then work some more so you only see them in the hours that mushrooms grow."

He remembered the man he had seen outside. "Sometimes their boots fall apart. They don't dance expertly through the kind of finances that pay for chilled cream in late spring, limestone walls, and marble floors. This place is bigger even than the Steel Castle. Farmers don't put up buildings that cost more than even religion can afford!"

Endicott glanced at the farmers sipping their tea and then back at his uncle, who was smiling more broadly now than before. "Aren't they bound to get pushed out or bought out or just plain robbed by the real money people?" Endicott gestured around the room. "Isn't this the start of that?" His rising voice seemed to echo in the expanse of the room, which gave him a start. He realized that he had once again grown excited and spoken more loudly than he intended.

A few of the tea-drinking group of farmers were indeed looking over at him a little sharply. One of them got up and sauntered over. He was middle-aged and a little stooped. "So you like the Exchange, do you?" He extended his hand. There was dirt under his fingernails and Endicott saw that he had the distinctive dark skin and light eyes of old Engevelen.

"I'm Laurent. You must be young Robert Endicott." He nodded to Arrayn and shook his hand. "I'm old friends with Finlay, and I know yer uncle too. I've talked to them both many times."

"I don't remember ever having met you, Laurent." Endicott said, flat-footed and uncertain of the man.

Laurent smiled easily, his bright eyes twinkling. "Well, yer a lot younger than yer uncle or Finlay. You might not remember me, but we met once before when you were quite a bit younger than you are now. I've missed talking to you a few times since then because, as yer grandpa says, you don't sit still so well. You were always up to one thing or another when I've been by."

He paused and looked Endicott up and down. "And because of those itchy feet of yers, you may not fully appreciate that even though we old farmers sure do like to get the doings done, we also like little more than to sit around and talk . . . when we can. And because of that and one other thing, the question of whether *this* is the start of *that* remains to be seen."

"I'm sorry. I didn't mean to be rude. Sometimes I get carried away with a thought." Laurent reminded him of a younger, sharper Ernie, but that feeling of familiarity may only have been the green farmers' cap that Laurent wore. In any case, Endicott found himself liking this stranger.

How the trivial rules us so.

Laurent just chuckled. It was an easy, relaxed, unhurried laugh. "Don't apologize for a little passion. Passion or the truth, either-or, can seem rude if yer not in a like mind for it, Robert." He paused, sipping his tea. "But you ask a good question. This and that can be hard to know. Sometimes all that *this* is and all that *that* will be are not immediately . . . realized. Maybe they cannot be immediately realized, because *that* is not *that* until its season comes ripe."

The two men looked at each other, smiling in a kind of acceptance or recognition. Arrayn blew a big smoke ring up towards the high ceiling but made no other comment. The strangeness of the affable-seeming farmer's dialogue did what newfound mystery usually did to Endicott: it made him curious, and in his curiosity, silent.

Laurent continued, with a wink towards the lad. "Why don't you take a look around now and see for yourself what the doings are here while I catch up with yer uncle. Like I say, we old farmers do like to talk. Then maybe you can come back and explain to me what's happening here and whether *this* is going to be *that*."

"I think you have the advantage of me and my big mouth, Laurent, but sure." Endicott was not certain whether Laurent's suggestion was a challenge, a dismissal, or just an excuse to speak privately with Arrayn. He felt a little embarrassed but decided that going along with the suggestion in good cheer would be apropos. He also found it made him feel better to cooperate in this strange place with people who might have a similar background to his own.

What exactly is going on here?

He soon decided that the answer was: a lot. Every person in the building had their own story, after all, and besides the investment in chilled cream, fancy tea, expensive chalkboards, and the limestone and marble quarried and brought in from parts unknown to Endicott, there was also the fact that everyone here was willingly investing their time by participating in the exchange. *And time and thought are valuable.* Rising to the challenge, hoping there really was a mystery, Endicott found a space amid the action and became still.

Into Endicott's calm space came the realization that he didn't know enough about the place to do much more than speculate. He needed either some additional information or some way of breaking down what was going on around him. *Let's start with how people are the same and how they are different.*

Everyone is the same because, except for the tea drinkers, everyone else is focused on the wickets, the chalkboards, and the prices posted there. Why are some of the farmers so unconcerned?

It was too soon to say, but he felt that it must mean something. Endicott decided to momentarily ignore the loungers, as well as whatever went on in the upper floors. Most of the activity took place around the wickets and the chalkboards. He approached one of the chalkboards. There were prices for every major crop, but the board indicated an odd mark-up for wheat. One entire whole section was labelled *Futures.* Standard Vercors Triticale was going for ten knights a bushel, but the new Title Triticale was selling for eleven copper knights on present price, and thirteen and a half knights in one year. Its two-year futures price was seventeen knights, and its three-year price was twenty.

Someone thinks demand will go up in the next few years.

It was impossible to miss the unsustainability of the prices recorded in the futures section. Or the potential for profit inherent in the trade for something in the future.

Goose bumps broke out on his bare skin.

The future.

To some degree, everyone's efforts in the present had to do with what they thought would happen in the future. People built homes to enjoy in the future, planted crops to harvest and sell at the end of the season—which was in the future—or even went to the New School because they thought that somehow, beyond enjoyment in the now, it would benefit them in the future. It was not wrong, unusual, or inhuman to invest time now for the sake of some imagined future, but here the future was *traded*. The future, as much as the grain, was a commodity. Endicott's thoughts took flight, rising and expanding, full of passion.

What happens when the future becomes a commodity? We manipulate our understanding of the future? We manipulate the future itself? Does our whole view of time change? Do we accelerate the potential for profit?

Endicott had no answers to any of these questions, but he sensed that his initial vision of farmers being pushed out of their farms would turn out to be true. And he wondered who would do the pushing.

Enter the bankers. Enter the heralds.

Endicott felt a powerful temptation to herald the chalkboard himself and observe the future of the futures. He imagined a frenetic, chaotic dance of probabilities and prices. He imagined the rates of change to grow volatile as pressure to predict and profit from changes caused further changes, augmenting the magnitude of future uncertainty and the potential range of prices. He imagined a decoupling of value and product to a new coupling of value and prediction.

Should I look? He hesitated.

I shouldn't.

But why not?

What would happen if he was caught heralding? If they did catch him, would they shake their heads at him in disapproval or offer him a job? Or ask for his advice? *They won't even know.*

It was too simple and easy to be ignored. He turned on his heels and marched with celerity back to the tea service, refilled his cup with the steaming hot liquid, passed by the cream this time, and nodded to Arrayn and Laurent. They were still talking but had found themselves chairs. Endicott strode purposefully back to the chalkboard. Having made his decision, heated with the pride of thoughtless certainty. He bent his eyes onto the chalkboard.

Time to crack the sky.

His experience with heraldry was limited to what Grandpa had shown him, but he knew it involved two simultaneous and seemingly incongruent actions: a taut thrust of mental effort that felt like pushing a window with his eyes, and a relaxed openness to whatever images then came through the window. Grandpa compared it to an old man forcing himself to urinate in the midnight hours. Endicott pushed, then pushed again, careful not to grimace or show he was straining in any way. A trace of sweat trickled down his left temple, even as he began to feel chilled. The chalkboard blurred ever so slightly, and Endicott made what he hoped was the correct adjustment of attention. He needed to relax without losing focus and let the future appear. Suddenly he lost the window. It was gone, slipping through his inexperienced fingers.

The young man heaved the heavy sigh common to young people and the righteous minded at his failed effort. Like both kinds of person, he always expected things to go his way. But unlike many of the former, he was not easily discouraged. He pushed again, harder, straining towards the window to the empyreal sky. The transition came more quickly this time, but again he shifted clumsily and lost it. He shivered. He was truly cold now. Dangerously.

Endicott glanced down at his cup of tea. It was not steaming anymore. A thin veneer of ice crystals glittered on the surface.

One more shot. But different.

I need to be humble.

I need to let it happen.

Endicott paused and recalled the last time he had heralded with Grandpa. He had been relaxed at the forge. It was a place he knew well, a place he had spent countless hours working at, and he was comfortable there. Its heat replaced some of the energy lost in the act of heraldry. The object of prediction—his knife—was something he had wanted keenly to understand better, and he had formed no prior ideas or expectations about it, where it would go, or what would be done with it. The heraldry had been easy.

His grandpa had been there too, quiet and calm, laconically talking him through it, assuring him the sky was there with or without him, that he just needed to let it speak, let it be what it would be, his only task to bear objective witness to it.

Endicott closed his recollection, focusing on the mental and physical sensations of successful heraldry, and began pushing towards the window again. He opened himself once more to the empyreal sky. This time, when the window opened, he let himself watch without losing focus.

The chalkboard flickered once and then grew still. As it stabilized, the people around it began to change. They flickered, altering in appearance, sex, clothes, and position, zipping and fluttering in colorful waves like a deck of cards spilling across a polished table. Sometimes a single person would splash across his vision like the fan of a peacock's tail, flashing across the room and past the chalkboard in a riot of shifting positions, facial expressions, and clothing, all subtly different.

But the board itself did not change.

Here and there an armored figure would even appear before the board: men of Armadale. These imposing figures flashed sporadically in and out of the image space, but they never approached a trade wicket. It was a complex dance of people, clothing, and poses around a perpetual chalkboard dance floor.

Why aren't the futures changing? Nimrheal is gone, and in any case the future always changes.

From Endicott's perspective, the stability of the heralded numbers was an anomaly. Rather than being the volatile mess he had expected, the futures were as solid as the grain elevator they had built, as safe as houses. That did not make sense. The futures should have incredible entropy, an entropy magnified by the power of human greed and interference, but the boards changed less than the peacock fan splashes of even a single person, who each day arrived, acted, and left just a little different even when faced with the identical board.

Nothing stayed the same without some bounding parameter, not even a single person faced with the same data.

Endicott released the heraldry, shuttering the window, shivering. His cup of tea was nearly solid ice now.

"I don't recall seeing an iced tea before." Laurent was standing by his left shoulder, Arrayn by his right.

"You gonna be all right?" Arrayn's rough voice was a low rumble.

"Fine. Just thinking." Endicott lowered his left hand in a gesture that appealed for patience and returned the frozen cup to the back table before rejoining the older men. He stretched out a few kinks and shook out a passing shiver on his way and organized his thoughts. "How often do the futures values change?"

Laurent chuckled. "Not very often, young Robert. Not very often. Aren't allowed to change 'em except according to the rules."

Bounding parameters! "What rules?"

"The Bankers Ban as us farmers call 'em. The Realized Commodities Rules if yer the duke who instituted 'em. Allegedly came about because of none other than the great and ancient Keith Euyn, soon to be one of your professors." Laurent winked. "The great old wizard himself. The story is that he heralded what needed to be done one dark night a couple years back not long after the new wheat got invented."

Endicott shivered again, thinking of the staggering reputation of Keith Euyn during the Tower and Line War. "I thought he died a long time ago."

Laurent raised an eyebrow over a bright blue eye. "You should know these things, young Robert. To be fair, though, Keith Euyn isn't mentioned much of late when folk talk about the New School. Supposed to be retired or some such. But he's there in the background somewhere, and story is he didn't like what he saw looking into the future. Didn't like what he saw coming out of Armadale and didn't like some of the other things people were gonna use the new inventions for."

"So the duke legislated a set of rules based on Euyn's heraldry?" Endicott was trying to put the pieces together, but he felt out of step again.

Arrayn blew a smoke ring towards the young man's face. "Sometimes people listen to their elders, boy."

Endicott waved the smoky air away, his irritation spurring him to go further. "So these rules protect the farmers. They would have to protect land ownership, but it would take more than that to stabilize the futures board. It must have been a big set of rules."

"Saw it, did ya?" Laurent squinted at Robert gamely.

When the jig is up, the jig is up. "I think you know what I did, Laurent." Endicott stared back at the older man.

Laurent relented, carrying on as if nothing had been said. "Well, yer right, Robert. The rules do cover ownership, but they also control how long the futures contracts and prices are in effect for. Foreigners can't do much of anything with the new grain. Can't buy it, and sure can't buy anyone's farm around here. Buying a farm, even when yer allowed to, has a lot of rules about it. They even allow farmers to buy back their land—at the original price!" he paused. "But what really dampens down the changeability of it all are the rules around only trading what you physically own. You have to own a farm, or at least own the grain from a farm, to trade grain."

So that is how a lot of jiggery-pokery is avoided.

Endicott had no sophisticated knowledge of finance, but his heraldry had seen stability even when instinct and reason both told him that stability was far from likely.

And they still have a futures market.

The ownership rule may suppress speculation. But not kill it.

And the prices are still higher in the future. A lot higher.

Another thought flashed through Endicott's mind. "A big grain elevator is a good thing, then." He felt as if the ground was moving under his feet.

"Oh yes, it certainly is." Laurent chuckled. "Lucky timing, isn't it? Yer grandpa started building the Bron elevator *before* the Bankers Ban."

Lucky? Could Grandpa really have heralded that far?

Endicott marveled at the timing and the consequences of it. The connections between the exchange and his own elevator were falling into place, and they made the young man marvel at the foresight and talent of his grandpa in a way he never done before. His grandpa's heraldry was an order of magnitude—no, several orders of magnitude—beyond what Endicott could do. He gazed again at the polished marble floors and the bustling room and took a deep breath, proud of what had been done back at Bron, and prouder of his grandpa.

But Grandpa had not been alone. Clearly a lot of other people, Laurent for one, had been involved. And like Laurent, some of them must have known about Grandpa's talent for heraldry.

There was more to it than just his grandpa's heraldry or maybe, Endicott considered, his good luck. He took another breath and for a moment was able to let go of his own ego and his own imagined place in it all. He began to appreciate that there might be bigger things at work in the grain exchange and the little piece of the puzzle that he had so far seen and heard. The economics of an entire region were changing. Law, industry, and people were changing with them. *Where all the changes will take us is an open question.* How these changes would ultimately affect the duchy, let alone the individual outcomes of particular people, could only be guessed. He remembered the shabby man with the parted boots.

Ah Heydron, not everyone is invited to the ale wagon. Or the table of tea and cream.

Arrayn was smiling a big, ugly smile. Endicott recognized it as self-satisfaction. Laurent was still chuckling, perhaps thinking he could read Endicott's thoughts. "So, Robert, now that you understand a little more of what's happening here, do you think *this* will be *that*? Will we dumb farmers get bilked out of our land?"

This same argument again?

Irritated at having been pulled away from deeper thoughts and reminded of careless comments made—it seemed to him—so long ago, Endicott lost a little of his polite manner. "How would I know?"

Then remembering that he really had jumped in with both feet, and holding on to that humility, he added more softly, "I hope not. Laurent. The future isn't predictable, even to the best heralds. Or so I'm told."

No one said anything to this, so Endicott continued. "The duke's rules are sure to help keep the skolves at bay." He paused and looked over his shoulder at the group of farmers lounging at the back.

Those that are different.

He remembered wondering what had brought everyone to Nyhmes. It was so cosmopolitan compared to Bron, filled with such a variety of people. Even in the grain exchange, people were different, acted differently, maybe had different views of the future. There was a reason for this, many reasons. Something new had been added to the mix. He realized that at Nyhmes he had found the first intersection of the farming he knew with the commerce he did not. With that thought, he relaxed, feeling like he had brought something under control.

"Or at least that's what you and your friends seem to think." He clapped Laurent on the shoulder. "Let's have some more of that tea while the cream's still cold."

As he sat comfortably in one of the big chairs at the back, sipping his tea, Endicott's mood shifted again. He felt confident and relaxed. The duke's new rules *were* a good thing.

A future unmanipulated.

All was well in the world, at least for the moment. He doubted he would see the grain exchange again for a long while or even think about grain, elevators, farms, or relatives and their strangely erudite friends once he started school. For now, he only wanted to enjoy this moment. He could accept that the new grain-based prosperity would be what it would be. However well that might turn out for his family and friends back home, it would all be behind him once he arrived at the New School.

Chapter Five

The Battle of Nyhmes

VERCORS CITY WAS BUSY, LOUD, AND CHAOTIC, BUT ENDICOTT HAD A TRICK UP HIS sleeve to manage the commotion and his feelings of otherness.

When in a strange and busy place, find one moment of peace.

Some carried their peace or their certitude with them, like the Lonely Wizard. People like him were the same wherever they went, peaceful or not. Endicott too would find his own peace. Leaving the coach, he hoisted his luggage manfully and set out for Cardinal Square and the fountain he knew he would find at its center. The titanic figure of Hervor stood there, blowing his horn. Water cascaded from the horn, keeping the large pool in constant, swirling motion. He remembered something he had heard at Nyhmes.

"Have you paid?" What did that mean?

Not everything he observed in the world made sense to Endicott, and he tended to worry over unexplained moments, feelings, and people. The fountain was comforting in many ways after the strange people he had encountered in Nyhmes. On one level, it was a monument to the great Methueyn Knight, or angel, Hervor. The attachment to knights and angels, dead or gone, made little rational sense to Endicott, but he invariably had a visceral reaction to the stories in which they appeared. Religion and myth, both or either, were buried deep. Their effects could manifest unpredictably.

On another level, the fountain was simply an impressive engineering feat. He knew that water was fed by aqueduct through a system of catchment vessels and basins and pumped to fountains throughout the city. It impressed him that the duchy valued access to water so highly. He could only imagine what life would be like in such a large city if water were not so well managed.

He smiled to himself. The fountain was also comforting simply because the cool water soothed his bruised knuckles and sweaty feet. Four days had been a long time to be cooped up in a coach from Nyhmes to Vercors. There was still no shortage of mysteries bouncing around in his head, but as he enjoyed the fountain's freshness, Endicott began to relax.

"Well, we've got your bags now, boy. What are you gonna give us to get them back?"

Endicott whirled his head away from contemplating the cool waters to find two young women standing by his luggage. They could hardly have looked more different. One was enormously tall, with long, wild blond hair and calf-high, brown leather boots that went nowhere near as high as the mid-thigh hem on her short blue skirt. Her nose was just a touch too big, and more than a touch bent, but there was no doubt in Endicott's mind that she was beautiful. She also wore the most delightfully evil grin as she spoke.

The other girl appeared short at first, although in reality she was of average height. The first girl's unusual size skewed Endicott's initial perception of the second girl. She was thin and dark-haired, with the distinctively dark skin and light eyes—green, he noted with surprise—of the old Engevelen nobility. Her expression, unlike her giant friend's, was unreadable. She was dressed in a divided skirt and wore a tartan scarf of blue and yellow. Her ebony skin was flawlessly smooth, like a painting that had been smoothed gently by the artist, so perfect it was as if Endicott was seeing her in a dream. Both girls were around his own age. Endicott tried to bury the instant attraction he felt for them.

I must be smart.

"You," Endicott pointed at the giant, "are from Armadale." He did not move to take his feet out of the water or reach for his socks and boots.

She put one booted foot down on his big case. "My mam was. What of it?"

Endicott shrugged, trying not to stare at her long leg, profiled so smoothly and so muscularly above the boot. "I am told the people of Armadale value honor above all else. I wouldn't take one for a thief."

"Maybe I've fallen on hard times." She grinned and looked even more evil as she spoke.

"I don't think so."

"Maybe honor doesn't mean what you think it does."

"I know what it means." Endicott kept his voice cool, careful not to allow any trace of emotion to show.

"You vex me, boy. It's not always simple! Besides, now that I'm a citizen of Vercors, I've left all of Armadale behind me. And let's not forget my friend here. She obviously isn't from Armadale." She pointed a thumb at her silent, scowling friend. "She'll steal your bags." She pointed her thumb at herself. "I'll defend her honor."

Endicott scratched his chin and looked them over slowly. "It's just that you don't look much like thieves."

"Looks can be deceiving. We are simply the trickiest of them." This, finally, from the darker haired girl. Her voice was cultured and mellifluous, exactly as one might expect from Engevelen nobility. Endicott was intensely curious. She was even more of a puzzle than her tall companion.

They were both pieces of a larger puzzle, one that did not fit together . . . yet. He looked them over more closely, noting the dark one's tartan scarf.

"Ya! That's the point, stupe. We don't look like thieves so we can trick you," added the blonde more coarsely, her mouth wide with self-satisfied pleasure.

"I'll tell you what, ladies." Endicott rotated, pulling his feet out of the pool and facing the two girls. "I believe you are indeed sly, and I'll pay you something for your fierce protection of my goods. In fact, I'll pay you to haul my bags to where I am going."

"What will you give us?" The blonde leaned over her bent knee, peering hard at Endicott, who maintained his casual demeanor.

"I was thinking of telling you a story."

Their names, they revealed, were Koria Valcourt and Eloise Kyre, Koria being the shorter, dark-haired one. They conspired for a few moments, giving Endicott time to dry and organize himself without appearing flustered. They looked back at him darkly a few times before finally breaking their huddle.

Koria gave Endicott an appraising look. "What kind of story?"

THERE IS A TRAJECTORY THROUGH EVENTS THAT- FOLLOWED FROM START TO CONCLUSION- DEFINES the narrative of what happens. It is a personal trajectory, although not necessarily entirely unique. It is the chosen interpretation—or fated one, depending on whether you believe you control your own mind—that we apply to the facts. Its bias is made up of religion and philosophy, experience, culture, and, above all, the nature of the interpreter. I am going to tell you about my visit to Aeres Angelicus's business and the strange thing that happened

there. I won't just tell you the facts. I can't. Who could? We pick and choose the pieces we care about, forming a conscious—or unconscious—narrative.

I think that this narrative would seem, if not boring, at best a little mundane to most people. But I think it will mean something to you two. In any case, you'll let me know if it was worth your time by either helping me to carry my baggage or not.

"Knights alive! Decide if you're a storyteller or a pedant. Get on with it!" Acting against her tone and words, Eloise reclined her gigantic form against the edge of the fountain.

Koria found some shade beside her and added, leaning back, "I can tell you've read *The Lonely Wizard* a few times. It has gotten into your head—"

Eloise jumped in. "You aren't the Lonely Wizard, Robert!"

Koria laughed softly. "And just because you admit to some bias in your telling doesn't make you more believable."

"That's right," Eloise added. "No lying!"

Both girls laughed in a way that felt both superior and evil, informing Endicott that he had a big row to hoe.

As I mentioned, my Uncle Arrayn and I were in Nyhmes doing some family business before I caught the stagecoach that would eventually bring me here. For the New School. Now, my uncle is a big, heavy-set, grumpy man. Nothing like me. For all that, he was enjoying showing me the ropes in Nyhmes, educating me on the new business of farming, a thing that you know has changed a lot over the last few years. The final stop we made, the really important one, was at Aeres Angelicus's registered seed store.

Despite its name, it is more than one building. Several squat storage edifices, in fact, all in the limestone so prevalent in Nyhmes, plus one beautiful oak house, which is for trading. The whole complex is in a compound with a wide, gated entry to allow for loading and unloading.

Arrayn and I were just there to talk that first day, so we were on foot. The gate was iron, wide enough for two horse teams to go through side by each. A few flecks of rust on the gate told me it wasn't built yesterday, nor by my grandpa, who would have built it so it couldn't rust. But it was stout enough, and ornate enough to have the name Angelicus wrought fancifully on the high arch overhead. There was quite a bit of traffic through the gate. Wagons came and went, and people on foot passed through as well. A large group was also gathered outside the gates, fiddling about with some wooden signs. I didn't take much notice of them as we went in except to observe that they seemed to be dressed in an unusual variety of clothes for the trade and were absent the green caps of the farmers I knew.

Uncle Arrayn practically flew through the gates and headed straight to the big oak trading house, not bothering to look at the small crowd forming outside the gate. I followed along, examining the squat grain storage buildings and comparing them to our much taller elevator at home. The choice of limestone made sense to me. Limestone would not burn, but the cost seemed fat. I wondered what assumptions were made when it came to cost control in Nyhmes and why everyone in town seemed to assume the same things. Grandpa always said cost was a controllable factor, but I didn't see much control at all there.

"—And after much consideration, that's the offer from my patron, Lord Glynnis, in its *fullity.*"

Fullity? *I thought.* Futility? Fool? Who talks like that? Obviously, a man of pretense. *I guess I had missed a few things while I had followed Arrayn, lost in my thoughts over strange building standards and their costs. I pieced together a retrospective of our route into the building, into the large, crowded front room, past the numerous lines connecting client and agent, and then down a longish hallway to the double doorway that Arrayn and I currently darkened. We stood on the threshold, watching a man of contrived, near-comical punctiliousness in the middle or perhaps the end of his negotiations with a woman who I assumed must be Aeres Angelicus.*

Aeres was a tall, dark-skinned woman of straight back and wise expression. She had those crinkle lines around her eyes that came from a lifetime of skeptical expressions. She was of a height with the fussy-looking man, but seemed taller because, well, she didn't stoop herself with airs. She was strong, hard, and gorgeous in every way my brain could perceive in those sharp first seconds of seeing her.

Aeres laid out the papers that I assume the man had handed her and was taking her time looking them over. She maintained a straight-backed posture as she read and ticked off lines with a stylish feather pen as she went through the document. The gentleman opposite her struck a pose of beneficent patience, but he couldn't pull it off consistently. Soon enough—and we had only been at the door a moment—he started shifting around, rubbing at his eyes and scratching at his scalp. I swear his hand twice jerked abortively as he nearly scratched his groin, but each time he caught himself nervously before recrossing the median of his waist and good manners.

"Well? Will you sign? You will see no better price for this . . . small, nascent, little enterprise. You should sign while you are so fortunate to have such a good offer." *The man just could not wait.*

Aeres speared him with her dark eyes, holding his gaze for a moment to dramatic effect. I wasn't quite sure who was meant to be the benefactor of her dramatic timing. Possibly us, possibly her, definitely not him. Finally she spoke.

"No."

He couldn't seem to believe her response. He spasmed, unable to speak.

"Ah! My next appointment." She gestured sharply at the door. That she had noted our presence earlier there was no doubt. Now she used it to her purpose. "You can leave now, Terwynn."

Terwynn's head jerked towards us. Apparently we had snuck up on him with little cat feet. Especially big Uncle Arrayn, who stalked nice and quiet like a bull in a thunderstorm and breathed nice and quiet through his mouth like the gusty west wind. Some people live in the little bubble of their own world, their own concerns, and do not see others at all until forced to, and even then only as objects or obstacles. Terwynn might have been one of that type. He snapped his long neck back to Aeres without acknowledging us. Of course we said nothing either. Why interrupt an unpaid entertainment?

"But what should I tell milord about the offer?"

Aeres Angelicus rolled and tied the papers before forcibly putting them in one of Terwynn's hands. His hat went into the other, barely resisting, hand. Without further ceremony, she took him by his hat elbow and started walking him towards the door and us.

"Tell him that the offer is weak. And in purely legal terms, tell him that I am not negotiating with him." We stepped back as she pushed the spluttering man through the doorway.

Teetering on his way out, hat still in hand, Terwynn protested, "But Lord Glynnis wants to purchase your business!"

"That and a copper knight can buy you a beer."

Terwynn drew himself up, attempting to puff out his hollow chest. "I said, Lord Glynnis wants—"

"I heard you the first time." Aeres had no problem interrupting him. "And I didn't care on either occasion. Why should I entertain a weak offer? Glynnis's desires are not mine, nor will they be. Good day, Terwynn."

Aeres Angelicus turned her put-upon expression to one of better welcome, practically beaming at Uncle Arrayn. "Arrayn Endicott, elevator baron of Bron! Welcome." She gestured the big man into the room, and I happily followed.

Terwynn blustered outside the door, but Aeres was shaking Arrayn's big paw with two of her own and was so clearly ignoring him that Terwynn had little to do but leave. I watched him go, recognizing the voice of outrage in his stiff gate, and missed most of the introductions.

"—and who is the lad with you? A close relative, surely. He looks like Deryn or Finlay." I turned to find Aeres looking right into me, dark eyes evaluating.

Everyone on this trip had seemed to get the advantage of me, but I tried for a game recovery. "You have a good eye, Mrs. Angelicus. Those are my uncle and grandpa." I reached out to shake her hand, but she took me in for a strong-armed hug. Nice. There was nowhere better to go from there, so I didn't. What? I was simply being nice. Hugs are good.

"Meycal's boy!" Aeres practically cooed. She was soft and beautiful and deep, and nothing like how she had been with the Terwynn fellow. "You do look just like him. I am Aeres. Call me Aeres."

"He's going to get all soft if you mother him too much, Aeres." Arrayn pulled me back out of her reach by my neck, I thought a bit jealously and miserly.

"Well—" It seemed like Aeres was going to say something back to Arrayn about this but changed her mind. She winked at me and then took a half step back.

"You did a wonderful job finishing the new trading office." Arrayn vaguely gestured around. "Looks great."

"The only way to get the doings done are to get to it." Aeres's confidence owned the colloquialism.

"No one doubts you paid the price of hard work."

"You can say it again, if you like, Arrayn."

"Everyone says it."

"They had better. Do you know what was the hardest? These oak panels—" And a lot more in that vein.

I watched the two of them exchange their little comments on the compound, its build-ings, and recent history, mildly enjoying the entertainment. I found, as I listened, that I preferred when others did the entertaining than myself. That Aeres Angelicus had built an impressive business was clear. That Uncle Arrayn wanted her to know he was also impressed was even more evident. It could have been a sign of friendship or simply of flattery. It was likely some of both, and in this case the prelude to negotiation.

Aeres moved things along to the next step. "Have you seen any merchant pressure out Bron way to purchase your elevator?"

Arrayn shook his head. "We're a bit further out. So it hasn't happened yet."

Aeres laughed briefly and mirthlessly. "It'll happen sooner or later. And when it does, old Finlay isn't likely to be of good cheer about the bother."

That didn't sound right to me. "Don't the Realized Commodities Rules help you, Aeres?"

Aeres's skeptical squint was endearing when softened with the hint of a smile. "No, they do not, young Robert. They actually make it worse. Those late-to-the-game old-money types like Lord Glynnis can't very well buy up all the farms or manipulate the prices. The Banker Ban takes care of that. But it puts more pressure on other owners of grain, which we are here, and which your family and others are in Bron. Our storage can be bought up without the buy-back provisions, and the centralized wealth it represents is coveted by the late adopters. Grain is money, you know." She winked at me again. "You'll see soon enough."

"No, he won't, Aeres." I couldn't tell if Arrayn was being protective or proud, but for a moment he moved just a little into the space between Aeres and me. "Robert here has been invited to some special program at the New School. The Duchess's Program. He won't be bothered by all this at all."

Aeres eyebrows shot up. "Duchess's Program? I heard they ran one of those a couple of years ago." She paused, remembering or trying to remember something. "Well, congratulations, Robert. If I was the duchess, I'd have you doing all kind of things."

I did not blush. "What kinds of things?"

Aeres sat on the edge of her desk, long legs relaxed as she leaned back slightly and looked at me through long, dark lashes. "Designing bigger elevators for one thing. That's the business of the day, but your grandpa, and sometimes even your dad, got involved in quite an eclectic collection of projects. Finlay made this frictionless pump that still pushes most of the water here in town. He installed a bigger one in the central district of Vercors City. Not too many people know how it works, and fewer still remember it was him that did the work, Finlay being so quiet, but it is a thing that still gets everyone arguing. In my experience, the things that get people arguing are worth their trouble."

That seemed a bit elliptical to me. Once more I found I was in over my head. I had never heard of the pumps. Nothing is frictionless, not even old memories. And she might have been mixing my dad up with Uncle Deryn. I knew my dad more from farming than invention, but then again, I didn't know him very well at all, being that he died so long ago. Mostly I remember a vague image of a blackened face from the long days in the field.

"Maybe," grunted Arrayn. "I prefer to avoid trouble myself. Maybe we should talk about your elevator proposal then, Aeres."

Aeres gave Arrayn a funny look. Just then we heard the rapid patter of running boots getting louder and closer. A burly young man in the gloves, boots, and overalls of a work hand stopped in the big doorway.

"Mrs. Angelicus!" He was breathing hard. "Those form, I mean fomenters, have come back and are blocking the gate."

I didn't know what a fomenter was, but the three of us were following the hand out before I could ask, so I knew that I would soon find out. Without hesitation, Aeres picked up a heavy-looking cane of dark wood from a basket near her desk. Arrayn picked up another. I attempted to follow suit and wrapped my hand around the polished handle of what turned out to be an elegant umbrella. I had heard of umbrellas before but never owned one. Usually I just got rained on. This one had what looked like elements of a knightly pattern on its tan fabric. I was curious to see the whole pattern but refrained from opening the umbrella for fear of getting it caught in the hallway on the way out. Twirling my fearsome, furled weapon, I hurried to keep up.

There was quite a noisy commotion near the iron gates. As far as I could tell, two crowds had met there, and a kind of rolling growl was coming off them, as if the two small mobs combined to give voice to a single creature of noisy unreason. As we rushed across the yard past the storage bins, past wagons and horse teams, the situation resolved itself audibly and visually. But not more reasonably.

For the moment, the confrontation was limited to yelling and gesturing. The two groups used the line of the gates as their pitch. On the near side were Aeres's hands, as well as a few older, better-dressed workmen I took to be their foremen, and a scattering of very well-dressed individuals—both men and women—who must have come from the trading house. On the other side was a different, more motley group. None were dressed in the heavy, durable clothes of farmers or workmen, and quite a few of them had a rough look, as if they hadn't been eating enough or maybe had been drinking more than enough. Their faces and necks were red, the veins standing out as they shouted across the line. A handful of the fomenters were very well dressed—one even had a top hat—and looked like professionals. They must have left their high-paying jobs to come here. It was the only thing I could think of that made sense. The alternative was that this was their job, but that was ridiculous. I had never heard of fomenting as a profession. It has no direct connection to producing anything of value, but then I suppose I still haven't seen much of the world.

I felt excited. Surely I would learn something here, for I just as surely had no idea why these people had come or why they seemed so angry.

"Did you earn it!" one well-dressed fomenter shouted.

"Did you pay the price?" Another one hurled this question, which to me was entirely baffling if vaguely familiar. I couldn't quite place where I had heard the language before. Why was everyone yelling about cost and price? Was this a business dispute?

I saw that the fomenters had a few signs. One had these words written on it: "Did you pay the Empyrean for that grain!" The punctuation betrayed the lack of any desire for an answer.

Since grain was not the province or business of heaven, I wondered if there existed some, to me unknown and sinister, company called the Empyrean. Or were the fomenters confused about the relative and orthogonal jurisdictions of religion and commerce.

Another more lyrical sign read:

THE BOOK OF NATURE
DOES NOT ITS NATURE
CHANGE.

Was that from the Steel Castle? It sounded vaguely familiar too. As we crossed the remaining distance between us and the roiling crowds, I nodded my head in satisfaction. I well and truly had no skolving clue as to what was going on.

Aeres stepped through her people, who parted for her as well as for Arrayn and me flanking her, and came to a stop almost exactly on the imaginary line that ran under the arch of her gate. She held her left arm up. In her right, she still held her dark cane.

"What do you want now?"

The well-dressed fomenter answered with "Pay the price!"

"I have paid," she responded clearly, with a statesman-like poise. She was very upright, like Koria here.

"Who did you pay!" he shouted, not really asking.

Aeres was incredulous. "Do you think I owe you something?"

"The Empyrean!" he shouted, and turned to the crowd, raising one arm in a rousing gesture. "She never paid the Empyrean!"

I was now becoming a little more certain that there was no unknown and sinister company called the Empyrean and that these were certainly not the agents of any such entity. Then I heard another voice.

"Pay Nimrheal!"

Pay Nimrheal? That caught my attention. This shout was almost lost among the chorus of "Pay the Empyrean" shouts that rose at the same time, but it was strange enough that I picked it up and tracked it to a particularly grubby-looking man at the far corner of the fomenter mob. He was of average height but slouched shorter.

Matted brown hair, a short, scraggly beard, and a veiny, bulging red nose completed the picture of debasement. His left shoe had burst open. When I saw the stringy bit of cloth hanging out of the shoe like a sad and dirty tongue, I realized why the man was familiar.

Recognition reverberated through me.

I gathered myself to cross the line and go talk to him.

But Aeres's clear voice rose up and held me back. "These buildings didn't just appear out of nowhere. No building that I ever heard of just popped out of Elysium all built by angels for anyone. No! I built this business. I had a dream, and I put the work into it."

"Pay the price, bitch!" This witty, charitable remark came from somewhere further back in the crowd, from a homely and bitter-looking man.

I assumed Aeres had heard worse and wouldn't be deterred. I was right. She fired back without a pause, "What did you ever build that gives you license to tear down my house? And when you did build something, was I there kicking it and insulting you?"

For once there was no quick rejoinder. Aeres held her moment a few seconds longer. Then she answered her own question. "No, I wasn't. I know what it is to put effort into the world, and I believe that, if you do something, the doings themselves earn it."

The mob kept quiet for another moment, but then the well-dressed man started to chant "Pay the price! Pay the price!" The mob took it up. By now I had counted thirty-two of them against seventeen of us, and the chant was deafening so close.

I noticed some furtive movement in the crowd. Small bags were being passed about as the chant continued, "Pay the price! Pay the price!"

What is in those bags, *I wondered, with rising concern.*

Fear gripped me for the first time. Or was it anger? Either way, I gripped my umbrella tighter and rolled the handle around, feeling for the button on it. Aeres' people were outnumbered, but quite a few of them held shovels, rakes, or other tools. One lady from the trading house had a long feather pen in her hand.

This could get ugly, depending on what's in those bags, *I thought. No one seemed to have noticed them except me.*

Abruptly the fomenters reached into their bags and flung something out towards us. I reacted instantly, pressing the button, and opening the umbrella, holding it as a shield in front of Aeres.

"Aha!" I said, manfully.

A veritable storm of tiny objects sprayed across the pitch at us, deflecting off the umbrella—which I now realized was a beautiful print of Heydron holding a shield against Hati, how apropos—and flying in every direction.

I shielded Aeres Angelicus from the maelstrom of tiny objects, from the small seeds of grain that the fomenters hurled at us. I was a hero! I was an angel, a Methueyn Knight, the deflecting seeds forming my corona, my halo. Wait, seeds? I couldn't believe it at first. Seeds? The umbrella dipped slightly as I started to laugh.

Aeres Angelicus also laughed and even gave me a gratified smile, but then she frowned. She turned to one side, stooped down, and picked up one of the tiny seeds. As she held it up for examination, her eyes widened. The seed she held was not the new breed that was currently at the center of the futures market and that she both stored and traded. It was an older, much smaller grain.

"These are standard triticale!"

Aeres Angelicus is a beautiful woman, and a canny woman, but now I saw that she could also be a scary woman. Her transformative power stunned me. When she turned back to her employees, her angelic face shone with an awful mix of keen rage and angry delight.

"Our property is under attack! This is an assault on our pedigree!" she shouted at her people in a tremendous voice. Was the Steel Castle right? Was all change deadly? Even something as small as a variation in grain kernels?

Aeres then brushed my umbrella aside and stepped forward, cane raised high. In one stroke, she exploded the bag out of the well-dressed man's hand and walloped him across the hip, dropping him to the ground.

The battle was joined.

"This is Registered Seed, fucker!" she boomed. "Get your shitticale out of here!" And then she gave him a couple of extra muscular and meaty whacks while he was down. Defending the provenance and pedigree of her valuable product was demonstrably a passion for Aeres.

Her people immediately threw themselves into the fray. Bags of seeds flew everywhere as canes, rakes, hoes, and shovels connected with bags, hands, heads, and balls.

I wondered where the feather pen was going to end up. Perhaps it would prove mightiest of the tools.

A man with a purple top hat turned to flee but was tripped up by a long, stiff rake, then subsequently raked back into range for further grooming. His top hat rolled away unharmed, but it was the only part of him that managed to do so.

Another of the fomenters ran daringly towards the storehouses, mongrel seeds spilling from his clenched fists. If he manages to mix old grain with new, it could mean disaster for Aeres's business. *The man brayed like a mule as he sprinted, weaving from side to side to avoid interception until a long-handled shovel wielded by one of the storehouse hands caught him across the shins. He cartwheeled across the yard, crumpling into a wagon wheel. His neck twisted horrifically, and his body collapsed, unmoving.*

I turned to see Uncle Arrayn laying about him with his cane and his fists, apparently enjoying himself, yelling unintelligibly in a deep pitch. Here were some people he could actually run over, and he did not waste the chance. He certainly did not walk softly and behave congenially as he had advised me so earnestly to do on the road to Nyhmes. He was a bull in a playground, and it didn't matter—no it was better—that he was outnumbered. It meant more playmates to hit.

My excitement was turning to disgust at the whole, weird situation. I let the frenetic battle roll past me with only a few collisions. I had thought I might learn something, that the unfolding confrontation would naturally expose the motivations and underlying reason to me, but apparently I had been naïve. Events did not work out like that.

Or was it that I simply didn't have the stomach for the ugly realities of battle?

Most likely there was some truth in both these thoughts, but ultimately what changed my attitude was my suspicion that what was going on was just . . . stupid, that there was no underlying truth to be found in it at all. I was baffled. What could have given birth to such passion and violence? I couldn't understand it. It was irrational. It was insane.

Even more puzzling, how did so many insane people come to be here today? How could they organize? Why were some of them seemingly wealthy and well-connected? None of it made sense to me. Maybe there was no sense to be made.

Still, I couldn't let it go at that. Even an irrational story must have some internal logic or the semblance of such. These idiots had to at least imagine their cause made sense, and this meant there must be some elements of the struggle to understand. And so, disgust changed back to curiosity.

As strangely varied as the dress of the fomenters were their slogans. Who was to be paid and why? Outside of the Empyrean itself, Nimrheal had to be the strangest of the supposed collectors of the missing grain-tithe. Why would anyone want Nimrheal to be paid? Back before the Methueyn War, Nimrheal used to appear and kill first time inventors. Or so the stories say. But the two centuries and more that had passed since the war made me wonder if there had ever been a real Nimrheal, and, if not, why people would make up such strange stories. It isn't that I had never heard Nimrheal brought up in the context of new things. When we started building our elevator, some folks had joked about Nimrheal showing up to punish Grandpa or even me. I didn't take them seriously, nor did they mean me to. But here, as ridiculous as this fight was, everyone was taking their part seriously.

I looked up and saw the man who had called for Nimrheal to be paid. He of the burst shoe, the one chased from the Grain Exchange. He lay on the ground, seemingly overcome in the first few seconds of the battle. Now his other shoe was broken open too, and stringy bits of sock spilled out. His upper lip was swollen and his nose gushed blood. He had wide parallel gashes on his cheek. Someone had got him with a rake.

I felt such pity for the man, he was such a sad and forlorn figure, ruined, and abandoned. I crossed between combatants and reached down to help him up. He looked up at me with uncomprehending eyes, rheumy with tears. I pulled him to his feet, and he swayed for a moment, sobbing quietly as he gathered his wits. I smiled at him, feeling beneficent and pleased with myself for having helped the man, but at that moment, he came violently to life. He grabbed my shirt maniacally and hauled my face close to his.

"Have you paid?" he shrieked, spraying my face with spit and a storm of onions. I was horrified, caught between my own angry counter-reaction and tears of frustration over the inanity of it all.

"Have you paid!" he screamed even more loudly now, working himself up. I still could scarcely believe what was happening. I had always been relied on to react quickly to defend others—too quickly some have said—but when it came to insults or injuries to myself, I was slow to mete out violence.

"Have you—" Bwoof! His insane question was cut short this time as Arrayn smashed into him at a run, laying him out flat again, this time sideways and stretched out.

"Don't touch my nephew, fucker!" Arrayn roared, laying into him with fists and feet. The poor man's eyes glazed over again as Arrayn beat him and his clothes into a ragged mop. I sat on the ground, shocked.

Eventually the Nyhmes Guard came out and hauled the fomenters away to the safety of the town jail. Aeres made it clear she would press formal charges for assault, conspiracy, and malicious damage as well as sue for other damages against whichever of the fomenters had assets to go after. She even demanded that Lord Glynnis be investigated for potential involvement. I couldn't know where that might go, if anywhere, but Aeres was certainly not taking a passive stance about any aspect of the incident.

I watched passively, feeling I had done enough but knowing I understood too little. Apparently, though, I was a bit of a hero. The story of my umbrella shield had quickly become the favorite anecdote of the fight among Aeres and her crew rather than the blood and beatings that followed.

▽

Endicott blinked his eyes, coming back to the present again after becoming absorbed in telling his tale. "It's a small story, maybe. No Lonely Wizard, and yet . . ."

Endicott reluctantly stopped, still trapped in his own head and not sure of the girls' reaction. "After that, I spent the better part of four days in a stagecoach, unable to set aside the events of that day. The hug from a strange lady, the scorn of strangers."

He swallowed, turning deeper into introspection. "Nothing that happened was of any great import, but all of it has stuck with me. I've been wanting to tell this little story to get it off my chest. Perhaps I want some of the details of it to go away. The drops of blood on that man's swollen lip, his ruined shoes, they are hardly earth-shattering images, but they don't make me happy."

Endicott finally looked up at the girls to see what they thought of his story.

"What. The. Fuck. Was. That." Eloise was staring incredulously at Endicott. "*That* didn't happen. Not like that."

Koria started laughing.

"And you aren't really that bothered, that *haunted*," Eloise added in an affected tone, "by what happened."

"I know. It sounds ridiculous. And it was." Endicott looked at the girls again, holding up his hands.

"Put aside the weirdness of it for a minute." He marshalled a little dignity, he hoped, and made his confession. "People *did* get hurt there, you know. You ever get raked? I mean, hit by a rake?"

Both Koria and Eloise were laughing now.

It wasn't coming out as he had hoped, but Endicott tried again to explain his feelings. "It was skolving ridiculous to be fighting like that over some seeds and some kind of religious hysteria. That those people gathered like they did was disturbing. I've never heard of anything like that before, but I can tell you I didn't like it. I didn't like that shabby beggar-guy getting his other shoe ripped or getting beat up. Arrayn didn't need to thrash him like that, but how could there be any issue about *seeds* worth getting himself beaten so badly? You probably think I'm soft, but let me tell you something else: I don't like the unreasonable. I'm going to the New School because I want to learn new things, create new opportunities for myself and others. But I'm also going because I expect to either make or find new reason in the world, and the story of that man at the grain exchange was tragic and unreasonable. I think it stood out for me so much because I'd been hoping for something better."

Eloise was squinting at him incredulously. "Knights alive, Robert!" she laughed. "You know what your problem is, farm boy? You're too sensitive. Don't go to a circus and expect philosophy from the clowns. And don't feel bad when they drop something on their toes. That's what they do. That stupe isn't worth your time."

"He's still a human being, Eloise."

"As opposed to what?" This, in soft tones, from Koria, who was not laughing anymore.

Endicott treated the remark as rhetorical and said nothing. Eloise sighed, but not at Koria. "If you try to save everyone, you are going to spend a lot of time crying."

Koria was looking at the fountain. When she spoke, it was in her usual soft tones, and this time just audible enough for Endicott to make out her words over the burble of the fountain. "Do you know enough even to be bothered? I wonder if the beggar or vagabond, or whatever he was, is the point at all. There is every chance he is simply cracked. But we don't really know enough about him to be sure. Your story only tells us about *you*, Robert."

Endicott stared at her, his melancholy changing into something else, a roiling, visceral frustration that was hopelessly mixed up with the attraction he was feeling for the girls.

Perhaps I'm just in love and not sad at all.

"Sure," he said as lightly as he could. "That's the thing about narratives. If you want to learn something new, you need new facts."

"You haven't answered the real question, though, have you?" Koria was staring intently at him now, and Eloise leaned closer to her, also giving the young man a piercing look.

Aha! Endicott suddenly completed the change of heart that had started a moment ago with Eloise's challenge. In a flash his mood shifted from deeply sincere to sincerely coy. "What question could that be, ladies?"

Koria had sharp eyes, but she spoke with what Endicott was coming to learn was her customary mix of precision and softness. "Assuming any part of your story actually happened."

She glanced surreptitiously at his bruised knuckles before continuing. "Assuming that perhaps you twisted something that happened at this registered seed place in a way you thought would mean something to us. But why did you think that *narrative* would resonate with us?"

"Yeah! What do we care?" translated Eloise, glancing sideways at Koria.

Endicott laughed and sprang to his feet. "Because you are both also going to the New School." He studied their expressions as he spoke. "I'm not sure how you came to find me here, but somehow you guessed or deduced that I am going to be one of your peers there. It's amazing, really, that you went to this trouble. I mean, I know that everyone going to the school is going to be inquisitive by nature, but you two must be *especially* curious to have taken the trouble to intercept me and my luggage." He paused, drinking in the startled faces of the two young women. "I think you are a lot like me."

Eloise stood up and spat sideways. "What, arrogant about *reason* like you? Full of pedantic philosophy like you? Afraid to shove over a useless stupe like you?" Eloise squinted at Endicott. "You know, all kinds of people go to the New School, and not all of them are the same." She stepped forward and picked up his satchel. "I'll give you a little help though. I liked that Angelicus lady."

Koria picked up another of the bags. Not a very big one. "I liked your uncle. I wonder if he really is the brute you make him out to be." She stopped. "But how did you know we were from the school?"

Endicott grinned hugely, enjoying his moment and loving her attention.

"There were several incongruities about the two of you. Neither of you reacted in any way when I said I was on my way to attend the New School, when of course that is at least somewhat rare even here in Vercors. But there was more. Your clothes, your attitude, and then your diction—especially yours, Koria—were, to say the least, a little unusual. By themselves, these clues could have meant any number of things." Endicott pointed at Koria's blue and yellow tartan. "But those are the school colors, and you didn't come to wear them by accident. No more an accident than the invention of the grain that seems so stubbornly to have been at the center of my life for the last several years, the same grain that seemed to fuel the fight and inflame the imagination of one poor old bum. *That* grain came about because of research conducted at the New School. So you see, the trajectory comes back to us."

"Wake
End my slumber, wake my hunger to make
Just once for you, from nothing, something real
That shines in all our minds and calls Nimrheal
Fear not what I have wrought, the price is paid."

—Author Jennifer Reyland, struck down by Nimrheal,
neither anonymous nor forgotten

Chapter Six

Words in Two Media

"WELL THAT'S DEPRESSING. THANK *YOU* FOR SHOWING ME THAT, KORIA." ELOISE rolled her great blue eyes, but Endicott suspected she was hiding some discomfort.

He felt it too. The discomfort. It was a sharp stomach ache of a reminder of that day at the registered seed yard. That day of real violence for no real reason. The fomenters had also spoken of a price, and the vagrant had invoked Nimrheal.

But somehow I doubt the fomenters were poetry enthusiasts. The poem itself was ancient. It had been a long time since Nimrheal had killed, or allegedly killed, anyone.

And why would anyone want the demon to return and extract punishment for inventions, for acts of creation?

"I needed you both to see this." Koria's expression was inscrutable.

"Since when? We only met an hour ago." Endicott puzzled over the dark-haired girl, who looked away from him and down at the poem inscribed on the etched compass image in the stone of the center square of the great School of Vercors.

The New School was really four schools built around a vast central square on a broad rise in the city. Koria and Eloise had led Endicott away from the town center, over various stone bridges, and finally up a long slope to the sprawling plateau—called the Academic Plateau—that dominated the south quarter of the city. The four schools were laid out symmetrically around the square, at whose precise center the compass and poem were engraved. The Military School stood sentinel at the north, the Steel Castle of the Methueyn Church seminary faced it on the south, the School of Statics—or the Old School—bordered the east side, and the New School looked across it from the west.

Endicott shook himself away from puzzling over Koria and the fomenters and looked again at the poem. "I appreciate that it must have been important to people. They wrote it in stone, so they must have thought it necessary that the message endure." Endicott squatted down and ran his fingers over the etched words before standing up again.

"You should see the Methueyn Treaty. Similar idea, but . . . more interesting to me." Eloise's feet pointed away from the square.

"Let's stick to this for now." Koria's tone was firm. Eloise returned her attention to the poem but said nothing.

"Fine," Endicott said. "It's meant to be inspirational, right? That we can create new things, poems or whatever we want. That we *should* make them. Back in Reyland's day, they feared mortal punishment from the very act of creating." His heart beat faster, his enthusiasm rising with it.

"But now, absent Nimrheal, we don't have to be afraid, so we have a duty to create whatever we can." He looked at the two women, who stared back at him with two kinds of scorn.

"You're such a dreamer, Robert." Eloise spoke harshly, but she might have been smiling. A little.

"You should be afraid." Koria spoke softly but looked more serious.

"Why?" Endicott was almost offended. He enjoyed poetry, but he was also afraid of embarrassing himself with the two young ladies. There was something he did not understand about the way she spoke to him, something that was confusing. Others, he reflected, might say she was being a little overbearing.

As Endicott thought about it and looked at her, he felt a thrill.

She cares.

Koria's sincerity was certainly obvious. "There are always consequences for what we do," she continued. "Always." She glanced down at the poem and quickly returned her gaze to Endicott. "It doesn't have to be a murderous transcendental being; it could be subtler but just as profound. You may not even know it when it arrives, but the consequences always come to you or the people around you. The law of conservation of action is written in consequences."

Good knights! Endicott's mood changed again, transfixed on her point. Goosebumps tingled his bare skin. He felt love, the love of idea, the product of respect and enthusiasm, for Koria's insight. But he could not allow this momentary passion to slow him down or be expressed too plainly.

"You're not just some city ruffian, trolling the square for rubes to rob, are you?"

The intensity of Endicott's expression was lost on no one. Koria chose deflection as the safest response. "Well, Eloise is."

Eloise struck a mocking pose. They laughed and continued on their way.

▽

"IT'S CERTAINLY NICE TO BE GIVEN A GUIDED TOUR LIKE THIS, LADIES, BUT HOW DID YOU know to meet me at Hervor's Fountain? Seriously." They were passing behind the mathematics and physics building, a monstrous edifice of dolostone, heavy in fossils but with a light, almost sandy coloring. Well-worn stone paths led between all the main buildings of the New School. It was still early enough for this one to be partially shadowed.

Koria and Eloise looked at each other, an unreadable look passing between them.

"Who says we were looking for you at all? Maybe we just saw the lost look on your face and took a chance." Eloise winked at Koria.

Endicott knew he was being put off. "I don't believe in coincidences."

Koria looked suddenly triumphant. "Indeed!" She popped on her feet in a sudden movement that was like a cross between standing on her toes and making a small hop. For some reason, it made Endicott happy to see the thoughtless expression of joy, even if it was at his expense.

"Could you be any more egocentric?" she demanded, tone and words not as friendly as her body language. "Many, many concurrent events occur all the time, most of which have nothing to do with you. But people are always saying that—that there are no coincidences—thinking the world revolves around them, and all the while their minds are so very hard at work trying to tie a few of those many, many events together until . . . guess what? Some of them coincide."

Ouch. Am I egocentric now too?

It seemed to Endicott that people were heaping a fair number of flaws on him. Not to mention that some of Koria's comments, as well as some of her actions, seemed somehow premeditated. On the other hand, he did not fail to appreciate that the girls were unfailingly interesting company. And they were still carrying two of his bags for him.

They came out of the passageway between structures into yet another quadrangle. A massive building bordered the quadrangle in each of the cardinal directions. The math and physics building was one of these. In the spaces between the buildings stood collections of smaller, mostly stone and brick structures, with paths winding around them. The quadrangle itself contained numerous stone benches and four great, gleaming, polished stone and brushed steel rectangular monuments facing each of the main buildings. The monuments looked like some sort of free-standing door, tombstone, or massive signpost.

"And by no coincidence whatsoever, here we are at New School Square." Eloise gestured grandly. "Take a good look, stupe, because you won't always be so lucky to have us around to tell you what's what."

"What are the four buildings, ladies?" Endicott decided it was better to ignore being called a stupe than respond and risk proving that the name fit.

"You really haven't been here before, have you?" Eloise played at exasperation, her head tilted up and away in profile, showing that big nose, but all the same looked pleased. "Beside the mathematics and physics building behind us, arts is opposite, healing is on your left, and agriculture is on the right. The Aggies also have those greenhouses over there." Eloise pointed to a set of smaller, single-story, glass buildings on the far side of the square.

Endicott walked over to the monument in front of the math and physics building. As he approached it, he began to think it was a beautifully inlaid signpost. He was not far off the mark. Closer examination revealed that the polished stone and burnished steel bordered a tall, glass-encased message board. He looked at what was written on the thick, cream-colored paper inside.

"Welcome new students!

Question of the week.

Please address your argument with all relevant premises and calculations to Professor Annabelle Currik.

Which farm implement delivers the most damage when wielded as a weapon? Hoe, rake, shovel, or fertilizer."

Endicott stepped back, anxious, because despite what Koria had said, he still did not believe in coincidence. *At least there is no umbrella listed there.*

Koria was looking over his shoulder. "Some of us call them the heralds. Not like the wizards: the message boards. Each faculty has one. Some use them for news, others for challenges or commentary particular to the whim of the faculty. The other schools have them too. Outside the New School, people call them posts."

"You should write a response to this one, Robert." Eloise was smiling broadly, looking over his other shoulder. "I think you know something about it. You might not be the liar I took you for."

Endicott turned back to the two girls. His eyes were big.

Koria put a hand up in a calming gesture. "This posting must have just gone up. Literally. We didn't see it earlier this morning."

Slow. Be slow. Endicott took a deep breath and effected an approximation of serenity. "What news do they put up in statics?"

Eloise burst out laughing. "I've never looked! I've only been here a week. Nothing?"

Endicott was relieved by this diversion. "What do you bet that's right!" Endicott changed his tone to one of mock pretension. "There is no new knowledge in statics."

"Because all knowledge is eternal." Koria offered gleefully, then sighed. "Actually, they like to post classical poetry or philosophy from before the war."

You can't know that from being here just a few days!

Endicott almost spoke his thought aloud, but he remembered several things. He remembered his incautious words at the grain exchange. He remembered he could not afford to be a child. He remembered what his grandma and his uncle had said. Remembering these things, he fought against the impulse and chose to follow the advice he had been getting for most of his life. He chose to "be slow." He would save the mystery of Koria for later. He decided to focus for now on a more mundane, but still pressing, question. "I am to present myself to the Offices of the Registry. What is the eternal location of said building?"

Eloise leaned one arm against the "heraldic" monument, twisting sideways on one ankle. "Why, it is just by the agriculture building." She straightened her ankle, stood on her toes so that she towered even higher, and held up his satchel with exaggerated grace towards a brick and stone building in front of the greenhouses.

Koria sighed theatrically at Eloise's antics and began walking towards the registry. Endicott followed her, and, moments later, Eloise loped after them. They passed through the heavy cherrywood doors and found the interior lit by a set of large, fixed lanterns casting a pale-yellow light. A crowd of people his own age milled about in the room or were lined up in front of a set of wickets spaced around the room. Koria pointed to one of the wickets. A wooden sign was inlaid across the top border of the open window. It read: "Mathematics and Physics." There was no lineup for this wicket. Endicott looked around and saw all the other stations had lengthy ones, with arts and agriculture competing for the longest.

"That's the front line for the rest of your life, Robert." Koria said, setting his bag down. "From there you will be on your way."

Once more, Endicott felt a surge of excitement mixed with melancholy. He was finally here. The New School! All the possibilities for change and for the realization of unbounded potential he had dreamed of were right here in front of him. He had only been inside one of the many, many buildings on the Academic Plateau, and *barely* inside at that. He had *barely* looked through the window at this new world, and already it vastly exceeded his expectations. Every one of the structures, libraries, greenhouses, and laboratories that he had flown by on his rushed tour with the girls held knowledge and mystery for him. Now he would explore these buildings and breathe in their mysteries. The excitement was intoxicating!

Yet young Robert Endicott always carried just a little melancholy with him, though he did not always know why. The contrary feelings made an unsettling mix in his stomach, a weird elixir of the high adrenaline of excitement and the downward pull of its melancholy inverse. Strangely, though these pulled in opposite directions, if he for a moment chose not to name them, they might be mistaken for the same sensation. Endicott also felt more than a little sad to be leaving the girls. This feeling at least was unequivocal. They were an interesting, sometimes puzzling surprise that he certainly did not want to be parted from. Between the New School and all the other institutions, the Academic Plateau was huge, several times the size of the entire town of Bron. He realized it might be some time before he saw the ladies again.

Don't go!

I haven't even asked them what faculty or program they are in.

A wave of shyness threatened to overwhelm him, but he ruthlessly suppressed it and spoke his mind. "Will I see you again . . . soon? I would like to repay your kindness. You have been most helpful. Truly." Then he added, boldly, he thought, "What faculty are you in?"

Eloise howled and Koria laughed, though softly. "*Your* faculty and program." Koria said.

"And you're living with us, stupe." Eloise added, long hair suddenly a little wilder. She dropped Endicott's satchel beside the bag Koria had more gracefully deposited on the floor of the building. "So you can be sure we'll collect that debt."

The girls were out the door before a stunned Endicott could muster a word.

Living with you?

Chapter Seven.
Without Regret

ENDICOTT APPROACHED THE WICKET, BEHIND WHICH HE COULD NOW SEE A MAN STANDING, waiting for business. The man displayed the yellow and blue tartan of the New School as the pattern on his pressed and trim-fitting shirt.

"Name and program?" he asked, distractedly shuffling stacks of papers. Several of the stacks were impressively thick.

"Robert Endicott. Her Grace's Applied Mathematics and Physics Program." Endicott wondered which pile he belonged to.

The man looked at Endicott sharply. "Her Grace's?" He shuffled the stacks with what looked to the young man like excitement, then produced a single piece of paper. He ran a finger down the page until he found what Endicott assumed must be his name and looked up with a solemn expression.

"Robert Endicott. Do come in." The man unlatched a hidden catch and swung the wicket open so that Endicott could walk through what was now a doorway. Without the girls helping, Endicott struggled with his bags until the man came and took up the two small ones for him. When Endicott passed over the threshold, the man put the bags down and turned and latched the doorway. Then he reacquired the bags, stepped briskly in front of his young charge and led the way without another word.

Endicott followed him down a short hallway to an antechamber. An overweight young man of about Endicott's age sat on a well-padded chair facing the front of the room. The wicket man put Endicott's bags down beside another set of luggage, presumably the fat boy's.

"Take a seat, Robert." He waved to another padded chair, then rapped twice on a door at the far side of the antechamber, and after a pause, passed through it. The other young man, despite his size, sprang energetically to his feet and extended a large, fleshy hand. "Hi. I'm Davyn Daly." He spoke with a booming voice that reverberated around the otherwise empty room.

"I'm Robert." Endicott shook his hand, and they both sat down. "How long have you been here, Davyn?"

"All day!" he boomed. "Thank *you* for being so late." Davyn put his hands on his hips to admonish Endicott further. "What in Hati's Hell were you doing all these long hours? Don't you know there are people around here other than yourself? What, were you chatting up some girls?"

Before Endicott could summon a response, Davyn waved his hands up and down placatingly.

"Just kidding you, Robert." They both moved to sit, and Davyn continued without interruption. "I haven't been waiting long at all. I'm told there is a bit of a procedure here, and they like to go through it with a few of us at time. Apparently another group went through only an hour before I arrived."

Davyn's little speech startled Endicott no less from its energy than its accurate, but apparently random, shot at the truth of his encounter with Koria and Eloise. He had to smile. Here was someone as seemingly changeable as himself. And Davyn was sharp too. Endicott could see the intelligence in those quick eyes. He might be remarkably heavy, but he had a lively energy about him. When he had jumped to his feet, he had revealed a stature perhaps a little taller than average, but his neck was thick, and his brown hair was cut very short. Taken together, this created the odd effect of minimizing the transition between neck and head.

"Actually I *was* with a couple of other students. Girls. We were telling stories and arguing about poetry."

"Dear Knights in Elysium, you are already a professional student!" Davyn guffawed. His laugh had a funny *hew hew hew* cadence to it.

"Did you notice that our program seems to only have one page of students in it?"

Davyn's eyes widened, and he nodded in appreciation. "I *did* notice that. We might even be the last of them."

"Our program may be more . . . unusual than I had been led to believe, Davyn."

"Oh yes, let us count the ways!" Davyn looked ready to spring improbably from his chair again, but whatever was coming next was interrupted when the inner door abruptly opened.

A tall, slim young man dressed in a kilt of the New School's colors motioned them to come forward. He wore a sword suspended on a wide leather belt on each hip. "Gentlemen." He spoke in a soft voice. "Be welcome," he said, motioning for them to precede him through the door. He exuded an easy, confident friendliness.

As Endicott and Davyn passed through the door, they encountered the man from the wicket again. He smiled on his way by the two young men and exited through the same door, presumably returning to his station. Endicott turned from nodding politely and surveyed the room he and Davyn now stood in. It was about twice the size of the antechamber. In the center stood a long table towards which their tall guide waved them. Two women and another armed man waited near the head of the table. The man wore a thick tunic with hard leather forearm guards. He was almost as tall as his colleague, but boasted an extraordinary, imposing, muscular build. His hair was strikingly dark. On his right hip, he wore a short sword. This impressive figure stared at Endicott and Davyn with a skeptical expression, blinking at them in a way that almost persuaded Endicott that this powerful slab of a man must be myopic. Then he opened his mouth.

"What a pair! I can hardly tell you apart. You look like brothers, except that one of you's suffered the famine that the other caused." If he was joking, it did not show in his expression.

The younger of the two women shook her head at him. "Thank you for your insight, Mr. Merrett. Why don't you and Mr. Lindseth wait outside." Lindseth smiled and clapped the scowling Merrett on the shoulder. Merrett turned and followed him out the door, closing it firmly behind him.

"I am Lady Gwenyffer" the younger lady said, "And with me is Professor Eleanor, an associate of the program. We have a number of administrative matters to go over with you."

Eleanor was older, probably in her late forties or even her late fifties. She had long, thinning gray hair and numerous wrinkles around her eyes and mouth. Her skin looked papery and worn out to Endicott, but her posture was straight, and her eyes were alert and focused crisply on the two men.

"This is going to take some time, gentlemen, so please sit down." Eleanor's voice was gravelly. She passed each of them a feather pen and gave them a bottle of ink to share.

Slow. Be Slow. Endicott had to remind himself to be patient, to sit and wait quietly for whatever details were to follow. It was a familiar conflict for him, but he still had to struggle to manage himself.

"A test?" Davyn asked with some enthusiasm. He rubbed his meaty hands together.

"That will come soon enough." Eleanor said with a slight air of amusement.

Lady Gwenyffer opened a cabinet and pulled two stacks of paper from it. "Not a test. Expectations." She passed a set of papers to each of the young men.

"Read these documents, please."

Glad to be do something, Endicott eagerly began reading. There were two documents, each with execution pages, a list of definitions, and numerous, detailed clauses. The execution pages already had his name printed on them, as well as the name *Lady Brice, Duchess of Vercors,* and what Endicott understood to be the duchess's signature and wax seal.

"We are contracting with the duchess herself?" Endicott did not know how to feel about the documents other than surprised. While a part of him sounded a warning when viewing any contract, another part reacted enthusiastically. He liked the surprise. He liked the idea of having a contract directly with someone so important.

Eleanor leaned forward. "It is her program."

Endicott nodded and went back to reviewing the documents. The first was something called a confidentiality agreement. It talked of the secrecy of the program Endicott was about to enter and his responsibility to protect that secrecy. The second document concerned Endicott's role in the Duchess's Program and detailed his responsibilities as well as the duchess's. It was extensive. There were sections on terms of service, profit splitting for certain kinds of invented materials and not for others, sabbatical periods, and even mandatory terms of service in the military, along with his starting rank, should war be declared. Endicott had never seen anything like either document.

Complicated.

"This is not what I expected at all," Endicott whispered to himself. When he sat back, he detected Davyn looking sidelong at him.

"Let me count the ways." Davyn said in an undertone and with a none too subtle wink.

"Gentlemen," Lady Gwenyfer interjected, "do you have any questions?"

"So many!" exclaimed Davyn. "Some are even about the contracts."

"Let us hear them, then," said Eleanor evenly. "At least let us hear your questions about the documents."

Endicott spoke up first. "Why?"

Both women frowned at the ambiguity of this, while Davyn nodded, immediately catching his classmate's meaning.

Endicott blurted out, "Why such detail? Why is confidentiality so crucial in an institution of learning? Why such a prolonged period of service after the program? Why do we have to live here at this . . . Orchid place for the entire program?"

He swallowed, wondering if he was being too bold. "I appreciate the room and board, I am just surprised it's mandatory. It isn't that I—and I think Davyn too—aren't grateful for this opportunity. It isn't that we won't happily sign. I know I will sign and call myself fortunate. But this kind of expense and legal oversight must have taken some very serious thought, and that makes me curious."

"Right. Me too," Davyn added. "We understand the contracts, but they don't tell us why they exist." He had identified the same mystery as Endicott. "What are we missing? What isn't in these documents?"

"And why are there two armed men outside the door?" Endicott could not help adding.

Eleanor and Lady Gwenyfer had both looked rather stormy though the boys' list of questions, but at this last one Eleanor burst out laughing. She turned to Lady Gwenyfer. "Well, they are supposed to be sharp."

Lady Gwenyfer let out a breath and seemed to relax. "I'm surprised we didn't get this from all of them."

"Each in their own way, Gwen. And Koria didn't need to ask." Eleanor turned her attention back to Endicott and Davyn.

"The world has become more complicated, gentlemen. Not everyone in this wide creation, let alone this duchy is . . . shall we say, enamored with the New School, and those that don't like the New School would surely hate you too."

"But they don't even know us!" Davyn's tone was not completely humorous.

"If they knew of your rare and particular potential, they would know enough."

There it is. The Duchess's Program is a school for wizards!

Endicott cringed at his own thoughts.

What a stupid and childish-sounding thing. Wizards! Better if it were a circus school, a clown school. Stupid-sounding or not, Endicott was unsurprised. And still even now the words had not directly been said. Endicott realized that only *he* had used the loaded term explicitly, and only in his thoughts. *They* were still calling it Applied Mathematics and Physics.

"So they are for our protection? Those guards work for us?" Davyn asked.

Eleanor's brows knotted a little. "The New School has security for numerous reasons. Jeyn Lindseth and Bat Merrett are advanced students in the Military School, and they are helping us out with the Duchess's Program. But they aren't guards, and they don't work for you."

"Darn it." Davyn said. He put up his hand, but then spoke again immediately. "What program do we have to be in where we get our own guards?"

"And the confidentiality agreements are there for some of the same reasons as the . . . security forces?" Endicott interjected, ignoring Davyn's jest. He wanted to move the conversation along.

"Partly." Eleanor said. "There are significant economic implications for any discoveries made here at the New School. Some of those implications end up reaching further than originally expected. We need to maintain some control over the consequences."

"Is that why the terms of service are so long?" boomed Davyn, his voice echoing off the stone ceiling.

"Or why we would still be under contract even if we were to be *removed* from the program?" Endicott added, when Davyn's echo died down sufficiently.

"Also partly," replied Eleanor in her gravelly voice. "In the past, we have had a few students leave part way through the program to take up commercial work as heralds."

Endicott stewed on that for a moment, thinking of the futures board at the grain exchange. Even Davyn was quiet.

"And lastly there is the cost." Eleanor gestured to Gwenyfer, who pulled out two large bundles from the cabinet and slid them halfway to the men.

"This program is unusually secret but, even more so, it is costly. Your privilege here is unique, but reciprocally, so are your responsibilities." Eleanor gestured to the bundles. "But it isn't all contracts and legalities, gentlemen."

The two young men reached with equal enthusiasm to see what the brown paper wrappings contained. Each package revealed a tam, a pair of socks, and a scarf, all in the New School tartan, a set of keys, a pair of unremarkable looking woolen shorts, and a three-inch diameter gold medallion on a silver chain. The medallion showed the scroll-hung-on-maul symbol of the Methueyn Knight Darday'l. The medallion was breathtaking, and Endicott felt goose bumps break out on his arms once again.

Davyn had tears in his eyes. "This is lovely, just lovely," he exclaimed in his loud voice as he palmed the medallion.

"It is." Endicott dipped his feather pen in ink but paused before signing the paper. An inspiration rose in him, and this time he did not want to partition his words from his feelings.

"Can I tell you what most excited me about coming here?"

Davyn, Lady Gwenyfer, and Eleanor all looked at him expectantly.

"I want to be a better person." Endicott's voice rose with his excitement. He remembered his conversation with his uncle but did not let it hold him back. "Not the butt of a joke on aspirations, but really a better person who could help make a better world. It seems like we are in a time for it too. The world is changing. We can add our ingenuity to it and make those changes better. It is abundantly clear that this program means to make use of our empyreal abilities, which is also a good thing."

Endicott held up his medallion. "I appreciate the effort that has gone into this program. The duchess must really believe in it." He put the medallion down and gestured at the contracts. "But please tell me we aren't going to just be about contracts and paper. Tell me that when I sign this, we aren't making an agreement to be smaller than we might be. Tell me that our story isn't circumscribed entirely by ink. I would like to do more than have my signature beside the duchess's. I would like to meet her someday and show her that we made more of this than what's bound legally."

"You're such a romantic, Robert. So dramatic," Lady Gwenyfer said in a tone that might have been partially appreciative but was also most definitely condescending.

"But we like romantics." Eleanor looked older now than she did when Endicott and Davyn walked in. "We will tell the Duchess what you said. I am certain *she* will appreciate your feelings on the matter. I will also tell you that, whatever happens, it won't be paper or ink that determines the outcome."

Endicott nodded to Davyn, ready to sign, but the stout boy raised his hand again.

"I just have one more question."

"Is it as impassioned as Robert's?" Lady Gwenyfer asked.

"Let history decide that," Davyn said at almost the volume of a normal person. "What . . ." he drew the question out dramatically, ". . . is the purpose of the shorts?"

"We cannot tell you that until you sign the agreements, and even then you won't find out for some time." Eleanor's expression was one of mild amusement. "Not until after you pass a much more difficult test."

On another, earlier day Endicott might have regretted his speech to Gwenyfer and Eleanor, just as he might have regretted some of the things that he had said to Eloise and Koria by Hervor's Fountain. His regret would have been formed of too much self-awareness, and from that awareness, the fear that his passion was really pretension or indulgent sentiment. He might have feared that he had made a fool of himself, the clown in a clown school of his own making. Today Endicott feared nothing. He would act like an adult, but today he felt that he would never reach his potential if he let self-doubt and self-censuring rule him. Today he needed to be of one mind and without regret.

Chapter Eight.
Into the Soup

"THANK YOU, GENTLEMEN." LADY GWENYFER COLLECTED THE EXECUTED AGREEMENTS and opened the door. "Mr. Merrett will show you to the Orchid."

Endicott and Davyn followed the brick wall that was Merrett, leaving Lindseth and the two ladies in the room. This time Endicott was more careful in how he gathered up his luggage. He had the impression that Merrett was not the sort of person who carried other people's bags. In fact Merrett's expression as he waited for them to gather everything up was of undisguised, haughty impatience. As Endicott and Davyn followed the armed man down the hallway with their gear, they heard the women begin talking again through the still-open door.

"Knights alive! They are so yo—"

Endicott could not make out the rest of what Lady Gwenyfer said to Eleanor.

Merrett did not say a word. He silently led his young charges out through the wicket, past the lineups to the other programs, across the hall, and out of the building. This gave Endicott time to review what Lady Gwenyfer had said about the keys and the medallion. Apparently the medallion identified him as a student in the Duchess' Program and, among other things, would gain him access to the Lords' Commons for food. The keys would open the doors to the Orchid where they were quartered.

"So where is this Lords' Commons?" Davyn asked, almost as if he could read Endicott's mind. "I'm feeling a little hungry."

Merrett stopped and stared at him contemptuously. "What a surprise." He held the hard look for a long intimidating moment and then shook his head. "I'm hungry myself. But we'll have to wait."

The Orchid turned out to be a four-story building adjacent to the Tower of Mathematics. The first two stories were a library, while the top two housed the students of the Duchess's Program. A set of balconies sprang out from the top three floors. They were offset, so that none were underneath or overtop of another. To Endicott they had the vague appearance of flower petals.

"Well that's just wrong," Davyn hurled to the skies, gazing up at the balconies.

"What is?" Endicott asked.

"Orchids," Davyn explained loudly, "have three petals and three sepals, which some might mistake for petals. So the building should have three balconies per floor, six if we include the sepals, but this so-called orchid has eight balconies on each level! Who designed this thing?"

"Better put," Endicott interjected, "who named it?"

"I'm naming the both of you as idiots," Merrett sneered, as he led them towards the door.

"He's warming to me already," Davyn said, cheerfully unfazed by Merrett's hostility.

"Well, he's getting to know you." Endicott mused.

They bypassed the two library floors by taking a locked circular stairwell of gray stone that led up to the top two levels. Merrett stopped at the third floor, and they emerged from the stairs just in time to hear the tail end of a high-pitched rant.

"I am not an animal! These quarters are unacceptable. Far too small. Far too crowded. Too dirty. Musty. No good at all." As Merrett motioned them past a boot rack into the room from which these loud complaints could be heard, they saw that they were coming from a tall, blond-haired young man wearing an expensive blue cloak. "This might as well be a barn!" he finished.

"I think you might be an ass," said a short, skinny, brown-haired boy of the same age. "And isn't this better than what most asses get?" At that moment, he caught sight of Endicott and Davyn and seemed to forget what he was saying. Without paying any attention to Merrett, who glared at both him and his unhappy companion, he rushed over with his hand outstretched.

"I'm Heylor Style."

Endicott accepted the greeting with a bemused smile. "Nice to meet you, Heylor. I'm Robert." He noticed that Heylor's hand was clammy and that, even in the simple act of shaking hands, his movements seemed rushed and erratic.

Davyn shook hands as well. "Davyn Daly at your service."

Davyn looked around with exaggerated care. "So where do we keep our ani-mals? My doggie needs a spot to curl up in."

"Knights weep!" the complainer said, acknowledging Endicott and Davyn only with a doleful look. "More jumped-up peasants! Why am I trapped with peasants? Are there even more of you?"

Endicott fixed the tall boy with a cold look. "I am under the impression that, whatever we may be, we are the last."

The young man seemed to hesitate. "Well . . . good," he said, lamely.

He gazed around the room, taking everyone in. Finally he focused on Davyn and produced a disgusted expression. "Don't touch my mother's cookies, fat man."

Cookies? Endicott could not see the object of the random-seeming comment.

"Cookies?" Davyn said, incongruously encouraged. Endicott did not doubt that Davyn thought he was being funny.

"Don't make him more upset, please." A lean, dark-haired boy now spoke up from a seat in the center of the room. Endicott put his luggage down and took in what he could of the room and its occupants. The room was circular, dominated by a central sitting area with tall leather chairs, a heavy padded couch, and a work-table. Eight alcoves led out of the room, six with heavy doors and two without.

The recumbent boy had been largely enfolded by the leather chair he occupied, but he leaned forward and gave a truncated wave. "I'm Deleske Lachlan."

The complainer, looking peeved, picked up a circular tin from the table and rushed through one of the six doors, slamming it behind him.

"And there goes the Lord Gregory Justice with his mother's cookies!" Heylor announced in tones of glee and a volume of malice.

"Aren't you all just the greatest team?" Merrett was leaning against the wall adjacent to the stairs. "I'm leaving now. Don't make me come back because you've bothered the girls."

Merrett shook a harsh fist at them, gave a harsher glare, and stalked out. They heard his heavy, rapid steps as he raced down the stairs, presumably to some place he would rather be.

"He's nice." Davyn said wistfully.

Endicott had enough uncles not to react much to what he had seen of Merrett or his roommates so far. He also had enough uncles to know when to look after himself. He quickly explored the open doorways. One led to a small kitchen. It was absent a stove, but had plates, fired cups, carafes, and bowls of fruit. The other open doorway led to a small bathhouse. It had a stone tub filled with steaming hot water, towels, stone benches, a sink, and stalled privies. The water in the tub overflowed in a slow trickle to a narrow bordering channel with a drain.

Luxury beyond words! What is this going to cost me in years of service? The bath alone must be worth a year on the contract. Maybe two.

Endicott knocked on one of the doors, and not getting any reply, entered. To his surprise, this was a well-appointed chamber, with bed, desk, chair, wardrobe, and another door leading out to a private balcony with its own wicker chairs. The bed was stuffed with feathers. *Lovely. And not musty at all.*

Within moments, Endicott had moved his luggage in and begun unpacking his few possessions. His Aunt Ellys had made him several finely wrought shirts and pants with the stitching engine that Uncle Deryn had reverse-engineered. Uncle Arrayn had presented them to him in Nyhmes with an uncharacteristic flourish. One shirt was even made from South Harkness silk, with oversized, highly polished, petrified-wood buttons. All the shirts displayed the fine detail of the low-gauge thread and high frequency of stitches common to the very uncommon stitching engine.

After these gifts, Endicott only had a few other items to pack away: needle and thread, spare buttons, an extra belt, formal boots and pants, ink and feather pens, an expensive notebook, a gray cloak, his second cold-forged knife, which was even superior to the one Lord Latimer had bought, leather sheath for said knife, work clothes just in case he found a forge nearby, soldering kit, needle-nose pliers, pins, a small hammer, a pair of scissors, undergarments, gloves, a few miscellaneous knick-knacks, and finally his precious leather-bound copy of *The Lonely Wizard*.

"Good Knights! Do we have another country lord on our hands? *That* is a gorgeous shirt, Robert." Heylor rushed across the threshold of the doorway to run his thumb over the polished buttons and stroke the fine weave of the silk shirt.

Endicott raised his hands in a calming gesture. He had not heard Heylor open the door. "You shouldn't get too excited, Heylor. It's just the gift of an aunt with time on her hands and a motherly inclination."

Heylor reluctantly put the shirt down. "But it's gorgeous." He stared wonderingly at the other shirts. "They all are."

Endicott squinted at the skinny young man. It was not hard to see the boy in him. Heylor was still somewhere in the middle of the physical— and possibly emotional—struggle to leave that boy behind. Of all the roommates Endicott had met so far, Heylor had the most child in him, but it was not just because he looked boyish. He could not seem to hold himself still. He was loud and fast like Davyn, but he lacked Davyn's solidity and presence. There was simply no comparing him to Koria or Eloise. The girls were in a whole other world than Heylor in terms of poise. Heylor was physically small and awkward, and Endicott wondered if that made him hypersensitive to the kind of snobbish insults that Gregory Justice seemed to enjoy tossing around.

Let's find out. "Well, I wouldn't want you to get the wrong impression, given how you and Gregory appear to get on."

Heylor laughed. He seemed genuinely amused. "That was nothing. Gregory seems to think he's better than us. He's been going on and on about being trapped here with the likes of us. The peasants. That irked me, it did. I couldn't help it. So I ate one of his cookies."

Endicott stared silently at the cookie thief, not sure if he was happier that Heylor might be more confident than he had feared or concerned about his impudence.

"What?" Heylor said, still laughing. "He practically asked for it, the way he was brandishing that tin when he came in." He stopped chuckling. "We aren't any less important than him."

"I don't doubt that, Heylor." Endicott said evenly. He was thinking about something Koria had said to him. "But Gregory, who I don't know yet, may not really be talking about you at all."

"Huh?"

"This is all new to him as well. Like you and me, he just left home. Who knows what he expected?"

"What do you mean?" Heylor spoke so fast that his words almost tumbled over each other. Endicott found this unsettling.

"He might be the ass he makes himself out to be. But I wonder. Nobody likes being abruptly thrown into a whole new environment. Practically forced into it. Think about it." Endicott found himself speaking in a markedly slower cadence.

It was an almost unconscious balancing of the other boy's quickness. "Those contracts *were* something of a surprise."

"I'll say." The scrawny young man walked towards the door. "Who would have thought we would get paid a stipend for going to school?"

▽

"Tomorrow bright and early, is it?" Endicott asked the room.

Heylor fidgeted sloppily on the couch, while Deleske reclined into the tall chair he seemed to favor. Endicott sat in another of the same chairs. It was indeed very, very comfortable. Davyn was looking out through the kitchen doorway on to the balcony.

"That's what Koria said." Deleske sounded bored.

"I can hardly wait." Endicott said.

"Well said, Robert. Regarding that sentiment, have you noticed that it's getting dark out?" Davyn, returning from his silent scrutiny of the kitchen, crossed the room. "I don't want to make myself a caricature of the fat man, what with others already willing to do so, but I have to ask an important question."

"You're going to ask when we are going to dinner," Deleske said with an absence of inflection that nevertheless hinted at sarcasm.

"Good idea!" Heylor sprang from the couch and was already moving towards the stairwell. When he saw that nobody was following him, he stopped and seemed to vibrate there for a moment before giving up and settling uneasily on a bench beside the boot rack.

"Someone should speak to the ladies first," Davyn said, his loud voice echoing around the room.

Heylor snatched up his leather boots from the rack and bounded through the door, up the stairs, and out of sight.

The door to Gregory's room abruptly opened, and the tall young man stepped over the threshold. Endicott saw that his eyes were red. His face looked wrinkled.

Gregory stood where he was for a moment before speaking. "I overheard some talk of dinner." His tones were carefully even.

Awkward. Endicott had an instinct that an opportunity was presenting itself. He thought quickly. "Excellent, Gregory. Heylor has gone up to see about the ladies."

Gregory said nothing, so Endicott continued. "Why don't we wash up before we go?"

Endicott went into the baths first, hoping Gregory would follow. He did. Endicott found two towels and passed one to the taller boy. They stood at the sink.

Slow. Be slow. Against nature, Endicott kept silent, waiting. Heylor and Davyn had already held a mirror up to his own impulse to jump into things. He would practice patience just a bit more.

"Nice shirt," Gregory said, breaking the silence. It had only been a few seconds, but regardless of the cautionary examples around him, Endicott was still only eighteen. His sense of time was set very fast.

"Thanks. Stitching engine."

"You *own* one?" asked Gregory incredulously.

"One of my uncles made one."

"That would take a rare skill."

"We have a forge and a metal lathe, so it wasn't too difficult. The original idea itself, *that* was the beautiful thing."

"I suppose." Gregory had turned thoughtful.

"Perhaps we'll invent something even better together."

"Us?" Gregory looked at Endicott with a new kind of scrutiny. "Do you really think so?"

"Sure. It's why we're here, Gregory. Maybe you're used to living in a castle, but here they've given us our own tower right in the middle of the city. With hot running water. Hopes are high, my friend."

Gregory said nothing, but both eyebrows were raised high as he looked around the baths.

Endicott splashed hot water on his hands. "See this?" He held the still bruised knuckles of his right hand up for Gregory to see.

The blond-haired boy nodded pensively.

"This is the opposite of better. I was in a fight a few days ago. At Nyhmes. A bunch of . . . people . . . were taking exception to—protesting I suppose—against the registered seed system. They fomented the fight. I didn't actually do much fighting myself. I was mostly just horrified about how it escalated from words to fighting. It happened so fast, and once it started there was no stopping it. I think the protestors came with the intention of provoking a fight. I also think we gave them one too easily. It went from words to sticks and fists in a second. And for what? Perhaps we just didn't want to listen to each other."

Gregory was washing his hands now. "I heard a little about that this morning. People were calling it a riot. You were there, huh?"

Endicott just nodded.

Gregory's eyes gleamed. "You think I might commit some act of violence?"

Endicott shook his head, a small smile betraying his amusement at Gregory's reaction. "What? No. That was just a story."

He looked at his classmate directly. "Still, it's too bad that, back at Nyhmes, we didn't try harder to get along."

"You aren't very subtle, Robert."

"Perhaps it seems that way because you are a step ahead of me."

Gregory's brow furled. "You didn't even hear the worst of it." He threw his towel over a shoulder and splashed warm water on his face and hair. "I admit I haven't handled things well at all." His forehead relaxed. The redness in his eyes was beginning to fade.

Endicott washed his face and hands, rubbing the soft towel over his eyes. "It didn't look much like it."

"Nope."

"Everyone has those days."

"Yes, but I still did wrong." Gregory smiled and stood a little taller. "You might not believe this, but I am known for being fair and reasonable. I can't remember ever calling someone else a *peasant* before. I . . . don't know why I did," he added, drying his face. "I have made a poor impression."

"It will pass." Endicott said, hanging up his towel.

"I believe you." Davyn boomed from the doorway. "And it might also surprise you to hear that I don't even like cookies."

Endicott and Gregory turned as Davyn materialized next to them and joined Gregory at the sink.

"Really?" Gregory asked him. Endicott's struggled not to look skeptical.

Davyn erupted into his odd hew-hew-hew of a laugh. "No, I love cookies," he shouted. "But I only eat them when they are freely given. More importantly, I forgive you, Gregory. We can be friends now."

Gregory passed the towel a little sharply to Davyn. "What a relief. Shall we move on then?"

"You know, I think I could bring my doggie up and wash him in the big tub there," Davyn said as they left the baths.

"Shut it," said Gregory.

▽

THE LORDS' COMMONS WAS A BEAUTIFUL BUILDING. STYLED LIKE A LARGE MANOR HOUSE, it graced the northern border of the four schools, closest to the Military School, and was framed by large trees on two sides. A major thoroughfare ran behind the Commons, a section of the ring road that defined the boundary of the campus. Endicott noticed that two horse-and-carriage teams sat waiting there. They were well-maintained, open carriages with plush, leather bench seats behind the driver.

"Those are carriages for hire," Gregory said. "Some of the wealthier students live in their own estates within the city."

"Like you were expecting to?" Heylor jumped in a little too pointedly. He was walking a few steps behind Endicott, Gregory, and Davyn, keeping company with Koria and Eloise, who had joined them along with the third girl from the top floor, Bethyn. Endicott had only been introduced to her in passing. She had mousy brown hair and slouched. Deleske walked by himself behind the girls.

"Actually, no." Gregory turned and looked briefly at Heylor and the girls. "Truthfully, my family has no estate here in Vercors. We don't have the money for it. I could have stayed with my cousin Quincy, though. He is also a student here."

"Lucky for you that you get to stay with us instead, stupe." Eloise quipped.

Endicott did not know if he should be pleased he was not the only one Eloise called stupe, or jealous. All three girls were wearing their school tartans as scarves. It was a cool enough spring evening that the look was practical as well as fetching.

Gregory ignored the comment but stepped quickly to get the door and conspicuously hold it open for everyone. The girls passed through without comment, as did Deleske.

"Why thank you, my good man," Davyn said with a tilted wave and an exaggerated aristocratic accent as he passed through.

"Yes, indeed. The quality of the *peasants* has really come up. Thank you, my good man." Heylor flipped a coin jauntily at Gregory as he walked by. It bounced off Gregory's shoulder, fell, and spun crazily on the stone entryway. Endicott bent down to pick it up and saw that it was not a coin at all but one of *his* spare shirt buttons. The large, petrified-wood button shone with a red-gold tint in the fading light of the day. It was far more precious than most coins, having been textured by life and minted by the permineralization of time and experience.

That light-fingered little skolve! Endicott picked up the button, informing Gregory of its provenance as they entered the Commons.

The Lords' Commons was even nicer on the inside than it was when viewed from the cobble. The walls were done up in dark, stained wood and river-smoothed rock. No less than three oversized fireplaces decorated the main dining lounge, although they were all currently banked. In addition to the main dining room with its collection of oaken tables and cushioned chairs, there were four smaller dining rooms, one of them reserved for the duke and duchess on their rare visits. A small lounge sat dark behind the main dining room. It was open only on Ursday and Darday. There was even a cloak room with an attendant.

The food was laid out in a buffet heated by an intricately winding set of iron elements inlaid in the stone counter. Endicott decided there must be a stove under the counter from which the elements conducted heat. Several stoneware bowls of soup were set out, along with pans of sautéed potatoes and vegetables and a heated platter of beef. Cold items—cream, milk, chilled lettuce—were off the iron element in bowls of ice. A tall, red-haired woman of middle years dressed in a skirt of the school tartan stood behind the table, ready to assist.

Endicott sat with Gregory, Koria, and Eloise. His moderately filled plate lay untouched while he tried to ignore Gregory's clear fascination with Eloise, taller even than him by a fair margin. Instead of a fork, Endicott held the button and gazed across the dining room at Heylor, who was capering about as he bantered with the some very formally dressed men at another table. Several of the men wore swords.

Gregory tore his eyes off Eloise when he saw Endicott watching Heylor and leaned across the table. He spoke in a faint voice. "Why do you think he did it?"

"I don't know," Endicott mused.

"But you never offered him insult." Gregory said incredulously.

"No." Endicott said. "The opposite, in fact."

"Hey!" Davyn waved his hand in the air. He was sitting at an adjacent table with Deleske and Bethyn. "What are you two whispering about?"

Gregory readily outlined to both tables what had happened earlier, omitting nothing of his own poor behavior, Heylor's retaliatory cookie theft, and finally the strange detail of the stolen button.

"What do they do to button thieves back in Armadale, Eloise?" Davyn wondered aloud.

"Usually they chop off a hand," Eloise responded coolly, spooning soup into her mouth.

"For something as small as a button?" Koria looked disgusted.

Eloise shrugged. "In Armadale the size of the theft doesn't matter. How you do anything is how you do everything."

"So one punishment fits all crimes?" asked Davyn.

"Sometimes they have a duel instead."

"A duel?" Davyn's brow scrunched. "That doesn't sound like punishment. Why wouldn't everyone choose the duel?"

"Most don't. You see, the duel follows the concept of honor in arms: the strong get to keep according to their blessed skill." Eloise rolled her eyes before pointing her spoon at the uncomprehending Davyn. "The thief must fight the duel themselves, but the injured party gets to appoint a champion. For many of our greatest knights, there is no greater pleasure than beating a thief to death in a duel."

"Gahhh," said Davyn.

"Yes, gahhh," Koria mocked, then added firmly, "But Endicott isn't going to duel with Heylor." She fixed him with her green eyes. "Are you?"

Endicott said nothing. He was angry and frustrated with Heylor, but also confused. He wanted to grab the skinny young man right then and there and shake him until his teeth rattled. There was not much to the little man, so shaking him would be very effective. Endicott imagined all manner of other stolen items falling out of Heylor's pockets in a revealing, purgative rain. Abruptly, a new thought occurred to him.

"What would happen if Heylor stole something from those gentlemen?"

"Why would he do that?" Davyn said.

Gregory's eyes widened. "He would never. That's my cousin Quincy he's talking with now. And with Quincy is no less than Lord Jon Indulf, who has a cruel streak like you've never seen. They would beat him pretty badly."

"Into a mop?" Eloise asked.

Endicott glared at her.

"More like a broken mop," Deleske said laconically, leaning back in his chair.

"No less than he deserves." Endicott sharply pushed back from the table, his chair rubbing audibly as it scraped on the wooden floor. He stood up.

"Endicott!" Koria grabbed Endicott's arm. "It's only a button. Don't hurt him." Endicott looked down on her tiny fingers. The contact was a thrill, but another imperative ruled him now. He gently removed her fingers, regretting the loss of touch.

Endicott looked at Davyn. "Get the door for me."

Without waiting for a response, Endicott marched straight across the dining hall to Heylor, who was still speaking with the well-dressed students. Heylor saw Endicott's expression and flinched.

"Heylor, my good man!" Endicott said loudly, projecting his voice to a Davyn-like level.

Heylor looked confused, but instead of running away, which clearly crossed his mind, he hesitated long enough for Endicott to close the distance and get one hand on the back of his neck. Heylor's neck was clammy and cold. Endicott was only of average size, and lean, but he had extensive experience at the forge. Heylor was going nowhere.

"I need to speak with you about that formula from this morning," Endicott boomed and turned the smaller man in the direction of the door.

One of the men put his leg out to block Endicott. He had a cruel smile. "Don't take young Heylor from us so soon. He was just telling us the most amusing stories about the Orchid." Endicott thought this must be Lord Jon Indulf. Gregory's discreet pointing could have indicated him or any of the other men, but this man's air of authority gave him away. Endicott estimated that the young lord might be an inch or two taller than him, and he could make out the gleaming hilt of a longsword, which was hung on the back of Indulf's chair.

"Another time, if you please." Endicott pushed through his leg and walked Heylor towards the door. Heylor was stiff but did not resist.

"I do *not* please!" Indulf did not shout, but his voice carried clearly from his chair.

"Leave off, Jon. Other people have things . . ." Endicott didn't know to whom the last voice belonged, but he was happy to hear it trail into inaudibility. He had now reached the back of the room with his captive. Here Merrett stood watching, sword on hip, aspect like the black anvil head of a thunderstorm.

The dark cloud frowned at Endicott and broke his silence. "Nice blouse."

Endicott ignored him and continued marching Heylor down the hallway, towards the big entry doors, which Davyn held open. Gregory stood outside. Once they were through the door, Endicott turned Heylor around and pushed him up against the nearest wall. The button thief was shivering violently.

"I think you dropped this." Endicott held up the button and pushed it into the hand Heylor held up to ward off the imagined blow.

"No one is going to hurt you," Davyn said, noting Heylor's trembling.

"Much," Gregory added.

"I'm sorry," Heylor squeaked.

"I thought we were friends." Endicott pointed a finger at the skinny young man.

"W-w we *are*." Heylor pleaded.

Endicott sighed. "Did you need the button?"

"No."

"It's quite pretty. Did you *want* it?"

"N-no."

"Then why did you take it?" Endicott's frustration was all too evident in his tone.

"I d-don't know."

I don't understand.

"How often do you do this?"

"Often."

With a sudden convulsion, Heylor burst into tears. It reminded Endicott of a window of glass shattering. One moment pristine, the next an unrecoverable mess.

"I don't know why I d-do it," he sobbed. "I just do." He cried for several uncomfortable minutes into which no one spoke.

Finally Gregory held out an embroidered handkerchief. "You have some snot . . ." He gestured haltingly at Heylor's lip.

Heylor dabbed ineffectively at the viscous mess.

"Now Heylor," Endicott said firmly. "Did you steal anything from those men you were just talking to?"

"Why would you think— No!" Heylor looked from Endicott, to Davyn, to Gregory, and finally off over Endicott's other shoulder at something or someone else.

Endicott whirled around. Merrett was standing behind the group of them. The stocky man had an apple in his hand.

"This is really quite touching. Do carry on." Merrett said.

"This has to stay between us," Endicott said to him.

"We'll see." Merrett took a crunchy bite out of the apple.

Endicott left that problem and returned his attention to Heylor. "Stop lying! What did you take from them?"

Heylor's eyes jumped around from person to person again as if he was looking for support, or perhaps an escape route.

"Just tell us," Davyn said sympathetically.

"Those *Lords* in there won't talk, Heylor," added Gregory.

Heylor wiped his lip and nose with the handkerchief and cleared his throat. "Only this." He reached into a trouser pocket and produced with palsied hand a surprisingly large, jeweled brooch. It had several improbably large diamonds set into it.

"How in Knights' names did you get that away without being caught?" Gregory exclaimed.

"You have to give it back," declared Endicott. "Right now."

"Just walk up and give it back in front of everyone?" Davyn bellowed. "What part of *mop* didn't you understand?" Davyn shook his head. "No, we have to find a discreet way of returning it."

"We can't wait until tomorrow," Endicott pointed out.

"Whose is it?" Gregory demanded.

"Indulf's" blurted Heylor.

Gregory winced. "I hoped not, though it looked familiar. Jon Indulf is the worst of the bunch by far. He'll never accept an apology and a return. He'll want restitution for the insult, and he'll make sure he gets it."

Gregory looked up at the darkening sky, clearly conflicted about what should be done. "If it was Quincy's, maybe I could have gotten it back to him later and pretended it was a joke, but Lord Jon Indulf has no sense of humor, and he would love to have an excuse for beating a . . . peasant."

"I'm not a peasant!" Heylor threw back.

"No. What you are is fucked," observed Davyn.

Merrett took another loud bite out of his apple. "Oh yeah," he said while he chewed. "You're fucked all right."

Endicott gave him a questioning look.

Merrett chewed some more. "You don't want me involved." He spit out a seed. "You're supposed to be the geniuses. Figure something out."

"We better hurry up. He's going to notice it's missing soon, and then it'll be all peasants and mops." Davyn's booming voice took on a higher pitch.

I must be fast. Be fast. Endicott thought fast.

How much further can I expose myself for, and to, a group of people I just met? Making Heylor return the pendant seemed like the simple, moral action. Fearing a violent and disproportionate response by Lord Jon Indulf could simply be an excuse to avoid doing the uncomfortable but right thing. And what good would it do Heylor over the course of his life if he did not learn his lesson now?

Endicott looked at the young man, who was thoroughly miserable. Heylor was shaking, but he was looking at Endicott with something in his eyes. Was it hope? Was it trust? From a thief? No, not a thief . . . trust from a young man who stole things. He remembered Indulf's leg blocking him, and proud Gregory suggesting that Indulf was another kind of noble altogether. Indulf might be the kind of noble his uncle had warned him about.

When does apparent justice end up being no justice at all?

"This has been a long and strange day," Endicott muttered to himself

"Let me count the ways," Davyn added, more worried than ever.

Endicott made his decision, realizing suddenly that he had already made it when he decided to grab Heylor and march him out of the Commons. It was past time to embrace his commitment to roommates. He took the brooch from Heylor. "Indulf wore this on his collar, right?"

"Yes," said Heylor, followed by Gregory a split second later.

Endicott nodded. "It's a pity, then, that it fell into the soup when he was ladling up."

"Gorgeous!" Heylor exclaimed.

Davyn smiled. "It's big enough. It'll be found for sure."

Heylor vibrated on his toes. "Who's going to put it in the soup?"

"I'll do it," Gregory said, holding out his hand. "If I get caught, at least I'll have a chance. Quincy will probably help me."

"Nope." Davyn snatched the brooch from Endicott. "*I* will put it in the soup. No one will question the fat man going for another helping."

Chapter Nine

I Am Heydron

"**K**ORIA, WHY ARE YOU UPSET WITH ME?" ENDICOTT SPOKE SOFTLY, TRYING TO READ the withdrawn-looking girl. They were in the stairwell between the boys' and girls' floors. Endicott had asked Koria to talk with him privately after the pandemonium that had developed from the soup gambit. He did not think Koria disliked him but found her behavior towards him more and more puzzling. At dinner she had been so eager at first to tell him what to do—and what not to do— and then later, after the brooch went missing, she became quite reticent. On the way back from the commons, she barely spoke to him at all. He reached a hand out to hers and held it. She let him but said nothing.

The electric thrill of her hand compelled Endicott to speak. He had to do so, or where would the surplus energy he felt go? "Did you really think I was going to hurt Heylor? I am *not* a violent person. I was only trying to help him."

"Did you help him?" Her green eyes shone wet and bright out of the darkness of the stairwell.

At the end of the night, there in the stairwell, Endicott realized that it might be too early to be sure of the answer. But what else had there been to do?

▽

THE FOUR YOUNG MEN HAD SLIPPED BACK INTO THE LORDS' COMMONS- WITH MERRETT PRESUMABLY somewhere behind them and, with the exception of Davyn, resumed their seats. Davyn went straight for his second helping, dropping the brooch into the soup without anyone saying anything. None of those who had remained behind when Endicott marched Heylor out of the building could be persuaded that nothing strange was going on.

"Looking a little sketchy," Deleske said in a faint voice, half covering his mouth with a hand.

"What in the knight's names are you stupes up to?" Eloise asked with less subtlety.

Koria was staring a hole into Endicott's face.

Bethyn had a lazy, sly look. "I bet they were out there drinking."

"We weren't," said Endicott, "but that's a good story to go with."

"If you keep telling stories, pretty soon no one is going to believe you about anything." Koria whispered to Endicott alone. That stung, but he was in no position to explain matters to her. If anyone else heard her, they pretended that they had not.

"Wait till you see," Heylor chuckled to no one and everyone.

"Mmmm, this is great food. Let's just talk about dinner." Davyn looked relieved to be back, and his voice returned to its familiar depth and volume.

"Where do you come from, Bethyn?" Gregory said, perhaps to distract himself from anticipating events, perhaps just to find a safe topic in the meantime.

Bethyn shrugged and spoke with a marked lack of enthusiasm. "The great city of Auvigne." A moment or two passed, but she supplied nothing further.

That Gregory knew his attempt to draw Bethyn out had fallen flat was written all over his face, but he forged on. "You didn't like it there?"

"Not really," she said, once again with a total absence of inflection.

"Well, you must be glad to be here at the New School, then," Gregory persisted.

"I'm away from my folks." A flatter voice had never been heard.

"Were they unkind to you?"

"They were okay."

Eloise's hand came down on the table. "A little more feeling, please! Bethyn, you are boring the holy boredom right out of me. If these stupes are going to keep their little secrets from us, the least you can do is—"

"Who stole my brooch!" The thundering voice of Jon Indulf interrupted Eloise's harangue. Indulf spoke loudly enough to command the instant attention of every person in the hall.

"Which one of you sons of skolves took it?" Indulf was clearly apoplectic. Endicott guessed that he had already questioned his cronies in quieter tones and had worked himself up to a pitch of angry and injured dignity. He had circled his own table and was now shoving his way around the adjacent table, hauling other students out of their chairs and rudely shaking their jackets.

Endicott saw Merrett start towards them from his position at the back of the room. His taller compatriot, Lindseth, had joined him at some point that Endicott had missed. Lindseth was armed with two swords as before.

Indulf was patting down an older female student when he finally seemed to remember Heylor. He stopped his body search abruptly and absentmindedly shoved the red-haired lady away so he could fast-march over to Heylor's table.

"You! Heylor! Don't move." Indulf swept through in the wake of his extended index finger, two cronies from his table trailing hesitantly behind him. Indulf was advancing so aggressively that Heylor shrank away. Endicott instinctively stepped into Indulf's path. He found Gregory right beside him.

"Whatever is the matter, Lord Jon?" Gregory said with a sincere-looking, apologetic smile.

Indulf seemed to have just enough mastery of himself to stop before colliding with both Gregory and Endicott. "Out of the way, Bare Justice!" he growled.

"Bare?" Endicott said, holding his ground. "His name is Gregory."

Indulf scowled at Endicott, noting his polished, petrified-wood buttons. "He's destitute, don't you know? Poorer than most merchants and some farmers. I call him Bare Justice. Who the hell are you?"

"Robert Endicott at your service. Now what can we do to help you, Lord Indulf?" Endicott noticed Gregory startling at something but, with Indulf literally inches from both their faces, had little attention to spare.

"Never heard of you."

Footsteps sounded loudly beside Endicott. "That's enough, gentlemen. What in Halls of Elysium is the problem here?" Merrett's voice sounded bored, almost as if he was performing an impression of Bethyn. Lindseth's forehead, by contrast, was furrowed with concern.

"He," Indulf pointed between Endicott and Gregory at Heylor, "stole my brooch!"

"No I didn't!" Heylor lied, looking plausibly outraged. He pulled the pockets out of either side of his trousers and held his hands out.

"Did you lose your brooch?" Lindseth asked in quiet, earnest tones.

"No! He stole it!" Indulf's face was as red as a berry.

Lindseth's voice remained calm. "But he was a long way from you."

Indulf was not impressed. "He did it earlier. When he was talking with us."

"Why didn't you say something then?" Lindseth looked confused.

"I didn't see him do it." Despite his words, Indulf's voice lacked no confidence.

Eloise laughed loudly and long. "What a stupe!" she cackled. "He lost his jewelry. He doesn't even know when! And now he wants a whipping boy for his carelessness."

"Shut up, bent-nosed Armadale cow."

Endicott's temper shattered. His next memory was of Merrett wrestling with him to get his hands off Indulf's collar. It might have been his neck. The whole thing happened so quickly that it seemed like time had simply skipped or contracted. Endicott went from standing in front of Jon Indulf to, without any perceptible pause, grappling with him and Merrett at once. The three young men were suddenly locked in a comic dance, shuffling and spinning in a tight circle around the room. They bumped against a table, and a piece of cutlery must have struck a glass cup, for a high-pitched reverberation rolled across the otherwise silent room.

Indulf's two cronies reluctantly stepped forward, only to be faced by Gregory and Eloise. Bethyn, Deleske, and Davyn remained at their table, Davyn still eating, Bethyn performing eye rolls, and Deleske leaning back casually. Lindseth jumped to Merrett's aid and together they first separated Indulf and Endicott and then, back to back, took up a position between the two sides. Reluctantly or not, everyone stepped back a pace or two.

Out of the corner of his eye, Endicott saw Koria standing to the side of the fray, frowning at him. Were those tears in her eyes?

"That will be quite enough," Merrett roared, no longer sounding bored at all, possibly, it seemed to Endicott, enjoying himself. "If any of you throws a punch, I'll recommend you for expulsion. But only after my tall friend and I beat you into next week."

Lindseth shook his head gently. He was very tall. "He exaggerates. We won't beat you for that long," he said in his soft, unassuming voice.

"What about my brooch?" Indulf gasped hoarsely, his neck now redder than his face.

Lindseth sighed. "Everyone sit down. We will conduct a search for the brooch."

"Yes! Search everyone!" Lord Indulf wheezed on the way to his table, looking venomously at Heylor.

"We will search the room." Merrett said firmly but now settling back in the direction of bored.

It only took Merrett and Lindseth a few moments to organize the staff of the Lords' Commons in a search of the room. Two cooks, the cloakroom attendant, and the buffet lady scoured the room while Lindseth and Merrett talked quietly. The search went on for a long time.

After a while, Davyn put his hand up and immediately called out "Could we have dessert while this drags on?"

The room erupted in laughter, except for Indulf's table.

Endicott feared the brooch might not be found until the buffet was totally broken down, but the buffet lady absentmindedly gave the soup a stir while she inspected the various dishes and heard a suspicious clinking.

"Oh dearie. Mr. Merrett! I've got something here," she squealed.

Merrett and Lindseth rushed over to join her, as did the cloakroom attendant and the cooks. One of the cooks held a bowl for her and she ladled the object free. Indulf's brooch was stained red from the tomato soup. In slow dribs and drabs, the students filtered forward towards the buffet to see what had come out of the soup.

The brooch received a rudimentary wipe on the cook's apron and was then passed, still smeared with soup, to Merrett. He held it up. "Is this your brooch, Lord Indulf?" His tone was haughty and put-upon.

"Yes." Indulf was redder now than the stains on his brooch. A vein throbbed in his forehead.

"Well thank YOU for wasting all our time, Lord Jon Careless," Davyn boomed.

Once more, everyone laughed except for Indulf and his cronies, who variously seethed or stifled laughter. Endicott and Gregory both winced.

Indulf turned to say something to Davyn, but Merrett stepped in his way.

"That'll do, Indulf. Go home and cool off."

Gregory and Endicott did their best to dampen the reactions of their roommates on the way back to the Orchid. Eloise was almost as angry as Koria, although for a different reason. She did not appreciate having been left out of what she assumed was a carefully planned prank. Koria was angry, but she refused to speak with any of them. Deleske hardly seemed to have noticed the whole fiasco. Bethyn did not seem to care about anything. Heylor acted as if he had discovered a new set of heroes in everyone else. Davyn was surprisingly quiet, which made Endicott think his loud comments had been more calculated than they seemed.

Endicott was worried. He had hoped for much less chaos and bad blood. Now he just hoped that the whole incident could be forgotten, doubtful as this seemed. Koria's quiet outrage gave him no relief from this anxiety, implicitly validating his concerns. For very different reasons, he also felt sad that she seemed angry with him in particular.

$\triangledown$

ENDICOTT CAME BACK TO THE PRESENT, ALONE WITH KORIA IN THE STONE STAIRWELL. He felt a sharp pain in his chest just looking at her. Perhaps it was a product of his youth and his ardent nature that in the length of one long day the intelligent, dark-haired girl had become such a source of both hope and pain for him. He sighed and stopped himself from launching into a defense of his actions. Instead he said gently, "Koria, what is it you want to tell me? What should I have done differently?"

Koria gripped his hand and stood up. The stairwell made her taller than him. "Come with me. I want to show you something."

Koria released his hand, stepped around him, and proceeded down the stairwell. At the bottom they emerged onto the darkened grounds of the campus, and Koria locked the heavy doors behind them. A few students could still be seen making their way along the paths. It was not yet very late, but the sparse lantern light did little to relieve the shadows.

It quickly became clear that Koria was leading Endicott back towards the Lords' Commons.

Though Endicott doubted that Jon Indulf and his friends were still about, intent on revenge, he was uncomfortable to be returning so soon to the scene of the evening's drama. With some effort he pushed the revenge scenario out of his mind, along with the concern it generated, and his mood quickly changed. He started to enjoy the walk and to feel, misadventures aside, that he was exactly where he ought to be and with this intelligent and attractive young lady.

Just before they reached the Commons, Koria turned and led him instead to the Military School and its square. The square was dominated by a tall statue of Heydron in female form holding a shield over a child, iconography archetypical of that knight. There was a plaque at the foot of the statue. Koria gestured to what was written there:

"I AM HEYDRON
I shielded my sisters from early age
Against my sire's long alcoholic rage.
Instant insight is my eternal gift,
To defend, to step ahead, and shield lift.

For all those smaller or weaker than me,
I have the strength and the celerity,
Of those who straddled the Methueyn Bridge
And thus, with Empyreal Angel merge.

If you mean harm to those I champion
Beware my wrath, for I am Sir Heydron."

> — By Yeyncie Greene, a little girl, the third Sir Heydron of the Methueyn War. Lost somewhere in the Ardgour Wilderness.

Heydron always gets the best words. Endicott remembered the inscription for Heydron he had seen at Nyhmes' Steel Castle. He saw that once more he had broken out in goose bumps and his eyes had filled with tears of their own accord.

"Do you think you could be another Heydron?" Koria asked him.

His heart skipped a beat, but reason had reasserted itself by the time he replied,. "Not one grain in a bushel, not one chance of it."

"Why not?" Koria said.

"I cannot ken her face," Endicott quoted.

Koria's face clouded. "What?"

"There are no Methueyn Knights. Not since the Methueyn War. Not since Nimrheal left. No one has heard any voice, crossed any bridge, lifted any impossible shields, or seen any face they couldn't describe since that time. Perhaps the Methueyn Knights never existed at all, perhaps the stories of them are lies."

Koria looked up at the statue. "There were *definitely* Methueyn Knights, Robert. That little girl existed, and she became one. Yeyncie Greene and her exploits were mentioned in numerous texts, too many to have been faked."

"How can we trust two-hundred-year-old stories from a people who until that time had kept themselves in a perpetual dark age?"

Koria smiled for the first time that evening, but it was a sad smile. "Really? I don't know how you can be optimistic in so many ways and yet so skeptical in so many others. But for the sake of my question, let's ignore present circumstances and put aside the skepticism. Why *couldn't* you be one? You act pretty certain of yourself."

"Is that what this is? You think I'm too brash?" Endicott sputtered. For a moment he was overcome with frustration, but this passed, and he allowed himself to consider the question more openly. It hurt to do so. It meant looking clearly at his failures and shortcomings. He laughed, briefly, with the pain.

Koria did not laugh or say a word, so Endicott continued. "Well, I doubt that Yeyncie Greene would have resorted to lying. To even imply the possibility wasn't too knightly of me." He glanced up at the imposing statue again. "But honestly, Koria, I don't have the single mindedness the Methueyns were said to have. I am far too conflicted to be a Deladieyr Knight, let alone cross the bridge. I keep thinking that I have everything under control: how I think, how I act, what I say. I tell myself I'm thinking, acting and speaking exactly as I mean to. That I am of one mind. But I'm not."

He could feel tears forming again but looked straight at Koria as he spoke. "I have so many doubts, Koria."

She took his pale hand in her smoother, darker one. "Why did you try to choke Jon Indulf then? Why did you intervene for Heylor like you did?"

"I don't even remember choking Indulf. That just happened. I lost my temper, I guess. Lost? No, that's not right. It's more like it just evaporated. Instantly. One second he was insulting Eloise, and the next Merrett was trying to pull my hands from around Indulf's neck. But with Heylor it was different. I *decided* to help him, but I wasn't sure *how* to do it. The soup was the best I could come up with."

Koria tugged on his hand. "Look at me," she said. "You *must* control that temper of yours. It could kill you and everyone around you. You have to be smarter than you have been."

With Koria's small hand in his, with her standing so close, Endicott could not give voice to his astonishment over what he had just heard.

Kill everyone?

He decided that to object to her hyperbole was to miss her point. Instead he asked, "What would you have done differently?"

Koria laughed. "Well, I wouldn't have thrown his brooch in the soup for one thing!" In a more serious tone she added, "You should have dropped it in a salad and then pointed it out to Mary the buffet attendant. And you should have done that *before* Jon Indulf realized it had gone missing and humiliated himself. Now he feels he has been made a fool of."

"Next time I'll get you to come up with the plan," Endicott said, smiling.

"Do that," she said. "You have to be smarter, Robert. Slow down. Please."

Chapter Ten

Fatalities

HIGH ON THE TOP FLOOR OF THE MATHEMATICS BUILDING, HER GRACE'S APPLIED Mathematics and Physics Program had at last officially begun, but Endicott's feelings were still split between backward-looking anxiety over the soup debacle and forward-looking optimism for the start of the program.

The attitudes of his roommates occupied a similar continuum. Heylor was quiet and even relatively still at breakfast in the Commons, but his unstable boisterousness rebounded as breakfast drew to a close and no confrontation with the previous night's enemies seemed in the offing. Eloise was particularly sharp and alert, perhaps determined to miss nothing this time. Koria was in a better mood and smiled at Endicott, giving his hand a brief squeeze as she went down the stairs of the Orchid and off to the Commons. Deleske and Bethyn chatted quietly among themselves, apparently unconcerned with the recent past and immune to events that might yet occur. Davyn had rebounded overnight to his old self, although Endicott twice thought he caught the big man looking around for someone in the Commons. Gregory Justice wore his adaptation on his hip: he carried a longsword.

"Robert *Endicott,*" he said with a curious emphasis before they left for the Commons. "I would like to talk with you tonight." His right hand covered the sword hilt. Whatever was on Gregory's mind, he would not yet say, but he did clasp Endicott's shoulder in a brotherly way.

The sun was still at a sharp angle when the students climbed the stairs of the mathematics building, crossed a hallway, and faced yet another door to their future. Merrett and Lindseth stood at attention in an anteroom just outside the door. They were both armed. Endicott nodded to them. Lindseth smiled. Merrett did not.

"Try not to cause any trouble today," Merrett said with a hard expression.

Endicott did not reply, remembering Koria's advice about haste, care, and thought. Independent of that reasonable advice, Endicott had his own reasons for deferring any reaction to Merrett. The grumpy, muscular soldier was a mystery, a lesser one than Koria perhaps, but a mystery nonetheless. Endicott needed more information before he could decide whether Merrett was one of the best or one of the worst persons he had ever met.

For their lectures they were being given the loft-on-the-top, or the Lott, an expansive room taking up about a quarter of the top floor of the building. It had a series of windowed alcoves on the two outer walls, while the two inner walls were taken up with smooth slate boards on which chalksticks could be applied. It was a bigger room than they needed, yet still very private. The scuttlebutt in the Commons was that the Lott had often been used for staff parties in the old days but had been taken over by Keith Euyn a decade or two in the past. No other classes were held on that floor.

"I am Professor Gerveault," the gray-haired, dark-skinned man standing front and center announced. Gerveault might have been in his mid or early sixties, but he exuded a sense of vitality, particularly in his crisp manner of speaking. Like Koria he had the complexion of old Engevelen, but his gray hair seemed to make a halo for his bright blue eyes. He gestured at the other adults standing beside him. "With me are your other professors." He paused. "Except for Keith Euyn, who . . . could not be here today."

Endicott recognized Professor Eleanor but not the two other women with her. They were both at least a decade younger than Eleanor and wore amused expressions. Endicott took a head count. With four professors, and Merrett and Lindseth presumably still standing on the other side of the door, the ratio of student to professor-slash-security was rather high. He noted it as just another example of the incongruous cost of the program.

"Is this where we learn to be wizards?" Heylor shouted from his seat.

Heylor was as uncouth and abrupt as ever, but Endicott was happy to hear the question.

"No," Gerveault said, blue eyes hard. "If we have anything to say about it, *that* you will never be."

Endicott was reminded of the Lonely Wizard and his aversion to the title of wizard.

"In today's world a wizard is a risk-taker, a reckless gambler. A wizard, as rare as the talent for wizardry may be, is widely mistrusted. This is not because the ability to change things makes one morally untrustworthy, but because what wizards do is inherently unpredictable. Wizards are a thing of the old world, and this school is not about ideas that no longer work. A wizard, with only a very few exceptions, is also likely to live a very short life. We want to help you become something else."

"Why?" Endicott said.

Gerveault smiled at Endicott, who wondered if the smile was patronizing. "I'd heard that some of you like to ask that question." He paused. "It's the big question. Who thinks that young Robert Endicott is about to receive some manner of ridicule for his question?"

Heylor's hand shot up, as did Eloise's, Deleske's, and Bethyn's, albeit more slowly.

"Not you?" Gerveault asked Davyn.

"I don't know what you're going to do," said Davyn with his usual window-shaking volume, "but I'll know you better after you do it."

"Hmmm." Gerveault turned to Gregory. "What about you, Lord Justice?"

"No." Gregory's thrust jaw made him look confident.

Gerveault's eyebrows rose fractionally. He turned back to Endicott, who noted that the old man had not asked Koria. "The answer is no. Please ask your questions. If you ask them with integrity, we will answer them . . . charitably. None of us want you dead or someone else dead because you were reluctant to ask a question. We are not going to invest all of our time at all this expense only to cheat ourselves of what we want."

"And what is that?" Davyn's hand rose and then dropped as he spoke.

"You are going to become a person who can change the world in certain small ways."

Goose bumps rose again on Endicott's arms.

"And when you change the world, you will change it in the way you expected at the cost you have calculated. You will act with precision in an imprecise medium, and you will carefully pose your questions in an ill-posed science. You will not be a wizard. *That* we do not want. We want you to become an expert at manipulating the fundamental energies and states of our reality. We want you to become . . . dynamicists."

Gerveault let his words soak in for a moment before continuing. "To do this, you will require instruction from Meredeth Callum," Gerveault gestured to the taller of the two women beside him, who had long brown hair. "She will teach you the mathematics that you need." Gerveault then gestured to the other woman Endicott did not know, a short woman with long blond hair. "You will learn the physics you need from Annabelle Currik, Professor of Physics. And I think you already know Professor Eleanor, who will be looking on during some of your classes."

"It is very likely," Gerveault continued, "that you have heard of Keith Euyn, who is the original proponent of our method of empyreal manipulation. He is a resource we will use as much as we can throughout your studies here."

Endicott had heard of Keith Euyn, the so-called great man, but most of the stories about him had long become stale. He was more a figure of Ernie's or Laurent's time than of Endicott's. The *wizard* Keith Euyn had supposedly been quite instrumental in several of the duchy's military campaigns against Armadale, but the stories about the great man were very old. They were passing out of collective consciousness. Endicott remembered hearing at least as much about Gerveault, who had apparently turned the tide against Armadale in the War of Rose and Thorn, which had ended in the early adulthood of his grandfather.

"But let us return to young Robert's question of why. I said we would be charitable, so I am going to *assume* Robert was wondering about the most relevant of my first statements, which concerns itself with wizards being a product of the past, whereas dynamics is our shot into the future. *Perhaps* Robert was also wondering why wizards have a short life span. *Maybe* he even wondered why the results of a wizard's work tend to great uncertainty." Gerveault made little stabbing motions with his hand as he pronounced each statement.

"Is that what you were thinking, Robert?"

Endicott just nodded. He could see Gerveault did not want a long answer.

"Are you sure you aren't ridiculing Robert?" Heylor blurted out, shifting in his chair.

Gerveault allowed himself a chuckle. "Hmm. Yes, Heylor Style, I am sure. I think you may be mistaking pedantic with patronizing. You see, I am ridiculing *myself*, not Robert. No, gentlemen and ladies, we are spending time on the *why* of things because your *lives* depend upon it."

Well, that has my attention.

"Let us consider this: wizards and dynamicists do the same thing. They manipulate the empyreal continuum to change probability, rearrange or borrow energy, or perceive the future and occasionally the past. Both types of practitioner accomplish the same things, but the wizard does these things through what is essentially an instinctive sense of *feel*. A dynamicist does them through a mathematical framework. The *what* is essentially the same, but the '*how*' is very different."

Gerveault pointed a finger skyward. "But *why* do the dynamicists operate differently, and *why* do we think this is so important? And finally, *why* is this a mortal question?"

Endicott heard a small sound. He turned. It was from Koria, who sat at her own small table. She had grunted quietly but emotionally. Her eyes were just slightly wider than normal, and Endicott could feel the tension rolling off her.

"One answer that I could give you," continued Gerveault, "is that our way is better. But that's more a declaration than an explanation. The most important reason we must perform dynamics and not wizardry is that Heygan's Modulus has changed."

What?

"Well, thank you for nothing," muttered Bethyn caustically.

Gerveault must have heard her, for he pointed right at her. "When we herald, we observe the empyreal continuum. This act of observation is often termed a minor breakdown of the continuum, even though nothing is actually broken." He lowered his voice but continued to fix his stern gaze on Bethyn, smiling coolly. "We are only observing, but it costs us a little to do even that. If we want to do anything *to* the medium, the cost is much higher. When we *manipulate* the continuum, we must first truly break through the medium. We call that the greater breakdown."

He lifted his eyes from Bethyn, who looked back at him opaquely, and surveyed the whole class. "Heygan's Modulus defines the tensile strength of the medium, into which we must open a very small, temporary fissure. Every material act of dynamics or wizardry, except for heraldry, requires the greater breakdown. However, the tensile strength of the medium changed near the conclusion of the Methueyn War. It became much, much harder to achieve the greater breakdown."

Endicott wondered what could have caused such a change, but Heylor had other concerns. "Aeugh," he groaned, then shifted crookedly in his seat. The fidgety young man's frustration was all too evident. He looked as if he wanted to push through the back of his chair. Davyn watched this performance almost gleefully and quickly put up his hand. "What my esteemed colleague means to say is: so?"

Gerveault's smile tightened. "What is the significance of the breakdown suddenly becoming harder to achieve?" He glanced at the other lecturers. "We know this information is difficult to absorb with so little context. However," he added, giving Endicott a significant look, "we decided that this time we would tell you everything we could right from the start."

This time?

"The relevant point is this. Empyreal manipulation, or innovation if you prefer, has several kinds of energy cost. Ultimately almost all of what happens is only a rearranging of energy and probability, but there is still the initial cost to achieve breakdown, as well as losses with respect to efficiency and affinity. Most of those costs come from one source: you." Gerveault now looked grave.

"There is nothing magical about the costs. You don't suddenly age or lose some metaphysical life force. There is nothing *mystical* about it. The costs are purely physical. They are thermodynamic in nature. The cost of dynamics is mostly felt as heat loss in your body. If your manipulation is too inefficient, if you do a poor job or have deficient talent, or if the energy required for breakdown is simply too high, you will die of hypothermia."

Endicott started. He knew this already, just not with that vocabulary. His grandfather had taught him to offset small thermal losses with a cup of tea as he had done at the elevator and at the grain exchange. At the forge they had sometimes even used a large heat sink. In the process Endicott had learned a rudimentary skill for this thermal offset that was almost instinctive.

Gerveault gave each of the students in turn a direct look as he continued. "Each of you has performed some manner of empyreal manipulation or observation already. We know that. Your manipulations have almost certainly been largely instinctive. For most of you this has been simple heraldry, although there have been a couple of unexpected exceptions." He momentarily speared Endicott with his bright blue eyes.

"You will all have felt the chill. So to answer Robert's *why*, it is hard to do anything safely with your ability now. The old methods of wizardry are too dangerous given the current cost of breakdown. Those methods must be abandoned. Keith Euyn and I believe that dynamics is a superior approach for several other reasons, but given the mortal danger of wizardry, we demand—and the Duchess demands—a focus on dynamics exclusively."

Gregory's posture was very upright in his seat. He shifted just slightly before speaking. "And you know that this approach works? May I ask how many classes you have successfully put through under this program?"

"Five, Gregory." Gerveault shook his head. "Five and none. The program was quite successful though the first four classes, though we had some minor . . . incidents. Because nothing serious happened, we considered the program risks to be small. But last year's class was cancelled when two of the students died of hypothermia. A reassessment of our methods occurred. We have planned this class to be different from any of the others. We do not intend to have any more fatalities."

Oh. Certain details and oddities, hardly noticed before, now abruptly came to order in Endicott's mind. He tried to be discreet as he glanced Koria's way. She was looking down at the floor.

"I have to ask," said Davyn, hand going up briefly as it always did, "how exactly is this class going to be different? You've implied that you and Keith Euyn have had a longstanding desire to teach dynamics, so I take it that dynamics is what all the other classes were taught. What's different this time?"

"Thank you for being as curious, and impatient, as I expected, Davyn. You are a very good prompter. In a sentence we have chosen *you* more carefully and have a more careful plan for you." He motioned to his right. "I was just about to hand you over to Meredeth Callum. She will talk about the first phase of that plan and explain what your next few months are going to entail."

Meredeth Callum had a sincere smile and a warm, somewhat deep voice. "Thank you, Gerveault," she said and stepped to the center of the room. Gerveault and

Annabelle Currik strode from the room without a backwards glance at this point, but Eleanor took a seat at the back of the class.

"I am going to teach you aspects of mathematics that are useful to dynamics. I taught these same concepts in more rudimentary form to the previous classes, but you will be required to learn at a much higher level, and you will need to show that you have understood the lessons better."

Endicott had a sinking feeling. *A test?* He had thought he was accepted into the program. Why should there be a test?

Meredeth smiled again, seeing realization dawn on the faces of her students. "Yes, there will be a test. We have decided to call it the twenty-four-hour test, because you will endure challenges for a full day."

"What if we don't pass?" Heylor blurted out.

"Yah," Bethyn muttered almost inaudibly. She slouched, but in an easier, lazier way than Heylor's contorted posture, which appeared to be due to a nature unsuited to chairs, classrooms, or otherwise sitting still.

"Then you will not become a dynamicist. The duchess has decided that no one will be admitted to the actual dynamics classes unless they pass this challenge; we will not even *speak* further of dynamics until you pass the test. But you *will* pass, Heylor Style." Meredeth's dimples showed as she gave Heylor her full attention and her best smile. "We can't have you dying of hypothermia every time you steal some dandy's brooch, now can we?"

Endicott remembered Heylor's clammy skin and uncontrollable shivering. What he had thought was sleight of hand now revealed itself as something else. He remembered his button, and Heylor's admission that he stole items regularly. He turned and studied the skinny young man once more.

A compulsive wizard.

Heylor twitched but did not meet Endicott's eyes. There would be time to investigate his young roommate's curious habit later. Right now there were other things to consider. Meredeth's comments could only mean that Merrett had passed along a true account of the soup incident to the professors. What job, then, were Merrett and Lindseth really here to do? Were they guards, protectors, or spies? Certainly not friends. Still, Endicott was not angry with the stocky man. There had been no betrayal.

He never promised us anything.

Without any further exposition, Meredeth launched into a lesson on inverse problems. Before the lunch break the students broke into small groups to tackle their first equations.

"This doesn't seem much like wizardry to me," Heylor complained. "Where are the secret words and gestures?"

"I like it," boomed Davyn. "It's math. It's open and anyone can learn it."

"Maybe *you* can, skolve," Heylor huffed.

Davyn was not put off in the least. "Think about it. Would you rather we learned a bunch of dark, carefully guarded secrets, parsed out by the elite few to the supposedly worthy?" The big man smiled. "We are all peasants here. Well, maybe not Koria or Gregory, but the rest of us are. Do you want advancement to be arbitrary, based on birth or friendship? Mathematics are available to everyone."

And are objective, coldly precise, and uniformly knowable. Endicott was reminded of the Lonely Wizard.

Chapter Eleven.
Last Refuge

THE AFTERNOON SESSION WAS A CONTINUATION OF WHAT MEREDETH HAD CALLED THE beginning. It focused on objective functions and error minimization schemes. Some schemes were more robust to data outliers, but more difficult to solve. Others were fast, but sometimes less accurate.

"What is the physical significance of the difference in accuracy, Professor Callum?" Endicott asked.

Meredeth replied as she strolled between the chairs and tables. "First, what is accuracy, Robert?" She surprised him by casually touching his arm as she walked past him. "The answer to both questions depends on what the functions describe and how much noise exists in the data, or if the noise really is noise and not data."

"For the love of knights, what does—arrghh . . ." Heylor wriggled uncomfortably in his chair, not even finishing his question.

Davyn put his hand up, but before he could translate for his colleague, Meredeth motioned to him with a palm held downwards.

"It does mean something, Heylor. Rest assured it does. But I may not have a good general answer for you. Let me give you an example: height and weight data. If we are trying to solve for an equation relating weight to height, and we were to line up everyone in this room and take their measurements—excuse me ladies—we would see one aspect of the problem." She smiled kindly at Davyn. "You, Davyn, have a weight to height ratio outside the norm of the class sample, so if we chose a length two method of solving the objective function, your measurements would have a strong impact on the results. But if instead we used a length one minimization approach, your data would not count as strongly. The length one approach is costlier, however, and Heylor might have wasted away by the time we completed the estimate. So which approach is better? It depends on how important we think Davyn's contribution is."

Heylor laughed. "But we already *know* Davyn is fat!"

"Why is everyone making my prosperousness the most important thing about me?" Davyn bellowed.

"You do it more than anyone else," whispered Bethyn.

Endicott heard this and scowled at her.

Meredeth put a hand on Bethyn's shoulder briefly as she passed but winked at Davyn. "It is far from the most important thing about you, Davyn."

Davyn blushed.

"Here, here," said Gregory, in lordly tones, as if he had never insulted Davyn's weight. Of course, that had been a day and a shared incident with a brooch and a soup bowl ago. "But can you give us an example in dynamics where this would actually matter?"

Meredeth laughed. It sounded like the tinkling of bells. "Nice try, Gregory. In this class it will only be the math."

"Until the twenty-four-hour test," Endicott added.

"Just so." Meredeth said. "But I must confess that, even without the duchess's prohibition, I could not tell you about the dynamics part. At least I couldn't tell you from firsthand knowledge. I have no talent for it. It is a thing you either can or cannot do."

"Like math," groaned Heylor.

"No, Heylor. Math anyone can do, but you must apply yourself."

She clapped her hands together energetically. "All right everyone, please split up into groups. We are going to solve some problems that don't have to do with our relative measurements. Please choose a new partner."

Endicott had worked with Heylor in the morning. At first it had been a challenge working with the fidgety young man, but they had made excellent progress after Endicott suggested they work standing up at the chalkboard. At one point the two of them had even solved a problem while walking down the hallway of the building. Merrett had mocked them for it, but Heylor enjoyed the process hugely. It was something he had never before considered doing or been allowed to do.

This time the partnership was going to be very different. "We're partners," declared Eloise, marching straight over to Endicott. He had been hoping to pair up with Koria, but Eloise was not to be ignored. The tall blond girl took his hand

and led him over to her desk. For one awful moment as he was being led around the room, Endicott caught Gregory's eye and then, even worse, Koria's. But what could he do? Eloise was shockingly strong and fighting with her to escape would be even more embarrassing than just going along with her.

Plus, he liked her too.

Seated beside her Endicott could not help noticing her knee and smooth, strong quadriceps below the hem line of her tartan skirt.

"Your hand is sweaty, Robert," she whispered after they sat down.

Endicott's heart was racing. It thundered in his ears. Eloise was beautiful, close, and staring boldly at him. Her slightly large, subtly crooked nose suddenly seemed perfect. She was who she was, and what she was, was a gorgeous, powerful female. He was also eighteen years old and needed little incentive to arousal. He tried to think about grain.

Grain, grain, grain. Grain in an elevator, Eloise in the elevator. In that skirt. No! Grain, grain, grain, Eloise, grain, grain. Koria, grain. Koria.

Koria.

Eloise was gazing directly at him as he struggled to achieve some measure of calmness. "Last night when Jon Indulf insulted me, you almost tore his head right off. But his feet came off the ground instead of his head from his shoulders. It was impressive. It took two strong men, Indulf and Merrett, to break your grip. Did you know that back in Armadale defending an unmarried woman has consequences?" Eloise's tone may have been sweet, but her eyes were wicked. "What you did last night was an old and honorable way of announcing your intentions towards me."

Grain, grain, grain.

"Uhh, no," Endicott said with all the wit he had left.

"Stupe, no! We aren't barbarians. Fighting for me was not a marriage proposition," she said loudly, followed by "it was" more quietly.

A single bead of sweat ran slowly down Endicott's cheek toward his jaw.

Eloise reached across the very short distance separating them and stopped the bead of sweat with one long finger. She placed that hand on his near shoulder as she leaned in and whispered in his ear. "I know that Koria likes you, and honestly you are both kind of alike. So I told her I would give the two of you a bit of time. But not much. You had best be about it." Eloise then pushed away from him and said in a louder tone, "Until then, please stop distracting me. Let's get to work on this problem."

She turned out to be astonishingly adept at mathematics and kept Endicott on his toes throughout the problem set. She seemed very pleased with herself.

"Surprised?" she chimed as they finished up their work and gathered their things to leave.

"I promise that I will no longer think that you being my fiancée is the most important thing about you," Endicott said, having recovered some portion of his misplaced poise.

"That's a start," she said, hands on hips. "Fiancée. I like that."

"R-right." Endicott noticed Koria and Eleanor walking out the door. "Would you excuse me?"

As Endicott jogged towards the door, Gregory called out to him. He was talking with Davyn, Deleske, and Bethyn at the far chalkboard.

"Robert. Can I have that word?"

"How about in an hour?"

"Where?" Gregory's voice was fading as Endicott hit the doorway.

"By the statue of Heydron?"

"One hour." Endicott just caught Gregory's affirmation as he passed through the antechamber.

"Hello, Professor Eleanor, hello Koria," Endicott said as he caught up with them in the hallway. He thought he saw Lindseth smiling and Merrett shaking his head at him. The two of them followed on his heels.

I don't care if I'm transparent.

"Did you enjoy your first day in class, Robert?" Eleanor said in her gravelly voice. She was so lean and stiff that she walked like a stick man, but Endicott nevertheless got a welcoming, warm-blanket feeling from her.

"I did, Professor."

"Eleanor, when it's just us."

"Eleanor. I did. Some might call it dry, and it is definitely work, but I have faith it is going somewhere."

Eleanor laughed easily at this. "You have no idea. Yet. It will take a long time, Robert, so hold on tight to that patience."

Koria smiled at Endicott, and in the warmth of this he imagined he really was a patient man. They passed down the stairs and exited the building. Endicott noted that Merrett and Lindseth continued to walk a few steps behind him.

"Lady Eleanor? Would it be okay with you if I borrowed Koria for a few moments? That is, if Koria is willing to lend me some of her time."

Koria smiled softly but said nothing, but Eleanor had a knowing look as she spoke. "Certainly. Koria, I will be at the Commons. Find me there." She turned to the two armed men behind Endicott. "Come on, gentlemen, I don't think our young friends want you dogging their every move just now. Let's see about something to eat."

The professor strode stiffly off to the left, Merrett and Lindseth, broad and tall, following obediently in her footsteps.

"Where would you like to go, Robert?" Koria asked.

"If it's with you, anywhere," Endicott replied, as his eyes wandered over the smooth, perfect skin of her face and settled into the startlingly bright, green pools of her eyes. Koria blanched, which fractionally narrowed those green eyes, slightly unsmoothed that perfect skin, and loosed a very big butterfly in Endicott's stomach. For a small eternity of time, Endicott yearned to take back his cliché. But then he realized he did not care how foolish or hackneyed he sounded; he would rather be honest with her.

Time to embrace the butterfly.

"Koria, I know I sound the fool, but I am in a predicament and don't see any way out of it except through it. Eloise claims I'm her fiancé, so unless I want to get trussed up by cousins or brothers or what have you and taken off to a wedding, I need to put all my grain in the bin. I . . . *like* you. I know we just met, but I have no doubts about it. I think you're wonderful and beautiful and smart, and you've shown that you care for me. This isn't a marriage proposal, in case you think I am crazed or from Armadale, but I want you to know how I feel about you. Plus, there is the thing with Eloise that I want to avoid any confusion over. So please, please, let's be honest about matters. Or I'll have to keep a lookout for the cousin-brothers."

Koria laughed so hard she cried. Still laughing, she took his hand and led him off onto one of the school paths. They walked in companionable silence for a few moments, Koria still giggling from time to time.

"Eloise is just teasing," she finally said. "Surely you know that, don't you?" Her voice was merry but not mocking.

Well, my body doesn't know any such thing.

"Easy for you to say, Koria. But given Eloise's size and ferocity, I really don't look forward to meeting her cousin-brothers."

"I heard she has a great-uncle in Vercors somewhere. A knight, I think. *Hemdale.*"

"Hemdale! Oh, Knights, why? That sounds *so* much better." Endicott had heard nothing but horror stories of the fierce Sir Hemdale, but he refused to be distracted by the prospect of an encounter with the legendarily volatile Deladieyr Knight. He had more pressing issues in front of him. He gave her hand a squeeze. "Koria, I want you to know something: I understand better now what you were talking about yesterday."

Koria looked up at him, and Endicott took her other hand, turning to fully face her, holding both hands. "You were in the last class, weren't you?"

Her hands spasmed, but he held on. "How did you figure that out?"

There had been quite a few clues, but the young man knew listing them would only be another distraction. "You know campus a little too well." He smiled softly. "When Gerveault brought up the dangers of dynamics, you reacted. You lost your friends last year. It hurt you."

He closed his hands firmly over hers. "That's why you've been so worried and watchful. I will do anything and everything, I will do whatever I can to help you with this class." Endicott said this as if it was a solemn vow.

"Why do you feel so strongly?"

Endicott never considered turning the question back on her. He knew his emotions tended to run away with him, but a visceral fear abruptly gripped him. *Does she think I'm a madman?* "I can't help myself," he blurted, because it was true, madman or not.

She frowned. "We really just met."

"It feels like I've known you a lot longer." It really *did*, despite sounding like a romantic cliché, but Endicott could not say why.

"Try again, Robert. Why do you care?"

He had only his youthful ideals to answer with. "There is no why to caring, no mathematics to be calculated in the classroom or measured in the lab."

"Hmmm. That sounds familiar. Did you read it somewhere?" Koria closed her eyes and after a moment leaned into him, speaking even more softly. "Have you ever had a dream that seemed so real that, when you woke up, you were convinced it *was* real? And the feelings from that dream remained with you, stronger than the strongest memory, even though you knew that the ephemeral events of the dream never actually happened."

Endicott had no answer except confusion, but then she kissed him. She smelled like lilac. Her lips were soft. He felt as if he could leap over the mathematics building. His energy felt enough for that, but the desire to stay right there, kissing the strange, brilliant, beautiful, dark-haired girl was stronger.

$$\nabla$$

Endicott walked the paths of the New School in the euphoria of new love. He felt that he had won a triumph. A great ball of passion and feeling rose within him and rotated through his being. The great convolution centered in his gut, but as it churned under the power of youthful intensity, he began to feel other confusing emotions. It was not just that love, lust, and infatuation were hard to tell apart, especially at his age. He was confounded by a very different set of feelings, ones not normally associated with romantic passion. As he walked on, Endicott realized that one of those feelings was a strange sadness, an eccentric melancholy. Perhaps when others loved, they felt only love with no admixture of melancholy, but Endicott felt them both together.

How is it that love and sadness can be so alike?

He pondered this, remembering how fear and anger also felt similar. Without context the two emotions could not easily be distinguished, but without context all meaning was lost from feelings. He certainly felt love now, and even if love made him sad too, he wanted to continue feeling it. He also felt relief. His feelings for Koria had developed with an abruptness and intensity uncommon even to youth. He knew this was irrational. He also knew his feelings should have seemed strange or even frightening to Koria. But she had reacted as if she understood and accepted his feelings. And reciprocated them.

How fortunate am I.

He floated on, meandering the pathways of the Academic Plateau.

Heydron was never far away on campus, so it did not take very long for Endicott to follow the cobbled paths to the great statue where Gregory waited, sword at hip. Gregory was no longer the upset, noxious boy-man of the day before: homesick, wrestling with pride, or simply lost in a new place. He had an upright, assured look about him now, and perhaps having found his place again, a natural generosity was showing. Or so Endicott thought as he saw him waiting there.

Gregory stepped forward, hand extended. "Excellent, Robert. Excellent. I am glad we could meet here."

Endicott could not help but be caught up in Gregory's enthusiasm. "Me too. It feels good to be up and about after being cooped up all day, doesn't it?"

"Without a doubt," Gregory said, "even in as nice a place as the Lott." Gregory paused momentarily. "That was a clever idea you had with Heylor, I mean, getting him up on his feet and moving around. Before that I thought he was about to run mad!"

"Or kick over the furniture," Endicott chuckled. "We are going to have to keep a close eye on him."

"A very close eye," Gregory agreed. "Jon Indulf looked daggers at him this morning at the Commons and even muttered something to him at lunch. Indulf doesn't normally *take* breakfast at the Commons."

Endicott had missed that.

Is this going to fade away or fester? Fester, I think.

But while Endicott had been reflecting on this unwelcome news of Indulf, Gregory had evidently been busy with his own thoughts. "Robert, I wonder if I could buy you a drink?"

Gregory had heard of a place just off campus called the Apprentices' Library, so they headed off to find it. The day was just now fading into dusk, and there were many other students on their way to the ring road. Gregory pointed to a dark stone house on the corner of Apprentice and Ring. "That must be it."

Huh, Endicott thought, *I won't forget how to find this place.*

They were about to step onto the street when Gregory caught sight of something so odd he grabbed a handful of Endicott's jacket to stop him.

"Look there."

Endicott could not immediately see what Gregory was pointing at, for a large covered wagon with "Vercors Ice Company" painted on it rolled by just at that moment. As it passed it revealed two large, middle-aged men standing on the corner across from the Library. They both had bald heads that gleamed in the dimming light and carried crude signs over their shoulders. Passersby were avoiding them, stepping sharply aside as if buffeted by a sudden wind. The two men called after some of the passersby. Endicott could not tell if they spoke good naturedly or cruelly. Endicott and Gregory shared a glance and by unspoken mutual consent moved closer to the two men. They could now read the signs. The first man's was written in red and black in thick, angular paint. It read:

"You will reap what you sew.

Nimrheal will git you!

Your Duchess is in leege with Nimrheal

You will be another Ardgour Wilderness!"

The second man's sign was as crude as the first. It read:

"Evil grayn, heretical Skool!

Stupid studints

If you don't pay the price, we will collekt!

Skoll and Hati will take you to Hell!"

"That's entirely uncheerful," said Gregory in a cheerful tone of his own but with an expression of disgust.

"I think they're already in a hellish wilderness," Endicott said with as much charity as he could muster.

"What do you suppose is the point of this . . . display?" Gregory sounded sincerely baffled.

Endicott remembered the fomenters in Nyhmes. Their signs had expressed similar admonitions, though not as manic or as poorly spelled as the wrecks of literature before him now. He thought about the *Heydron* poem by Yeyncie Greene and *Wake* by Jennifer Reyland, considering the messages they conveyed and the care the two women must have taken in writing them. Endicott knew he couldn't judge the relative passions of those two women and these two men, but he could see that one group was hopeful, brave, and uplifting, while the other was malicious and controlling. Reyland had wanted people to wake. Greene had shown the value of courage. These two men just wanted to punish.

What the hell good are they adding to the world?

"Perhaps we should go talk to them," Gregory added.

Endicott was conflicted. He was curious, and some part of him wanted justice for the insulting signs, but it was also not hard to imagine the conversation that would likely ensue. The possibility of bloody fisticuffs or worse was high in his assessment. Koria would *not* be proud.

"Have you heard that proverb that says that violence is the last refuge of the incompetent?" he asked Gregory.

"Yes, I have. I always thought it was one of their first refuges as well."

"Because they can't do any better, right?" Endicott's breath whistled through his teeth. "I'm starting to think these short little messages are the *second last* refuge of the incompetent." Endicott felt hot. "Signs! At best a shallow and pithy joke, at worst a hateful admonition, and as usual, not looking for any kind of real dialogue."

Gregory could not miss Endicott's red face. "Maybe we'll skip talking to them, then?"

They crossed the street opposite the two men and entered the Apprentices' Library. Candles and lantern light bathed the bar and eatery in a warm golden glow. Gregory led Endicott to a corner booth with an unobstructed view of the other patrons and the interior. Shelves filled with books lined all the free wall space, and Endicott noted that some of the other patrons were reading at their tables as they drank beer, wine, or even tea.

Nice.

Gregory ordered two beers, and when they arrived, raised his tankard and looked at Endicott. "I am very glad to have met you, Robert Endicott."

Endicott found that he felt the same. It seemed like he had known everyone in the Orchid for months rather than days except for maybe Deleske and Bethyn. "Me too."

"Did you know we have a connection, Robert?" Gregory asked.

That we are both attracted to Eloise?

Despite this random thought, Endicott had no real idea what Gregory meant, and he certainly did not want to talk about Eloise after kissing Koria, so he just spread his hands in a gesture that said, "Tell me."

"We do," said Gregory with enthusiasm, taking a drink from the tankard. "Behold!" he said with a Davyn-level of volume, jumped to his feet, and drew his longsword.

The leather scabbard had the word "Justice" deeply embossed on it. The sword slid out with a ringing sound, its blade curiously reflecting the amber light of the room.

A ripple went through the room at the sight of the drawn sword, so Gregory hastily set it down on the table. The metal of the blade and hilt had a distinctively shiny, glass-like look, as if made of some bright liquid instead of a metal alloy. "Look at the hilt," Gregory whispered.

Endicott did not really need to. The glassy metal had already told him the origin of the sword. He peered at the hilt nevertheless, making out the raised letter E that he knew he would see at the cross guard.

"That's right, Robert. This sword is an Endicott. Your grandfather made it for my father."

"He made very few of these," Endicott said with wonder. He knew how difficult and dangerous it was to make a sword of the type he suspected this one was. As far as he knew, Grandpa had never made one in Endicott's lifetime. The closest that Grandpa had come to doing so was in helping with the two long knives that Endicott and he had made. That effort had been a long and careful one. The second of the knives was in Endicott's room in the Orchid, and he knew that if Grandpa had used the same methods on the sword as they had on *that* knife, this longsword would have been a monumental undertaking for one man.

"Do you mind," Endicott gestured, "if I take a closer look?"

Gregory nodded enthusiastically and Endicott opened himself to the empyreal sky. He now knew that the phrase for what he was doing was a lesser breakdown. It came easily to him, and he had no trouble viewing the secret structure of the metal in the sword. There were seven kinds of metal in it, ordered in a complex, unique weave. If you could call the forced structural arrangement of the molecules in the sword a kind of randomness, this sword was *perfectly* random. Such a work of art required both probabilistic and thermal manipulation on a magnitude Endicott had never seen and could scarcely imagine.

"Amazing, isn't it?" Gregory cooed. "I can see it too if I try. Sometimes. It is every bit as good as any Deladieyr Knight's weapon. I bet it is as good as any of the lost Methueyn blades."

"How did your father convince my grandpa to make this?" Endicott had seen his grandpa turn down vast amounts of money to make swords of this nature.

The knife Endicott kept in his room could probably buy the entire elevator they had built in Bron. It was better than the one Lord Latimer had purchased. That knife had only used thermal manipulation and four elements.

Gregory sighed and took another sip from his tankard. "It's a long story. I'll shorten it for you. You heard Jon Indulf call me "Bare Justice" because my family are not so well off? Well, he isn't far wrong. My father can herald. The talent is in the family, as it is in yours. But as in most of the families with the talent, heraldry is about all my father or I can do. And unfortunately we don't do it very well."

The tall young man paused, fingers playing along his tankard. "You'd think being able to herald would give you an advantage, right? That you would buy the right goods, plant the best crops for the weather, make all the right decisions. Not so for my father." He shook his head. "For some reason, the decisions he made through heraldry always turned out to be poor ones. Our fortunes declined."

Gregory raised his tankard and looked at Endicott over the top as if wondering how to best tell the next part of the story.

"Well, one day a few years before I was born, my father has a heraldic dream. An actual heraldic dream! He had never had one before; it just wasn't in his wheelhouse. We aren't like you Endicotts. Our blood gives us only the *title* of nobility, not real talent. What we do have is determination, though, and heraldic dreams are not to be ignored. This one, from how my father describes it, was . . . intense. He had to act on it. It told him to ask *your* grandpa to make this sword, and so my father did, despite knowing that Finlay Endicott only made these swords for . . . certain people. He also made one a few years later on for Sir Hemdale when he visited Vercors. I think this may have happened just before Hemdale defected from Armadale. That would have been . . . oh, when you and I were about three. Did you know that?"

"I have *no* memory of any knight visiting us," Endicott said shrugging, "let alone Sir Hemdale or of Grandpa making a sword."

The veins stood out on Gregory's forehead. "No? Well, it made a difference. Without that sword, the song "March of Sir Hemdale" would be missing that stanza about limbs flying. Maybe Sir Hemdale wouldn't have made it out alive."

Endicott took a swig of his beer, amazed. He had never imagined that Finlay was as famous as Gregory made him sound. He also had not known that he had *two* connections to the legendary Sir Hemdale. *Eloise's uncle was at my farm!* That was worth thinking about after Gregory finished telling his story.

"So my father asks Finlay, and amazingly, he does it." Gregory shook his head in wonder. Endicott wondered too. *Grandpa wouldn't make an entropic sword only because of someone else's dream.*

"He makes this sword," Gregory continued "It's probably one of the most precious objects in all of Vercors, and do you know what Finlay charged my father for it?"

"I sense you are going to tell me," Endicott said under Gregory's expectant stare.

"I am. Finlay *did* charge him but only for the metals, some of which were hard to come by. He sold this sword at less than a thousand thousandth of its true value. In all the years since then, all the years of being called the Bare Justices, my father would never hear of selling it. We didn't have enough money to seed all our crops, but he wouldn't sell it. We almost lost the last manor house, and he still wouldn't sell it. The other lords start calling us *peasants*, but he doesn't sell it. And then he gave the sword to *me*, his *second* son, as soon as I'm accepted into the Duchess' Program and commands me to wear it here."

Endicott could see the powerful emotions seething in Gregory as he told the story of the sword. They were all over his face, in the tight set of his shoulders, and in his normally still but now trembling hands. "That is quite a story, Gregory."

"Yes, it is," Gregory said, taking another swig of beer. "Yes, it is. I didn't know who you were when we met yesterday. I was acting the biggest shit in the outhouse when you first laid eyes on me. And despite that you *still* helped me recover my dignity before we went to dinner. *Then* you had only said your name was Robert. When you introduced yourself to Jon Indulf at the Commons as Robert *Endicott* my eyes must have just about came out of my head. I probably looked at you then like Koria does all the time. I couldn't believe it. Knights, I'm so glad I stood at your side against Indulf before I knew who you were, or I would have doubted my own character. It wouldn't have been the same if I had known your last name."

Endicott felt more than a little strange, and strangely fortunate, to have his family at the center of a story that meant so much to Gregory. It was discomfiting, and even if he did not understand what had motivated his grandpa, it was also inspiring. "Well, I'm glad too, Gregory. Who knows what would have happened if you hadn't been there? I needed you."

Gregory waved this away. "Ahh, no. Those guards, Merrett and Lindseth, had their eyes on the situation. From what I've heard, that Lindseth fellow is hell with his swords and could handle three Indulfs. You didn't need me. But you have my help now, brother. I'm with you. And not just for the sake of my father. From what I know of you already, for the sake of what's right."

The beer helped damp down Endicott's embarrassment, but not his gratitude for this warm and generous declaration. He did not think it likely that he would need more from Gregory than his friendship, but he knew when to accept a kind gesture with good grace. He raised his tankard in a toast. "For the sake of our fathers, Justice."

Gregory's faith in "what's right" stuck with Endicott as he and Gregory finished their beer. He began to reconsider the two protestors they had left on the corner and to wonder if he had been too judgmental. Certainly the men made a miserable impression with the language and the spelling of their signs, but he wondered if there might be more to them than bitterness and bad grammar. He even wondered if *he* had been the desperate, incompetent one by assuming that any discussion with them would end badly and not even attempting to speak with them. *The third from last refuge of the incompetent is not even trying.*

"Gregory, I would like to talk to those two gentlemen with the signs."

"Really?" Gregory's eyebrows rose higher than Endicott would have thought possible, but when the young aristocrat saw that his new comrade was serious, he quickly drained his tankard. "Okay."

Endicott tried to pay because, he said, Gregory had been far too kind to him, but Gregory would not hear of it. The cupboard was not completely bare yet, he said, laughing.

When they got back out on the street, the two men were gone.

"Oh well," said Gregory, clapping Endicott on the shoulder. "We'll talk to them next time. "I'm sure they'll be back," he added with a laugh.

Endicott only nodded, feeling a little deflated all the same. As they made the short journey back to the Orchid, he told himself that, aside from the two men with their signs, it had been a splendid day. What more could there have been, after all? He had experienced the first day of classes in a course of study that promised to be as exciting as it would be challenging, a walk with Koria that had ended with a lovely kiss, and now this curious and inspiring connection with Gregory. He reflected on Gregory's story of his rare Endicott sword. Once upon a time his grandpa had done a favor for Gregory's father that many years later was having a positive effect on the here and now, and for all he knew, would have a decisive effect on some unknown later day. It was almost as if goodwill from the past was reaching across time to pave the road into the future.

But then a corollary thought suddenly darkened the picture.

What bad will from yesterday's fiasco with Lord Jon Indulf is going to reach across time and threaten us?

Chapter Twelve

The Lonely Wizard

When most people kill another person, they feel guilt or sadness. I do not.

In yesterday's battle, I personally killed thousands, starting with Armadale's wizards. I always kill the wizards first. For my hand in all those deaths, I feel no remorse.

Why should I? It is what I chose to do. What sentimental fool would choose to kill even one person and not be sure that is what should be done? What monster would kill thousands and not be sure?

I was sure. I am always sure. I chose to kill them. I knew why. I calculated the energy required, the probabilities to be manipulated. I waited for my moment, and in an act simultaneously surgical and intuitive, I cracked the sky. One does not reach into Elysium on a whim, without reason or with regret. One may only breach heaven with an unequivocal resolve.

Some might say that it is a gross incongruity that I should feel so badly about the possible death of one person, and such equanimity over the killing of an army. I feel sorry for the feckless, the fearful, and the lost who go through their lives misunderstanding such issues. Such people should avoid taking actions of consequence, for surely they will only feel regret whether they fail or succeed. When I act, I act with purpose and with no internal conflict. When I kill, I feel no remorse, but I am not uncaring, nor do I desire the random death of innocent people. I pursue necessary justice, but I do not think my mother's suffering is necessary, or good or just. She is my mother, and I will return to her side.

"How much further, do you think?" Feydleyn's mournful voice rolled over the sounds of the horse's hooves and broke me out of my thoughts. I had taken his company for granted. Wherever I went, Feydleyn was axiomatically sure to follow.

I must have looked cross to him, for he cringed. "The horses won't last much longer!" he offered as explanation for interrupting my thoughts.

"Take a drink of water." I checked my gear, securing my sword scabbard a little tighter to the tack while Feydleyn complied. When I saw he had drunk, I held up my hand and we stopped.

"Off." We both dismounted.

"Run." We ran, pulling the reins of our horses.

I knew Feydleyn would soon be thinking again about how much further it would be.

⦾

"Mount." We mounted and rode.

"Run." We dismounted and ran.

And so it went for the day, repeated again and again as the minutes, hours, and heartbeats pounded away, echoing a counterpoint to our gasping breaths, footfalls, and hoofbeats that together told of our labor across the quiet grasslands.

It was easier for me than for Feydleyn, in every way measurable and immeasurable. I had the full strength of a Deladieyr Knight, drawing power with my purpose. I was virtually indefatigable so long as my conviction held. He had only the strength of his body and his heart. As the hours wound down, and as he tired, the effort to keep going drew more and more from that heart. Once past easy endurance and trainable distance, it all comes down to injury avoidance and heart. Heart becomes all when every step is a step further than the nervous system can thoughtlessly enable. After that each stride requires a conscious effort, and the spiral to eventual defeat only lasts as long as that heart can pound another willful beat.

If I loved him, I would have stopped.

Finally we reached a shallow stream where we could water the horses. Feydleyn fumbled with his canteen, a viscous stream of snot hanging off his sagging face. His breathing was coming in hoarse gasps, and his eyes were bloodshot and dull. He stumbled sideways and fell sprawling into the water. I yanked him up before he drowned and sat him on the bank to recover.

You might wonder if Feydleyn would have been better off as squire to someone—anyone—else. He was suffering, of that I had no doubt. I had never ordered him to accompany me. In fact I couldn't easily have ordered him away. His pain was the result of an act of freedom and choice. If I took from him that choice to serve me, then I would injure the man's dignity, for even with dirt and snot on his face he retained merit for himself.

Think you that dignity is about jewelry, a clean face, and an upright posture? Look upon the ruin of my squire and learn otherwise. He was more dignified in the wretched now of his choice than in clean clothes and at his leisure. I worked Feydleyn harder than the horses because of this: they had no choice and therefore no stake in the ethics of the action. We had to be ethical on behalf of the horses. For ourselves we reserve the choice to suffer. When Feydleyn was so far gone that he had to exert an effort of mind to move forward another step, he became for me a paragon of virtue. He was at his best: every step a choice, every hoarse gasp authentic.

Still, his dying would not help my mother to live.

I would have to leave Feydleyn behind. But not here. He would die here. I decided to slow down and see him to the Line, and there leave him on one side while I crossed to the other.

⦾

Hours and, for the exhausted, an eternity later, we caught our first phantom glimpse of the Castlereagh Line, a shadowy arc, an indigo warning shimmering insubstantially from the darkness of the nearly absent light of a spent day. It stood between us and Nehring Ardgour's folly, between us and the wilderness.

Do you imagine I speak in metaphor? I do not. Try measuring a metaphor. The Ardgour Wilderness is just that: a wilderness. It is a land wasted by arrogance, filled by monsters and gods. Or better put, not gods but the demons Skoll and Hati, still there even after killing all the Methueyn Knights and, I presume, burning their precious bridge to Elysium. It is objectively ruined, measurably overthrown. These things can be quantified by area and demographics. Area: forty thousand square miles. Industry: none. People: none alive. Skolves: tens of thousands. Demons: two.

The Castlereagh Line was built to reinforce the previous border with Ardgour's county in the northern country of Novgoreyl. When Armadale made their attempt on the Engevelen strip, a peninsular wedge of country bordering both Armadale and the Ardgour Wilderness, we worried that they might weaken the Line and force us to fight both them and an army of skolves. They did damage seven outposts along the wall, killing or capturing all the soldiers garrisoned there, but they did not damage the Line itself. As our army passed through the strip, we left behind small, independent groups to rebuild and regarrison the outposts. I had aimed us squarely at one of those groups and could just now make out the light from their torches.

I pulled our horses towards these yellow flickers of humanity. Feydleyn was sprawled across his horse, but he must have sensed the change in pace and direction and scrambled upright.

"Feydleyn. We're there."

We had been spotted. A group of soldiers approached, hands on the hilts of their swords. One tall woman had a loaded crossbow at her shoulder and was flanking left. A faint smell of baked beans reached us, and in the silence I could feel the radiant heat from the torches and hear the tiny perturbations of their uneven fire.

"Hold it right there while we get a good look at you, sirs." This came from a short female soldier, who held a torch of her own. I could hear the quiet footsteps of additional soldiers unseen, moving around behind us.

"Do you not know us, Captain Ectyn?" I said loudly.

She squinted, and then her eyes widened. "It's you!" She peered around. "Who is with you? Is the army at your back, sir? Did you engage Armadale?"

I dismounted without waiting for Feydleyn's customary attendance and stepped forward, handing the reins of my horse to one of Ectyn's men. I could see all the places this conversation was going to go. Best to get there quickly. "Just us, Ectyn. And yes, we engaged Armadale and annihilated what they sent at us." A spontaneous cheer went up at this. I let it die down and continued. "We have to resupply and clean up, and then I will pass over the Line. Quickly."

They did move quickly for me. The outpost was still far from restored, but it did have a rebuilt corral and reasonably well-stocked camp. For bathing they had two full rain barrels on a platform by a trough. After making sure our horses were tended to, Feydleyn and I each bathed quickly in the rain barrels and wolfed down a plate of beans and pork. I washed my own clothes and hung them, while Feydleyn simply pulled on a newer set from his saddlebags. He sat back, rubbing raw and blistered feet. The soldiers were very curious about us, and except for those on watch, crowded around to hear whatever we had to say.

"Is the war over, then, sir?" This obvious question came from the female crossbowman, who in the light turned out to be redhaired and tall.

"No. They still have two divisions that were uncommitted in the fight yesterday."

"But we won?" she persisted.

"Decisively."

Feydleyn coughed. "There were fewer survivors than you have fingers and toes."

This produced a moment of silence. Feydleyn continued eventually. "He did it." He pointed at me. "He turned the tide."

All eyes were upon me now. Someone shouted out, "Tell us!"

Feydleyn half stood up as if preparing an enthusiastic narration, but then grim memories returned, and he slouched back down. The grim events had been nearly forgotten but not forgotten nearly enough. "If the angels of Elysium had come again and rained down death, it couldn't have been worse . . ." He trailed off, too much detail returning. "You would not have wanted to see it."

Some of them *did* look like they wanted to see it. They did not know better. They had not been there. The lull in conversation was welcome to me.

"You are really crossing into the Ardgour Wilderness from here?" Ectyn took the cue to change the subject. My plan was further from the norm than even the camp's barrel baths.

"Yes," I replied laconically, then decided to be more forthcoming. "It's the shape of the Engevelen strip. If I cut across the Wilderness here, that takes seventy-nine miles off my trip."

Ectyn scratched her head. "But you'll lose time avoiding skolves. Let us at least give you a head start by organizing a provocation further down the Line."

"Thank you, Captain, but that will not be required. I will cross alone and quietly as soon as my clothes are dry."

"Tomorrow morning surely?"

"Tonight, definitely." I looked directly at Ectyn so she would feel this with the force of an order. "You will outfit Feydleyn here with fresh supplies and, when he is recovered, send him along the Line to Engevelen City."

Captain Ectyn nodded, saying nothing, but Feydleyn protested. He hobbled painfully to his feet. "No! I should go with you."

I shook my head, thinking about the road before me. "You can't, Feydleyn. You won't be able to travel for at least a day, more likely two."

Feydleyn's face reddened and crumpled with the misery of realizing that he was being denied moral responsibility in the matter. I hoped his protest was over, his argument defeated. But not every hope succeeds.

"No one goes alone into the Wilderness," he said hoarsely. "No one."

Feydleyn was so sincere. If there was ever a sad and dutiful Methueyn Knight, surely it was he. I laughed his histrionics off as gently as I could. I do not normally care to be gentle. Life has been a series of dichotomies for me, black or white, but I knew I was taking Feydleyn's choice away from him. I remembered his face, covered in grime and snot just a few hours ago. How much prouder it was then as opposed to the grief it held now, clean but crumpled. "I am not like other people, Feydleyn. Leave off. Besides that, someone—that being you—has to carry my report back to command in Engevelen."

He pulled himself erect despite his weary feet, though his face remained in a state of collapse. "It is my duty to come with you," he pleaded.

I said nothing. Feydleyn looked to Ectyn for support, but the captain was clearly uncomfortable and gave him none.

"You think I can't handle myself out there?" Again I spoke as gently as I could.

Feydleyn made a sputtering cry that was almost a laugh. "None better! That's not it. You don't have to go alone. Give me a day and I'll be fine."

My patience was running out. I started to turn to shake out my drying shirt, but he lunged forward, grabbing my shoulders. "You don't have to be alone out there!"

I removed his hands from my shoulders. This was my choice, but I could not allow him his. "My mother cannot wait on your weakness, Feydleyn. It is as simple as that."

Those words ended his objections. I did not regret their cruelty. I am not a fool, nor am I a monster. I only do what I mean to do.

Chapter Thirteen.
The Great Man

MOST PEOPLE ARE BOTH IMPRESSED AND INTIMIDATED WHEN THEY MEET THE GREAT man, Keith Euyn. Endicott was no exception. After several weeks of increasingly difficult mathematics lessons, the Emeritus Fellow finally arrived to deliver a lecture on the long-awaited Lessingham transformation.

"Who the—who was Lessingham anyway?" Heylor asked. Only a moment before he had been nodding off at his desk, which seemed to be a new habit. Gregory had kicked Heylor's chair, which roused the fidgety youth enough to reengage with the class. Heylor had not stolen anything as far as Endicott knew since that night at the Commons, but he continued to struggle with sitting still in class, at least when awake. Lord Jon Indulf and his friends had also kept Heylor on his toes, bumping him or giving him a shoulder whenever they caught him alone. These intermittent soft threats had made Heylor even jumpier than usual, and he seemed to be losing sleep over it. Neither fidgeting nor dozing in class were any help in his comprehension of advanced mathematics.

"Eydith Lessingham was a mathematician, as you may have guessed, Mr. Style." Keith Euyn was old, very old, but despite that he was still terrifically tall, and his voice had lost none of its commanding vigor. His only noticeable concession to age was an antiquated fashion sense. He was an imposing presence in an old-fashioned cloak in the New School tartan and a deerstalker hat.

So far he had been firmly polite in his lecture style.

"Was she a dynamicist?"

"No, she was not." It was hard to tell what the old man was thinking while he answered Heylor's questions. In that respect he reminded Endicott of his grandpa. "She did not invent the transform for *our* purposes, Mr. Heylor. She did die for it, though. Lessingham was killed by Nimrheal in the year 442 Before-Methueyn War."

The students had been hearing about the untimely deaths of mathematicians for weeks. A great many of the iconic figures had supposedly been killed by Nimrheal, each in grisly fashion. Each by the demon's dark spear.

As tall tales go, the stories of Nimrheal are certainly numerous and eerily similar.

"Well, what *did* she invent it for, then?" Heylor asked, perhaps for once in his life choosing his words almost carefully. Endicott thought he was about to ask again why they were learning math unrelated to wizardry, a phrasing that would have gotten him into two kinds of trouble, both familiar.

Keith Euyn drummed his fingers on Heylor's desk, looking not at the young man but two rows behind him at Professor Eleanor.

"If Eleanor will forgive me, I will answer you. The truth might do you some good, Mr. Style."

Heylor shrank in his chair under the steely glare of the old man.

"The Lessingham transform is of enormous use in the laboratory. Not so much if you are in a duel or if skolves are leaping after you through the tall grass. It is a tool of control and precision when applied correctly and with proper analytical tact. The transform also has deep connections to the Kinetic Equation, which you will all study in considerable detail later."

Keith Euyn again looked back at Eleanor, who must have frowned. "I know what we agreed to, my dear, but we mustn't forget that rules are for those that cannot rule themselves."

"Shall we return to the subject, Keith?" Eleanor's sounded moderately irritated.

"This *is* the subject, my dear Eleanor."

"Are the Lessingham coefficients unique, Professor Euyn?" Koria asked, her question coming between what was starting to look like an argument between Mom and Dad.

"Yes they are, Miss Valcourt. The coefficients are unique and trivial to solve for, provided the phenomena being studied are appropriately periodic and continuous. People do, however, sometimes misapply the transform, much to their chagrin." There was a low titter from Deleske and Bethyn at this comment. Keith Euyn continued without pause, speaking over their snickering. "But that is another story. This uniqueness property is dependent on the orthogonality of the coefficients and is indeed quite easily provable." He launched into a long, three-chalkboard discourse on the proof of the orthogonality relations. Bethyn was going for a new, personal eye-roll record before it was done.

"Why did you ask, Koria? Why?" This would have sounded more urgent from Bethyn if anyone believed she really cared, but Endicott had yet to see Bethyn engage fully with anything.

Endicott's heart leaped as he suddenly realized that the transform had a different, an intuitive, kind of symmetry. "But Professor Euyn, can't the proof be done by simple visual inspection?"

"Ha!" boomed Davyn. "I can imagine that! You just visualize a full period, right?"

"That's what I see," said Endicott.

"It's obvious once you say it out loud." Davyn was smiling happily.

"Which you certainly did, stupe," said Eloise.

Keith Euyn's eyes widened momentarily. "Yes, Mr. Endicott, the orthogonality is indeed graphically obvious, though this manner of proof is absent from the literature. Expect to have to present *both* styles of proof in the twenty-four-hour test."

"Thanks, *Mr.* Endicott," whispered Deleske sarcastically.

Endicott had thought the old man's hearing might be failing, but Keith Euyn surprised him. "Yes, Mr. Lachlan, you should thank Mr. Endicott."

Deleske sat up straighter, forced to sincere attention by the direct gaze of the great man. "But we don't understand the Endicott proof, sir."

"Don't call me sir," Keith Euyn snapped, cold eyes wide. "Let this be an assignment for the group of you, then, as a team. Figure it out together. *That* will certainly be on the test."

This sort of threat had been applied in enough of their classes that Endicott had come to assume that *everything* would be on the test. But twenty-four hours seemed like an outrageously long time for a test, and he doubted that any of the professors would let themselves be cheated out of asking their favorite questions.

Why twenty-four hours?

Endicott wondered how Heylor would survive having to sit still for so long.

"That will be enough for today. You are dismissed. Except for you, Mr. Endicott, and you, Mr. Daly. Please come by my office one floor down, if you would."

"I don't get it either," Heylor said after Keith Euyn had left.

"I don't care," said Bethyn with a yawn. "Anyone who says mathematics is worth all this bother is a liar or is hiding something."

It was a comment Bethyn had made often enough in other classes. She had spoken this way so ubiquitously that her complaints had come to be treated no more seriously than background noise to the mathematic detail she so clearly underappreciated. As evidence of this, Koria ignored the quip but gave Endicott a quick smile and a head tilt in Heylor's direction that told him she would help the skinny young man. Eleanor had not moved from her seat at the back of the class yet either, which he understood to mean she would also stay and help with the follow-up to the new proof.

Koria doesn't need me here.

"Let's go find out what the great man wants, Davyn." Endicott was up and on his feet in an instant, the big man right behind him. As he passed through the doorway, he saw that Gregory, Deleske, and Bethyn had stayed in their seats, Gregory to help Koria and Eleanor or perhaps just to listen in, Deleske to help himself, and Bethyn for unknown reasons. Possibly simple inertia.

Lindseth and Merrett stood silently in the anteroom, their usual station, as Endicott had come to understand, when class was in session at the Lott. Lanky Lindseth nodded affably at them as they passed. Massive Merrett did not.

"Nice blouse."

Endicott looked down at his shirt. Merrett seemed to find the shirts his aunt had made for him with her stitching engine affected and never missed an opportunity to make his disdain for them clear. *How quickly some things become familiar.* Endicott wondered if he would have been disappointed if Merrett had broken the predictable nature of their relationship and said nothing.

Strange to come to expect abuse and think it friendly.

"I think he likes your shirt," Davyn said.

"I am going to write my aunt and see if she will make one for him." *That'll fix his wagon.*

"Can I have one too?" Davyn might even have been serious.

"Sure. But then I'll have to get one for everybody." They skipped down the stairs and emerged in the lower hallway.

A rich female voice overrode the sound of their footsteps. "You can come up to my room later and get the measurements for *my* shirt, fiancée."

Endicott whirled. He had not heard Eloise come up behind them. She was an agile, athletic girl, but he had not known she could move so quietly. She was smirking at him. He could feel his face redden, partly from the surprise, partly from embarrassment, and partly because he was still young, and Eloise was still gorgeous. His developing relationship with Koria did not fully immunize him from a healthy, autonomic response to the blond girl; it only made him even more embarrassed about his physical attraction to Eloise. For her part Eloise seemed to delight in putting him off stride.

"You're coming with us, aren't you?" Endicott asked resignedly. It was hardly a question. Endicott knew that Eloise never hesitated to go where she wanted, when she wanted, and with whom she wanted, regardless of the situation.

"Why? Do you have a problem with that?" Eloise's smile turned fierce.

Davyn put his hand up, then lowered it as he started speaking. "*I* don't have a problem with it."

Eloise put an arm around his shoulder and kissed him lightly on the temple. Davyn did not blush, but he did look happy.

Endicott shook his head and continued down the hallway. "Of course not. You know I like you." He smiled, doing his best to find his own leverage. "But just as a fiancée."

The door to Keith Euyn's office was open. The ancient professor sat behind a massive, beautifully stained desk. His office was enormous but crowded with mementos and objects of an eclectic or esoteric nature. Swords, axes, and spears adorned one wall. A full suit of armor in the fashion of Armadale stood in the corner next to the weapons. Eloise gravitated immediately to this and the other martial paraphernalia. Davyn was transfixed by the book collection on the opposite wall. It went from floor to ceiling. The bindings were rich, with meticulous craftsmanship.

"Eight knights! An original edition of *The Lonely Wizard*." Davyn practically yelled with excitement, pointing at the creased leather binding of a particularly large volume.

Original edition? Endicott had heard of the children's edition, but never the *original* edition.

"Correct, Mr. Daly. I am surprised you even knew there was such a thing, so few of that edition were ever printed. Too many big words apparently. They made Gerveault rewrite it so more people could enjoy it." Keith Euyn sounded disapproving.

"Professor Gerveault wrote *The Lonely Wizard*!" Davyn's eyes were as big as saucers.

"Indeed. Shortly after the War of Rose and Thorn, when he first joined the New School, although it was not called that back then."

"Gerveault is the Lonely Wizard?" Endicott walked over for a closer look at the book.

Keith Euyn laughed darkly. "There is no Lonely Wizard, gentlemen and lady. It's only fiction. Please don't suggest such a thing to Gerveault. He would become quite wroth with you." The old man's lips twitched, and he added, "Borrow it if you like, Mr. Daly." His eyes narrowed. "You should *all* read it." His head turned like an owl's. "Do you like that armor, Miss. Kyre?"

Eloise's voice sounded strange when she spoke. "I've seen its like before. But these aren't the gauntlets of a Knight of Armadale." She pointed at the two mounted gauntlets. Each had a single word etched on it, across the top of the metacarpals.

"True," said Keith Euyn.

"Hope and prayer," she read. "What does that mean?"

"It's an old jest from our days in Novgoreyl, Eloise. It isn't as strange as you seem to think, if I may judge by the expression you are wielding. We used to name all our weapons and even some of our armor. You really should see Gerveault's collection."

Endicott noticed that a long, heavy-looking sword was propped on the other side of the armor. It had the word Likelihood etched on the blade. *An old Methueyn blade?* The young man looked for one of the archetypical sigils but found nothing. He achieved the lesser breakdown nearly instantaneously and examined the molecular fabric of the alloy. The artificial, cold-forged nature of the weapon was obvious.

"You are very quick, Robert Endicott. You lost no discernible level of heat there. But you could perceive it clearly, could you not?" Endicott nodded. "So you see," Keith Euyn added, "it was not only your father and grandfather that could forge Deladieyr- or Methueyn-class arms." He sounded almost smug.

Endicott left the empyreal sky as abruptly as he had entered it. *How did he know?* "You knew my father?"

"We know *all* the lines with talent, young man. How do you think we directed Lord Latimer? I must say, though, that your family is especially well known to us for quite a number of reasons. Your grandfather spent a few years here in his youth."

He did? How come nobody in the family seems to know this or talk about it? Endicott was shocked. He could think of nothing to say.

Davyn stopped tracing the embossed leather cover of *The Lonely Wizard* and reentered the conversation. "But why did Lord Latimer test us, then?" Endicott did not remember Latimer doing anything more than asking a few questions. To him. The Duchess's man had asked just as many questions of the rest of the townsfolk of Bron if Ernie was to be believed.

Keith Euyn leaned forward. "Because we didn't need to make last year's mistake twice! Those twins and their idiot brother were nearly the ruin of us."

All three students flinched at the great man's harsh tone. Endicott had not noticed that Eloise had moved next to him, but when her hand brushed his for a brief moment, he noticed that.

Davyn's hand went up. "Twins? Idiot?"

Keith Euyn's smile was too sharp to be sincere. "Yes. The reason we are here, at least in a roundabout sense. The gift is often correlated with intelligence, but there are exceptions. The twins committed the sin of mediocrity. It is not a gift limited to politicians; it can happen to anyone when their confidence outstrips their worth. They weren't quite smart enough, didn't work quite hard enough. They lacked the truly remarkable *affinity* that we need. Above all they weren't nearly humble enough. Their imbecile of a brother was better off than them, stuck in the middle like they were. They are all lost now."

He looked at the three students sharply. "But you two, sorry, you three—Miss Kyre, I'm too old to be distracted by your looks and your flirting to miss what is inside—you three, and the others as well, are all highly intelligent. I called you here to give you something to ponder."

Davyn clapped his hands together enthusiastically, misreading the mood of the old man, Endicott thought.

"Wizards and dynamicists do the same thing with a different methodology. One has an intuitive, spontaneous gift, the other a managed, quantitative process. At the limit of mastery the wizard and the dynamicist can be the same. But *only* at the limit. There is nothing worse for either wizard or dynamicist than to be mediocre within the wheelhouse of their chosen style but then attempt the method of the other. They are *so* different, you see, *except* at that limit. It is like the Lessingham transformation. If you understand it fully, the mathematical proof and the visual intuition of Mr. Endicott will be the same, but *only* then."

Davyn raised his hand into the silence of Keith Euyn's pause. "I may not be intuitive enough to know what you are advising us, Professor."

"Unsurprising." Keith Euyn sounded oddly satisfied. "Think on it. But think more about working hard at mastering what we *do* teach you, which is dynamics. You may go now."

They turned to leave, but the great man spoke once more. "I had hoped for more integrity from you, Mr. Endicott, not less."

Endicott frowned, confused and alarmed. "What do you mean, Professor?"

"Your grandfather would never have spoken a word of a lie, but *you* did. Of omission. It would have been more honest to simply give Lord Jon Indulf his brooch back and probably even easier if you had just kept it. Why didn't you do either?"

Will this never go away?

Endicott saw Davyn shrinking unconsciously towards the door. Eloise also seemed to know better than to say anything, but he knew he had to. "We aren't thieves."

"Not thieves, but not exactly honest either. Are you sure you know what it is that you are?"

It was difficult for Endicott not to swallow. "I had hoped to defuse the situation."

"Why?"

Endicott sighed, at which Keith Euyn seemed to frown. "Because of Jon Indulf's reputation for cruelty and overreaction."

Keith Euyn stood up. "His reputation? So you did not know him, and yet you perpetrated dissemblance based on that paltry evidence. For all you know, Jon Indulf is a great man. A great man. Easy complacence to ease a lie. You can do better than these half measures. They do no one any good."

The posture of the three students made wilted flowers look fresh. "We will do better next time," Davyn said at the volume of a normal person. Davyn's attempt to help was an unexpected respite for Endicott, but it only lasted the two hundredths of a second that it took for Keith Euyn to respond. He chuckled mirthlessly. "*This time is still in play!* If any of you wish to be great, you will need to think either more quickly or more deeply. Preferably both. But if you refuse to think at all, at least stick with your integrity."

$$\nabla$$

"That was excessively harsh," Davyn said as he dished up a heaping plate from the buffet at the Commons.

Endicott did not reply. He had been brooding over the rebuke since they left Keith Euyn's office.

Eloise speared a hard-boiled egg from off the ice chips. "I think that old man is just jealous of you. Come on, let's go sit with Koria and Gregory. They have been waving at us since we got here."

Endicott ignored them all and marched in the direction of Lord Jon Indulf's table. He held his plate in his left hand in case things went poorly. One of Indulf's cronies bumped the lord on the shoulder when he saw Endicott approaching. Indulf stood up.

"You stay away from me, Robert Endicott," Indulf said.

Endicott raised his right palm in what he hoped was a calming manner. "I only wanted to say something to you."

"And that is?" Indulf's arrogant face had a suspicious twist to it, and something else Endicott could not identify. *Fear?*

"I regret what happened here with you. With your brooch. I didn't mean for you to be . . . discomfited." He had thought to say "embarrassed" but thought better of shaming the young lord a second time and putting them even more firmly on the wrong foot. Endicott kept his voice calm and low, even though he was angry. He was not angry at Indulf or at Keith Euyn, only at himself for taking so long to do the right thing.

"It was a poor way to treat you," he finished.

This seemed to make Indulf even less satisfied. "It *was* poor!" His volume and tone stopped all conversation in the room. Again.

"But don't think you can fool me." Indulf's expression turned sly and cruel. "I know it was that skinny little skolve, Heylor, and his fat friend. I'll have satisfaction from them, you can be sure."

Indulf's threat to his friends redirected some of Endicott's inward-facing anger toward the aristocrat. He made a snap decision. He roared out a response at the top of his voice, not to Jon Indulf but to the crowd. "You all may remember the night when Lord Jon Indulf's brooch went in the soup. That was *my* fault, *not* Jon's! He was correct to be upset then. I am sorry about the disruption to your dinner then and now."

Lord Jon Indulf stared at him incredulously. He had nothing to say to this.

Endicott took a half step towards Indulf, who took a whole step back. Endicott spoke quietly to him. "I am truly sorry about what happened. *That* was your apology. Give up any thoughts of revenge against Heylor and Davyn. If you want further *satisfaction*, come to me, sir. What happened before was *my* fault, but what happens next is on *you*."

Endicott turned on his heel and left Jon Indulf to his thoughts. He could see Gregory and Davyn watching aghast, Koria's anger hardening her smooth skin, and Eloise smiling widely. Heylor had his head down and was eating ferociously.

Well, I sure made that better, he thought, feeling simultaneously disappointed, angry, and satisfied. None of those emotions had a remotely similar feel to them.

"Robert. Come join me," Eleanor said.

Endicott saw thin Eleanor sitting alone at a table. He noted that her plate was half empty. The empty half was clean. *I wish she would eat more.*

No other students had joined her. No one had cared to cross the line that separated professor from student. He sat down and waited for her commentary. Eleanor surprised him by saying nothing. Endicott decided not to flaunt the fact that they were on a first-name basis, so he spoke carefully. "Could you pass the pepper, Professor?" She did. Pepper was not exactly rare, but it was a bit of a luxury. There was plenty of that at the New School, Endicott thought, and all the freedom to make good or bad decisions. But was good or bad an outcome, a process, or just a way of thinking? If decisions were difficult to judge, how much more complex were people? What made a woman or man good or bad? Or great?

Endicott closed his eyes and enjoyed his second bite of the roast beef. He heard someone sit down on the other side of him, but he kept chewing. He knew what Koria sounded like and even recognized her faint scent.

"It will be okay, Robert." Endicott opened his eyes. Eleanor's hand rested on his shoulder. Koria placed her hand on his other shoulder. One rough and papery hand, one soft and smooth hand, both comforting.

"Thank you." Without thinking, he put his head on Eleanor's shoulder for just a moment. He had expected a lecture from both ladies and was deeply grateful for the moment of peace.

"Eloise and Davyn told us what Professor Euyn said to you. As if you needed incentive to act . . . like you just acted." Koria sounded angry, but this time perhaps not with him. Endicott wondered why, since she seemed to agree with the great man about his poor handling of the brooch incident. Perhaps she felt that admonishing Endicott should be her privilege alone.

"What did Keith say?" Eleanor withdrew her hand.

"He said I should either tell the whole truth or become a better liar. He told me I had treated Jon Indulf prejudicially, and that for all I know Jon Indulf is a great man."

Eleanor laughed. "Maybe for all *you* know, but from what *I* know, the answer is *no*." Eleanor's eyes sparkled in her wrinkled face.

Endicott nodded. "I suppose we'll see. At least now we aren't playing games."

"*You* aren't, Robert." Koria said, not looking relieved.

Eleanor chewed on her last piece of lettuce and put her fork down. "With the exception of mathematics and dynamics, you should be wary of advice from Keith Euyn, Robert."

"Why? Isn't he the great man of the program?"

Eleanor sat back and smiled patiently, her wrinkles somehow looking sympathetic. "Yes, he is, but that does not mean you should try to *become* him or act like him in all things. These dynamicists are . . . complicated. Keith and Gerveault both are what you might call idealistic. Neither of them really understands the little things that can seem so big here in the Commons where we come together and break bread. Their world has always been about ethics and ideas, best practices and proper procedures." She paused and pushed her plate to one side.

"They lack, shall we say, a sense of humour or joy in the day-to-day. Keith has always been more passionate about ideas than people. And now he is old and even less flexible than he used to be, though a decade ago I wouldn't have thought that possible. I think he is suffering the curse of the old, which I say gently since I am getting old myself. He *used* to be a great man. And the used-tos tend to judge the might-becomes a touch harshly."

Koria shook her head. "All this talk of *great* men seems a bit of a waste of time to me. I would prefer it if you could be described as a *careful* man, Robert, but that is proving unrealistic." Koria smiled to take some of the harshness off what she was saying. "Who can say what makes a man or woman great? Probably the best we can hope for is to be great sometimes or in some things."

▽

ANOTHER COVERED ICE CARRIAGE ROLLED BY THE CORNER OPPOSITE THE APPRENTICES' Library. Koria's hand in his, Endicott was about to step across the roadway when he saw someone he recognized. Or thought he recognized.

Could that be him?

It was indeed the bum from the registered seed fight, the man with the ruined shoe, but Endicott had to look twice to be sure. Some things had changed. The man was better dressed now, not in expensive clothes, but he had a relatively clean coat and his shoes were mended. There was also something else familiar about him, something from far further back in Endicott's memory, something that preceded that day in Nyhmes, something Endicott could not identify. Whatever it was, pathos came with it. The man turned and began to walk past the Apprentices' Library and further away from the New School.

I must speak with him.

"Koria! Do you trust me?"

Koria smiled, not knowing where the question was coming from. "Well, I want to." She hesitated. "I trust your intentions." She frowned suspiciously. "What is it that you want to do?"

Why are you so wise?

The words came tumbling out of Endicott. "There was a man there. He was the vagabond my uncle beat. The one who kept bringing up Nimrheal. He just left. Down the street!"

"And you have to catch him?"

Endicott kissed her quickly. "I'll meet you in the Library." He was off at a run, across the intersection, and down the street. He rounded a corner and saw the man walking alone not far ahead.

I must be smart.

Endicott tucked his medallion under his shirt, slowed his pace, and gradually closed on the man, who was whistling tunelessly to himself. As Endicott came up on him, he noted the smell of turnips and then saw that the man's coat had more than a few threads hanging off it. He also limped slightly in his left leg. Endicott passed him and pretended to only just recognize him then. "You! I know you sir!"

The vagabond stopped and squinted at Endicott. "You do, young sir?" His voice had a strange tonality to it, reminding Endicott of the color green.

"Yes! We were in that fight at Nyhmes together. At the seed place." Endicott smiled encouragingly at the man, not wanting him to think a further beating was in the offing. The man squinted again and hit the palm of his right hand to his forehead twice. "I don't remember you, young fella. I am so sorry. I took an awful knock on the head that day. Sometimes I just can't recall. Yer vaguely familiar, but sorry, that was a rough day."

Endicott felt pathos swelling again. He did not know why he always felt so sad when he saw this fellow. Other than the certain fact that his life was a sorry one. He raised his hands placatingly. "It's okay. That was a difficult day. I'm sorry you took one on the head. There was a lot of wood flying. Almost as much wood as grain."

The vagabond smiled. There was a smudge of dirt on his face, and in a shocking flash of recognition, Endicott understood at last why he always reacted so emotionally to the stranger.

He looks like my father!

Indeed the bum looked very much like his father, or at least like the image Endicott remembered from all those years ago before his dad had died. The resemblance had an immediate, visceral effect. Endicott found himself clutching the man in a strange parody of the grapple they had that day in Nyhmes. He came to his senses almost instantly, but when he did, he found the man was patting his shoulder. "Hey, now, young fella, it's all in the past now. Those pot-lickers at the Seed ain't here."

Good knights, he thinks I was on his side! Endicott thought about Keith Euyn's advice, and then Koria's advice, and decided to go his own way. He let go of the man but said nothing to clear up the misunderstanding.

The man straightened Endicott's shirt at the shoulder and seemed to hesitate. "I have a meeting to go to now. I don't want to run off on ya, but . . ."

I have embarrassed him.

"A meeting?"

"Yes. I got a job here. We ain't done with them pot-lickers, I tell ya." He laughed.

Endicott felt as if he had been punched in the stomach. He spoke on instinct. "Do you think I could get a job too?"

The vagabond scratched his head. "Maybe. Come by the Black Spear on another night. That's where I'm to go. I'll look for ya."

The man turned away and began to walk off. "I forgot your name!" Endicott called out.

"It's Conor."

"I'm Robert!"

Endicott watched Conor disappear around a corner before turning back the way he had come. He jumped, startled. Koria was standing no more than eight paces away. *How is it that women are always sneaking up on me?*

"How long were you following me?"

Koria smiled primly. "It isn't the first time, Robert."

On the way back to the Apprentices' Library, Koria would explain nothing about the stalking she had just admitted to. Instead she demanded an explanation from Robert. After shaking his head at her unfairness, Endicott explained his strange emotional reaction to Conor. Unaware of this at the time, Koria had thought he was starting another fight when she had seen him grab the man. By the time they found a booth at the Library, Endicott hoped he had convinced Koria that he was not loose in the head. They ordered tea with cream.

"You've never spoken about your parents." Koria had evidently decided which part of the day's events were most important.

Endicott took a sip of his tea. "I hardly knew them. They both died when I was . . . three? Four? I'm not even sure." The realization that he could not even be certain of the year of their deaths brought a wave of melancholy. "Their faces faded. First, I think, into an idea, a form. Eventually I lost my mother's completely."

"You don't remember your mother at all?"

He reached but could not find her. *Where is she?*

"When I think about my mother, I only remember standing by a slough with my dog. I don't know what that means. But my mom herself? Her face? The sound of her voice or what she smelled like? Gone. Evaporated. Like mist in the sunlight."

Like a hole in my mind.

"My father had faded to a smudgy sort of blur, but then Conor reminded me. *That* was what my father looked like."

Koria held his hand. "Tell me something that you do remember about your dad." She smiled impishly and added, "Was he a great man?"

Endicott laughed sorrowfully. "Like Indulf? Or Keith Euyn? I wouldn't know. By now I probably know those two, or even Conor, as well as I knew my father."

He closed his eyes for the second time that day, trying to remember, taking his time to recall what he could, letting his feelings carry the memories like a stream carries a small boat. "I remember fresh bread from Mom's kitchen. The smell of it. I remember sounds too. From the kitchen. Work being done, food cooking. But I don't remember *her sounds* or *her*." He trailed off, still reaching for memories.

"I can remember Dad better, though. His boots crunch, crunch, crunching in the snow. I remembered his face tonight better than I have in years. It was often dusty or smudged from metalworking or the fields. I remember the smell of dirt and oil and the smithy's deep, grumbly sounds and overwhelming heat. I remember seeing if I could arc my pee as far as his in the snow, and that my feet would always get cold before his, but he would carry me in when they did."

Koria smiled her wise, small smile. "He sounds like he was a great man to me."

Chapter Fourteen.

Call it Coincidence

*A*NOTHER WEEK—ANOTHER THREE DEAD MATHEMATICIANS.
Endicott adored the New School. He was excelling in his classes. He enjoyed the mystery and unpredictability of the new and luxuriated intellectually in the gift of learning every new concept. It was why he had come to the New School, or a large part of the reason. Some of his classmates were not quite as enthused about spending day after day in the Lott learning about mathematics, particularly Bethyn and Heylor. Heylor usually tried to pay attention but failed in character-istically messy ways. Bethyn treated the program with all the enthusiasm of a cat lover receiving a stinking, three-day-dead mouse from her pet. Gregory seemed to appreciate the classes as a sort of duty, Eloise as a battle, Koria as a solemn vow. Deleske was unreadable. Davyn exhibited the closest attitude to Endicott's, and the two sometimes comically interrupted each other in rushing to answer the professors' questions.

In every other way that Endicott could think of, life was proceeding with dream-like beauty and smoothness. There had been no further trouble from Lord Jon Indulf and no more strange sign bearers or fomenters. Endicott put aside the memory of the vagrant who reminded him of his father and acted and behaved in all the ways that he imagined he should. Koria seemed to relax after her worried reaction to his public apology to Jon Indulf in the Commons. She even jumped joyfully up to brush the low-hanging leaves of a tree with her hands as they passed under it. Endicott was as happy as he could be.

But the dead mathematicians were adding up. Each major new transform or new inversion method had its own inventor, and each of these geniuses had apparently paid the price of a fatal visit from Nimrheal.

Endicott reclined on Koria's bed. It was time for him to either go or, for the first time, stay. He paused on the boundary, the melancholy prospect of saying goodnight bringing a sudden thought from nowhere. "Koria. Can I ask you a question?"

Koria looked at him expectantly, her green eyes bright and widening. Her smooth, dark legs lay across his, bare to the hem of her night dress.

"Do you believe in Nimrheal?" he asked.

She looked surprised. "Nimrheal?" She smiled mischievously. "That's not what I thought you were going to ask."

Endicott knew the question was strange, and hardly appropriate to the mood or moment, but he persisted. "Most of the mathematicians we have studied did not die of old age, apoplexy, or tooth decay," he pointed out, trying to introduce his point with some humor. Then he grew serious. "They all supposedly died by the spear of Nimrheal. Could all those violent deaths be a coincidence? There must be a common cause. And how about Jennifer Reyland, the one who wrote the poem in the square that you wanted me to read? It is written there, in the very stone of our school, that Nimrheal killed her too. So it must be true, right?"

Endicott stroked Koria's foot in a soothing gesture. "Professor Euyn loaned us the original edition of *The Lonely Wizard*. In that version, but not in the version I own, the Lonely Wizard says that Nimrheal is real. But the book, says Euyn, is fiction. So is Nimrheal real or not? Do you think people only *want* Nimrheal to be real? Do they want him to come back?"

Koria's look was sharper than he expected, then sadder and wiser too. "We don't need Nimrheal to make horror, Robert. Our successes are all too ephemeral, but our mistakes stay with us forever."

She's so wise, but also somewhat . . . forlorn.

Endicott leaned across her legs and kissed her long and deeply. His hand moved along the outside of her leg and over her hip. "I love you."

"You can stay if you want," she breathed.

Endicott moved his face back just far enough to gaze into her eyes. "Our good decisions can stay with us forever too." He smiled. "You still trust my intentions more than my actions, don't you?"

It hurt to ask the question. Part of him did not want to ask it, did not want to have it confirmed that he was not the hero in her eyes that he hoped he was. Maybe he was no hero at all. Koria's face turned a different kind of serious. "Yes." She wiped a tear from her eyes. "I worry for you."

It hurt to receive the answer too.

Endicott kissed her again, though not for as long or as deeply, then gently disentangled himself. "I don't blame you, Koria. You probably trust me more than I trust myself. I will stay the night with you on the first day that *both* of us believe in me all the way through."

Endicott closed the door to her room behind him and stepped out into the girls' common area. Eloise was coming out of the baths, wrapped in a big furry towel. The towel was large, but Eloise was very tall, and it only covered her from shoulders to mid-thigh. Her long hair was wet and straggly, hanging down her back. She frowned at him, then smiled. "Are you cheating on me again, fiancé?"

Endicott walked up to her and stood on his toes to kiss her on her slightly damp forehead. "You know I love you, Eloise."

"At least you're not a total stupe."

Endicott was at the stairwell door when she spoke again. "Send Bethyn up when you get down. It's getting late."

"Will do."

As Endicott trotted down the stairs and the door slowly shut, he heard Eloise's fading voice. "Koria, what the—"

As the lovely female voices faded behind him, Endicott started to pick up the contrasting tones of his male roommates. "Twenty-four hours of hell, my ass! How about all the time we've spent in the Lott? That's two hundred and forty hours of hell. That's what we're in!"

Ah, the dulcet tones of Heylor.

Dulcet, Heylor was not. Calm, Heylor was not. Happy, Heylor was not. Right now he was pacing frenetically in front of Davyn, Deleske, and Gregory.

Deleske watched him with his sly half smile. "Don't forget the next two hundred and forty hours, Heylor. We're only half way through."

Heylor jumped up and stood on one foot on the arm of Deleske's chair. "Who in the hells of Skoll and Hati said this would be so much work? Work, work, work, work, math, work, work, math. When are we gonna get to the magic?"

Four voices answered as one, "There is no magic, Mr. Style, only mathematics and the laws of physics."

Deleske absently swatted Heylor on the shin, sending him wobbling off the chair. Endicott took his own seat and sat back with a sigh.

"How was the *studying*, Robert?" said Davyn loudly.

Deleske, immune to worry, slouched back in his chair. "He wasn't studying."

"I bet you learned a lot," snickered Heylor, back on his feet. "All three girls?"

"Leave him be, gentlemen." Gregory deepened his voice as he did on the odd occasions when he wanted to sound authoritative. When he acted as a lord.

"What have you gentlemen been doing other than ranting?" Endicott looked around. *All three girls?*

Someone was missing.

"Where is Bethyn?" he asked, over top of their grumbled responses.

"She went upstairs two hours ago at least," said Deleske.

"No, she did not," said Endicott. "Eloise was just asking after her."

"It's pretty late," hedged Davyn.

"She's just out drinking," said Deleske lazily. "I wouldn't worry about it."

"Alone? I don't think so." Gregory looked worried. "Heylor, go tell Eloise that she isn't with us."

The next few minutes were dominated by Heylor running to and from the girls' floor relaying messages. He only commented on Eloise's towel five times and tripped on the stairs in distraction over it once. Finally the decision was made, over Deleske's lazy protests, that the boys should go look for Bethyn. The idea of notifying or involving Merrett and Lindseth was reluctantly discarded given the commonly held suspicion that the two military students were acting as spies for their professors. Endicott was surprised that Eloise did not insist on accompanying them, but she had always been unpredictable.

It was decided that Deleske, Gregory, and Davyn would go search the east half of the Academic Plateau, while Heylor and Endicott would take the west half.

"You should bring your knife, Robert." Gregory was strapping his longsword on to his hip. His face was dripping. He had, perhaps as some sort of ritual, splashed water on it in the baths. Endicott went into his room to find his knife. The belt for it was there, but the blade itself was missing! He turned around, walked into the common room, and kicked open the door to Heylor's room.

"Robert, what are y—" Heylor called from behind him.

Endicott marched over to Heylor's mattress and unceremoniously flipped it. A collection of trinkets lay exposed: miscellaneous jewelry, Davyn's small stuffed dog, items of cutlery, a pepper shaker, and various objects of mysterious provenance. Endicott's knife, too, had been stuffed under the feather mattress.

"That's my doggie!" Davyn boomed mournfully into Endicott's ear as he walked through the doorway.

"I'm sorry, Robert," Heylor pleaded.

$$\nabla$$

"I am thinking of a double-wide plank contraption with wheels," said Gregory. He had switched groups with Heylor after the knife incident. "When we go out in public, say to the Commons, we strap him to it—arms, legs, and body—and push him around. When he's bad or acting the particular peasant, we can accidentally bang him into things."

"I'm not feeding him," Endicott rasped.

They had searched the Apprentices' Library and most of the west half of campus and were now standing not far from where they had started in the Field. The Field was another name for the Agriculture Square. Its monument sheltered a wooden signpost, which had two roughly etched planks nailed to it. One of the planks contained the list of futures prices at the Vercors Grain Exchange, which was much bigger than the one in Nyhmes. The other plank only said:

"The Book of Nature is penned

Deep in everything you ken.

Its language is mathematics,

Its medium, genetics."

"We all like to think we are the center of the Empyrean," Gregory said flatly, pointing at the plank. "I do sometimes think we might be part of something larger than ourselves. Do you ever think that, Robert?"

Endicott was listening for the footsteps he had noted before, which seemed intermittently to follow them about campus. He had not heard his friend's question clearly. The footfalls had stopped again. It was getting late, and few people were about. Perhaps the other walker had at last turned in. He sighed.

Endicott was not feeling hopeful, and his anxiety over Bethyn was steadily increasing as dusk gave way to night. Only Deleske was really close to her, but she was still one of Endicott's roommates, and he had sworn to help Koria get everyone safely through the twenty-four-hour test. That did not account for all his anxiety, though. He had two other reasons for concern.

"Robert?"

Endicott shook his head. "Sorry, Gregory. I *hope* there is a reason and purpose for our program. It would be a strange waste of resources if there weren't."

"It had better become clear soon. With Bethyn out here somewhere alone and Heylor starting to steal things again, we need some progress." Endicott would have never thought Gregory was a worrier when he first met him, but he had learned that his tall friend was both worrier and romantic. There was a kinship between them in this respect as well as in the story of Gregory's sword.

"It really hasn't been all that long Gregory. I think we need some patience. Even if our history is one of stutter steps rather than smooth progress, it's still a long history. We should expect to have to put some work into getting ahead of the past."

"Everyone wants progress to be quick, I suppose. That's been my father's mistake. Except for this one thing." Gregory patted the scabbard of his sword. "Where else can we look?" he asked, reverting to their immediate objective.

"My Uncle Arrayn wrote two weeks back asking me to visit a friend of his from Bron. She's the manager of a tavern called the Hanging Man. It's not far from here. Supposedly it's an upscale alternative to the Apprentices' Library."

Gregory smiled, the light from a hung lantern reflecting suddenly from his eyes. "You think Bethyn might be drinking there instead of the Apprentice? Let's go. Do you know this friend of your uncle's?"

Endicott chuckled. "Sure do. I beat up her cousins."

They set off at a trot, but as they worked their way through the greenhouses that marked the boundary of the Field and that of mathematics and physics, something caught their eyes. One of the greenhouses was glowing yellow by its own internal lamplight.

"That's wasteful even for here," Endicott said.

"Yes . . ." Gregory trailed off, uncertain.

As the two young men rounded the corner of the building, they almost ran headlong into two guards standing near the greenhouse doorway. Both guards were in full chainmail. One of the men put a hand on his sword, and the other raised his hand and held it up, palm out.

"Stop right there, gentlemen. We know you not," he said calmly.

Endicott thought fast, remembering something. He pulled out his medallion, which had been under his shirt. "You know this, don't you, sir?"

The guard took a careful moment examining the medallion and without betraying either surprise or uncertainty, nodded to his companion, who promptly opened the greenhouse door.

Endicott and Gregory stepped inside. The interior was lit by a line of lamps hung on a long horizontal metal pole and suspended by two small stands, each of which had wheels. A woman and a man stood amid this lighting contraption, examining the shoots of adolescent grain which were planted in rows of wooden boxes. The lady was holding an undeveloped wheat head, her eyes closed.

Endicott opened himself to the empyreal sky, achieving the lesser breakdown nearly instantly. The immature wheat head was surrounded by a nimbus of probability fed from elsewhere but manipulated and groomed by the woman. Goose bumps rose on Endicott's forearms and neck. He had manipulated molten metal at his grandpa's forge, but what was this?

The Book of Nature? Could it be?

Endicott did not know. He could not know. He had manipulated the dead molecules of metal, but could it be they were manipulating the living? If true, this was entirely different. This was a step across a very different line. This was the manipulation of life itself.

What confidence must it take to do this? What fear must they be feeling?

Endicott wanted to confirm his intuitive leap by asking them what they were doing, but that would have revealed that he did not belong there. Instead, motioning to Gregory to keep silent, he asked, "How many do you have left to do?"

"Almost there," she said distractedly before stopping to look at Endicott and Gregory. Her eyes widened, and she released the wheat head. "I know you. You're Robert Endicott. You have a heavy footstep. I saw you and your friend in the Commons, playing games with Jon Indulf."

The man beside her frowned, shook his head, and said, "They can't be ready yet." He then glared suspiciously at Endicott and Gregory. "Did Gerveault send you?"

Gregory shook his head, "No. We were looking for a classmate and saw the light here."

"Well, she's not here," the man said. He turned his attention back to the wheat, but the woman did not. She smiled and casually approached Endicott and Gregory. When the man saw what she was doing, he followed her.

"So it's just chance that brought you here, then?" the woman's eyes shone wetly. "A strange piece of luck. I don't believe in coincidence, you know."

You should meet my friend Koria.

She held out her hand and said, "I am Elyze Astarte. This is Vern."

"Vyrnus," he corrected.

Gregory stepped forward, leading with his open hand. "Gregory Justice." Endicott followed suit with his hand but not his words. He had made his name known to everyone, apparently, through his big mouth in the Commons.

Elyze studied Endicott and Gregory carefully, not appearing to be in any rush despite the time of night. She was dark haired, of medium height, perhaps just a bit taller than Koria, but older. Endicott guessed she must be in her late twenties. Her eyes were a cold, sharp blue. There was something in them and in the set of her face and shoulders that suggested a predator. Vern looked about the same age, was perhaps Endicott's height, and might have been considered handsome, but the two younger men paid him very little attention.

"Which class were you in?" Endicott asked, guessing.

Elyze did not answer, but Vern was more forthcoming. "The third. Half your lifetime ago."

Elyze continued watching the two young men with a slight, knowing smile.

"You're manipulating the grain," Endicott said, though he still had trouble imagining the daring it would take to do such a thing, let alone the skill. Gregory started. Endicott guessed that he had not achieved the lesser breakdown. Elyze betrayed no discomfort at his speculation. In fact her smile broadened. "Let's just say that we are standing directly in the way of statistics, young Robert." She waved her arms expansively at the rows of wheat. "There will be no regression to the mean while *we* are here."

You are *overwriting the Book of Nature.*

"You are manipulating probabilities in the developing seeds," Gregory hazarded. Elyze blanched.

Good guess.

Endicott doubted that Gregory really understood what Elyze was doing. Endicott knew that *he* did not either. But Gregory had not even seen it. What Endicott saw, and what he surmised from it, made him feel curious and excited but even more afraid.

"That would be one way of describing it," said Elyze

"Are both of you doing it?" Gregory asked.

"I wish," complained Vern. "Elyze is the only one from our class who can safely achieve the greater. I'm just confirming the results."

"We haven't done anything yet in our classes," Gregory confided a little apologetically.

"It will come soon enough," Vern muttered with a shudder.

"Somebody already did do something similar, class or no." Elyze pointed at their armaments, her eyes defocusing strangely. "Something wonderful."

Is this what I look like when I view the empyreal sky?

"I have never seen a probability blade before. You could be of help to us," she continued, staring intently at Endicott now.

He seized the opportunity to satisfy his curiosity and, if he were lucky, quell his fear. "There are two problems with that."

He raised a finger. "First. Gerveault and Keith Euyn would kill us if we did even one thing, good or bad." But he was really thinking of Koria and, unexpectedly, of Eleanor.

He raised a second finger, but Gregory broke in. "And second, we don't know what you are doing." His voice dropped to a confessional volume. "Not really."

Vern's shoulders dropped slightly as if he had been holding tension. "Very wise." He patted Gregory's shoulder. "As you say, Gerveault and Keith Euyn would kill us all. This is tightly held information, so—"

Elyze cut in. "So we cannot tell you what we are doing either. It would seem that we are at an impasse." She touched her lips with a finger. "And yet there is the coincidence to consider. It should be respected. Why don't you guess?"

Endicott disliked games, but despite his heart huddling low, his curiosity leaped. "You are controlling the variation of the seeds of grain. Their size primarily, but possibly other attributes. Perhaps you are attempting to grow a viable seed population for a new strain."

And you are doing it with ever so much control and at a rate that is orders of magnitude faster than selective breeding. You have absolute control, which makes your selection absolutely efficient.

"Actually most of that has already been done," Elyze said with a satisfied smirk. "But you get the idea. When you're back in class, think about the design of experiments and you'll understand better." Her smile faded. "You can't have a control experiment without control."

Her feet turned away from Endicott and Gregory. "But everyone here is correct. We will be in a great deal of *hot water* if we are found conspiring." She chuckled to herself for reasons that neither young man understood. "Still, I will ask our betters to send you to help us the moment you are ready." Elyze's head and torso followed her feet as she fully turned from the two young men, walking back to the row of plants and her lighting contraption. Vern was close behind her.

"It was great meeting you both," said Gregory to their backs, somewhat put out. "But we should get back to looking for our friend." Endicott was not sure how to feel about the strange, coincidental meeting, but he was just as happy it was over. It was time to go.

"Good luck!" said Elyze with a long laugh, which Endicott and Gregory continued to hear even as the door closed behind them. The young men gave sighs of relief and irritation, respectively, as they passed the two guards and returned to their mission.

"She treated us like peasants," Gregory huffed.

Elyze had seemed very sharp and knowing, strangely welcoming, but then more than slightly dismissive. She had made Endicott feel like a boy, though not in a cruel way.

"A little sensitive perhaps, *Lord* Justice? At least she didn't actually *call* us peasants," Endicott rallied with a smile. "That would have been rude." Gregory hit him lightly on the shoulder.

They trotted past buildings, lone walkers, over the grass field that bordered this part of the campus, and finally to the ring road. They stopped momentarily before crossing. There was a noise in the distance. It was caused by something big moving towards them down the road. It was a covered carriage. When it came closer, both men could see that it was rocking slightly from side to side and swerving wildly but slowly down the empty road. Something fluttered in the carriage window facing Endicott and Gregory, and a shout sounded from within. The carriage slowed and stopped opposite the two young men. The driver, a thick-bodied man, waved to them with exaggerated care.

"Ho there, merry gentlemen! Care to join us in our travelling party?" His lips fluttered disturbingly, and his words slurred to the limit of intelligibility. A smoking fag drooped from his mouth, the red stump somehow not falling out while he attempted to speak. A foul smell wafted from the fag.

"You must be mocking!" said Gregory disdainfully, turning his back on the man.

"Nope, lords, we're not a joking. Join us!"

"Why?" Endicott said, wondering why he and whoever was in the carriage wanted their company.

"We have a girl."

Endicott's heart skipped a beat. It was not a sentence he had ever expected to hear. It was an alien idea, and for one still instant his naïve young mind could form no clear conception of what "having a girl" might portend. This uncertain millisecond was followed just as suddenly by a new realization and just as quickly by rage. His heartbeats hammered in his ears, and he tasted copper in his mouth. Only his recent experience with Jon Indulf stopped him from locking his hands around the wide neck of the drunk. Instead of losing time and memory to rage, he was able, just barely, to think, and thinking, to ask a question.

"A girl, you say?" he grated, breathing in gasps, and looking at Gregory who had whirled around at the fellow's invitation.

"Yes, yes, gentles, a girl in the carriage. She's sloshed, smoked, and slack. He he he. Have a drink with us and you can play with her. She don't care no more."

Endicott's fists pumped at his sides as he attempted to hold onto sentience. Gregory's forehead was creased with two kinds of concern, one for the girl and one for Endicott's white faced, apoplectic state. "Why don't you have a drink with the gentleman, Robert, while I check on the lady."

"Come on out, Lynal!" the drunk called. "Bring the Neverclear and another fag. These fine gents want to drink with us!"

Endicott took a long, slow breath, fighting for calm by breathing as if he was. Another thick-bodied man slithered haltingly out the carriage door, bumping his knee as he came. Endicott could see that this fellow had to be a close blood relation, perhaps even a twin, of the driver. He had a bottle in one hand about a third full of some clear liquid.

"Aghh, I gots no cup, Vard, we made her drink right out of the cock," Lynal said, stumbling but holding the bottle clear and high as if he had almost dropped it. He stood blocking the door. Gregory's hand was on the hilt of his sword.

"No cups! No cups? *You* are in your cups, brother. Pass him the bottle. He's a brother gentle and won't mind sharing." Vard climbed slowly and with care down from his perch.

"Sure. I'll have that drink." Endicott took a half step back, making Lynal take a step from the carriage door to pass the bottle. It was surprisingly heavy and had a long neck. Endicott nodded subtly to Gregory, who released the hilt of his sword and opened the carriage door.

Endicott wiped the bottle on Vard's shirt, further distracting the drunk as Gregory climbed into the carriage. He tilted the bottle back as if to take an enormous swig of the unknown liquor but held his throat tight and only allowed a small amount into his mouth. It was hot and peppery. He coughed a spray of the poison out and up into the air.

Grain alcohol?

Both Vard and Lynal stood laughing in a great and childish joy from seeing Endicott apparently taking in more of the ethanol than he could handle.

"We call it Neverclear, 'cause you're *never* clear after," one of them said. They both guffawed in the way only the simple or the addled could. Endicott could hardly tell them apart and did not care to. Gregory emerged from the carriage and caught Endicott's eye. He shook his head, tight and worried, eyes big. "It's not her, Robert."

Not her?

Endicott had trouble processing Gregory's report.

It has to be her!

They had left the Orchid on a mission to find Bethyn. Endicott blinked, a new shock running through him as he realized all was not as he thought. It was worse.

Worse because the situation could be ignored, would be so easy to thoughtlessly ignore. He saw that Gregory did not know what to do, did not know if action was called for or if they had a moral imperative. He understood, too, that his young friend's mental processes were out of step not from any ethical ignorance but because of a lack of experience. And because the situation no longer related to the mission they were on. Surprise, ignorance, and preoccupation worked to obscure what, objectively viewed, was a deeply moral crisis.

Endicott's semblance of calm boiled away as a new imperative materialized.

"But there *is* a girl in there?" Endicott's volume rose with each word. "Sloshed, smoked, and slack?" He shouted, "*Not caring!*"

The two brothers did not seem to take Endicott's violent shouting amiss. "Have another drink, gentle friend," Vard said, fag finally dropping out of his mouth. He grubbed clumsily about on the cobbles to retrieve it.

Endicott ruthlessly thrust down the urge to kick Vard in his teeth while he grubbed for the fag. He thrust the bottle into Gregory's chest. "My friend will have a drink with you." Endicott shook his head minimally at Gregory. *No.* "I want the girl."

"Have at her, brother," one of the drunken brothers slobbered out.

Endicott entered the carriage and his pounding heart dropped out of his chest and into his stomach. A rumpled girl lay on the back seat, curled up, languid, barely conscious, with eyes half closed. She had medium length, dark hair, and was perhaps a year or two older than he. Booze, ejaculate, and some other viscous liquid were splattered in streaks on her once white dress and in her hair. She was not Bethyn, but she was *someone*. Endicott kneeled, facing her, trying to determine if she could even see him. On gazing into her face, the horror and rage that had been coursing through him was overwhelmed by love.

"Ahhh, we knew you gentles were students of the school. It isn't just that we're right by the school. We can tell, you know. We were students once too." Endicott could hear the two idiots yelling out their best impression of human speech against the quieter tones of Gregory, which he could not make out. Only the feeling of love enabled him to overcome his rage, block out their ravings, and focus again on the girl.

"Hello?" he said gently. "Can you hear me? I am Robert. I'm a friend."

A slow smile spread languorously across her face. "Hi, Robert." Her eyes closed.

Endicott reached out and shook her shoulder gently. Her eyes opened again. "What is your name? Where can I take you where you will be safe?"

"Safe?" she breathed softly, reminding him of Koria earlier. His hands shook again, but he squeezed them into fists until the shaking subsided.

"Yes. I'll take you to where it's safe. Where is your family?"

"Jain."

"Your name is Jain?" Endicott kept his voice encouraging, holding her shoulders gently again. "What's your last name, Jain?"

"No," she laughed at the limit of perceptibility, "Jeyn. My cousin Jeyn."

Endicott's heart leapt, hoping. "Your cousin's name is Jeyn? What is his last name? Where can I find him?"

"Jeyn Linds . . ." her voice trailed off, and her eyes closed again.

Jeyn Lindseth! Another coincidence, but a better one. Endicott knew where to find *him*.

He scrambled blindly for the door handle and popped it, then scooped the girl up in his arms. He pushed his way through the door, maneuvering her carefully one way, then the other. She was unexpectedly light. He could hear a roaring, but it was not his heart.

"Aghh. Maybe we shouldn't have her out of the carriage there, brother," Vard or Lynal called, then laughed, holding the mostly empty bottle up to his flabby lips. "We might have to share her."

Endicott ignored the two drunks and faced Gregory, whose sweat-covered face betrayed his own crisis. "I'm taking her to Lindseth. If they try to stop me, give your sword a reason for being. Cut them in half."

Endicott turned, and carrying the girl, walked north on the sidewalk towards the Military School. He heard the brief humming sound of Gregory drawing his probability sword.

"Hey there, you aren't taking our girl!"

"I *will* cut you in half, bastards! Stay back."

A hollow ringing sound clattered behind him. Endicott turned, fearing that Gregory had been hit on the head by the thick glass vessel. He was relieved to see Gregory on his feet, sword drawn, backing carefully towards him. One of the idiots had fallen and dropped the bottle, while the other looked on in horror.

"Now you've fucking done it, brother. You've spilled most've the Neverclear. Knights damn you to hell, skolve!"

The one who had dropped the bottle, and who Endicott now saw was Vard, lurched edgewise and improbably to his feet, stumbling and spitting. "You'd drunk most all of it anyway! Shut your gob, ff- *brother*! Mom was right about you, yer a selfish prick." They started hitting each other and wrestling wildly. The bottle rolled away into the gutter.

Gregory caught up to Endicott, who could not believe what he was seeing. "Let's get out of here while they're distracted." Gregory swung his sword around, so he could sheath it, making it hum again briefly as it cut the air. "Do you want me to take her?"

"You keep watch. I'll try to run. That Neverclear's turned half her brain off. If it concentrates much more, she'll be dead." Endicott pulled the girl tight and increased his pace to an almost unsustainable level. The sounds of yelling and fighting echoed faintly behind them. "Why Lindseth?" Gregory said, puffing, holding his sword hilt with one hand to keep from tripping on it and looking over his shoulder. Endicott could not answer immediately. Snot was mixing with sweat and running into his gaping mouth. His throat burned. "Lindseth's cousin," he gasped.

Gregory said nothing. A moment passed. Endicott took a chance and half turned to see why. Gregory was looking back and drawing his sword again. "They've stopped fighting," Gregory panted, squinting. "I think they found the bottle, of all things, and are getting their carriage turned around."

We don't have time for this!

Endicott stopped and turned to face the carriage, which was now coming on at a galloping pace. He knew from the incident with his uncle that running would not work out in the open, where they unfortunately were. His uncle had only been joking in his reckless way, but he knew that the brothers were capable of anything. And part of him did not want to run. The carriage picked up speed, swerving wildly.

"You go, Robert," Gregory said, "I'll hold them off." Gregory started walking in the direction of the carriage.

Robert let his rage slip the leash and reached through the empyreal sky. He calculated nothing. Righteousness and fury were his formulae now. He smashed through the boundary with heart rather than mind and roughly, dangerously, achieved the greater breakdown. Without stopping, he pushed and broke through some other, unfamiliar barrier. Beyond it, he felt all the endless fire in heaven. It was there, ready to be bent by his passion. He shook with it. It raged in step with his heart.

I will remove them from this earth!

"Step back, Gregory. Please! Now!" Endicott shouted, struggling to maintain control of the energy. He felt the power, but feeling was all he had. Part of him knew how perilous this could be. He was operating by instinct but had nothing to base his instinct upon. Another part of him gloried in the finality of what was to come. A definitive, objective example would be made of what happened to people like the brothers. "I don't know how wide this is going to be."

Gregory turned to him, confused. Then his eyes widened, and his mouth opened in shocked realization. "I can see it!" he exclaimed. "Good knights, Robert, don't!"

A tall blond woman abruptly ran out from the grass of the school grounds towards the carriage. She reached the roadside and stopped. She pulled up the hem of her tartan skirt to expose a long, smooth, muscular thigh. The carriage skidded, bucking and rough, to a halt. The horses screamed.

Eloise! Then he saw Koria only thirty or so paces behind her! With a cry of frustration, he released the empyreal sky and shivered violently, biting cold washing over and through him.

"Can I have a drink of that, boys?" Eloise called loudly, leg still exposed.

Both brothers stumbled out of the rig, fighting over the nearly empty bottle. Finally one of them won free and passed it to her. Eloise quickly reversed her grip so she had the bottle by the neck and smashed him viciously on the head with it, a hollow glonk marking the first blow.

Glonk, glonk, glonk.

She hit him three more times in the head in rapid succession. He tottered for a moment and collapsed bonelessly to the ground. He made a sloppy puddle. Eloise then turned to the other brother, who was backing gracelessly and ineffectively away.

Glonk, glonk, glonk, clishhh.

Endicott started running again, nearly falling on frozen shins. His thoughts were sluggish, he was so cold. His normally robust mind could hold onto only one option: reaching Lindseth and the medical group at the barracks by running as fast as he could. A few moments later he heard the carriage coming up on him again.

"Get in, Robert!" It was Koria. He turned and saw her sitting beside Eloise, who had the reins, on the driver's bench. Her eyes were red, but she smiled at him. Endicott stumbled to a stop and climbed up, balancing awkwardly so he would not drop the girl. He sat between the two women, still cradling the girl in his arms. Gregory squeezed in on the other side of Koria.

"You're frozen, stupe!" exclaimed Eloise.

"You w-were both stalking me," he stammered. "Again."

"You're welcome," Koria said calmly, snuggling awkwardly close to him and lending him some of her heat. "It is a very good thing that we were."

"Wh-why?"

"Because you're an idiot," chimed Eloise.

It took only a few moments of galloping to arrive at the spartan stone and brick buildings of the military barracks. The statue of Heydron stood off in the middle distance. A surprising number of armed men were milling about near the entrance, including Merrett and Lindseth. Within seconds of their shouting, frenzied arrival, they were able to hand Lindseth's brutalized cousin, whose name they now learned was Syriol, to medics, who rushed her away to the infirmary. It had been fortunate that the staff had already been roused by some other incident. Apparently, only a few moments before they arrived, there had been reports of a carriage stolen from campus grounds. Merrett gave them all an unreadable look before joining three other armed men to collect the two brothers that Eloise had left bleeding on the ring road.

"They might be dead," Eloise said without emotion, even though Merrett was already out of earshot. "That bottle didn't break easily."

"Hati take them," said Gregory into the night.

Endicott was still shaking, despite Koria's arms around him. "It was just such a strange coincidence that she was your cousin, Jeyn."

"I wish I could believe it was a coincidence, Robert." Lindseth's mournful eyes were pointed skyward. He had touched Syriol's crusted hair and tried to smooth it before they took her away. Then he had cried, but now he was quietly philosophical. "But this sort of . . . assault happens more often that you would think. It happens so often that I don't think it should be called a coincidence at all."

Chapter Fifteen

Hero

ENDICOTT WAS STILL SHIVERING WHEN HE AND HIS THREE FRIENDS ARRIVED BACK AT the Orchid. The four of them rushed past the reclining but surprised form of Deleske, slouching on one of the chairs, and into the baths. Gregory, Koria, and Eloise helped Endicott up and into the hot bath, clothes and all.

"Didn't Elyze say something about hot water?" Gregory mused.

"Another c-coincidence?" Endicott closed his eyes, still shaking.

"Take your clothes off," said Koria. "In the bath."

"Yes, take 'em off," Eloise amplified.

Endicott smiled, eyes still closed. "Are we all betrothed now?" he murmured.

Gregory's right eyebrow climbed. "The four of us?"

"I am going to evaluate that in just a minute," Eloise said brightly.

For once Endicott was unfazed by Eloise's innuendo. He sluggishly pulled his shirt off. He considered his pants, but belatedly realized his boots were in the way and had to take them off while sitting in the hot water. They floated. He closed his eyes. Time passed silently except for the breathing of the four of them. Endicott opened his eyes and held his hands out over the edge of the bath towards his friends. "Take my hands. All of you."

With some shuffling, Koria, Eloise, and Gregory crowded around the vessel to hold hands with Endicott, who remained in the tub. Four heads crowded in with the hands. Endicott could feel the others were shaking, though not from being cold. The troubles of this night might be over, but they would never truly be gone. He knew neither he nor Gregory would soon, if ever, forget the nightmare memories of poor Syriol crumpled up, used up, and dying in the coach. Dying alone in the dark. Would the rage over this ever go away? It was inchoate in its swelling size and its pure, truthful, frustrated awfulness.

The terrible death Endicott had almost brought down on the two criminals might have given his fury appropriate voice, but the victory of such an eloquent response would have been pyrrhic. He knew he had nearly killed them all.

Was rage even the correct response to such an atrocity? What did *correct* even mean in the context of what they had seen? Endicott wondered whether he or Gregory would ever be able to take an innocent view of their fellow man again. Would the horror of what the brothers now seemed to represent ever leave him? At an intellectual level he knew that to generalize their predatory brutality to all men was wrong. It was prejudicial as well as unfair, but as he shook in the tub from both hypothermia and emotional shock, he felt shame. He knew he did not deserve to, but he could not help the feeling. He also worried that this night had only primed him for even worse responses in the future.

How would the girls feel? They had not seen Syriol in the coach. They had never faced such a situation uncertain about what should be done. They would never have to ask themselves if there was a version of the world where they had not looked closely enough but had simply gone on their way to find Bethyn.

But how had the girls known to come in the first place? Why had they arrived to save the situation? When they reflected upon the night, what would they feel? Did they see a mother or sister in place of Syriol? Did they fear the same thing could happen to them? Did even Eloise, as strong and fierce as she was, fear that it could happen to her? Endicott knew that he and Gregory were closest to the events of the night, but he also knew that these events must strike the girls in a more deeply personal way. And so his thoughts continued to torment him. The only thing that made it bearable for Endicott was that the other hands and heads were there.

Thank the Knights that Koria and Eloise came. The sweetest sound Endicott had heard that night was the glonk, glonk, glonk, glonk of the heavy bottle.

"I hope they're both dead," someone said.

"Yes," someone else said.

Finally, as if achieving some release, they all opened their eyes and looked up. They still held hands.

Tears streamed down Gregory's face. "I reached the lesser breakdown. I *saw* you, Robert. You had punched a hole in the Sky and held it open. Fire—"

"Stop, Gregory." Endicott felt an overwhelming lethargy. "We can talk about it later. Just give me some time."

They slowly released each other's hands, and Koria turned back towards the door. "Deleske, where is everyone else? Where is Bethyn, and where are Heylor and Davyn?"

A long sigh answered her enquiry. A couple of moments later, Deleske shuffled into the baths, stretching. "Robert, you know you're in the tub with your pants on, right? What happened to you?" He frowned at the rest of them arrayed around the tub. "You all look a little raggy."

Koria shook her head. "We'll tell you later, Deleske. First, please, what happened with the rest of you?"

Deleske scratched his head. "Not much." He turned as if to leave them, then pivoted back. "Well, not much that I saw, anyway."

"What does that mean?" Gregory asked, suspicious now.

"Nothing was going to come of it, so I left them." Deleske walked into the common room and slouched back down in his chair. Gregory and Eloise followed him with twin expressions of disbelief. Koria stayed with Endicott.

A climactic fit of shaking seized Endicott. Koria gripped his hand until it passed. When it was over, he knew the worst had passed. Koria helped him with his soaked clothes. His boots were ruined from all the running, from the wave of cold on the street, and finally from the bathwater. Koria turned them upside down on a ledge. She hung his shirt and pants and came back to the tub. Endicott turned in the bath so he could rest his forehead against Koria's as she leaned against the outside of the stone vessel. Neither of them said anything, luxuriating in this moment to themselves. But the rest of the world soon intruded again. They could hear a developing argument in the common room.

"And you just left them?" Eloise's voice had a steely edge. "Not much of a teammate, are you?"

"It was boring and a waste of time." Deleske's voice was not quite as relaxed as it normally sounded. "Hey, let go of my arm!"

"You really don't care about anyone but yourself, do you, Deleske?" Gregory sounded weary.

"What is everyone so upset about? There's no reason for all this drama." Deleske sounded patronizing now. "Robert has got you all acting just like him. Alternating between being madly in love or just mad at the world. There is something not right about that. Ough! Let go!"

"Shut your mouth, you . . . I would call you a skolve, but skolves at least look out for each other." Eloise's voice had an uncharacteristic flatness to it.

"I didn't do anything wrong! Please let go!" Deleske's voice became pleading. "I'll explain everything."

"Let him go, Eloise," Gregory said. "Please."

Endicott and Koria emerged from the baths, he wrapped in a towel and she in one of his arms. They crossed the common room and flopped onto a couch together. Deleske was rubbing his arm. With obvious reluctance, Eloise stepped back from him and sat down. Gregory took the chair beside her. They all fixed their eyes expectantly on their recalcitrant classmate.

"Listen," Deleske said, "We *did* look for Bethyn. But she wasn't anywhere to be found. I know you are all very excited and worried. You care, and I appreciate that. Don't hate me because I don't wear every feeling I have on my sleeve."

Deleske settled back, assuming his casual slouch. "I never thought she was in any danger. Bethyn just doesn't like school, or she likes it well enough some of the time but not others. She drinks. I told the others that Bethyn was just off somewhere drinking. Like you four, they didn't believe me. Like you four, their heads were full of a fear that came from I do not know where. Why all the drama, I thought, so I took my leave and came back here. And sure enough, she was upstairs, wondering where everyone had gotten to."

"Really?" said Gregory.

"No, not so much," Deleske allowed, looking up and to the left as if for patience. "She was drunk and didn't give a hoot. When I told her you'd all gone out hunting for her, she just pulled a pillow over her head and burrowed face down into the couch. So you see, I was right all along."

"You didn't know that for sure when you abandoned Davyn and Heylor," Koria said evenly.

"No, but I knew *her*," Deleske said with exasperation. "So, please, all of you lay off me. I *did* wait up for you, you know."

"You're a real knightly hero," spat Eloise, blue eyes hard, big nose scrunched.

Deleske nodded, rubbing his arm and grimacing at Eloise. "Yes, I am. All this upset is over nothing. *I* made sure she was here. *I* made sure she didn't vomit and choke. *I* stayed up to tell you about it. I wasn't really expecting thanks, but I certainly didn't expect a beating."

"You don't know everything yet, Deleske," Gregory said in a low, weary tone.

"Wiser words were never said. But I *do* know that a few beers never hurt anyone. We don't need to be under guard every slow minute of our lives. There is no great risk in going out at night here. The campus is about the safest place anyone could be."

At that instant there was a great clatter in the stairwell. Moments later a thoroughly disheveled Heylor and Davyn ran gasping through the doorway. A thin stream of blood ran down Davyn's face. "We were nearly killed out there!" he boomed.

$$\nabla$$

"I WILL TELL YOU THE STORY NOW," DAVYN SAID AFTER HE HAD CLEANED UP THE SCRAPE on his forehead and heard an abbreviated version of the events surrounding Syriol and the two drunk men. Deleske was still clutching his arm and sulking at Eloise.

"No, wait. Something is missing!" Davyn looked around frantically. "I think I need one of those Justice cookies, because as you are about to hear, Heylor and I are the real heroes here. Heylor wants one, too."

When he had his cookie, Heylor offered it to Endicott in what could only be an apology for the theft of the knife. Endicott took a bite. It was shortbread, a favorite of his, particularly with tea. Meanwhile Deleske had assured Davyn and Heylor that Bethyn had indeed made it back safely and was wedged tightly in the soft, safe embrace of the girl's couch upstairs. Then, just as Davyn opened his mouth to start his tale, Endicott looked down at his plate to see that there was a second bite missing from his cookie.

As Robert mentioned in his oft-repeated story of the Battle of Nyhmes, everyone lies a little when they tell their tales. Let me just say that the only exceptions to this obfuscation of narration are the mathematicians. They can't even lie about who really discovered the important theorems, because the real discoveries have each been verified by the deaths of the discoverers. Of all of us, the mathematicians tell the truth the most, so long as you ask them to tell you about something mathematical. Take one step from mathematicians and you get the physicists, who you would think can't lie, because, hey, we are talking about the laws of physics, right? No. You would be wrong.

Can I have another cookie? No? Okay, the physicists. In so far as laws go, no, it's hard to lie, but then again, the laws change under the crucible of the scientific method, and even the physicists are proven wrong in celebrated fashion. But mostly the laws themselves don't lie. A poor experimental design can make a lie, whether the design is poor because of incompetence or not. So when we speak as physicists, we must be very careful about the experiment our thesis relies on, for we would hate to speak a thing that might be a lie. Hew, hew, hew.

Engineers? Don't get me started. They lie for whoever is paying them. It is easy to apply the simple laws of physics to the complex world and, ignoring nuance, tell any lie you like. Bureaucrats? Nimrheal never kills them because there has yet to be a bureaucrat who created value, let alone something new. And anyway, nobody can tell if they are telling the truth or lying, because they keep their own books and hire their own people.

Poets? They are admittedly confusing. Their passion can be absolutely authentic. Who can call a feeling a lie? Still, not even death by Nimrheal can prove a poet was actually telling the truth, for after all their death by Nimrheal is one of originality and thematic truth, not absolute truth. And who knows less about the objective world than poets? They are about as educated in math and physics as a six-year-old.

What? No, I'm not trying to be negative or malicious. Bring on the poets and the engineers! I love them all whether they are telling the truth or not. My point is that you cannot trust anyone's story. Except for the ones told by me and Heylor. Actually, just me; you can't trust Heylor not to steal the truth or the lie right off your cookie plate. So pay attention.

Quiet, Heylor.

I stood unmoving in the eye of the hurricane. My stuffed doggie Rupert had been found and tucked in, but Bethyn had not. In this storm everyone took up their role and followed their trajectory. Heylor had been buffeted and rejected by the winds of his own compulsion. Robert and Gregory, cocksure and certain, had practically flown down the steps on unequivocal wings and were already gone. Moments later Koria and Eloise crept down the stairs in time to little gusts, cautious and quiet. I walked to my room and out onto the balcony to see them following, wraith-like, fluttering after the boys at a distance.

Was it chaos? People were rushing about. Deleske was certainly calling it chaos, warning against excessive reaction. But was the rapid unfolding of events unpredictable? Was the rush to search for Bethyn an overreaction?

I considered in those first few moments that there were reasons for every action being contemplated and for every position being taken. The wind blew for a reason. I simply did not understand those reasons. There was rationality to be found there if one knew enough about the motivations, fears, and values of the actors. Did it seem likely that I would discover enough or infer enough to unravel the mysteries driving my roommates and friends? Yes, I decided. I had already deduced some of their secret hopes and fears and someday would likely know them all well enough to make sense of the developing storm. But would I learn enough to answer all questions on this night? No, I thought not.

I did, however, realize that I already knew enough to make informed decisions of how and where to look for Bethyn. That I would eventually be proven wrong about the timing of her whereabouts does not prove my process false. I did after all just miss capturing her in her lair.

Deleske would solve the problem of sending someone back to the Orchid to wait for Bethyn if she eluded us. A real boozer, which she is, requires care. Deleske could do that in his understated manner, and there was no chance that he would endure a long search. He thought he knew Bethyn best and was sure she would be fine. He has lived a life of emotional denial that reads to everyone like detachment, but that is a lie. He has denied that he loves her, denied that he worries about her, and would deny that she was at any risk. To accept any of these things would be too painful, sharp, and hot for our cool Deleske. This was not a conscious process for him. He was following the nature of his mind. He cares not too little but, when it comes to Bethyn, too much. So back here Deleske certainly would come. He would feel forlorn at heart but pretend it was all simply disinterest. Even if Deleske finds it too painful to know himself, he will be better off if Bethyn knows him.

Okay, I must admit that I don't know if Deleske really harbors a secret love for Bethyn, nestled within an equally well-concealed and deeply sensitive nature. But I like that explanation better than the theory, even if backed by all appearances, that he just doesn't care about anything. Either way I knew he was going home early.

The strange foursome of Robert, Gregory, and their two stalkers were of no concern to me. Why did the girls stalk the boys? Why do they act as a team? Probably not relevant to the search and certainly not a wise topic of conjecture. Neither Robert nor Gregory were going to stop until they had finished, and the girls weren't coming home without them. As four, they should be in no danger whatsoever, and I expected them to carry out a long, thorough, and orderly search for Bethyn in their half of the campus.

This left, or would eventually leave, only Heylor and me. Heylor had already let down his heroes, but his failure was one of compulsion, not conscience. Heylor's heart is not in question, just his twitching need to steal. I knew I could count on him. We would steal Bethyn away if we found her.

Did I know enough? Let me tell you what happened.

"Can you believe he just left us?" Heylor exclaimed, vibrating this time with indignation. "Heydron's tits, Davyn, what a shitty thing to do."

This would be blasphemy if you were in the Steel Castle, but common enough in the streets of the city, which had to be where Heylor hailed from.

"What in the hells of Hati do we do now? We've looked everywhere there is to look. No wonder Deleske up and ran off home." If Heylor was a dog, his ears would have laid down low.

"It's really quite simple, my dear Heylor," I said manfully.

"Hervor's horn, Davyn. How so?" Heylor responded attentively, head darting about, staring at shadows.

"What do drunks do?" I asked my young friend.

"Yell and scream?" Heylor said bitterly. "Run off on you?" he said more bitterly still. "Disappoint you in every way possible? When you think they have brought the most shame and humiliation upon themselves, when you think they have sunk to lows you wouldn't imagine, they surprise you with worse. In the end they leave nothing unspoiled: no love, no friendship, no family member, no material possession. You have to forget about what drunks do, Davyn, and you have to get away from them."

What could I say to this? He had shocked me. It was no matter for humor and, more to the point, he was right. Not everyone who drinks becomes a drunk, but every drinker knowingly or unknowingly walks upon a high wire. Most can keep their balance: for some the wire is very broad and for others it is as narrow and slippery as a fishing line. If they can stay on the line, all is well, but if they fall they become a drunk and eventually, absent a miracle, all the things Heylor had said. The worst thing about drinking must be that, unlike the man on the high wire, drunks do not even know when they are falling. To everyone else, the fall of the drunk is as obvious as that of the high-wire artist.

I usually avoid thinking about such things. I don't look for confrontation and would normally have tried to come up with some humorous riposte to Heylor's bleak rant. I have also never been directly affected by this issue, though I am aware that the struggle of the high wire goes on all about me. I wanted to hug my friend. I wanted to shout: is this why, Heylor? Is this why you put yourself on a high wire of your own devising? *But who knows why? And since we are talking about drunks, we mustn't make excuses. I still wanted to thank him, though, for making me face this truth. In his grief Heylor had given voice to an eloquence that showed his usual crude patter to be a deception.*

Are you surprised? I warned you that everyone lies. Everyone but me of course.

I digress. The matter of Bethyn was still unsettled, and she was not the drunk that Heylor was speaking of. I led him in the direction we needed to go, giving him some moments of peace while I framed my response.

"Let's talk about Bethyn, Heylor. She is young and maybe just starting the slide towards the fall you described. Where might she be? What do drunks do?"

Heylor said nothing. He was looking down at his feet, wrapped up in his own world. He did not see the enormous, upright sword that we approached.

"I think drunks do one of three things, my dear Heylor. First they find a place where they can drink more. Not at the Orchid, and Deleske has that covered now anyway. At an earlier hour we could look for an event, but now I think a bar of some kind. Second they wake up loved ones or friends to fight. You alluded to this. Failing friends, they might fight with strangers. But I think we must eliminate this line of possibility for Bethyn. She is not the fighting type, and her family lives some distance away. The third thing that drunks might do is find some quiet place to drink or reminisce. They might choose a sentimental or evocative location."

I whirled about grandiosely, waving my hand at the Methueyn Treaty. Heylor's eyes followed my expansive gesture, and we both looked at the twelve-foot-long, metal sword of the Treaty. It was etched in the words of the Methueyn Knights, the words that all Deladieyr Knights spoke before hanging in counterbalance to the massive sword. This sword was a monument to the Steel Castle on the south end of the Academic Plateau.

"She isn't here," *Heylor muttered, coming back to himself.*

"A bit big for even you to steal, eh, Heylor?" *I said, pointing at the massive weapon.*

"Maybe," *he laughed.* "I don't know where I would put it."

"We have a spare room up in the Orchid."

I let the moment hang. I did not feel there was much reason to rush the search, and I was pleased to see Heylor recovered from his introspection.

"By the great black spear of Nimrheal," he said, still smiling, "where to next, then?"

That colloquialism seemed a bit over the line to me, but no one likes a quibbler. "Where I think she would really hide is the small lounge in the Lords' Commons. It is Ursday, and it should be open late. Neither Robert nor Gregory drink much at all, and I think they are barely aware that the bar exists. So we will go there next, and failing that, to the more . . . romantic statue of Heydron."

Off we went, down the dark paths of the campus.

"Nimrheal's nuts, Davyn, someone's following us!" Heylor hissed.

I couldn't hear any footfalls behind us over my own huffing and puffing. We were putting on quite a pace, I have to say, and the sound of my own breathing filled my ears. I grabbed Heylor by the scruff of his neck and pulled him around the next corner. I crouched low, below eyeline, and poked my head around the corner. No one was there. Heylor didn't believe me until he had seen for himself. We laughed at the false alarm and continued on our way to the Commons.

The lounge was still open. Sir Urieyn's day was known for late drinking on campus, and quite a few students still haunted the room's dark recesses. Bethyn did not appear to be among them. In keeping with Urieyn's love of music, a flutist serenaded the remaining drinkers in low, soft tones, while a young woman recited a poem of her own creation. It was Jennyfer Gray, who we had seen about the Commons before. She was a lovely, blond woman, but a person, I had concluded, of only modest means. Tonight, however, she had the attention of none other than Lord Jon Indulf, Lord Quincy Leighton, and Steyphan Kenelm. Their state of inebriation spoke to the likelihood that they had been at the lounge for some time. They could tell me if Bethyn had been here. I started to step forward to speak to them, but Heylor clutched at me.

"Knights alive, Davyn, what do you think you're doing? Indulf hates us!" Heylor's eyes were wide.

I shook my head ruefully. "That is all in the past, my dear Heylor. We're all friends now."

"How can you be so naïve? He's not our friend. He's just scared of Robert."

I did not know if I agreed with "scared," but Robert had certainly made an impression. Still, I was far less at the center of the controversy than Heylor. "I prefer to ask, "why can't he be our friend" rather than "why isn't he." Don't you think that is a better way to approach life, Heylor?"

The poem ended, but Indulf and his crew were so impressed and enthusiastic that they pressed her for another. This one was very short and much older, a traditional composition. I remembered it from Leysday at the Steel Castle when I was but little.

"Price
We may have paid a price,
That does not make it right.
Take heart in your battle
Against Nimrheal's evil.

Rage against the demon,
Enemy of reason."

Jennyfer had a lovely voice for oration, and I could see that her performance had put everyone in fine spirits. It seemed the time was right, so I broke Heylor's grip on my arm and approached Indulf's group. Lord Jon held a beautifully wrought crystalline hip flask in one hand and was speaking softly with Jennyfer. She noticed me coming and smiled in my direction. With her blond hair and good looks, she was like a much shorter, far less fierce, and somewhat friendlier version of Eloise. They all turned to look, everyone smiling or looking indulgently confused except for Indulf, whose face was unreadable.

"Excuse me, lords and ladies," I said with as much gentility as I could project. "I wonder if I could trouble you with a question."

Lord Indulf did not smile, but he also did not shout. "As long as that thief Heylor keeps his skolve paws over there, fine. Ask your question, big man."

I knew we could all be friends. "I was looking for my friend and classmate Bethyn. We were to meet here, but I seem to have missed her."

The gentlemen gave me back only blank looks, but Jennyfer brightened at the question. "You just missed her, Davyn. She was sitting in the back and left not a quarter hour ago. I think she was heading home to your Orchid tower."

I thanked them profusely and gathered up Heylor to leave. Maybe she was going home, and maybe she wasn't. But she couldn't be far away. I decided we should follow our initial plan and check on the monument to Heydron.

"And no comments about Heydron's . . . boobs or other parts, Heylor," I warned. The great statue was not far away. We would reach it in just a few moments.

Clop. Clop. Clop.

Less worried now after learning that Bethyn had indeed only been out drinking, we were walking at an easier pace, and this time I could clearly discriminate the footsteps of a stalker behind us. I put a hand on Heylor's shoulder but gave him the subtlest of head shakes to indicate that we should give no sign of having detected someone following us. Was it one person or two? I wasn't sure. Two, I thought. I suspected I knew who it was and whispered my suspicions to Heylor. But why, I wondered, had Koria and Eloise switched to following us?

We waited until we came to a corner, around which we crouched in wait, giggling. The footsteps sounded closer and closer. Strangely now, it did seem to be one person. Then, just as I realized that something wasn't right, the stalker rounded the corner. Before I could say anything, Heylor leapt forward to surprise his assumed classmate.

He bounced painfully off the seven-foot-tall, hooded, and robed figure, which we now saw held an enormous black spear. I swear its eyes were glowing bright red in the dark.

"Skoll's scrotum!" Heylor exclaimed in his rudest vernacular yet. "It's fucking Nimrheal!"

"Run!" I bravely shouted. And ran.

We ran like the heroes we were, fast, wild, and scared. I could hear the pursuer behind us, breathing hard but weirdly, unlike any human breathing. Heylor should not have uttered such blasphemy of Nimrheal. The chase led us around buildings, between them, around the Heydron monument, and back towards the Commons. We rounded the same corner where we had originally waited in ambush and collided violently with someone else. It was Indulf and his crew. I felt something wet on my chest. I reached to touch myself. I was wet. Blood? I tasted it off my fingers. It was whisky.

We had run at full speed into Jon Indulf and his companions. I had smashed chest to chest with Indulf himself and broken his crystalline flask. Heylor was spilled like a farm sale across the path, having tripped on someone else. I helped Jon to his feet and cried, "It's Nimrheal! He's right behind us!"

Nimrheal was not right behind us. Our pursuer was gone. All that was left was us, Indulf, his cronies, and the broken flask. Some silences are good, and some are not good. This was not a good silence.

"Uh. I don't know where he went," I said lamely, knowing how matters looked. "Can we still be friends?"

Indulf shoved me back, roaring, "I'm going to kill you, fat man. You and your pet skolve!" He glanced at his companions, who grinned and nodded.

If he was really planning to slaughter us then and there, I reflected, surely he would have simply commenced to killing. Why shove me and then talk? He hadn't even drawn his sword. What I saw before me was a man who needed to pronounce his intentions before acting. He was righteous, and the righteous like to say so. At length. What I saw was an opportunity—to run. Again.

And so we ran. I admit I am a big man, but I can move when I must. Heylor was right behind me. We had a bit of a lead on our pursuers. They had perhaps not expected us to flee until they were done terrifying us. But what to do? They would catch me eventually. I am not equipped to run indefinitely. Heylor might get away but maybe not; Indulf and his crew were athletic looking, to say the least. I needed a solution that could be executed before my wind gave out like the air from a pig bladder.

I remembered something. I turned past the Commons and made for the carriage for hire waiting there. It was white, with two beautiful, white horses. The driver, a man in expensive livery, sat tall on the front bench looking out across the ring road. He did not see me as I dived head first onto the bench, scraping my head on something. My stinging head was in his lap. Heylor flew into the back seat.

I looked up at the shocked face of the driver. "Drive!" I gasped.

The driver leapt out of the carriage.

Clop, clop, clop, clop, clop.

He was running off. I sat up, skootched over, grabbed the reins, and gave the horses the whip. We had just got up to a gallop when Indulf and his gang appeared. I drove the carriage over the lawn and through our pursuers, scattering them, and then got the horses under control and back onto the road. Heylor clung to the back, laughing.

"We drove back around the east side of campus, hid the horses, and then made our way here," Davyn finished, face red with excitement.

"That. Was. Such. Skolve. Shit." Eloise said. "You are an even bigger liar than Robert."

"I never said any of that," complained Heylor, head hung low. "That's not how I talk. But that *is* pretty much what happened."

"I am *not* sensitive. Or in love." Deleske walked off to his room and shut the door behind him.

"You never saw Nimrheal," said Koria softly, snuggling with Endicott.

"And you never stole a carriage for hire," added Gregory.

Davyn clapped his meaty hands together with satisfaction. "And that's *exactly* what you are all going to say tomorrow if you're asked."

Chapter Sixteen.
Desperation

ENDICOTT WOKE UP WITH A WOMAN FOR THE FIRST TIME IN HIS LIFE. HE HAD NEVER been in love before, so this was fitting, but the reason they had stayed together was for a consummation of a different sort. Neither of them had wanted to endure their dreams separately after what had happened.

Eyes open, Endicott knew that the events of the night were not magically behind anyone. The slightest remembrance of those events accelerated the young man's heart. He wondered about Syriol, if she was physically okay and if she remembered much of what had happened. He hoped she did not. He did not want to remember, but memory is a thing to be reckoned with. Bad memories in particular have a life of their own, wanting to be reviewed again and again as if they have only just happened. Memory can multiply injury repeatedly, never letting it heal. Good remembrances are different. They are soft, comforting, and easily forgotten once time has moved onward a sufficient distance. They are like a soft light in a dark night.

The image of a quiet field and a still pond came to him. It was old, from childhood, but he could not place it or understand its context. He did, however, remember love and who he was with. *That,* Endicott wanted to remember. He sat up, kissed Koria's forehead, and looked past her. Gregory and Eloise were tangled in the other bed, both in nightclothes, heads side by side. Eloise's long, blond locks were fanned across Gregory's face. The look of ultimate happiness on his young friend's sleeping face confirmed Endicott's long-held suspicions about the feelings of the tall young man. Gregory was in love too.

When did we move Gregory's bed in here?

Endicott carefully got to his feet, avoided tripping over beds, legs, or heads, and approached the door. Before opening it, he looked back at his friends, sprawled and innocent-looking. He felt a tear threaten, so he turned back to the door and poked his head into the common room. Davyn was stretched out on the couch reading the original edition of *The Lonely Wizard.*

"I didn't sleep with Heylor. Just so you know," boomed Davyn.

▽

THE LORDS' COMMONS WAS UNUSUALLY QUIET, EVEN WHEN TAKING THE SMALLER breakfast crowd into account. Merrett and Lindseth came but left quickly, apparently off on some errand. As they went out, Lindseth came by and clapped Endicott and Gregory on the shoulders. Merrett gave their table a sharp nod. The big slab of a man for once did not sneer at Endicott's "blouse," nor did he comment on the sandals Endicott wore in consequence of his ruined boots.

"I'm sorry," Bethyn whispered again, though only into her oatmeal. Her eyes were red and her face puffy. She admitted to a headache but claimed to have no memory of the night before except for some scraps of Jennyfer Gray's poetry. She had been shocked to hear about the adventures of the night before. Nobody, including her, *believed* Davyn's heroic tale, and no one *wanted* to believe what Eloise, Koria, Gregory, and Endicott had gone through to rescue Syriol.

"I didn't know you would all come out and . . ." she trailed off into her porridge bowl.

Deleske put an arm around her. "I told them you were fine."

Bethyn shrugged his arm off and said nothing further.

"People are staring at us," Heylor whispered, returning from the porridge pot with another bowl. "I heard them at the buffet. They say Robert and Gregory hacked up Jon Indulf and two of his friends because they violated Koria. Apparently the Duke's men have been all over campus since last night trying to find all the body parts. Which makes sense, even if it isn't true. Have you seen all the guards and constables roaming around out there?"

That is mixed up. Endicott wondered which parts of Davyn's story might be true, if any. Then he saw Koria's reaction to Heylor's report, which was one of mute horror. Her dark face paled, and she seemed unable to look up. A slow heat built again within him. He did not want to imagine that what had happened to Syriol could have happened to Koria. The thought was unbearable.

That people would make up stories of events they knew nothing about added to his building rage.

"Let's go," he said, pushing away from the table and taking Koria's hand.

ANNABELLE CURRIK DID HER BEST TO PRESENT THE SUBJECT OF THE THERMAL CAPACITY of various substances to a class of obviously tired, distracted students. Bethyn's head was buried in her arms, Deleske slouched and stared at the ceiling, Koria's arms were crossed and her eyes still downcast, Eloise frowned at the corner of the room, Gregory stared at Eloise, and Heylor looked as if he was getting ready to crawl under his desk. Endicott tried to release his anger by pushing thoughts of the previous night from his mind. Perhaps if he listened hard enough to Annabelle's dry discourse on physics, he could move on. Only Davyn behaved relatively normally, asking pertinent questions and taking notes diligently.

"Should we be most concerned with volumetric or mass-related thermal capacity, Professor Currik?" Davyn held his long feather pen poised, ready to record her answer. Annabelle breathed out in obvious relief. Endicott guessed that she was unaware as yet of the source of everyone's malaise, but he doubted she was enjoying teaching such a tepid crowd.

"Both, Mr. Daly. As a dynamicist you may choose to manipulate the energy or temperature of any number of things, but you will need to understand the amount of energy required to balance the equation by mass or volume." She smiled, and it was like a cool glass of water to a tired and still angry Endicott. "This is no less true for the physicist. The relationship of heat and energy is a beautiful, real thing. It is measurable, testable, and under identical conditions, always behaves the same. These properties should not to be rushed through to pass a test, even our twenty-four-hour test, but should be studied from every perspective so that you can appreciate all the dimensions of how they operate in this world." Endicott finally began to reawaken, an answering enthusiasm rising within him. Both her smile and her enthusiasm for the cool rationalities of physics resonated strongly within him.

What an intelligent woman. Math is beautiful and objective in and of itself. The world is still beautiful despite some of the people in it. The physics are inviolable.

Endicott's hunger to understand was reignited and his capacity for the joy of learning roused itself again. Perhaps few would have understood this emotional sublimation. It was an almost spiritual response that most would have found strange. But Endicott felt better at once, and his behavior reflected this.

"What about the relationship to state, Professor Currik?" he said with some of his usual enthusiasm. "How does the heat capacity of water versus ice versus steam change?"

"Very good, Mr. Endicott. The differences are profound. We will discuss this in—"

At that moment Eleanor, Gerveault, Merrett and Lindseth walked through the door of the Lott, their expressions serious. The three professors huddled in conference. Merrett returned to his station in the anteroom, but Lindseth approached the students. He locked red-tinged eyes on Endicott.

"Syriol is doing better. They pumped her sto—" He stopped, clearly struggling to collect himself. "She is sitting up and is able to speak normally." Lindseth forced a smile through his grief as he finished. "Thank you for helping her last night."

Endicott was not sure if he should say anything. Lindseth's raw emotion was palpable. Endicott himself began to feel the weight of his own memories of the night again. At the same time he recognized that he had suffered much less than Syriol, or even than Lindseth was suffering now. He realized he should try to help.

To say nothing is not enough.

"Jeyn. Could we visit her?" A thought occurred to him. *I think we need to if we are to put this behind us.*

Lindseth's old, gentle smile returned. "Yes. When the time is right."

Gerveault cleared his throat. His two colleagues stood silently beside him "Lord Kennyth Brice, the next Duke of Vercors," Gerveault announced, "has arrived. He is waiting in the Lords' Commons to speak with you about last night's events."

"I'm sorry," Bethyn whispered.

"No." Gerveault had heard her and raised his bushy eyebrows. "Do not be. The facts are mostly known. Witnesses have come forth. Keith Euyn himself performed an exhaustive act of heraldry at the crime scene. He saw what happened and even some of what might have been," he added, looking straight at Endicott. The old man's gaze swung to the others. "Tell the truth when you are asked for it."

They filed quietly out of the Lott and made a quiet a procession down the pathways towards the Commons. The flatness and brevity of Gerveault's words had done nothing to lighten anyone's mood. Eleanor asked Endicott, Gregory, Eloise, and Koria to walk with her, so they followed some distance behind Heylor, Davyn, Bethyn, and Deleske. Further back, Annabelle Currik trailed, flanked by Merrett and Lindseth.

"Thank the Knights for you girls," Eleanor said quietly, so that only her group could hear. "You pulled that one out of the fire. Literally." Eloise looked up, proud, but Koria blushed.

Eleanor reached out and gripped Endicott's hand on one side and Gregory's on the other. "But you did well too, boys. You were very brave, and you saw what needed to be done. It's easy to be asleep in your responsibilities to your fellows, you know. So easy." She squeezed their hands. "But you're my boys, and you did right. Heydron herself would have been proud of you."

"Thank you, Professor Eleanor," said Gregory clearly touched.

Eleanor squeezed their hands once more. "You *cannot* manipulate the Empyrean until we give you leave to do so." Her voice dropped even lower. "You *must* not. It's too dangerous. Don't let yourself become so desperate." She let go of their hands.

Clap!

Endicott had been about to reply, but the sharp sound shocked them all. It was the sound of a slap.

They had been so attentive to Eleanor's quiet words that Endicott's group had missed the collision up ahead of Davyn, Heylor, Bethyn, and Deleske with Lord Jon Indulf, Quincy, and Steyphan Kenelm. Bethyn and Deleske had been pushed aside. Indulf slapped Davyn a second time.

Clap!

The big man did not respond other than to hold his reddening cheek with one hand. Steyphan held Heylor by the scruff of his neck.

Jon Indulf tore the long feather pen from Davyn's hand, saying something to him, and bent it between fingers in opposite hands. The pen broke, the sharpened end flipping rapidly through the air towards Eleanor's group. Endicott's hand flashed out, seemingly of its own volition, and caught the pen nib two or three inches from Eleanor's face.

Indulf threw the other half of the pen on the ground and slapped Davyn a third time.

Clap!

Endicott handed a shocked Eleanor the broken piece of pen and charged at Indulf, Gregory and Eloise a half step behind him.

"Robert, don't!" Koria's familiar voice sounded an all-too-familiar admonition behind Endicott. Jon Indulf saw him for the first time now and drew his sword with a panicked expression. Steyphan Kenelm did the same, but he held his to the side, staring at it as if he did not know what it was. Quincy stepped back, stiff, as if frozen.

"You stay out of this, Robert Endicott!" Jon Indulf yelled, sword up and poised.

"Put it away, Steyphan!" Gregory roared. The sound of running feet echoed off the path. Clop, clop, clop, clop.

Endicott closed with Indulf before the aristocrat could react further, right hand grabbing his neck and left reaching for the wrist of his sword arm. Beside him Robert heard a sharp ringing sound followed by a metallic clatter. Steyphan's sword was in two pieces, Gregory's intact, brightly shining, blade pointed at his face. Quincy was splayed wide on the ground, eyes the size of teacups, with Eloise standing over him. Her fists were clenched, and she was smiling.

Indulf started to move his sword arm, but Endicott caught it with his left hand. He squeezed without thought or effort, and Jon Indulf's hand opened. His sword fell with a clang. Indulf gasped.

Being desperate is a state of mind, and Endicott wrestled with his. Even the most self-aware person is not self-aware always. Otherwise self-awareness would be a curse, a recursive cycle that would make action slow or even impossible. Still, Endicott knew he was in a poor state of mind, fighting between sadness and anxiety over Syriol, a manic desire for immediate and violent justice—even though the brothers had been dealt with—and a frustrated desire to simply get on with his education. He was aware enough to ask himself, holding Jon Indulf's wrist in a crushing grip. *How desperate am I? Is this person where the problem lies?*

Words. I need words.

And still he squeezed Indulf's wrist, but still harder.

"Is this who you hoped to be, Jon?" Endicott spoke through gritted teeth.

Indulf's expression screamed confusion.

"This?" Endicott continued. "Someone on one side of a series of one-sided conversations followed by acts of petty violence. Is this what you dreamed of?"

Endicott turned, Indulf's neck and wrist still held tight in his grip, the man himself forced to turn with Endicott. "Do you see Professor Eleanor over there?"

Indulf's eyes flickered to Eleanor and back to Endicott.

"You came a hair away from putting her eye out with the tip of Davyn's feather pen. Would you have been *proud*? You already hit Davyn, who from what I have seen is a better man than you."

"It's okay, Robert," said Davyn, his voice not loud.

"He provoked me." Spit flew as Indulf gasped. "He—"

"He irritated you? Ran into you accidentally last night?" Endicott interrupted, squeezing a little harder. "So? Are you a lord or not? Aren't you bigger than this? Or is this how small you came here to be?"

"They stole, they broke—"

"What! What did they steal? What did they break that gives you license for this?" Endicott squeezed harder still with both hands. "Why does this matter so much?"

Indulf's knees had sagged, but now he straightened. "They said I violated Koria." He shuddered as a discontinuous emotion abruptly emerged. It came with twin tears. "I would never do that!"

"Not these two. They never said that."

"No. People. In the Commons."

Endicott closed his eyes and let go of Indulf's wrist and neck. Jon sagged but stayed on his feet. "Set you off a little more this morning, did it?"

"I wouldn't do that!" Indulf's tears were a torrent now.

Endicott bent and picked up the fallen longsword. He handed the hilt to Indulf, who mastered himself and took it with his left hand.

Endicott did not look away from Jon Indulf's eyes. "I know it, but do you wonder why people find it so easy to believe that of you? You show a love of yourself and no one else. You show a man full of arrogance, indifferent to becoming better. They think you are small and mean because that's how you act."

Lord Jon Indulf had to try three times to sheath his sword with his left hand. His right was only good for wiping his red and runny face. He turned away from Endicott and said. "I am sorry Davyn, Heylor. Professor Eleanor, I'm sorry."

Jon nodded to his friends. Quincy stood up, brushing off dirt. He had the wherewithal to smile at Eloise. Steyphan Kenelm gathered up the pieces of his sword, wrapping them carefully, almost reverentially, in his cloak. His eyes were wide. Gregory stood watching like a statue, then sheathed his own sword, which emitted its customary hum as it cut the air.

"I *do* love, you know." Jon's words were barely audible as he walked away, Quincy and Steyphan following him.

Lindseth looked a question at Eleanor. He had rushed to her when the fight started.

"No, it is okay, Jeyn." She held the pen tight in her hand.

Merrett shifted, sheathing his own sword last. Endicott had not fully registered his presence even though Merrett had closed to within arm's distance shortly after he had grasped Jon's wrist. "Straight out of the library, blouse." Merrett shook his head.

"Straight out of the library."

▽

Lord Kennyth Brice had set up his enquiry in the Duke and Duchess's Lounge, which everyone agreed made sense. The professors, and a tall knight in shining plate armor, arranged themselves at the front of the room, while assorted guards moved in, out, and around on obscure errands. Everyone else waited in the big buffet room, where tea was served. A large crowd of students eventually gathered there, including Jon Indulf's group, Jennyfer Gray, and a multitude of others Endicott barely recognized. The young man could feel a host of eyes on him. He could see others staring at Eloise, Koria, and Gregory. All around him was the low murmur of hundreds of voices, but no one approached Endicott to speak to him. Perhaps the ice bag around Jon Indulf's right arm was a warning not to. Perhaps the story itself carried a certain stigma. One by one, each of Endicott's classmates were called into the lounge. Endicott was called in last.

The duke-to-be was quite young. Endicott guessed him to be in his very early thirties. He had dark hair and stood just above average height. His eyes were bright and attentive, his voice, as he thanked Koria for something, was sonorous. Kennyth was not alone. The tall knight in shining steel armor stood only one large step away from him. Endicott's professors, except for Keith Euyn, sat in chairs nearby. His classmates, including Koria, were arrayed on chairs as well, just a little further from the young duke-to-be.

Kennyth Brice nodded at Endicott and turned to stare down at something in his left hand as the young man approached him. It was the remains of Davyn's feather pen, the piece that Endicott had caught out of the air. "Robert Endicott at last," Kennyth Brice said extending his free hand. "I've been hearing so much about the Endicotts lately. My mother says such good things about you."

The duchess!

"She does, sir? I do not know her."

"She knows *you*, Robert." Kennyth paused as if he was about to say something, then switched directions. "Be at ease. We have talked to just about everyone, examined physical evidence, heralded, and even taken a confession. We *know* what happened last night. Everything, even down to your ruined boots." His eyes focused on Endicott's sandals.

Endicott sighed. He did not want to talk about that terrible night anymore. He did not wish to speak, and in speaking, remember.

Kennyth laughed freely, probably still thinking about ruined boots and sandals. "We even know about the temporary theft of a carriage for hire. I liked that story. Your friend Davyn is a gifted teller."

"He has . . . an optimism, sir."

"He does at that, Robert. Listen, we are going to go out there and talk to everyone in the Commons, but I wanted to ask you one or two things first." Kennyth's forehead crinkled.

"I will answer you, sir."

Lord Brice nodded. "Do you like it here, Robert?"

"Yes."

Kennyth let out a breath. "I understand that you do. But how do you feel about your time at the New School?"

"Confused." The word came out before Endicott could think at all. It was the right word. It was not just that Endicott was confused as to why Kennyth Brice was asking him about his feelings instead of the events of the previous evening, although that was indeed confusing to him. Endicott was confused in all sorts of ways.

"About what?"

Endicott struggled for a moment to dredge up the meaning behind his own word. His insights clarified as he started to speak again. "I thought we were here to learn, to invent. That's what I wanted. And in many ways the situation is even better than I expected. Far better perhaps than what I deserve. I love my classmates and my professors. But I never expected these other things, horrible things. Last night was unimaginably more horrible than anything I thought to see here, sir. It was terrible. But on my way here, and around here, and even within the school, there has been the occurrence of something I did not expect."

Kennyth leaned forward, towards Endicott. "An occurrence of what?"

"The absence of reason."

Kennyth rocked back on his heels. "Ah, I have that problem too, Robert. More than you know, I have that problem. But I have reason to hope for better. Do you know why?"

Endicott shook his head.

"*You*, Robert. *You* make me hopeful." Brice twirled the broken feather pen around his thumb. "You know, my mother and father argue quite often about getting too close to our subjects. Personal attachments can sometimes make certain duties and decisions more difficult, at least according to my father. My mother disagrees." He looked at the pen. "On this point I agree with my mother. It might seem . . . awkward, in some ways, getting close, but it is better to know and enjoy people than to think of them as mere objects. Even if knowing them better might eventually be painful. Look at you, Robert. Last night you helped save the life of a girl you had never met, and then you," he held up the feather pen, "somehow caught *this* out of the air today. Knowing you gives me hope." Lord Kennyth Brice smiled at Endicott and turned to the knight. "Could you get everyone ready out there, please?"

The shining knight jumped to it and was out the door before Endicott could wonder what was coming next. "Robert, you need to prepare for something.

Although our investigation is over, there must still be a trial. You and the others may be called to testify."

"Syriol too?" Robert asked, feeling the floor fall out from under him.

$$\nabla$$

THE RESIDENTS OF THE ORCHID AND THEIR PROFESSORS FOLLOWED KENNYTH BRICE OUT into the Commons. By now the crowd had grown even bigger. Endicott held Koria's hand and was pleased to see Gregory standing next to Eloise.

"I am glad you are well, Bethyn. You have some very good friends." Kennyth spoke quietly to her as their group settled into place near the buffet. Bethyn simply nodded in response, looking down as if embarrassed. Kennyth waited a few more minutes, making easy small talk with Heylor, Deleske, and even Bethyn while a few latecomers from the faculty and student body trickled in. When he was satisfied that all was ready, he smiled grimly and raised his hand for silence. The murmuring of the crowd ceased at once.

"One of the two men who assaulted a woman on our campus last night is dead. The other will be tried in three days before a magistrate. He has confessed, so it should not be a long trial. I ask that you leave the criminal matter to our investigation and the judgment of the court. A few unrelated incidents also occurred last night. One carriage was damaged severely. The owner and driver will be compensated, and we will forget the event." A few chuckles followed, some even coming from Jon Indulf's group.

Kennyth took a deep breath. "I am distressed about what happened to the young lady last night. But I am pleased that worse was prevented. I am proud of four of the students here. Very proud. Something happened that we do *not* have a course for. They made a special effort to care for a stranger and for each other. I, my father, and my mother would like to see that happen more often. Even a small act of kindness is a beautiful thing, and what happened last night was not small. It was terrible, yet it was also beautiful, and it was brave. It all started with care. Gregory Justice, Eloise Kyre, and Robert Endicott will all be made Knights of Vercors immediately. Koria Valcourt will be elevated to the rank of a Lady of Engevelen in a more public ceremony in the Citadel. Announcements will be posted at every monument and every square of the duchy. Come forward, knights, and take a knee."

Gregory, Eloise, and Endicott lined up on their knees.

"Could you lend me your sword, Sir Christensen?" Kennyth looked back at the armored, shining knight behind him.

"Gladly, my lord," rang the even tones of the knight. "But perhaps we should use the superior blade of young Justice?"

Gregory startled, but quickly regained his poise and proffered his sword, hilt first, to Lord Brice. Kennyth took the sword in his hands, eyebrows raised momentarily as he gazed on the strange, brightly reflecting, liquid texture of the metal. "You are hereby granted the powers and responsibilities of a Knight of Vercors. You may be guided by the First Precept of the Methueyn Treaty within this duchy, and you may ask for aid from any constabulary, garrison, or magistrate. You may follow your conscience, but you are not made knights *for* yourselves. You are in service to others and the duchy." He smiled. "Use your powers for reason—and carefully."

He touched the sword upon each of their shoulders. "You will also report to Lord Arthur Wolverton of the Military School at the end of classes every school day for training. We cannot have our knights exhibit a lack of skill."

As they filed out of the lounge, Lord Kennyth Brice called Endicott over. "Robert, although only you three knights are required to go for training with Lord Wolverton, any of your classmates are invited to join you if they wish. Will you let them know?"

"Certainly, sir." Endicott turned to leave, then stopped himself. "I was wondering something, if I may?"

Kennyth smiled. "You are going to ask why. I have been informed of your nature, Robert. Why such a rare and public response to this situation? Why training at the Military School? Why indeed?"

Endicott waited out the rhetorical moment.

"There is always more than one reason, Robert. In this case, please trust me that the reasons are many. I could tell you that the Steel Castle has not raised any Deladieyr Knights in several years, and we have raised no secular knights this year. That is not important. The chief reason is this: I don't like what happened to Syriol

Lindseth. I don't like it at all. And I *won't* have it happen here again." Kennyth's eyes blazed, and his mellifluous voice turned hard. "Part of that is making it known how such acts should be treated. I would beat them both to death myself if Eloise had not made a start on it and the law had no remedy." He softened again. "You and your friends deserve our support. I want the next person of conscience to know they have my support as well. Reason and ethics must prevail."

"And the other reasons, sir?"

"You need more than just dynamics to draw upon when events turn physical, Robert. Next time I don't want you to feel so desperate."

Chapter Seventeen.
Who Must Remember

"SYRIOL," THE ATTORNEY SAID EMOTIONLESSLY, "PLEASE TELL THE COURT HOW YOU CAME to be in the company of the two defendants."

▽

"THIS IS NOT GOING TO BE A GOOD DAY," GREGORY DECLARED. HE WAS DRESSED IN HIS best clothes and jacket, sword belted on his hip. He did not wear the Knight of Vercors cape he had been given but selected another one of deep blue instead. They were all as formally attired as they could be, even Heylor, though his clothes did not seem to fit him well, and failed to stay tucked in, on straight, or buttoned properly. The two constables escorting them wore their dress uniforms.

Endicott understood why Gregory had said what he said. The mood of the group was understandably somber. No one said anything in response to their tall friend's assertion. They all just walked on, leaving the Academic Plateau, passing the enormous Citadel where Koria had been made a lady, and striding on towards the circus where the court would shortly be in session.

Feeling a pleasant heat on his face, Endicott looked up. He saw that the sky was bright blue and that the early morning sun was already blazing. "I think you are wrong, brother. It *is* going to be a good day."

"You're crazy," muttered Deleske.

"You're a stupe," asserted Eloise.

Endicott looked to Davyn for his response, but the big man held his hands up. "I'm waiting to hear why it's going to be so good."

"I as well," added Koria, frowning at Endicott. "You know what we are going to hear today, don't you?"

Still enjoying the sun on his face, Endicott looked around for support. Bethyn stared back at him aghast, and even Heylor scowled. The escorting constables watched him sidelong. Endicott held his lonely smile a moment longer before saying anything. When he did speak, the smile was gone. "I know very well, Koria. But we will only ever need to hear it once more and then never again. Once more and he will be hanged."

"If the bottle hadn't broken, we wouldn't even have to hear it this one last time," hissed Eloise. "I should have sawed his head off with the shard."

"That's a lot of sawing," whispered Deleske under his breath.

Heylor's face was pale. "Tell me you're joking, Eloise."

Eloise stepped in front of Heylor and stopped him with a finger on his chest. "Do I look like I'm skolving joking?" she growled.

Another deep growling sound came from not far away. *Is it coming from the circus?*

The high court was a large, circular building in gray stone with a wide, round inner courtyard. They were only a block away, and they could just see the lane into the inner courtyard, or circus. There seemed to be people moving about accompanied by a roiling, low-frequency buzz.

What is *that sound?*

A small knot of constables passed through the lane and marched rapidly in their direction.

"Just hold up here a second, please," said one of their escorts, looking at the approaching group.

"What I mean is," Endicott cut in, trying to rescue his point, "this is going to be tough, *very* tough for some, but it is going to do some good. Better than a summary decapitation, Eloise. Justice will be done. The rule of law will be served. Because of today, skolves like Vard will know what happens when they assault a woman. They'll know that justice will find them. This day's trauma will make tomorrow better. *That* is why it's a good day."

Eloise shook her head and sneered, "You are too romantic to live, stupe."

The mockery rolled off Endicott. He knew what he sounded like, and personal insults had never meant much to him. Besides, he understood Eloise's anger. He felt it himself, but he was trying to resist his own rage with a convincing narrative. Words: to turn his own mood, to make something better out of something horrific. What had happened was *objectively* terrible; he worked with words to alter what it *meant* to him and his friends.

Can I?

What Eloise had said about finishing off the surviving brother, Vard, had crossed Endicott's mind. He had fantasized hitting Vard again and again until the man's fat head was paste. He had no doubt that is what Vard deserved.

Vard deserves to die and be forgotten, and here I am making up another, more pleasant fantasy about what it all means.

Endicott looked up at the blue skies above him and then back at Eloise's fierce expression. *I cannot be so ruthless.* The young man tried again to find a narrative, tried to remember where he had come from and where he hoped to go. Not angry and heartless, but happy and hopeful. He had walked down quite a few roads and pathways since meeting Lord Latimer and being invited to the New School, usually with a buoyant optimism and a spring in his step. He understood that this was no time for hopping and skipping, yet the funereal tread of their current march did not seem quite fitting either. "We should walk proudly at least, with our heads held high for all to see, even if the task is grim."

"You have to stop right there," ordered a red-haired constable in a heavily decorated coat. She was of medium height and might have been in her mid-thirties. She had a golden badge on her chest. "The crowd is too excited. We are going to have to sneak you in a side door."

▽

AND SO IT WAS THAT THEY MADE A LESS THAN DIGNIFIED ENTRY TO THE COURT THROUGH a back alley, a basement passage, a secret stairwell, and finally a side door.

"Someone really got the mob whipped up for this one," said Chief Constable Eryka Lyon to no one in particular. The sun shining in through one of the antechamber windows made her red hair look on fire.

"Do you see that one?" yelled Heylor, pointing past her into the circus. An old woman held up a sign in dark black paint. It read:

"Why punish the victim?

Set the innocent free,

Hang his attacker!"

Deleske stood beside another window. "I think that's about you, Eloise," he said laconically. Eloise crossed her arms under her breasts but said nothing.

It was not the only sign suggesting that some thought the two brothers had been mistreated. Others clearly felt differently. "Justice comes with a bottle," another sign read.

Some pushing and shoving began to take place between the factions.

Gregory shook his head. "What can you expect from a mob?"

"It's okay," Endicott said, trying to calm everyone down, not least himself. "They don't know the truth yet." He smiled. "And even those two idiot brothers have a mother. Perhaps that's her down there," he suggested, pointing to the woman he had privately dubbed the hang-Eloise sign lady.

"That's odd," rejoined Davyn. "I always assumed their parents must be brothers."

"Hey, here come Gerveault and Keith Euyn," announced Heylor.

Bethyn looked sideways through another window. "How come *they* didn't have to slink in through a side door?"

A muted growl leaked through the windows. This was a new sound from the protestors. *Not much for sneaking, I guess.* Endicott looked over at Eryka Lyon, who was frowning at this news of the old men using the main door.

BANG

The windows shook violently, once.

"Did you see that!" shrieked Heylor.

Endicott turned back to the window. A large gap had opened in the crowd. Gerveault and Keith Euyn stood in its center with the shattered remains of a sign lying to one side near the edge of the gap. Beside it was a prostrate human form, presumably the carrier of the shattered sign.

"What happened?" asked Eryka Lyon.

"One of the protestors tried to hit Gerveault with his sign!" shouted Heylor.

"And?"

Heylor looked at her with eyes wide. "I-I didn't see it clearly. It happened too fast, but he's on his ass now."

"I couldn't make it out either," added Davyn.

Deleske snorted. "Well, I don't know how that unfortunate . . . gentleman is, but his sign isn't going to make it."

"He *still* hasn't got up," Heylor whispered.

"You know what that makes me think?" mused Davyn. When everyone looked at him, he continued. "All those times in class, Heylor, when you goofed off in front of Gerveault. *That* is what could have happened to you."

After the laughter trailed off, Endicott clenched his hands into fists. *It's time to get serious.* The trial would certainly get underway soon. It was time to forget the fascinating but disturbing mob that had come to bear witness, some to support the process, others to denounce it. It was time to put away the jokes and make peace with what was going to happen, to calm down and prepare to do what needed to be done. As he so often did, Endicott spoke the advice he most needed to hear. "Let's put all that commotion outside aside, everyone. We are in the court now. We just have to tell our stories and everything will be fine."

"About that," said Eryka firmly, "you are all going to have to be very, very careful about what you say out there under questioning. No *stories*. Keep your suppositions and speculations to yourselves unless asked." She closed her eyes for a moment. "Can you do that? Vard is going to plead guilty, so hopefully you will only be called to give impact statements." She looked at Koria. "I think your professors are . . . indisposed now, but Lady Valcourt, you have been through an enquiry before. Help me out please, if you would."

Koria smiled sadly and came to stand near the constable. "You need to understand that a trial is procedural. It is like an experiment from physics class. Hold to that discipline. Imagine Gerveault is giving a lecture on what you saw, if that helps frame it for you. Speak only to what you saw, only to what you *actually* observed. The good physicist makes the most parsimonious conclusions, so limit your inferences to what the facts you observed tell you directly. Be objective, be quantitative if you must, but do *not* tell stories or add narratives. Don't feel in a rush to answer. Be slow, and be sure your answer is what you want on the record." She looked at Endicott, green eyes unreadable. "Your beliefs mean very little here, and your feelings mean even less."

"Good pep talk," declared the long-necked constable from the open doorway. By the decoration on his uniform, he appeared to be Chief Constable Lyons' direct subordinate. "We need to go in now. We have a spot at the balcony ready for you until you are called."

▽

FROM THE FRONT ROW OF THE BALCONY, ENDICOTT COULD SEE ALMOST ALL THE MAJOR players. Vard and his attorney sat at their desk, the Court Chairman sat in her high chair, and the prosecutor stood by his lectern. Meredeth Callum, Annabelle Currik and a group of other professors sat in a box near the back of the room. Gerveault and Keith Euyn shuffled to their seats among the faculty last.

They were probably held up by the incident out front.

Of Eleanor there was no still no sign. *Where is she?* Endicott began to worry that she might have also run afoul of the protestors out front.

Off to the side, in a raised box, sat Kennyth Brice with an older man and woman, whom Endicott assumed must be the duke and duchess. The duke was a big, craggy, fierce-looking man. The duchess had long braided hair—a wig?—and a stiff brocade dress. She wore long, dark gloves and was heavily powdered in the dark tones common to the nobles. Looking along the wooden railing of the balcony, Endicott noted Lord Jon Indulf's crew as well as Jennyfer Gray seated on a bench near the far wall. Indulf and every one of his friends nodded in Endicott's direction. Jennyfer had a notebook in her hand and was furiously scribbling on it. Syriol was absent. Endicott wondered if she planned to come in only towards the end during sentencing. That was the least of the things Endicott turned out to be wrong about.

"My client pleads not guilty."

▽

"MY BOYS WERE ALWAYS GOOD," VARD AND LYNAL'S MOTHER WHIMPERED ON THE WITNESS stand. "They had some ups and downs, no one will deny, but I'm proud of them. They just got new jobs. They had a happier outlook. They had a promising future. Until they were attacked."

"A promising future as rapists and murderers until they were stopped!" shouted Eloise, spittle flying from the balcony onto the professors' box below.

▽

"Thank you for that testimony, Professor Euyn," the prosecuting attorney said. Keith had explained the images and events he had heralded, including what had happened in the carriage before and after Gregory and Endicott had arrived, as well as what would have happened if they had not.

The defense attorney stood up. "Professor Euyn, thank you for coming here today. I have heard that heraldry is uncertain, that it varies with the practitioner, that it fades with time. I have heard that heraldry is subject to interpretation and is in fact subjective. How can you expect the court to determine this young man's future on something so equivocal?"

"I expect the court's decision will not depend on what you have *heard*, young man, but upon the known facts and behavior of dynamics." Keith's face was unreadable, but his tone and words were not so opaque.

"Answer the question, professor," ordered the court chairman from her high seat.

"Which one?" Keith Euyn replied coolly. "The defense made a series of declarations to which I object, since he is neither standing as a witness nor under oath."

"Your objection is valid, professor. The defense will refrain from rhetoric." She stabbed her small dagger into the cork board in front of her. "There was, however, a question buried in the rhetoric. Would you like the defense to restate it?"

"No need, Madame Chairman, I remember it precisely. Let us be charitable and answer the defense's question as if he is not simply casting aspersions upon subjects in which he has no expertise." There was a titter of laughter in the courtroom. The great man continued. "Heraldry of the future is uncertain to some degree, depending on how far into the future one looks."

The defense attorney, looking put-upon, asked, "Why?"

Now Keith smiled. "Because the future is *not* set."

"And the past is open to interpretation too, is it not?" the defense attorney asked with oily tones, the scolding he had so recently endured from the older man apparently having rolled off him.

"Only to liars and the ignorant," Keith Euyn shot back. "*You* may be one or both, but *I* am neither. The past is *set*. It does not change at all, though information from it may fade with time unless recorded."

The defense attorney smiled now as if he had scored a point or was about to. "But it must have been hours before you reached the scene. Might the information from the past have faded before you could get out of bed, get dressed, and walk over there?"

"I was not *in* my bed, young man, I was returning across campus from my office when I heard the ruckus. I arrived only moments after the incident concluded. The images were quite stable and clear."

The attorney's jaw clenched momentarily, but he seemed to rally after a moment. "You said that information from the past fades unless recorded. Did you write down what you saw?"

The great man's bushy eyebrows furled. "What I saw will never fade from my memory."

▽

"Swear on the Methueyn Treaty, swear on the Methueyn Knights and the angels in Elysium, to tell us only truth," intoned the court steward. He held out a miniature replica of the Methueyn Treaty. Even as a miniature the six-foot sword still required two strong hands to hold up sideways. Endicott gazed on the metal, trying to see if the writing etched into the blade was the same as what was written in steel upon the twelve-foot-long monstrosity of the true Methueyn Treaty. He found the first words of the First Precept. *You are Free.* They were larger than the others, just as they were in the real sword. Endicott had never understood why those particular words were given such prominence; they were never adequately explained on the few occasions where he had attended the Steel Castle's service. It seemed strange to swear oaths he did not understand to an extinct order of knights on the replica of a holy object, but he did so.

"Sir Robert Endicott, Knight of Vercors, student in Her Grace's Applied Mathematics and Physics Program, tell us what you saw and did on the night under examination."

I must be slow. Be slow. He knew that he would never be allowed the latitude the court had given to Keith Euyn. Only the great man could get away with such arrogance.

I must be careful.

The young man looked up and caught Koria's eyes. He looked across at Kennyth Brice and the duchess in her wig and powder. Then he answered the prosecutions' questions slowly and carefully, as parsimonious with his words as he had been with Lord Latimer that day months ago in Bron. He spoke the words and hoped to forget what they described.

The defense hoped to do better with this young man than they had done with the great Keith Euyn. "Why were you out in the first place, Sir Robert?"

"We were all looking for Bethyn."

"Why?"

"Because it was very late, and we were worried for her."

"That seems a bit strange, Sir Robert. Was it because she is a drunk?"

"No." Robert saw the trap. He understood the attorney intended to connect drunkenness with recklessness, exchange Bethyn with Syriol, and blame Syriol for what had happened to her. But "no" was the honest answer.

"No? Really? Why then? Why so worried about your classmate?"

"Because I love her."

Eloise hissed "stupe!" from the balcony, and some in the court laughed. Endicott could not see Bethyn's face. Endicott did not care if people laughed, or if Bethyn thought less of him for his childish declaration. He *did* love her. He loved Eloise, too, and Eleanor. He loved Koria most of all. If he was asked, he would say so.

He was asked, and he did say so. Apparently his answers remained funny, but they gave the defense attorney nowhere to go. Love was not an answer or a sentiment he had prepared for.

ENDICOTT'S CLASSMATES EACH FOLLOWED HIS LEAD, DECLARING EITHER THAT THEY ALSO searched for Bethyn out of love or because they were pulled along by Endicott's concern. Heylor named the upcoming twenty-four-hour test as one motivator. Endicott was especially interested in Koria's testimony.

She'll have to say why she stalks me.

She did no such thing.

"Sir Eloise Kyre and I were searching for Bethyn when I heard a commotion," Koria explained, her words precisely enunciated. "We saw a carriage swerving dangerously and bearing down upon Sir Robert and Sir Gregory. Sir Robert was running with a woman in his arms."

Eloise backed up Koria's testimony. No mention was made of heraldry. They claimed to have acted only in defense of their classmates.

▽

ENDICOTT REMEMBERED VERY LITTLE OF THE REMAINING DETAILS OF THE TRIAL. The evidence mounted inexorably against Vard and his now-dead brother, Lynal. What followed was largely the slow, boring work of procedure, easily forgettable despite its ultimate importance. The prosecution had an enormous lineup of additional witnesses, many of whom Endicott himself had not noticed on the terrible night. They also had copious amounts of physical evidence taken from the carriage, from Vard and Lynal, and from Syriol. Finally they had Vard's confession.

Only one essential element of the prosecution's case remained: the testimony of Syriol Lindseth.

The questioning of Syriol was searingly unforgettable. It was burned into Endicott's mind and soul. He doubted he would ever forget her wooden movements as she approached the bench, the desolate look on her face as she spoke, and the quiet, dead tones with which she produced her testimony. Endicott realized, as he watched her in the witness box, that the organization and design of the court was such that witnesses were *made* to feel isolated and alone. His hands made the wood of the court balcony railing crack as he gripped it and listened haltingly to her recount what had happened. He could not take his eyes off Syriol, he tried to smile and nod to her, he wanted desperately to let her know she was supported, but there was little he could do except watch and burn the sight into his mind forever.

▽

Tʜᴇ ᴅᴇꜰᴇɴsᴇ's ᴇꜰꜰᴏʀᴛs ᴛᴏ ᴜɴᴅᴇʀᴍɪɴᴇ ᴛʜᴇ ᴘʀᴏsᴇᴄᴜᴛɪᴏɴ ᴡᴇʀᴇ ᴘʀᴇᴅɪᴄᴛᴀʙʟᴇ ᴀɴᴅ ᴜɴɪɴ-teresting. Of course they attacked the witnesses' ability to see anything with certainty on such a dark night. Unsurprisingly they attempted to have Vard's confession thrown out and attacked the impartiality of Kennyth Brice and even of the court itself. Surely making three new knights out of the event guaranteed that there could be no fair trial.

None of their attempts surprised anyone or went anywhere. The defense was anticipated everywhere, almost suspiciously so. Endicott wondered if the prose-cution had used the services of a talented herald to anticipate what would be said at the trial. Or was it possible that the defense's attempts to attack the witnesses, to attack Syriol, were trivial for anyone to predict with or without a herald? In any case, those efforts at obfuscation were seen through by everyone except per-haps the mob out in the circus. Out there they continued to chant, grumble, and fight amongst themselves. There was only one detail of the defense that Endicott remembered distinctly.

"I don't remember what happened, sir. She hit me over and over again on the head with the bottle." Vard pointed at his grotesquely bruised forehead and temple. "She murdered Lynal. How can I be guilty if I don't remember what happened?"

It was beyond odd that Vard could remember *who* beat him but apparently not what *he* had done that night. Endicott reasoned that it was possible Vard was speaking the truth. Memory could be strange and pernicious. Vard might be a murderer and a rapist, but he might *not* be a liar. If so it seemed an evil and unfair outcome when the predator could not remember what he had done but the victim was not *allowed* to forget.

Chapter Eighteen

Hand-to-Hand Combat

"It's a good thing Eloise isn't here," said Davyn, loudly enough to make Endicott wince.

"I almost wish *I* wasn't here," Endicott replied, frustrated. *What should be done about the two bald men and their signs?* His time in court had not increased his tolerance for protestors. The first sign had been only slightly altered, but the alteration was personal.

"You will reap what you sew.
Nimrheal will git you for
Murderers of young men.
Should hang THEM instead."

The second man's sign had also been changed, but his alterations made less sense.

"Evil grayn grows, people die!
Wizards kill people last week
If you don't pay the price, we will collekt!
Skoll and Hati will take you to Hell!"

"These guys really do keep up on current events," Davyn said helpfully.

"Yes." Endicott frowned. "They are right up with the news posts. What do you think I should do?"

"Are they breaking any laws?" Davyn asked.

"In a vague sense, I suppose it could be argued."

"But maybe not so much yet, hey?" Davyn made an expansive arm gesture at Endicott. "It's tough to know what a knight should do, is it not, sir?

"I think I'm not the kind of knight who knows what he should do all the time."

"I feel a little, I don't know . . . disappointed."

Me too.

Endicott closed his eyes and considered. *What is the right thing to do?* Being knighted had not magically added years of experience or maturity to him, only the painful awareness of his shortcomings in both regards. He had optimistically vowed to try talking to the two sign bearers next time he saw them, but he knew something about the subject matter of their protests this time. Their irrationality made his blood boil. What were the chances of actual communication?

"I am going to herald it, Davyn."

The fat boy's head snapped back. "No. We aren't *supposed to,* Robert. We promised that we would wait to be trained. *You* have been warned particularly."

Endicott smiled, feeling the rightness of the idea. "This isn't desperate recklessness, big man. Why shouldn't we get a little intelligence before we expose ourselves?"

"Why? Why expose ourselves at all for that matter? Your name may be famous, but your face isn't." Davyn smiled. "We can just scuttle on by and be about our business."

"Like sneaking into court through the side door?" Endicott winked at Davyn. "I need to know what's going on with these two." His eyes returned to the two protestors and their hateful, misspelled signs.

"Really?"

"Really."

Davyn's nose scrunched. "I thought you were going to go meet that fellow with the shoe problems—the one who reminded you of your father—and sift the grain right out of him."

"*Conor.* I haven't had time," Endicott admitted, now a little embarrassed. "And these two miscreants are right here. Besides," Endicott clapped Davyn's shoulder, "using heraldry will be much safer than walking to some unknown tavern in the wrong part of town to meet someone under false pretenses hoping they don't remember which side of the Battle of Nyhmes I was really on. These two gentlemen won't even know we looked into them at all."

Davyn laughed, but his laughter quickly slid into a groan. "If heraldry is so much safer than talking, why have we—and by we, I mean you—been expressly told not to herald?"

"Because it's not practical to tell us not to talk?"

"Very funny. Eleanor asked you not to perform dynamics. Gerveault *told* you not to. He said we should change the world in the way we expect at the price we have calculated. *After* we are trained. *After* the test. Right now, we don't even know *how* to calculate the cost!"

"My grandpa taught me how to herald, Davyn. I've done it a hundred times." *Well, maybe a dozen or two.*

"Perfect! If *Grandpa* says it's okay, go right ahead." Davyn looked up at the sky, exasperated.

"I will."

I am a knight now. I can do things.

And he was no longer constrained by the rules and procedures of the court. He was less constrained even than the constabulary who he had come to understand during the trial were limited by law and a customary reluctance to interfere with civil demonstration.

There was no law against heraldry, only a tiring list of warnings.

I've been held back too long.

"I wish Koria were here," Davyn muttered, shaking his big head on his short neck.

Endicott frowned and looked at him. "Why? To stop me?"

"No," Davyn boomed. "Well, yes actually. I'm pretty sure she *would* stop you. But also Eloise says that Koria's a natural at heraldry."

That makes too much sense.

It also came very close to his one big concern with their relationship. There had been many opportunities for Koria to explain why she had followed him that night and the nights before. She refused to discuss it, even in court, always deflecting to other subjects. She would eagerly, if quietly, tell him about her family, her sisters, her childhood, her dreams, but not about this one thing. He had his suspicions, and now Davyn had given him a new clue.

She follows me because she heralds. She heralds because she does not trust me. Just as she said.

Endicott pushed the troubling thought aside with some difficulty and considered how he should attempt his own heraldry. If he went down to join the two big, bald sign holders, he could herald in detail. He might even hear some of what was being said. Unfortunately, coming that close might also start the chain of events he only wanted to predict. He decided to stay where he was. From here he should still be able to obtain an overall picture of the consequences of approaching the two protestors. For now this was preferable to the risk of provoking the consequences directly.

No tea this time. No thermal cushion. I must take this piss on the first try.

He opened himself to the empyreal sky, quickly achieved the lesser breakdown, and with an elementary ease, hit the sweet spot of heraldry. A riot of images, colors, and impressions sprayed across his consciousness. A covered horse and carriage bearing the word "ice" rippled by, and the men with signs vibrated in place, then ran away in triplicate as two Endicotts arrived. Five versions of the three of them fought in a blur of fists, feet, and signs. Endicott's borrowed sword vibrated and flailed, blood spattered in a multidimensional pitch and hue. Davyn was mixed up in the mess, vibrating, falling, being jumped on, holding someone's head. An old lady ran. She was run over by two men—or was it one man—on a horse. One of the sign holders was run down by the ice carriage, which rolled by like a deck of cards. A crowd gathered like a rippling organism, plunging into and recoiling from the action in an insane, periodic melee.

I wonder what three-dimensional Lessingham coefficients best describe that crowd?

He shook his head. Most of the energy would be in the first two dimensions if he defined his coordinate system properly. He shook his head again.

Focus! This is too chaotic.

Endicott knew he was seeing too much; it was a mess of piled and compressed probabilities. The heraldry was uninterpretable. He pulled back in an attempt to see only one line of future at a time. His grandpa had said this could be done but was much more difficult. If heraldry was like an old man trying to piss at night, following one line of heraldic probability was like the same old man trying to write his name in the snow. Of course, Endicott reminded himself, he was not his grandpa; he did not have over sixty years of heraldry behind him, and he did not herald so often that he regularly had heraldic dreams. He struggled to release his anxiety.

I am still my grandpa's grandson. I am an Endicott!

He knew what he had to do: follow the twisting signature of one possible event-set through its loops and turns and intersections with other sets, follow the twisting passage of a potential reality like a signature in cursive.

I know how to write my name in snow.

He did, and it came to him more easily than he had feared it might.

He saw himself approach the two men. They spoke for a few moments. One of the men tried to hit Endicott with his sign. He responded by drawing his sword, but the other man tackled him, and the two of them laid boots to him. Davyn ran up and was also beaten.

Next.

Wrenching himself from one line of probability to another was like stopping the piss mid-stream and starting the signature over. Endicott made the attempt, and the image exploded again into the old multiple probabilities of standard heraldry, uncountable images and possibilities fanning out and overlapping across his consciousness. With the curious effort-not-effort his grandpa had described, Endicott reacquired the single line of what might be.

He saw himself approach the two men. They spoke for a few moments. One of the men tried to hit Endicott with his sign. Endicott stepped back and, drawing his sword, took off most of the face of the second man as he attempted to make the tackle. The other man ran away while the first man rolled about clutching his ruined face. Davyn ran down and tried to hold the bald man's face together, blood squirting between his sausage-like fingers.

Next.

It was becoming easier.

He saw himself approach the two men. They spoke for a few moments. One of the men tried to hit Endicott with his sign. Both men burst into blue flames, running in circles. One was run over by the ice carriage, which tipped over and fell, blocks of ice sliding across the ring road. Endicott collapsed, frost engulfing him. Davyn ran towards him, tears on his face.

Next.

Effortless now.

He saw himself approach the two men. They spoke for a few moments. One of the men tried to hit Endicott with his sign. Endicott stepped back, hands raised. The second man tackled him, and the two of them laid boots to him. Davyn ran to help and was also beaten.

Endicott decided that he did not want to see the scenarios he had glimpsed but not followed where the old lady was run down or a mob formed. It had been enough. He released the Empyreal sky, and the shivering began, but only moderately now.

Not even too cold this time.

He smiled ironically and looked over at Davyn, whose taut face betrayed his concern. "I should do this *all* the time. Let me explain what I saw." He stamped his feet, shook his shoulders, and related the alternate futures. He took particular care in describing the Davyn-cries and Davyn-gets-beaten-up scenarios.

"Well, none of that sounds too good, Robert." Davyn mused, hand pensively on chin, after hearing all the potential results. "Maybe we should both go down there right from the start."

"Were you not listening? I don't think even *you* can make friends with those two, Davyn," Endicott said.

But how does knowing an outcome affect the morality of a choice?

He realized that it did not, but also that it was not immoral to consider a more effective approach. "Do you ever feel like a passenger in your own carriage, Davyn?"

"Oh, all the time. Especially when I'm with you," Davyn boomed, then laughed. "No. Not really, even when it's not my carriage." He winked. "However, I may define control a little less aggressively than you do."

"Well, I like driving."

"I've noticed."

Endicott ignored the jibe. "There is something going on here, Davyn, and I'm going to find out what it is."

"How? Do you really want *any* of the ugly outcomes your heralding showed?" Davyn frowned, a rare expression for him. "We have to behave righteously, Robert. You can't just assault them or arrest them."

Endicott smiled wolfishly. "No. I'm going to be smarter than that. I am going to follow them and see what they do, who they see. I am going to find out if these signs are all their own work or if they are getting their ideas from someone else." He paused and sighed. "But it cannot be tonight. Syriol is expecting us, and we can't leave her waiting. Not there."

They crossed the ring road as far from the strange protestors as they could. Syriol was waiting at a booth in the Apprentices' Library. She wore a cream-colored dress and gloves. When she saw Endicott, she rushed over and embraced him. She held him a long time and breathed contentedly.

"I still don't remember everything from that night. Was I drowning?" Her voice was small, a faint whisper in his ear. "I was submerged for a long time, it seemed. But then you came. You said your name, Robert Endicott, and you held me. It is a strange memory, like a dream, and it carries…" she seemed to search for the right word, "an inertia of feeling, almost like a tide."

She did not say that *in court, thank the knights!*

In court she had spoken of different memories from the time before Robert and Gregory had arrived. Those memories had an altogether different inertia, horrifying and almost unspeakable.

"I'm sorry I couldn't talk with you at the circus," Endicott confessed, holding her.

Syriol smiled wanly. "I know. We couldn't risk losing the case by appearing to collude, could we?"

She still held him.

Endicott caught Davyn's eye. This was why he had brought Davyn. He had not known if Syriol would want to avoid seeing him altogether because he reminded her of the horrible things that had happened to her, or if she would want to see him because he had rescued her from that horror. Either reaction would have made sense. The never-ending embrace answered his question more clearly than any words could have done.

It also worried him. He did not want to take advantage of Syriol's gratitude, and above all he did not want to confuse or hurt either her or Koria. He felt as if he was on one of Davyn's high wires. If he fell, his clumsiness would hurt both women more than himself. Making matters worse was the fact that he *did* feel something for Syriol. She was sweet, she was beautiful, and she appeared to trust him completely. He could not escape comforting and carrying her that night without a tidal change to his own emotions.

Finally she let him go. A little awkwardly Endicott introduced Davyn, and they ordered tea.

"How was your week?" Syriol asked intently.

"More mathematics, more dead mathematicians." Endicott was counting items off on his fingers. "Someone sent me these splendid new boots," he said, lifting one foot out from under the table to show off the polished leather. "I think it was the duchess because they had a note with a D clipped to them. They just showed up in my room at the Orchid."

He grinned at a clearly impressed Syriol. "In other news Davyn here has been taking dinner *most* nights with Jon Indulf, our former sworn enemy, and I have been getting beat on *every* night by your cousin Jeyn and my classmate Eloise, but she might have some sort of a mental problem. She beats up all the boys."

"I have been paying Jeyn to give him a few extra shots each night," Davyn added. "It turns out that punches come cheap. Eloise charges nothing."

"How about you, Syriol?" Endicott could see she was amused by Davyn. He also noted that she kept her hands hidden. The few times she briefly revealed them, they trembled.

"I'm thinking of getting a job." She paused and her expression grew inward-looking.

"You are very brave, Syriol." Davyn said, quieter than normal.

She smiled at him uncertainly. "What do you mean, Davyn?"

"Coming back here," Davyn said, a little haltingly. "This is where they spiked your drink. While you waited for Jeyn."

Syriol added some cream to her tea, hand shaking. "I am creating positive memories of the place. It will not be safe for me until I make it so."

Endicott felt uncomfortable, and it must have shown, for Syriol's face crumpled. "Why are you looking down, Robert? Are you embarrassed for me?"

"No, Syriol. Never!"

"How *do* you feel about me, then, Robert?" Her eyes were liquid.

Since being knighted, Robert, Gregory, and Eloise had spent two hours a day at the Military School. They had been accepted without comment but with a refreshing and open familiarity by students and faculty alike. Lord Wolverton was revealed to be another member of the old Engevelen aristocracy and, like Koria, had light eyes—though his were the more typical blue rather than her green—and dark skin. He had been fastidiously correct and careful in the one brief address he gave the young men before passing their training to Merrett, Lindseth, and the somewhat strange Eoyan March. Every day, those three young men had taken Endicott and his friends through grueling training in hand-to-hand combat. Thinking of that, Endicott decided now that he was not on a high wire with Syriol; he was in hand-to-hand combat, and of the most delicate kind. It was a combat of care.

"My feelings are complex, Syriol. I still barely know you, but like you I have had . . . feelings from the moment that we met." Endicott cringed at his own words.

I sound like I'm giving a lecture!

He knew he had to try to explain himself more naturally, but he feared the consequences of explaining the complex truth.

To hell with it.

Endicott plunged in. "Do you know what I felt when I first saw you?" Their eyes were locked.

Davyn's expression was one of dawning terror. He was making tiny shaking motions with his head.

"I felt *love*, Syriol. I felt love for you when I saw you. I love you." He smiled at her. "But I am not asking for your hand in marriage. It turns out that I may already be doubly betrothed." He held up a hand. "Don't ask please. It's complicated."

Davyn groaned, reminding Endicott of Heylor in class earlier that day, but he pushed on, committed now to the idea that the whole truth was needed.

"I love you without knowing you, Syriol. I mean, I love you in a pure way. Not like a lover or even a friend. *They* love you knowing you. I love an *idea* of you. You *evoked* love from me, the love of protecting something valuable and worthy."

"Like Sir Heydron," she offered in a quiet tone.

"I don't know. Maybe. Heydron *must* act out of love. I'm not sure if I have a choice or not about how I feel." Endicott took a breath. "So there, Syriol. I love you. Count on it. But I will not take advantage of the feelings of either of us from that terrible night. You are your own person and should be loved for yourself. I don't want to be creepy or weird about this."

"Too late," muttered Davyn, his hands over his face.

"We will not be a romantic couple. Ever. That's not what I mean at all by love. We *can't* be, given what lies between us. You might feel safe with me, but I will always be a reminder of that awful night."

She cried, and Endicott let her do so. A bead of sweat rolled down Davyn's face. After a few moments Syriol looked up at Endicott and tried to smile. "You say the word *love* a lot. Did you know that? It's nice." She swallowed. "Why don't we try for friends?"

Endicott, unembarrassed, reached across the table and gave her hand a squeeze. "Definitely."

"Don't waste your time on him, Syriol," Davyn interjected, this time loudly. "Love, love, love, that's all you'll hear from him, and frankly it is really boring and a little uncomfortable. You hit it on the head. He's no good for you." Davyn pointed a thumb firmly at himself. "*I*, on the other hand, have no confusing emotional baggage or set of fiancées hanging off me. *I* am free and clear. Love? Maybe someday. But if it happens, I promise to keep it bottled up properly like a man should. Let's start with the fact that *I* think you yourself are fantastic!"

He leapt to his feet, hand reaching out to Syriol. "May I walk you home?"

In that moment Endicott also loved Davyn. He *did* love Syriol, and in a very particular way, but he knew that saying it had every chance of seeming strange or even sinister.

How to act correctly? How best to help her?

Endicott knew he was doing well in mathematics and physics, that he was getting ready to pass some horrendous test so he could learn dynamics. He also knew he was no expert on trauma or what it could do to the mind. That realization told him that maybe he should have been more cautious with her.

A wave of heat surged through him. He did not know how he should have spoken to Syriol, if he should have told her how he felt so bluntly, or what would have been better to say instead. The anger that simmered as he thought about this was not comprehensible right now, but it was also not to be denied. Whatever fueled his rage had required that he meet the young woman and try to explain his feelings to her. Not an hour earlier he had willfully broken the rules for heraldry that his professors had laid out, but he was certain this dangerous transgression had been safer than his words to Syriol. In any case he knew could not have stopped himself. He could not have refused to meet her or, having met her, not told her how he felt. He accepted there could be some element of ego involved in his decision, but he was more certain than ever that refusing to talk to her would have been more damaging than staying aloof. To both of them.

∇

Endicott arrived back at the Military School hoping to catch the last of the day's training session with Gregory and Eloise. He could see that training was shutting down as the dinner hours approached. Most of the other young men and women nodded affably to him as they passed. Merrett strode by with his usual "nice blouse" comment. The stocky man's attitude towards Endicott had not changed. Tall, strange Eoyan March sauntered up, hand extended. Eoyan always seemed to have short stubble on his face and an expression that often baffled Endicott. It was darkly serious one moment and brightly comic the next.

"Hoy, Robert Endicott, come to see Uncle Eoyan!"

They shook hands. "You still have that blacksmith grip, Sir Robert." Eoyan took his hand back, affecting a grimace that Endicott did not believe. "It's a good thing you've got that going for you, because the rest of your sword work is a little . . ." He paused dramatically. "Shitty."

A chuckle burst out of Endicott's mouth. In comical mode Eoyan always made him laugh, and the man was not wrong about his sword work. "I was hoping to work on it. Sorry I missed the session today."

"I know where you were," Eoyan said, not smiling now. "Don't worry about it, Sir Knight. Lindseth's still in the pit if you want to catch him."

Endicott continued past areas cordoned off for weight training and unarmed combat to the wood-railed sandpit where Lindseth and Eloise were sparring with weighted, wooden swords.

Clack, clack, clack-clack, clack.

The quiet, gentle man had said that Eloise was the strongest woman he had ever trained. From sparring with her, Endicott felt that he might just have the edge in upper body strength, but she was significantly taller and had longer reach. He was certain that her long, muscular legs beat his in strength by a fair margin. Her smooth, toned quadriceps showed in fascinating relief beneath the protection of her heavy sparring skirt. She never seemed to become physically exhausted and certainly never grew emotionally tired of training.

They stopped, and Eloise smiled broadly. Lindseth took a step back and approached the rail, hanging his sparring vest on it. "Wrists, Eloise. That was good, but your wrists need to roll with your footwork or you're going to lose that sword to someone more massive like Merrett or your uncle, Sir Hemdale."

It was familiar advice, and Endicott appreciated it just as much for himself as for Eloise. Strong forearms or not, there was always someone stronger. Against greater strength one had to fight in a unity of parts, rolling and turning joints, shoulders, feet, and torso to find advantage somewhere.

"Come give me try, Robert," she said.

Endicott pulled on Lindseth's heavy vest. It covered him to mid-thigh. He took up a practice blade and approached her.

"What did you say to Syriol?" She chose that moment to lunge forward. Endicott blocked, mostly with his wrist, and riposted skillfully, forcing her to step back.

Endicott shrugged. "The truth." Eloise darted forward, attacking high and low in a smooth, ceaseless barrage, knees dropping and rising in turn, pressing him as he blocked, somewhat desperately evading her.

"This is sensitive, you know."

She came on again in a series of short body strikes that he caught and one leg strike that he missed. Endicott winced, stepped back, and gave her an abbreviated bow to acknowledge the hit.

"You're sensitive about everything, stupe." She attacked again, and he turned with her, blocking and returning.

"I'm honest. Life is too short to hold back what's in my heart." Someone behind him laughed. He had thought they were alone with Lindseth. Their swords locked. He hooked a leg behind her, but she smoothly stepped over it and backed out of range.

"So what is *your* truth then, stupe? You must know how she feels about you. What did you say?"

He glanced as briefly as he could afford at Lindseth. "I told her I loved her." He paused to let that sink in, then added, "But that we could only ever be friends. Davyn, however, made great poetry to her and is escorting her home."

Looking at Lindseth was a mistake. Eloise shouted "Love!" and rushed him, sword blurring. He backed away, but she pushed forward, hit him hard in the chest, in the right leg, and on his wrist, knocking his sword out of his hand. It spun with a whup, whup, whup before it struck the wall with a loud bang. She pinned him against the wooden rail, pressing up tight against him.

"You love everyone, don't you Robert?" she hissed into his ear, breathing hard. Strands of her long hair tickled his face. "But you can't save everyone. You can't love *everyone*."

Endicott had no idea where her sword had gotten to, but he could feel just about every part of her body up against his. He had no idea what to do. "Not everyone," he said lamely.

"What about Koria?" she said in a low tone. Endicott had never heard her breathe so hard before.

"Yes."

"Why aren't you with her?"

Endicott knew Eloise was not literally referring to the present moment. He and Koria had not slept together since the night they had rescued Syriol, and that intimacy, though blissful, had been platonic. Eloise knew this because she had been there in the adjacent bed with Gregory. Endicott was conflicted about the prospect of making the final commitment with Koria. She still only trusted his *intentions*. He held on to the hope that he could one day win Koria's trust fully and still felt strongly that he *must* win it before they could truly be together.

"She doesn't trust me, Eloise." Endicott struggled to keep his mind on the question at hand and off the sensation of being pinned by his nubile classmate. That sensation felt wonderful but also uncomfortable and wrong.

"Hah!" Eloise pushed harder against him, grinding now.

"She's keeping secrets from me." He could not seem to let it go.

Eloise stepped back and released him. Endicott almost fell. His knees trembled. He could see through the strands of her wild hair that Eloise's face was red. "All women keep secrets, stupe."

She turned away from him, took two steps, and turned back. "This your last warning, Robert." She pulled off her vest, unbuckled her heavy skirt, and walked to the baths.

"Uhh, that looked like fun," said Eoyan March, pointing at Endicott's painful arousal, which was apparent even through the sparring vest.

"Hervor's horn, what was that?" Endicott said, frustrated, embarrassed, and ready to explode. He had not even known that Eoyan was there. *That's who laughed.*

"Ha, ha, ha. Hervor's horn all right." Eoyan started laughing again, doubling over.

"Must we?" Endicott said, wanting to move on and glad that Gregory had not been around to see what had just happened.

Eoyan was still chuckling. "We must. I think I might have gotten pregnant just watching. Wait, I think my water just burst." Eoyan looked down at his groin. "Oh darn. That's wasn't my water."

Lindseth shook his head at Eoyan and helped Endicott with his vest.

He hung it on the fence and turned Endicott by the shoulders towards him. "You don't know, do you? What you did that terrible night. Carrying my cousin away. That struck a chord in everyone, Robert. Everyone was changed by it. You're a hero."

"Yes!" interrupted Eoyan. "Even *I* want to have your babies."

Lindseth frowned and continued. "For someone from Armadale, what you did was the pinnacle of heroic chivalry. And you said the right thing to Syriol. Thank you, Robert. She cannot help how she feels; probably doesn't *understand* how she feels yet. *However.*"

Suddenly Endicott realized he had never truly looked at Lindseth before. He had many times noted something watchful about the taller man. Lindseth was always polite, always smiling gently. Now Endicott looked at him and saw that Lindseth was not just acting as a guard, that the tall man was not simply doing a job. Lindseth cared, and he was wise. Wiser than Endicott.

Lindseth took a breath and finished his train of thought. "However, it's the same thing for Eloise, but with *no* confusion or injury."

"But she's the strongest, most independent woman there is!"

Lindseth looked over at Eoyan, who had stopped laughing. "That hardly matters. There is what you *say* you feel, what you *think* you should feel, and there is just the *way* that you feel. She was brought up on chivalry, which is everything for our noble neighbors."

"I'll tell you one thing," said Eoyan over his shoulder as he retrieved Endicott's practice sword from wherever it had landed. "You better sort things out with Koria, or Eloise is going to sort you out. Combat style." He laughed again, enjoying himself immensely.

Chapter Nineteen

The Hanging Man

A WEEK LATER TWO OF THE DUCHESS'S PAGES ARRIVED AT THE ORCHID CARRYING AN enormous bundle. It was heavy, wrapped in thick brown cloth, and tied elaborately and tightly. "D-delivery for Sir Robert," said one of the young women. Heylor rushed over and helped Endicott take the package from the wide-eyed pages.

"Thank you, ladies," Endicott said softly, wondering at the openly curious expressions on the young women's faces.

Heylor didn't ask to help unwrap the package. He simply set his nimble fingers flying over the knots, untying the package at a remarkable rate.

"Finally!" Endicott exclaimed, guessing what might be taking up so much space. The weight of the package did not fit his guess, though. It was too heavy to be just clothes.

"Aha!" exclaimed Heylor as the outer wrapping fell away to reveal two paper-wrapped, rectangular bundles and one long, thin package wrapped in a blanket. The third package was where all the weight came from. A note was pinned to the blanket. Heylor snatched up the note and passed it to Endicott. It read:

"Little Puke,

Your aunt has sent shirts and such for your friends as you asked. She sends another set for your professors and whoever else you would like to have them. She has opened a store in Bron and would like the good word.

Eight men tried to burn down the elevator last Volsday, but your grandpa had a heraldic dream, so your cousins, other uncles, and me were ready to deliver a mighty beating on them. One was so surprised when we burst out of ambush that he soiled himself and lit his own pants on fire! We captured two of them alive. One was a religious nut, but the other seemed more interested in money. The duke's men have them now and should get the story entire from them.

We heard you are made a knight. Don't get righteous on me now. You can't control the outcome for the entire world, remember? I am proud of you.

Grandpa is too, and he sends you a cold-forged present.

No fighting!

Love,

Your Uncle Arrayn."

Endicott wiped something from his eye and passed the note to Heylor, who had clearly been trying to read it over his shoulder.

"He lit his pants on fire!" laughed Heylor, reading the note twice.

"This one is for you," said Endicott, passing a small shirt to Heylor. "I made sure it has the buttons you like."

Heylor clutched it to himself, hugged Endicott, and then tried it on, all in a jumbled rush.

"If it goes missing, that's just because I stole it," Endicott added for good measure, but Heylor was not listening. The skinny man was flitting about in his shirt, which did not match his school shorts at all.

"I'll go show the girls!" Heylor was halfway to the door before Endicott's words stopped him.

"Put some pants on first, Heylor, and remember it's still early."

Davyn, Gregory, and Deleske emerged from their rooms and gathered around, attracted by the commotion. Endicott passed them their shirts and dug around in the parcel, organizing the skirts for the girls and trying to delay opening the third item. When he found he could endure the anticipation no longer, he slowly unwrapped the long, heavy bundle. As he had expected, it was a leather-sheathed sword. Unlike conventional swords this one was made of a glistening, glass-like alloy similar in appearance to the blade that Gregory carried. Endicott achieved the lesser breakdown and examined the blade. It was an impressive, costly, seven-element mix just like Gregory's sword, but its randomization had not quite the perfection that the Justice weapon boasted. This sword was cold-forged but not probability manipulated.

Almost as good at a quarter the effort.

Endicott was relieved: he did not want to think of Grandpa risking himself fighting so far past the point of diminishing returns. It was a beautiful weapon: light, strong, hard, sharp, and virtually unbreakable.

Gregory was overjoyed and drew his own sword to hold beside Endicott's. Gregory's was slightly longer and heavier.

"Don't feel bad about it, Robert," boomed Davyn. "That's just genetics. Just polish it lots and who knows, maybe it'll get bigger."

"You, sir, have been spending too much time with that pervert Eoyan March," declared Gregory, looking pointedly at Davyn.

The day after Davyn walked Syriol home from the Apprentices' Library, he had presented himself to the Military School for physical training. Some of the soldiers-to-be had at first made fun of the fat man, but Davyn rapidly won them over, including the irascible Eoyan March. Heylor had joined up the day after that, which left Deleske as the odd man out. Davyn had lost some weight already. At first Endicott assumed his jolly friend was motivated by the scenarios he had heralded in which Davyn was beaten by the bald protestors. That theory did not hold up. Even in training Davyn showed himself to be a pacifist. Now Endicott thought it more likely that the big man's budding relationship with Syriol was the real reason.

"Nice sword!" gushed Eloise. Koria and Bethyn were right behind her. Endicott passed the weapon over and handed Bethyn and Koria their new shirts and skirts. The girls' clothes were made from a special, smooth, iridescent silk from southern Harkness. Even Bethyn liked hers.

Koria wrapped him up in a hug. "Take that sword with you today, Robert."

He frowned a question at her, but she kissed him and made for the door. "No time, we have to get ready for the day."

KORIA WAS RIGHT; THE DAY PASSED QUICKLY. THEY WERE COMING CLOSER AND CLOSER TO the twenty-four-hour test, and the professors were working them mercilessly. Heylor and Bethyn were the focus of particular attention, and while Bethyn was skilled at ignoring both the pressure and the material, Heylor struggled in every way.

"What in Hati's Hell does it matter if we use a Cornell vector or a second-power polynomial to describe the inverse?" He kicked Gregory's chair while he said it.

"It matters," said Meredeth Callum. She had immediately donned the outfit from Endicott's aunt, using the antechamber as a changing room while Merrett and Lindseth turned away. Merrett did not say anything when Endicott gave him his shirt, but Lindseth clapped him on the shoulder.

"Everything matters, Mr. Style." She now sat on the front of his desk, which he could not ignore. The skinny young man went completely still, eyes locked on her. "One day when you completely master the material, you may even take it for granted, but right now these details are crucial." She looked up and surveyed the rest of the group. "There is no gray area, class. This is life and death." Then she hopped lithely off the desk and slapped a hand down where she had been sitting. "I will *not* lose another student because he could not be bothered to apply himself!"

$$\triangledown$$

IT WAS MORE LIFE AND DEATH AT THE MILITARY SCHOOL. ENDICOTT'S SWORD WORK WAS slowly improving. For several days he had tried to herald surreptitiously while sparring with Merrett, but every attempt had ended in a disaster of confusion and missteps. His technique failed in many ways. He would confuse his own footwork or the whole sequence of movement when attempting to apply probabilistic insight to an actual fight, or Merrett would do something Endicott had not heralded. Often Endicott's anticipation would cause him to mistime his responses or inadvertently betray his intentions to his massive instructor. Ultimately his surreptitious attempts to gain a heraldic advantage had to be abandoned, and he was forced to improve using conventional time and effort.

"Why don't we swap swords, Robert?" Gregory asked the question for the third time as they washed up at the end of training. "It is not right that *I* should have the better weapon from *your* grandpa."

"My sword is excellent, Gregory. I doubt even Sir Christensen's weapon is quite as good as it." Endicott smoothed his hair and tucked his medallion out of sight under his shirt. "Grandpa made yours specifically for your family. It's a special case for some reason. Why don't we trust that reason? I have rarely known Grandpa to make a mistake."

"It just doesn't seem fair."

"He is not as young as he used to be." Endicott thought that was the real reason why his sword was not a full probability blade. "*That* is not fair." He pulled his towel off his shoulder and hung it up. "I have a way you can make it up to me."

"Name it!" Gregory declared, hanging his own towel up.

"I want to see what happens with those bald protestors that lurk around the Apprentices' Library. Assuming they show up today."

Gregory looked left and then right, eyes narrowed. "We better sneak out then. There is no way that Heylor will miss out on this if he sees us go."

Endicott smiled. Heylor was not suited to patient work. "I asked Davyn to distract him."

$$\nabla$$

THE BALD, THICK-BODIED MEN WERE THERE ON THE STREET CORNER WITH THEIR SIGNS, which this time were unchanged. Endicott and Gregory set up shop in the Apprentices' Library, where they could watch the two malcontents unseen, but with tea and food at hand. Endicott had predicted that, if they tried to arrest or question the two men, it would almost certainly end in an ugly fight. He described what he had heralded that day with Davyn. Gregory was astounded but never doubted the veracity of his friend's heraldic technique.

"Do you think you should speak with Gerveault or Keith Euyn about that trick you used?" Gregory said cautiously.

"Why? It worked for my grandpa." Endicott's eyes were fixed on the two protestors.

"Koria might not like it," Gregory mused, eating a gravy-covered hunk of bread with peas stuck to it.

Might not?

Endicott would have indicated that he did not disagree with his taller friend, but the two protestors chose that moment to pack up and leave. They walked right by the window of the Library. Endicott fumbled with some coins from their monthly stipend, leaving them spinning on the table, and both young men walked swiftly towards the door. The two bald protestors were loud and self-absorbed, making them very easy to follow. They accosted half the people who walked by them.

"Your Duke is a murderer. You're no better, bitch!"

It did not improve from there.

The two malcontents worked their way to the far side of the academic plateau and approached a large estate home surrounded by a high stone wall and stopped in front of its imposing wrought-iron gate. A guard opened for them at once, and the two obnoxious men walked up the cobble to the door and disappeared inside without knocking.

"We will find out who owns this palace, Gregory," Endicott said excitedly as they walked back towards the Academic Plateau. "And then we'll know something. It surely isn't the—"

"Endicott!" Gregory whispered urgently. "Don't turn around. We are being followed."

"Is it Koria and Eloise?" Endicott hissed back, head stiffly forward, but with a small smile.

"I don't think so. I bet it's one of the protestors from the courthouse."

"Really?" asked Endicott. "I didn't think they noticed us at all."

They turned back towards the heart of the plateau where houses and shops crowded the streets. One shop window was all it took to prove incontrovertibly that their stalker was not Koria or Eloise. Both girls together could not account for the massive size of the cloaked individual following them.

"He's even bigger than that uncle you described! Should we turn and fight?" asked Gregory, hand on the hilt of his sword.

Part of Endicott very much wanted to, the part of him that longed to express itself through violence, the part of him that needed that release. The terrible night, the trial, and then the fraught meeting with Syriol, all carried an accumulating burden that begged for release. But another part of him knew that provoking confrontation and drawing steel would take him to a whole new level of recklessness. They had no idea *who* was following them or even if the colossal cloaked figure was following them for certain.

The Hanging Man!

Endicott saw the sign of the tavern ahead. He knew where they were and what they should do.

"No. We'll go in here and see what he does."

The tavern was warm, well-lit, and welcoming. They shot through the wooden door and immediately spun to peek out the nearest window. The cloaked figure was gone.

How?

They searched the street with their eyes, staring out the window, first one way and then the other. It was as if the cloaked figure had vanished.

"Robert? Robert Endicott from Bron way?" a deep, rich feminine voice called out loudly.

Endicott turned just in time to be engulfed in a powerful hug. The hugger was a tall, broad, brown-haired woman in her early twenties. She had an open smile and a robust physicality. She did not release Endicott quickly but held the crushing embrace through a long five count or more. "Rhiain?" he finally squeaked.

She let him go and nodded her head, grinning. "Who is your lordly looking friend, Robert?"

Endicott bowed to her. "Rhiain Height, may I present Sir Gregory Justice, Lord Justice to some, and my friend and classmate."

Gregory beamed at the introduction, kissing Rhiain's hand, which she obviously loved. "Are you an old friend of Robert's, Lady Rhiain?"

She held a hand to her face, waving as if she was hot. "Oh, Robert's my hero, don't you know? He beat up my two turds of cousins. A well-deserved beating." She turned to Endicott and frowned. "*Sir* Robert now, I understand. Why did you take so long to come visit me?"

They took a table with Gregory sitting close to Rhiain the entire time, and the big-boned woman finished telling the story of how Endicott had fought off her two cousins, who were harassing Endicott's friend, Mair.

"Gavin and Taryn were both bigger than young Robert. Gavin is quite a big lad actually, but Robert picked him up and threw him in the crick. Just threw him! Then he hit Taryn upwards of, oh, fifteen times in the face, as quick as you can say busted nose. They buggered off right quick after that." Rhiain made pugilistic gestures with her hands as she spoke, smiling at Gregory, clearly enjoying his reaction to the story.

"He is fierce when it comes to defending the ladies, isn't he?" Gregory said with a knowing tone.

"He is indeed. It's kind of a sad story, told all in all. Gavin and Taryn were beat by their daddy. Mine was prone to the switch a bit much himself, but I did the smart thing and moved out here. Now I manage this place. But those two are the more typical turds. They got beat, so they think when they get bigger that they should do some beating. It's kind of . . . morbid, is what it is. By acting as such, they tell the world they deserved to be beat, that beatings make sense and they're the right thing to mete out. But nobody needs the switch brought to them by their daddy, 'less it's done out of love to save them from some horrible thing they need to remember."

One of the serving girls hollered a question to Rhiain, and she hollered back an answer.

"I guess we should get back, Gregory. It's a school night." Endicott could see Gregory was in little hurry.

"We'll come back soon," Gregory said, kissing Rhiain's hand again. "I promise." She engulfed him and then Endicott in a hug and rushed off to attend to her tavern.

"How come we never visited her before, Robert?" Gregory asked as they walked home.

Endicott ignored the question. "I thought you liked Eloise."

"I do," Gregory said firmly, hand on Endicott's shoulder, halting him. "But I think she's in love with someone else."

"She likes you just fine," Endicott retorted, then added more softly, "You were there, too, on the terrible night. You are a hero too, Gregory."

Gregory looked unconvinced. "Am I?"

"Yes, but listen," Endicott said wryly, trying a different tack. "Just don't ask Eoyan that question. He'll want to have your babies."

No one followed them, and they passed by the ring road without incident. In a few moments they could see the Orchid.

▽

LONG DAY. ENDICOTT WENT STRAIGHT UP TO THE GIRLS' FLOOR, WAVING GOODBYE TO Gregory, and asked to see Koria. "I love you," he said, holding her tight.

Koria backed them both into her room and closed the door behind them. Her shining, green eyes spoke a wicked promise that ignited him. She pressed him against the door, her hips grinding on his erection through her night dress. Panting, he spun them both and pushed her against the door, one or both of them making a whoof sound as they pressed up against each other and the door. Koria kissed him deeper, tongue probing, and pushed him backwards to the bed, which they fell onto together.

When night drew a little deeper, Endicott rose up from on top of her. She smiled at him and said "stay."

"Soon," he said, kissing her gently. "I should speak with your parents. Let's talk about that tomorrow." He tried to forget her disappointed expression. One more kiss of her improbably soft lips, one more touch of her impossibly smooth skin, and he closed the door gently behind him.

Eloise was standing in the common area, eyes fixed on him. Endicott tried to ignore the fierce shaking of her head as he passed her by and made for the stairs.

"What is *wrong* with you, Stupe?" she called after him, the familiar insult echoing in the stairwell.

It is not time yet. She still doesn't trust me completely.

He was more than a little melancholy for having left Koria, but it felt wrong crossing that last line with her when she still did not completely trust him. He tried to ignore the slightly sour feeling of hurt pride that also lay behind his decision.

I just want it to be perfect.

Endicott did not want to feel conflicted when he and Koria were finally, fully together. He was also mentally and physically exhausted.

It will come. It will all come in time. Just be patient.

He was making progress on his goals. Despite having missed the evening study period, the young man felt satisfied that he and Gregory had learned something for their time. The constables would be able to tell them whose estate the bald protestors went to. They would somehow get Heylor and Bethyn ready for the twenty-four-hour test. He and Koria would be together.

All would be well.

He nodded to Deleske, who slouched in his chair, reading something, and went to bed. Dreams came quickly to him, but with more power and vivid detail than ever before.

He stood by the slough, his dog beside him. It was intensely quiet and peaceful. A solitary duck squawked from the reeds.

What?

Koria and Eloise were walking the dark paths of the campus. The paths were empty except for the two glorious girls. Endicott's heart soared looking upon them, their beauty, grace, and what he could not see but knew well: their hearts and minds. He did love them both, but differently. Eloise was everything he could hope for: a man's strength and ferocity, the pinnacle of female beauty, and an enormous, hidden heart. But Koria was his soul mate, darkly elegant, melancholy with a secret, deeper sadness, smarter than him, and much more mature. Wiser. He knew, watching her in the dream, that he would eventually prove himself worthy of all her trust and they would be together. He longed for it, and the longing hurt him a little while he slept.

If he could have hummed a song while he watched them, he would have, but he could only observe them in his dream. He loved them so much. They passed the agricultural greenhouses. An enormous, cloaked figure stepped out of the shadows and followed them.

No!

Koria looked over her shoulder and cried out silently in terror. Endicott could not hear her, but just seeing her expression evoked an answering horror in him.

No!

The girls ran, but the hulking mass closed on them. At last they turned to face it. A wall of blue flame sprang from the cloaked figure and rolled soundlessly towards the two girls. Koria raised a hand, and when the flames passed over the girls, it did not burn them, but Koria shivered, frost covered her, and she fell to a knee.

No!

Eloise drew her sword and lunged forward, striking at the shadowy attacker. The cloaked figure stepped back, producing as if from nowhere a long, black spear. They dueled, the hulking figure fighting with a peculiar, otherworldly style. Eloise struck again, fast and hard, but the creature caught her sword with the blade of its spear. Eloise's sword shattered, but even holding only the jagged hilt, she did not back down. She stepped in front of Koria, challenging the colossus. The spear went through her chest and drove her into Koria.

NOOO!

It was real. Endicott knew it was real. He could watch it no longer. With a powerful effort of will, he wrenched his consciousness away from the scene, only to find himself elsewhere in the same dark night. Bethyn was coming out of the Lords' Common. The figures of himself and Gregory ran up to her and spoke silently for a moment. They walked back to the orchid together.

No!

Syriol was curled up in the back of the carriage. They roughly violated her and made her drink from their bottle.

NO!

Endicott and Gregory were back at the Orchid.

Eight Knights, no!

His dream returned to the carriage and he watched Vard and Lynal tire of their sport and dump Syriol's broken body on the side of the road. Three different persons walked by but each one ignored Syriol's bleeding, stained, and violated form. Her poor, battered body remained on the curb until morning, breathing no more.

NOOO!

Endicott snapped awake screaming and covered in sweat. He rushed through the common room, crashed through the boys' door before Gregory could fully emerge from his room, and sprinted up the steps to the girls' floor. Their door was locked.

"Koria! Eloise!" he screamed, hammering on the door. It came off its hinges and fell to the side with a tremendous crash. He burst into the common room, as Bethyn, Koria, and Eloise stepped out of their doors, eyes wide in alarm.

"Knights, oh Knights, oh Knights, you're alive!" He rushed to Koria and hugged her with crushing strength. "I love you, I love, I love you, Koria!" He let her go and rushed to Eloise, picking her up in a frenzy. "Oh, Knights!! Help me, help me, help them, someone. Someone help them!"

He dropped her, screaming unintelligibly, and ran in a circle around the common room.

He hit a wall and, staggering, collided with Bethyn, who he immediately mashed in a powerful embrace. "Oh, thank the Knights you're okay Bethyn. Thank the Knights. Thank them. Why couldn't you stick with us?" He abruptly let her go and charged off around the room again. Bethyn's hair was wet.

"I'm sorry, Robert," Bethyn wailed.

Eloise's face had lost all its usual wicked confidence. She looked for once more like a girl than a giant. "What's wrong with him?"

"He's had a heraldic dream," Koria shouted. "Tackle him before he hurts himself!"

Bethyn, Koria, and Eloise tried to corner their screaming, sobbing, frenzied classmate as he darted around the common room. At last he tripped on a chair and Eloise tackled him. The three girls piled on, but he wriggled and pushed and crawled, and they began to lose their hold on him.

Gregory flew through the ruined doorway with Heylor and Davyn right behind him.

"Help us, stupes," gasped Eloise. "He's mad, and we can't hold him!"

The three boys added themselves to the pile, and even the six of them struggled with the manic, distraught man. Chairs flew, Heylor was flung off over the couch, and Davyn was breathing like a bellows.

Finally, and without warning, Endicott went limp.

"Is he dead?" Heylor whispered, regaining his balance, horrified tears in his eyes.

"No," Eloise said. "He's breathing into my knee."

"What should we do?" Heylor asked clutching his hair. "Tie him up?"

Koria crawled out from the pile. "No. Put him on the couch."

They raised him up and laid him out on the couch with a pillow under his head.

At that moment Deleske walked into the room. "Why have you murdered Robert?"

Koria's eyes snapped to him. "Go get Gerveault." Deleske stood, frozen, not understanding. "*Run! Now!*"

"What's wrong with him?" Davyn asked, looking at Koria.

"It's called a heraldic dream, Davyn." Koria held one of Endicott's hands. "They can be quite overwhelming if you are not prepared. He saw something. It could have been a prediction of the future or something that might have been. They can seem as real as any memory. It's like living it. From how he acted, I think it is safe to say that Eloise, I, and maybe Bethyn were hurt in his dream."

"He must really love you," said Gregory. "I've never been so scared in my life. That screaming. He was so strong. I'm amazed he didn't kill one of us." Gregory took stock as if he could not believe everyone was unhurt in the struggle to subdue his friend. "If he fought like that in the fence, he would spray the sand with the lot of us."

"Look at the door," said Bethyn, eyes still wide and tear filled. The hinges and bolt were shattered. "How is that possible?"

"But why would he have a heraldic dream?" Davyn asked, looking at Koria again.

"Will you take his other hand, Eloise? I want him to see us both when he wakes up." Koria raised her reddened eyes to answer Davyn. "I don't know. It usually takes decades, even for the extraordinarily gifted. Most never have one. Most never want one. It's emotionally devastating."

Eloise put a hand on Koria's shoulder.

"He tried an unusual heraldry a few days or a week ago," Davyn confessed. "I wonder if that had something to do with it."

Koria stared daggers at him. "Why didn't you tell me?"

Davyn looked down. He was saved by Endicott opening his eyes. Contrary to the fears of all assembled, he did not immediately spring back to manic life. He did, however, sob for a very long time, clutching the hands of the girls.

He asked to see Bethyn too, and then each of the boys. He was distraught that Deleske could not be produced. Slowly he calmed a little and was able to describe both dreams. After speaking of Syriol, he begged someone to get her. He could not believe she was okay, so powerful were the images of the dream.

"Go get my sword," Endicott demanded after Davyn ran to find Syriol. Gregory returned promptly with it, and Endicott stood up. Everyone else in the room flinched, fearing another manic outburst.

"Eloise." Endicott thrust the sheathed sword to her. "Take this sword."

"No. You need it," Eloise said in a faint voice, clearly uncomfortable, backing away in tiny un-Eloise-like steps.

"You take it, Eloise. Take it!" He thrust it at her again, hand shaking. Eloise stopped backing away and with a vast reluctance, took the sword in her hand. "Yours will break. You'll die. I can't live with that. You kill that fucker, thing . . . whatever it is, with *this*. Stay with Koria, please. Stay with Koria! STAY WITH KORIA!"

Endicott hit his face with the palm of his hand. "I have to get out there. Syriol is out there. But if I go, who will watch Koria?" He burst into fresh tears, mumbling incoherently.

"I'll watch them, Robert," Gregory said with a forced calm.

Koria, Eloise, Bethyn, and Gregory forced Endicott back on the couch. "Just lie down, Robert," Koria said brushing his forehead.

Eloise held his free hand and sighed at him. "I told you, stupe, you can't save everyone. You can't love everyone. No one can." She kissed his hand.

Syriol entered the room with Davyn and Jeyn Lindseth behind her. She looked at Endicott and gasped. "What's wrong with him?" she demanded, sounding both shocked and mournful.

"He is very . . . emotional right now, Syriol," Koria explained, sitting on Endicott's chest. "Don't move. Just be calm no matter what he does or says."

Endicott saw her and pushed himself off the couch, inadvertently lifting Koria right off him. Eloise helped keep Koria from falling while Endicott rushed to Syriol and collapsed at her feet, clutching her legs and sobbing into her stomach. She struggled to keep her balance while he gripped her legs and moaned, "I'm sorry, I'm so sorry. I'm so sorry. I wasn't there. I wasn't there! I WASN'T THERE!"

Davyn pushed a chair behind Syriol so she could sit down. Endicott hugged her legs and laid his head in her lap. "Be okay, be okay, be okay." Syriol's leaned over him, her dark hair half caressing his head.

Gerveault arrived not much later, Deleske behind him, and took in the situation instantly. Koria described what they had just endured. The old professor did not need to be told that Endicott had been in the grip of a heraldic dream. He shook his head but knew the students needed comforting and reassuring.

"I have rarely had a heraldic dream. I was so old by the time I had my first one that I no longer cared about things as I did when I was young. When I finally had that dream, it was not about anything emotional. It was nothing that even mattered personally to me. But it was as real as any memory. It was exactly as if it actually happened. This one, though. Knights! He is too young for this kind of thing." He looked at Koria. "They can be devastating for anyone, but on the young —especially someone already so sensitive—and if death or worse is in the vision. I do not know."

"He has always had this thing about women," Eloise said into the momentary silence. "As sensitive as he is about everything, he is extra sensitive about us girls."

"His mother died when he was three or four," supplied Koria.

Gerveault mumbled noncommittally.

"Will he be okay?" begged Heylor.

Gerveault pursed his lips. "He might not even be able to stay in the program."

Groans and ruder exclamations filled the room at this remark. Gerveault put his hand up. "*Might* not. Right now he is as unhinged as that door, but I hope he recovers. The vision should fade with time like any memory. Stay with him. There will be no class tomorrow." Gerveault touched the back of Endicott's head. The young man was still clutching Syriol. "In life we may all be hung on the rope of our own consequences. But we can own those ones. We must. With a heraldic dream, you can see the consequence of *every* action before they happen. Whether they ever happen or not. You hang yourself on *every* possible rope."

Chapter Twenty

Before the Crime

ENDICOTT SLOWLY DRIFTED TOWARDS CONSCIOUSNESS WITH HIS FACE GENTLY RESTING on Koria's stomach. His eyes did not need to be open to know her. Someone was running their hands along his lower legs. *Lovely.*

"Every day since that night, I have felt . . . wrong, like something is wrong, just out of sight, around the corner, in a shadow." Syriol's voice floated by from somewhere near. "It's like a weight. I can't see it, but it has been on me, pushing, pushing down. Sometimes it would seem heavier than I could bear, and my heart would race. I would feel fear, but worse, I would feel sick, wrong in my stomach. I could not walk with confidence or feel happiness. The sun changed color. It wasn't really yellow anymore. It was washed out, it was wrong. Sometimes, I was even afraid of Davyn." She laughed ruefully. "Davyn! He wouldn't hurt a skolve. Who could be afraid of him? Me. I was the idiot who got in the carriage. I felt a victim, I *made* myself one. I felt *ashamed.*" Syriol paused for a moment before continuing. "I feel different now. A little. A little better. I cannot explain why, but I feel more at peace with everything that has happened. Released."

"Because of this?" Endicott could feel Koria speaking through the vibrations of her stomach on his face.

"Yes," Syriol breathed, barely audible. "Seeing him like that made me feel better." Her voice dropped even lower. "Seeing how he *suffered.*"

"How does that make any sense?" This was Bethyn from somewhere off to the side. "It's not about *him.* *You're* the one who was assaulted." Despite her words, the inflection was largely interrogative.

"How come you're asking, Bethyn?" Eloise's strident tones were unmistakable. "I haven't seen you so engaged. Ever."

"Why do you have to bitch on me all the time, Eloise?" Bethyn again, but not really angry.

"Ladies, please." *Lovely, lovely voice.* It was Koria again. "How about we skip the fighting? In any case deep down we all know why."

"Do we?" asked Syriol.

Endicott felt Koria take a breath. "Yes, we do. We know why you feel just *a little* better, why Bethyn feels more alive, after Robert's . . . breakdown. But it's not really about him. Syriol. What happened to you was not your fault. It had nothing to do with who you are. You have been incredibly strong and," she laughed softly, "we've just seen that men cannot handle what we can."

She paused. "Forget I said that last part. What has helped you heal, Syriol, is this man's—"

"Stupe's!" interjected Eloise.

"This stupe's love," continued Koria, hugging Endicott's face to her, "His love, because that's what the dream and his reaction was about. It reminded you that you are worth something. Love is a powerful thing."

"Powerfully bad for him," muttered Bethyn.

Endicott struggled to awaken fully. He knew he should not be eavesdropping, but he could form only a vague and distant idea of what the ladies were talking about. He pushed himself to focus, and, in flashes of awareness, a picture of where he was and what had happened to him started to form. He began to remember his heraldic dream.

"When all this has passed," Koria hugged Endicott's head again, "remember it is not about Robert. He just carried the message. There is wickedness in the world, violence, unreason, prejudice, rapine, ignorance. Of those horrible things there is no shortage. We ourselves are capable of violence. But there is love as well. Even from people who have never met you, as Robert had not that night." Koria shifted. "Love even despite your sour moods and destructive choices, Bethyn." She paused. "There may be things we would all be better off forgetting, but we should remember love. Remember that we are worthy of love."

Endicott's trickle of recollections turned to a flood. *Dear knights, no! Koria, Syriol, Eloise, no!* With overwhelming speed, he remembered his dream in its full horror. Endicott opened his eyes and screamed, "Noooo!"

He tried to sit up, a cold sweat flashing over him, but eight hands held him down. He saw that he was on the couch, his upper body pinned under Koria and his legs under Eloise. Bethyn and Syriol sat close by on two chairs facing the couch, leaning forward with their hands pressing down upon him.

"Easy, Robert," said Koria. "Go slow."

"Why won't you let me up?" Endicott asked, still pushing. His head darted from woman to woman. He reached to cup Koria's face. "May I?" She smiled gently and inclined her head toward him.

"Come closer, please." He gently caressed each woman's face and then lay back. "Thank the Knights. Was all of it really just a dream?"

"Yes, stupe, it was all a dream." Eloise replied, still gripping his legs.

"What happened? Why are you all here?" He closed his eyes and then opened them again. "This is really nice."

Koria laughed. It sounded like little, tinkling bells.

Thank the Knights, thank them, thank them.

The ladies took turns explaining the events of the previous evening. It was already well past noon the following day, they revealed, and they had all stayed with him since he had exploded from the dream and gone on his rampage. Even lying there listening to the soft, high voices of the girls, memories assailed him. Every detail hurt like a knife his gut.

It was so real!

"I'm okay now," Endicott claimed. "You can let me up."

The hands still pressed down on him.

"We'll be the judge of that, stupe." Eloise declared.

Endicott frowned, not understanding.

"You have woken up and said this twice before Robert," Koria said. "It has *not* gone well. Let's just see how you are for a few moments before anyone goes anywhere."

Endicott started. "Did I hurt anyone?" he asked anxiously.

"No," said Bethyn, "but we've had to call Bat and Eoyan over to help us hold you down."

Endicott twisted his head to look for Merrett and Eoyan March. They were standing by the ruined door.

Did I really do that? How?

Endicott was horrified by the thought of his violent frenzy but thankful he seemed to have hurt only the door.

"Are they here to restrain me?" he asked.

"Only if we ask them to," said Eloise with a hint of her usual wickedness. "You are *our* job."

"They are here to guard the door until it can be fixed," explained Koria. "Professor Eleanor thought it would ease your recovery."

"You're safe," he breathed reaching out for her cheek again. He saw alarmed expressions on the girls' faces, so he rushed to add, "I'm okay. I'm just glad you are all safe. What else has been happening during my . . . absence?"

"I'm staying here for the week," Syriol said happily. "Until you are better. Then I start a job working for the duchess."

"I would like to meet her," Endicott said, which seemed to amuse everyone. "What?" he asked.

"You'll figure it out eventually," Bethyn said, smiling.

"Hmm. What else has been going on?" Endicott was starting to feel guilty; lying back under Koria was deliciously enjoyable.

"Sir Hemdale visited," Syriol declared with some awe.

Sir Hemdale?

"All your professors were here too," added Syriol, "except for the really old one."

"Keith Euyn is not well," Bethyn threw in.

Keith Euyn was often under the weather, so this news was not unusual.

Koria feels so nice. A familiar physical reaction warned Endicott that he really should get out from underneath the girls. "I really am okay now. I better sit up, ladies."

Eloise glanced down at him, saw what was happening, and started laughing. "We had better let him up. He's starting to look like himself."

Released at last, Endicott sat up, still a little woozy, and held Koria. The dream was still reverberating in the back of his mind, and he spasmed, holding her tighter. *Why can't I forget?*

"It will pass, Robert," Koria whispered. "Tell yourself it wasn't real and *allow* it to pass."

How are you so wise? "Koria, I think I should stay with you tonight. I'll sleep on top of the blankets, I just need to know you are okay. I know I sound like an infant, but—"

"It's okay, Robert," breathed Koria, silencing his doubts with a kiss.

Endicott let her go, not swiftly or easily, and stood up. He could smell his own sweat. "I think I should go get cleaned up." He gathered the four women into a group hug, something he never would have imagined doing before the dream.

"Honestly," Endicott said in wonder, "this is the best and the worst therapy I have ever heard of. I don't know how you have all put up with it."

He remembered dimly the conversation he had overheard as he had struggled to awaken and felt a little ashamed and unworthy of all their compassion. He knew very well that Syriol was the only one who had actually been hurt. *Had she been so well looked after? Had she had four friends hold her in the dark until she woke from that terrible night? There may be no fairness in the calculus of suffering.* He pushed down these thoughts in case he should start weeping again and alarm the ladies once more. "Shall we talk later?"

Endicott walked towards the ruined door. Still standing guard there, Merrett and Eoyan watched him impassively. He paused on the threshold, looking back at the girls. The dream was still there, rumbling deep in his mind, and he found it difficult to let them out of his sight.

"Don't worry, blouse," said Merrett in his rough tones. "Nothing is getting past us." He was dressed in full mail, his sword close to hand.

"I'll walk you down, Sir Robert," Eoyan added, smiling.

They started down the stairs, Endicott walking with reluctant slowness. "It almost seemed like he didn't hate me."

"Who? Bat?" asked Eoyan. "You're almost all he ever talks about." His eyebrows narrowed. "That might not quite be right. You come right after food, training, girls, maintenance of his sword, and maybe a couple other things I can't think of right now. That's still pretty high."

"Hmm. If that's true, why is he always scowling at me?" Endicott asked.

Eoyan stopped. "That's how he looks at everyone he likes. Actually that's how he looks at everyone he hates too, so maybe don't go by that. And who cares about that grumpy skolve anyway? He can look after his own worries." He hit Endicott on the shoulder. "I told you that you're *my* hero: you just slept with four women. And they were all smiling afterwards!"

As they started walking again, Endicott became aware, for the first time since waking, of a deep soreness throughout his body. He felt like he had been run over by one of the ubiquitous ice carriages. They were almost at the boys' door when Eoyan spoke again.

"I would give a lot to see Koria as happy as she used to be, Robert, so you be good to her."

"I love her, Eoyan."

Used to be?

"What do you mean? Did you know her before all this?"

"Everyone knows you love everyone, Robert. It's in the records at court." Eoyan March stopped again and gazed at Endicott, his mischievous face turning serious. "But yes, I met her more than a year ago, even before those boys in her class died. She used to run everywhere, flitting about. She would do this thing when she saw a fence. She would jump straight up on it and balance there like a circus acrobat. She even climbed up some of the school monuments. If ever I saw a sprite, it was her."

"Koria?" Endicott couldn't believe Eoyan's story. That was not Koria.

"No word a lie. She had as much fire in her as Eloise, in her own way, and I know that's saying a lot. You couldn't find better company anywhere. Either of them really. You are one lucky skolve." He hit Endicott on the shoulder again.

"So she changed after the boys in her class died?" Endicott persisted.

"No, Robert," Eoyan shook his head slowly, frowning. "Well, a little. She became more thoughtful. But about a month after they died she took sick, and when she came back to school she was different. Melancholy."

"She was here that long before classes started?"

"Sure," said Eoyan. "She helped the Duchess and Gerveault design the new plan for you lot."

Endicott thanked Eoyan at the boys' doorway. The tall man jogged back up the stairs, chain mail jingling. *I guess I sort of knew she had helped design the class, but what changed her?* He had a terrible suspicion.

He found all four of his roommates in the boys' common room, along with tall, thoughtful Lindseth, who was wearing his aunt's finely stitched shirt again. They scrambled to their feet. Endicott waved them down with a hand, but they ignored that and crowded around him instead.

"I am okay, gentlemen. Please."

"Truly?" said Gregory with a worried frown.

Endicott had at last hit the point of emotional saturation. His restless, continually working mind was revolving somewhere else now. It was turning to thoughts of action. "As true as that blade at your hip, Gregory."

"That reminds me." Gregory stepped aside and took up a bundle that had been leaning against his chair. It was his cold-forged sword. "Eloise sent it back to you, Robert."

"When you were asleep," interrupted Heylor, "you threw me over the couch!"

"I'm sorry about that, Heylor." Endicott refused the sword. "I was mad, no doubt of it, gentlemen, and I am sorry for all the trouble, but we are going to make something good out of this."

"Sayeth the madman," said Deleske sardonically.

"I do say it." Endicott stood firm. "Glad to see that you haven't changed, Deleske. I want to talk with everyone. But I need to clean up first. I smell like a sty." Without another word, he left them there, grabbed a change of clothes from his room and stepped into the baths. His shaving kit was missing.

"Heylor! I need my razor."

Gear back in hand, Endicott took his time shaving. His arms and hands felt stiff and sore. Even standing straight to shave produced an ache in his back. When he took his night clothes off, he was shocked at the mass of contusions that bloomed all over his body. *How on earth did I get all these?*

As he shaved and bathed, his mind worked, making connections. He considered everything he knew about the protestors with their signs, the people who had tried to burn down the Bron elevator, and going further back, the fight at the registered seed compound. He thought about his heraldic dream and the horrible deaths of Eloise and Koria it augured, and then he thought about the cloaked figure. The future he had seen was only a partial glimpse of things that *might* come, dependent on unknown changes in circumstance, auguring the possible deaths of his friends.

All happy people wrap themselves in a cocoon from which they perceive their lives as implicitly on the right track. They feel content in their comfortable, changeless equilibrium. Even in the New School, learning new things, Endicott had felt that false sense of security about the future. In his youthful naiveté, he had assumed he would somehow always be the master of his fate, that good things would come naturally as long as he worked hard. They always had, and like most happy people, he implicitly assumed not only that they always would but that he deserved those good things. Certainly there would be changes, but he would be on top of them. He would be *part* of the change that would come.

He now realized that assuming you would get what you deserved was foolish. Even thinking about what was deserved or undeserved was of little use. The future could be horrible as easily as it could be good. The realization was frightening. Change could be good, but it could also be unfair and cruel. And final. The thought of Syriol, Koria, and Eloise potentially meeting such cruel, unfair, terrible fates threatened to unhinge him again, but he managed that bottomless fear with the beginnings of an idea. The future might not be an entitlement that he was born to inherit, but he could try to own it.

The future is coming whether I like it or not, but I can be ready for it and make a better one.

I hope, I hope, I hope.

▽

IT DID NOT TAKE LONG FOR EVERYONE TO ASSEMBLE IN THE GIRLS' COMMON ROOM. THEY seemed eager to appease Endicott. They walked around him like he might break and watched him closely. Very closely.

It will be well.

"I am okay now, and I know," he looked at each of them, suppressing the knot in his stomach, "that *you* are as well. Thank you for looking after me. I am also glad our friends from the Military School are here. There is something I need everyone's help with."

"You can't sleep with me," hollered Eoyan from the doorway.

"Noted." Endicott glanced over at Davyn, who was holding Syriol's hand. "First we need to agree on a few vital facts. Davyn, were you and Heylor really pursued by a large, cloaked figure that night you stole the carriage for hire?"

"Yes!" Heylor burst out.

Davyn let go of Syriol's hand and covered Heylor's mouth. "Upon the instruction of Kennyth Brice, I must say we don't remember that part of the night, the part with the carriage anyway. But someone very large certainly did follow us."

"It was Nimrheal!" shouted Heylor, fighting with Davyn's big hand.

"How do you know that?" Merrett demanded with obvious skepticism from just inside the doorway.

There was a brief, comic struggle between Davyn and Heylor that involved hands over mouths and much slapping. "Shut up, Heylor," Davyn said, victorious, before looking up at everyone. "We don't know who it was. But the person was definitely well over six and half feet tall, which means probably male. He was strong. He had inertia enough that Heylor bounced right off him. He wore a cloak. *That* is what we know."

"That sounds like the same person who followed Endicott and me the other night," added Gregory.

"And it sounds like the person in my heraldic dream." Endicott said, coming to his point. "The person who threw fire at Koria and Eloise like a wizard from before the Methueyn War. The person who had a spear that could break swords."

"What are you driving at, Robert?" Bethyn asked.

Endicott was surprised to see Bethyn so involved. He nodded to her, which earned him a smile. "Just one more detail, Bethyn, and you'll know." He turned to Koria, who had been silent. "Does heraldry ever lie, Koria? Does it show things that do not exist?"

Everyone looked at Koria, who did not answer quickly. "We have not studied that yet, Robert."

"But *you* have studied it."

She nodded reluctantly. "Heraldry does not make up images or events that *cannot* exist. Their likelihood is a more complex issue. Your question is whether the hooded giant exists. The answer has to be yes."

"And he is capable of empyreal manipulation." Endicott took up his sheathed, cold-forged sword and thrust it at Eloise. "Take this, Eloise. You might need it."

"No." Eloise forcibly held her hands away from the weapon. "I see it, Robert. I see what it is, but it would be wrong for me to take it."

"Listen everyone," Endicott said confidently. "I understand less than half the foolishness that goes on in the world, or even half the fools we have met these last few months, but I am certain of at least one thing: we have an enemy. He is big, he is stalking us, and he has a Deladieyr-class spear. My dream may or may not come to pass. But we need to be ready. That means we must pass the twenty-four-hour test, we must learn the new dynamics, and we must become experts in combat against someone with a spear."

Endicott thrust the sheathed sword at Eloise again. "You're better than me, Eloise." *And I can't live with my dream unless that sword is in your hands.*

At first Eloise did not move. Her frozen, uncharacteristic, immobility lasted so long that Robert thought she would refuse him again. Eventually she smiled and took the weapon. "You finally said something smart, stupe."

Endicott smiled. "Let's make a plan, then."

▽

"WE HAVE TAKEN STEPS TO CATCH HIM, ROBERT, BUT HE WILL HAVE TO SHOW HIMSELF first." Gerveault watched the younger man closely as he spoke. He shared a look with Eleanor, who sat in the tall, high-backed chair beside his desk.

"You passed my description to the constabulary?"

"Yes, I did. Unhesitatingly."

"The duchess made certain that it was a priority for them," Eleanor added in her gravelly voice.

Endicott let out a breath. "Thank you for believing me, Professors."

Gerveault chuckled "Oh, there's no doubt you had a heraldic dream, young man. We will keep an eye out for this cloaked giant."

"Who do you suppose he was?" Endicott asked.

"Who *will* he be, you mean," corrected Gerveault.

Eleanor sat back in her chair, almost lost in its shadow. "The New School, and the duchy itself, has many enemies, Robert."

Slow, be slow.

"But we have to wait?"

*We cannot wait. Cannot. We cannot wait. If we wait, he'll have the advantage. He'll
kill Koria and Eloise.*

Eleanor reached from her chair and took Endicott's shaking hand. He had not
noticed the palsy. "It's okay, Robert. What you dreamed has *not* happened."

He gripped her papery hand tightly. "It feels like it has!" he cried, tears falling.
He grunted, forcing himself to stop crying, forcing himself back under control.

Gerveault nodded dispassionately from behind his big desk. "Heraldic dreams
are the only continuum in which the punishment precedes the crime."

"Robert," Eleanor said, still holding his hand, "there is precedent for simply
taking a breath and resuming dynamics next year. You could stay with the duchess
until you feel better."

"Really? I don't even know her." Endicott said it out of politeness. There was *no
way* he was taking any kind of break. That was not what he had come to Gerveault
and Eleanor for. He needed to continue with his plan. He had ensured that the
constabulary would do their part, but now he needed to do his. He needed to
be there at the Orchid. Eloise and Koria died in a dream in which he made no
appearance. He could change that. He could learn dynamics, and he could be there
to stop the cloaked figure.

I must stop him. I must. I must. We must.

"We could certainly do that," Gerveault said softly. "Take a break, Robert."

"No! I mean, *no thank you.*" Endicott patted Eleanor's hand and gently let it go.
He stood up. "No breaks. I'm okay. I wouldn't know what to do with myself if I
had extra time, and I think I am better off staying with my classmates. We are
going to get through the twenty-four-hour test together and stay together."

Chapter Twenty-One

No Place for Whistling

"**G**ET OUT!" HISSED THE LIBRARIAN. "THIS IS NO PLACE FOR WHISTLING, SCREAMING, OR carrying on." Her eyes bulged as she involuntarily glanced once more at the bizarre, and almost certainly never-before-seen tableau of Heylor Style strapped to the chair and being tended to by Bethyn with a willow switch in hand. "And untie your friend! He especially must leave."

▽

"HOW DO YOU VANQUISH SOMEONE YOU HAVE SEEN VANQUISH YOU?" ENDICOTT SMILED AT his friends. "In my dream the cloaked figure overpowers who we were *going* to be. We have to change who we are going to be; we must *become* something else. We must be better than we would have been. We must *exceed* ourselves." He saw Koria frowning at him. "But carefully, of course. Carefully."

"Why don't we begin in the library, then?" Koria said. "How much trouble can you get into there?"

And so the plan started not much later that same day in the library. While it eventually moved to the Military School and on to other places, it started in the library. No secret documents were uncovered, rules of magic discovered, or commercial plots exposed. There was only mathematics, plus the issues and idiosyncrasies that the students brought with them.

"Pay attention, Heylor, your eyelids are drooping," admonished Bethyn.

"Sorry," the jittery young man said.

"Why can't you pay attention?" Bethyn persisted.

"I don't know."

Bethyn smiled sourly at Heylor. "You know, math is the one class I would think you would appreciate, Heylor. The numbers don't care who you are, who your family is, what you are, the mistakes you've made, how poorly you fit in, what you steal, or that you have poor personal hygiene and smell bad."

"Some of that seems a little unfair," mumbled the young man, looking down.

"Bethyn," said Davyn. "you are being a little harsh."

Harsh, but interesting. Endicott had not been paying much attention to the argument until this point.

"No," Bethyn said unrelenting, "math may be the only fair thing in his life."

"It's hard to be excited about mathematics," Heylor complained.

Eloise raised an eyebrow. "It's not as exciting as it was in the old days when new mathematics might get you murdered by Nimrheal."

"Well, the rest of us manage." Bethyn scowled at Eloise and turned back to Heylor. "Just what is your problem?"

"Don't know, my mind just wanders."

"On to what?"

"Oh, I daydream about things. Girls." Heylor ducked his head "Even about you, Bethyn."

"Gross!" she punched him in the neck.

"Gah!"

Even though they were camped out in a private room at the library, Endicott could hear numerous shushes from outside. Both Heylor and Bethyn's faces were red. She was still scowling at the skinny boy.

"Nobody should be fantasizing about anyone," declared Gregory. "Let's just get back to work. This math isn't going to learn itself."

Heylor clutched at his neck, face still red. "W-what about him?" he wheezed, pointing at Endicott. "Robert gets to declare his love for everyone."

"Yes, Heylor, but I d-don't th-think about the girls that way," stammered Endicott, unprepared for this turn in conversation. *Not when I'm doing math. Not recently.* Lately, when Endicott's attention slipped, it went in only one direction: down the dark alley that ended in his heraldic dream. His fantasies these days were nightmares that he tried to keep to himself.

Eloise snorted, and Koria even looked up from the book she had been studying.

"You know, that has got to be true," chipped in Davyn, looking up from his page of scribbling, "because if Robert thought it, he would for sure say it."

"Okay," Endicott snapped, impatient that they were losing precious time, "we should try something different. We know that being passive doesn't work for you, Heylor. Let's try something more active."

"With my fantasies?"

ENDICOTT COULD NOT STAY ANGRY WITH HIS FRIEND FOR VERY LONG. HE KNEW THAT Heylor simply could not study in the traditional way. His mind wandered, he twitched, he whistled, and sometimes he stole things. A bored Heylor was a bad Heylor. A bad Heylor would not pass the twenty-four-hour test. The skinny young man had not been in the heraldic dream. If Endicott could ensure that Heylor passed the test, it might be the difference needed to defeat the cloaked figure. Probably not—what could Heylor really be expected to do?—but maybe. Any difference from his dream, any change, however small, was good.

The first attempt at helping Heylor *did* end in them being banished from the library for the day. Apparently it was both far too loud, and way, way too inappropriate for Bethyn and Davyn to strap Heylor to a chair and give him short, sandglass deadlines to solve problems or be tweaked on the nose with a willow switch. Their claims that it was only light tweaking went unheeded by the librarian.

The disruption of their first attempt with Heylor only encouraged everyone to try harder over the following days. They soon came to understand that there would need to be a rotating team to work with the jittery young man. Heylor had to move about, shout, write things down boldly on printed books, or paraphrase the meaning of the work himself. His team included everyone, even Syriol. Heylor was tasked with explaining a list of mathematical concepts to her until she also understood them. Later Davyn and Deleske took positions on topics within inverse theory and estimation, one position correct, the other incorrect, and challenged Heylor to determine who had the right answer and explain his reasoning. Even Bethyn seemed to enjoy the unorthodox approach they were taking, and her own readiness for the test also took a noticeable jump in the right direction.

Endicott, Eloise, and Gregory worked on mathematics and physics as well, but the plan required that they also step up the intensity of their training at the

Military School. Eoyan March was recruited to teach them how to fight some-one with a spear. Endicott did not want to remember the details of his heraldic dream—thinking about it made him feel sharply ill—but he forced himself to reproduce every movement he had seen the cloaked figure make. Eoyan helped break down the style, which was apparently quite old, and showed them the best counters to every move.

Koria designed the extramural lesson plans, wrote the mock tests and lists of subjects for Syriol and Heylor to work on, and coolly evaluated everyone's progress. She also watched Endicott carefully and quietly, as always.

Some concessions had to be begged from the professors.

"Please come down off the desk, Mr. Heylor," Gerveault ordered ten days later. Heylor was crouching on his desk and whistling.

"I don't understand the use of the dipole filter, Professor Gerveault," he said, not moving from his crouch. He whistled again.

Merrett looked in from the antechamber and shook his head. Lindseth's hand reached around and pulled the big man back out of view.

"Could you stop with the whistling, stupe?" complained Eloise, whose patience was rapidly wearing thin.

Gerveault rubbed his forehead. "What do you mean you don't understand, Mr. Style?"

Heylor jumped off the desk, walked past Gerveault, and put chalk to chalkboard. "The dipole is small in any spatial domain. It's two samples." Heylor drew a dipole with two ticks of chalk. "But in Lessingham space, all dipole filters are of infinite size." He drew the Lessingham domain representation of his chalk dipole, a long, long curve. "They aren't likely to represent an exact inverse to anything except one other specific dipole."

That's a very good point. A fresh insight leapt into Endicott's mind. "But it's fast, Heylor. It isn't exact, it isn't likely to be an inverse, but a dipole operator is incredibly fast."

Davyn's hand shot up. "But not accurate, so you use it when you already know the direction in which you want to change things."

"That actually makes sense," Heylor said, then whistled and handed the chalk to Gerveault.

Gerveault was unimpressed. "Yes, Mr. Endicott, Mr. Daly, if fast and loose is how you like to play, the dipole filter is indeed your best friend. But has that not worked out rather poorly so far?"

Heylor whistled again and jumped on a table at the back of the room.

"I'm getting the willow switch," muttered Bethyn.

Eloise jumped in, smiling for once at Bethyn. "I'll tie him up."

On an impulse, Endicott opened himself to the empyreal sky, achieving the lesser breakdown. From that vantage point, he could view the thermal properties of the room. He imagined dividing the room into a square grid and averaging the thermal properties within that grid to points for each grid space. He then imagined applying a dipole operator to the space. The exercise was similar to how his grandpa had taught him to rapidly heat or cool objects at their forge, only on a much, much coarser scale. *If I could just—*

"Robert Endicott!" Gerveault barked at him, making him jump in his chair. "Leave the Empyrean this instant, young man!"

Endicott let it go, chagrined. Koria's face was a storm cloud. There was little to be gained by telling them that he had done this before with his grandpa. Gerveault was yelling at him as it was.

"You *must* wait, Robert!" Gerveault's face was bright red. "You have a genius, but it could be a genius for getting yourself killed or driven mad. And if you killed only yourself it wouldn't be so bad—"

"And you'll go blind," whispered Davyn unquietly, smiling and making a rude hand gesture under the table. Everyone but Gerveault, Koria, and Endicott laughed.

"I'm sorry, Professor, I was just curious where this was go—"

"Patience, Mr. Endicott. If you even want to be here to take the test, wait until we teach you properly."

Heylor whistled.

Chapter Twenty-Two

The Book of Nature

"THE BOOK OF NATURE IS WRITTEN IN MATHEMATICS, LADIES AND GENTLEMEN," declared Meredeth Callum with an incongruously enthusiastic smile and sweet voice. "Its language is the same for everyone and makes no allowances for the fact that you are going to do today what you have done every day since you arrived here." She thumped a hand dramatically on the table in front of Heylor. "The mathematics do not care that you are bored." The twitchy young man was so tired from the extra studying they had been doing that he hardly even jumped. Meredeth frowned, obviously disappointed at the attenuated reaction.

"What? Are we going to learn about some more dead mathematicians?" Bethyn's dry, lazy voice rose up from the back of the room.

Has she started drinking again? Endicott's stomach fell at the thought. Bethyn had been doing so much better until something had gone suddenly wrong during a late-night study session the night before. She had abruptly yelled at Deleske over some triviality and stormed off. Her dramatic exit left had them all stunned. It was not just her mathematics performance that had improved recently, but her attitude had as well. She seemed to have started feeling as if she genuinely belonged and acting as though she finally, really cared. The dark, sarcastic shield that she held up against the world seemed to have been put aside. But not last night. And not today either.

What is wrong with her? Endicott turned around to look, trying to see into her eyes, but her head was lowered.

"Yes, Miss Trail, you are," said Meredeth said with obvious satisfaction. It seemed Bethyn had said something that served the purpose of the lesson. The professor continued with a beatific smile. "The lessons they taught have not changed. They apply with equal validity to everyone."

"What lessons?" Bethyn rejoined, looking up now with hooded eyes. "That curiosity killed everyone?"

▽

"Do you really wish you were somewhere else?" Endicott asked Bethyn as the two of them took a circuitous route back to the Orchid. Meredeth Callum had asked her that exact question earlier.

"Not really," she said quietly, not looking at him.

Endicott put his right arm around her shoulders. "Well, we're glad you are here."

She leaned into him for a moment and put her head on his shoulder before stepping away. "Thanks."

Endicott ached to get through to her without crossing a line he knew he should not. He imagined a line with his sandy footprints all over it. *I should not cross it again.*

Thinking that, he risked a very small step further. "What do you think of this Book of Nature that Professor Callum goes on about?"

"What about it?" Bethyn continued walking.

"I looked for it in the library but couldn't find it."

"Really?" She smiled slightly. "You do *know* it's only a metaphor."

Endicott scratched his chin. "I *did* know that, but I *had* to look anyway. What do you suppose the point of the book is, then?"

Bethyn kept walking, head pointed down. "The point? It's another made-up concept, a fictional attempt at putting a structure we *can* understand around a reality we *cannot.*"

Endicott blew out a breath, impressed. Bethyn did not speak up much and most of what she said when she did speak had the sour-sharp bite of sarcasm to it. Now and then, though, she came up with something unexpected and insightful. It showed there was more going on with her than a less interested observer would ever notice. "That sounds about right," he replied.

They walked a little further, and he made another attempt. "So the notional idea of the Book of Nature could be useful sometimes."

She shrugged. "Maybe."

Endicott persisted. "But not useful at other times, like if its concept of structure couldn't meaningfully mirror that reality you mentioned?"

"If you say so." She still looked down as she walked.

"Of course," Endicott spoke softly, looking at her, "sometimes the book is all wrong, written by the wrong people or written so far ahead of or behind the event that it isn't useful at all. We should get rid of a book like that, shouldn't we?"

Bethyn stopped and turned to face him. "What metaphor are you working at now?"

Endicott smiled tightly, looking her in the eyes. "Whatever people told you before, or whatever you have told yourself in the past, is not the tale of you, Bethyn. You can start writing your own book any time."

"So my book has been written by outside forces? There's something *wrong* with me?" Bethyn scowled. "No one has *damaged* me, Robert, if that's what you think. I haven't been beaten or abused. You're always trying to save people." Her eyes blazed, scary and wide. "I don't *need* saving."

"I'm sorry, Bethyn." Endicott placed both hands palm out towards her. He was confused and a little embarrassed. "You haven't been drinking as much as before, but here you are today hung over and picking fights with Meredeth. You still sound so melancholy sometimes. And I'm worried about the twenty-four-hour test. We need your help. *Heylor* needs your help. *You* need to study for *yourself.* Tell me: why are you so sad, Bethyn?"

One side of Bethyn's mouth curled into a smile while the other stayed flat. "Maybe not everything I like is according to the Book of Nature, Robert. Maybe some things are not so easy even now. New stitching machine? Okay. New grain? Fine. Kiss a girl? How embarrassing. We better call Nimrheal."

"Oh," Endicott blinked, surprised and off balance. The way Bethyn had always fought with Eloise, he never would have guessed.

"Apparently that's against the Book of Nature."

Endicott was pretty sure that nothing of a sexual nature had been written in steel. "Who said kissing a girl isn't in the book?"

"One of the protestors did. Down by the Apprentices' Library yesterday."

Endicott had not seen it. Not the signs, and not Bethyn's sexuality. The signs changed quite often after all, and he did not pay attention to every protestor he passed by. How could he? The list of supposed crimes against nature seemed to be growing; he had only paid attention to the ones with a close bearing on his own interests, the ones that hurt him. *That* was the truth. He felt sick.

Am I selfish? Shouldn't I be looking out for Bethyn, too? Shouldn't I be upset about everything *that's wrong?*

This was a new weight, a new problem. The realization humbled Endicott. He was not the hero he thought he was. He was not helping *all* his friends. He saw that Bethyn was looking at him. "I'm sorry. I never noticed that particular admonition. Do you think the protestors are still there?"

He took a deep breath, heart rate rising, body readying for action. Every time he had considered confronting the protestors something had stopped him: heraldry, or Koria's advice not to look for trouble, or just bad timing. But he felt Bethyn needed him. "I could go talk to them."

Endicott was brought up short by the force of Bethyn's hand as it suddenly landed on his chest. Her bloodshot eyes were locked on his. "Don't you think we have enough problems already, Robert? The test, remember? Your crazy temper, remember?"

Everything's a test. Endicott tried to control his warring impulses and pay attention to the girl in front of him. He pulled Bethyn into a tight hug. "I don't care who you like to kiss. It's . . . it's fine with me."

Bethyn snorted, her head resting on his chest. "That's a relief, Robert."

"I still love you."

I do.

"It really doesn't matter to me," he added.

"You had *better* still love me, idiot," she said, breaking the hug and stepping back from him. "And maybe it doesn't matter who I want to kiss. Perhaps I was going to be a malcontent anyway. What if melancholy is just the way I am?" Her eyes narrowed. "Maybe my nature isn't to be happy *all* the time. Not everyone is the enthusiastic maniac you are, Robert. I can tell you, I am far from the only one who wonders whether you are going to burn yourself out the way you rush from idea to idea at full speed and no hesitation. You looked ready to try something reckless in math class the other day. Do you have any idea what could have happened? Think about it. Are you even going to finish half of what you've started?"

Ouch.

Many things had indeed been left undone, some simply the casualties of prioritization, while others by their nature might never really be completable. But injuring or killing himself through some premature and impulsive action would definitely affect his ability to achieve his goals. He could not save Koria from the cloaked figure if he was dead.

Endicott was ready to admit that Bethyn was right about everything when she pointed a finger at him and continued. "Not everyone has to be saved."

He had heard shades of that comment before and knew there was some truth to it. "I am *not* sorry for caring, Bethyn. But you have a point."

"There isn't anything wrong with me." Bethyn's face had become red.

It is so easy to alienate a friend.

"You are who you are, Bethyn." Endicott, trying to sound conciliatory. "We *are* friends, you know. I didn't mean to patronize or pry, but I do worry about you and whether or not you are happy."

"Oh, Robert." A tear ran down her face. "You worry about how happy *I* am? What about you and your own metaphorical book? How is that heraldic dream you keep laboring under any different?"

Chapter Twenty-Three

The Smallest Thing

THE NIGHT BEFORE THE TWENTY-FOUR-HOUR TEST, ENDICOTT ASKED KORIA TO A private dinner at the Apprentices' Library. He had slept with her every night since his heraldic dream, but they had not had sex. It was maddening lying there beside each other and not crossing that last distance, but Endicott held back, still wanting to be sure of her complete trust. He loved her in every way, and wanted to *love* her in every way, but he could not overcome his misgivings about trust. When they did finally express love physically, he wanted to hold nothing back, no doubts, no conflicted feelings. No secrets.

In the final week before the test, Endicott tried to show he was worthy of her trust. He had worked conscientiously to keep both Heylor and Bethyn engaged. He had controlled his impulse to resort to any act of heraldry or dynamics. He had even refrained from surveilling or stalking any of the protestors who still circled the campus. Endicott hoped that for once a week had passed in which he had not worried the woman he loved. He hoped they could now finally resolve the trust issue over dinner. There was just one thing that still needed to come out into the open.

Dinner away from the Orchid, away from their friends and all their burdens, was just what was required. In some sense they needed to break the pattern of their relationship. Still, looking at Koria, Endicott wanted nothing to change. She wore a blue silk skirt, and he was in his Knight of Vercors formal cloak. As their expensive dessert of strawberries and cream arrived, Endicott reached across and took Koria's hand.

"How were you able to put up with me when I went mad, Koria?" he asked with stupefied sincerity. It was beyond him.

Koria smiled. "Why wouldn't I, Robert? I love you; you know that."

Endicott released her tiny hand and took a small spoonful of the straw-berries. "You were such a good leader too. You always are. Look at how far Heylor and Bethyn have come. And you read situations so well. Bethyn was amazed at how quickly you diagnosed the problem I was having when I woke up from that dream. It's almost as if you have personal experience with heraldic dreams."

Koria looked down, saying nothing. Endicott scooted along the booth to sit right next to her. He put his arm around her shoulders. "I'm sorry if that sounded like an accusation. Let's walk off some of these worries."

After paying for dinner, they walked slowly back towards the Orchid. When they neared the statue of Heydron, Endicott steered them over to the monument. "Do you remember when you asked me if I thought I was Heydron?" he said gently.

Koria looked at him.

"Well, I think *you* are the only Heydron around here." Endicott took both of her hands and faced her so he could see her eyes in the lantern light. "You have been looking after me ever since I arrived."

"I meant it to caution you about your recklessness, Robert." Koria looked down as she spoke.

"I know. But you are *my* Heydron." He pointed to the shield of Heydron. "I heard you used to climb on the monuments here. Did you climb the shield?"

Koria laughed. "Maybe. That was so long ago."

Endicott took her hands again, a little more tightly this time. "Before you had your first heraldic dream?"

Koria started pulling away, but Endicott held her fast. "That's what hurt you, isn't it, love? You had a heraldic dream. You were sick for a long time after it. I heard that. I heard that the Duchess took you into her care until you were better. You herald all the time. I hope you don't continue to have the dreams, but I know you are heralding. It must be how you always know when to follow me. It's why you're always frightened for me. You have also seen something you never wanted to see. Something terrible."

At that Koria burst into tears. Endicott waited, holding her hands more gently now. She freed herself to wipe her eyes, then looked carefully into his. After an uncomfortably long time she nodded as if she had made a decision. "I have an affinity for heraldry, Robert. After the boys in my class died, I was upset, but I was managing. We weren't close like this class is. We didn't live together and barely knew each other. I took on the task of helping Gerveault and Eleanor design a different, more patient approach for the program. Eleanor let me stay with her."

Eleanor is the Duchess! A bell went off in Endicott's mind. He almost laughed at himself. Between Eleanor's true identity and Bethyn's sexuality, he had missed quite a lot.

"I had the list of people most likely to be invited when the next year rolled around. I saw your name. It had asterisks beside it. You were coming though I'm sure you didn't know that yet. Then I had a heraldic dream. It wasn't about my dead classmates. It was about a man I had never met. It was about you. I saw *you* there with me. In the dream, I loved you. We were lovers. And then you died. You burned. It happened over and over in dozens of ways. You died. You died by spear from a giant, hooded man. In a fire, you died saving me. You got expelled from dynamics and you died. You *always* died."

"Dear Knights," Endicott said softly, reliving the power of his own heraldic dream, trying to imagine the punishing effect hers must have had.

How did she endure it?

Endicott could hardly endure the thought of it. Sympathetic pain nearly buckled his knees. Imagining Koria suffering under the kind of pain he *still* suffered under made him want to cry out. "I'm so sorry, Koria. That must have been . . . unspeakable." Then lamely he tried to inject some humour into the conversation. "No wonder you couldn't resist my charms."

"It was so unfair!" she hurled at him.

"I am so sorry it happened to you," he said, meaning it deeply. For some reason he remembered Conor and how that poor man's strange resemblance to his own barely remembered father had affected him so profoundly.

Dreams, memories dim or vivid, even secondhand associations, have such power over our feelings.

"The dreams stopped then. For a while. We finalized our plans for the new school year. Eleanor decided to house us all in the Orchid where we could be protected.

She brought in more security for campus. We hoped that maybe we had changed the circumstances enough to avoid what I had dreamed. It seemed like maybe that was so. I didn't have a heraldic dream of you again until the night before we met at the fountain. I dreamed of you there, and then of you burning. It hurt, and it scared me. Nothing had changed. You still died. When I met you, I felt as if I had been stabbed in the heart. The sight of you caused agonizing pain. You were just sitting there with your feet in the fountain. No one does that, Robert, except you. That is *drinking water*, for Knight's sake. But my love from the dream was *so* real."

She wrenched a hand free and punched him. "I would have loved you anyway. That first night with Heylor and Jon Indulf, I didn't want you making trouble, but I loved you for trying to help Heylor. You had only just met him. He stole your button, yet there you were, pulling him out of trouble."

"How have you endured it, though? I managed all of a half second of sanity after my heraldic dream." Endicott searched her eyes. *How has she endured the extensive list of my misadventures and mistakes, knowing what is to come?*

"I was staying with Eleanor the first time because we were working out the plan for this years' class. She helped me. She knew what it was and what to do. Then at the Orchid, Eloise was there for me."

"Eloise!" *No wonder she has always been so angry with me about Koria!* "Is that why she is so strange with me?"

Koria laughed, leaning into him. "You are the source of so much consternation for her, more than I can really even say. She thinks you owe me. But you don't owe me anything, Robert."

"I am not sure about that, Koria. What I don't deserve is you." He held her close, thinking about the trauma she must have endured for him.

"It is interesting, don't you think, that we only ever had heraldic dreams about people we love or about things that are emotionally important to us." Her words were muffled by his chest.

Endicott thought about that. *Does it make sense in my grandpa's case?* "Grandpa never seemed to get agitated over his dreams," he mused. "And he had them regularly." He shook his head. "The subjects of his dreams were always vitally important to him."

"What kind of man is he?" Koria asked.

"Quiet and calm. Not much like me, I'm afraid."

"Older," Koria speculated. She looked up abruptly. "Gerveault said something strange. He said he never dreamed about anything he cared about."

"Hmm. Maybe he lied."

"Perhaps. Perhaps such dreams are meant for the old."

Endicott was not sure about that. They were quiet for moment, and the young man took the opportunity to review what Koria had said. One thing in particular snapped into clarity.

Nothing they did changed her dreams. His hands around her waist involuntarily clenched at the unwelcome thought.

Nothing. Changed.

"Koria? If nothing *you* did changed what *you* dreamed, we are in trouble. It may mean nothing we are doing *now* is going to change what *I* dreamed."

Oh Knights, oh Knights.

Koria's green eyes were liquid. "Maybe *we can't* change the outcome, Robert. We might not even be together after the test. They are thinking of failing you, you know."

"Failing me?" Endicott could not believe that. "I know the math as well as anyone. I'm going to pass the test!"

"Perhaps fail is the wrong word," Koria confessed, looking down now, "but no matter how good your math is they might hold you back for your own good and that amounts to the same thing. They are *worried* about you, Robert. I think they're scared that if you learn dynamics before you fully recover from your heraldic dream, you could bring on the disaster we both dreamed about."

"That is ridiculous," Endicott declared. "I don't—I can't—cause the cloaked figure to kill you."

"I'm sure that's true, but they are still worried about you. They lost everyone in last year's class except me, Robert. They are frightened of losing you as well. You need to be calm. You need to be careful."

"Story of my skolving life." Endicott pinched the bridge of his nose and started laughing. "What else is new? I must be more careful. Nimrheal isn't going to appear because of that revelation!"

"All change is equally deadly, Robert. Did you know they still say that at the Steel Castle?" Koria smiled at Endicott. "Nimrheal comes to exact his price regardless. It's as dangerous to change the smallest thing—even yourself—as it is to change the entire world."

Dangerous? How about damned difficult? Maybe it is just as hard to change yourself as the world. Perhaps people would rather the world was changed than change themselves. The thought sent Endicott's mind chasing down a whole new path.

But how do I change myself?

$$\triangledown$$

ENDICOTT PROMISED TO TRY TO CHANGE, TO TRY TO WIN THE PROFESSORS' CONFIDENCE in more than his math skills. He was still curious about one other thing. "Let's talk a little more about you, Koria."

"Must we?" She burrowed into him under the shadow of Heydron.

"You had all those dreams, and then after you met me, you and Eloise followed me on several occasions. Did you have heraldic dreams then?"

"No," she said, letting out a breath. "Thank the Knights, no. I saw you were up to something and I heralded, focusing on you. The night with Syriol, that terrible night, my heraldry showed a high probability of everything going wrong. There was a strong likelihood you would die after immolating the carriage along with those awful twins. I saw that before you ever left the Orchid."

She is like some knight in a story, always saving me. What do I say to that?

"That must have been unpleasant," he said, feeling foolish for the understatement. "Thank you for stalking me, Koria."

"I do it out of love," she said, laughing softly.

Eight Knights, I have stayed apart from her for nothing more than prideful misunderstanding.

Remorse and elation made war within Endicott.

Pride makes us lonely.

He stepped back and kissed her left hand. "So when you said you only trusted my intentions, it was because of all the times you had seen me die. You feared for me. It wasn't because you didn't trust *me*."

Koria laughed again. "Yes, that, though you should admit that you do tend to run wild with some crazy ideas, Robert."

Yes.

He kissed her long and deep. "May I *truly* be with you tonight?"

"Yes."

"The Book of Nature
Does not its nature
Change."

— Steel Castle didactic

Chapter Twenty-four

The Twenty-four-Hour Test

"TELL ME HOW YOU WOULD APPROACH A PROBLEM INVOLVING FAILURE, MR. ENDICOTT."
Annabelle Currick's cheerful voice snapped Endicott back from delightful
memories of his night with Koria. Even now, during the twenty-four-hour test,
he found himself returning to thoughts of her. Professor Currik was still smiling
at him, so he must not have drifted off for too long. They had been together in a
small, high-ceilinged, stone-walled room in the military school for over two hours.

It was strange to be separated from his classmates during the test. No explanation for the format of the test had been given. They had simply been led to
separate rooms, each with a different professor-examiner waiting. In the first
session Endicott had been interrogated by Eleanor, who asked him an extensive
list of questions relating to the uses and limitations of certain models. After only
a quick break he had been hustled into a different room where Annabelle Currik
waited. He had only just managed to touch Koria's hand as she swapped rooms
with him.

How is Heylor doing?

Endicott had tried to calm the young man's nerves during breakfast in the
Lords' Commons, but Heylor was a difficult person to console.

"It's too late to worry now," Deleske had said sardonically, his usual affectation
of detachment fully intact.

The comment would have irritated Endicott less if it were no so obviously
true. It was unquestionably, irreducibly too late to worry. Only action, only the
performance mattered now. He could only hope the skinny boy was ready, but at
least, he assured himself, he did not regret the way in which they had prepared.
Putting Heylor through the grind had taught all of them. The active, aggressive,
and unorthodox methods they had invented to help Heylor had also helped each of
them in unexpected ways. By taking up the roles of actors and teachers, they had

mastered the material to a level that surprised each of them. Bethyn, aside from the Book of Nature debacle, had left behind her uncaring façade and appeared to take immense joy in punishing Heylor for every missed question.

"Let's hear your question, then, dear Professor," Endicott said with real enthusiasm. As sincere as his promise to Koria had been, he felt more himself than ever, and he felt happy with that.

Annabelle Currik tapped his desk, raising an eyebrow at his familiarity. Endicott smiled through this and eventually so did she. "A heavy iron-bound door is broken by a sharp blow. It fails at four places simultaneously: the three hinges and the barred door. How would you calculate the force required to break the door?"

Why does she always do this? Endicott remembered the question she had posted at the monument on the day he arrived at the New School. He did not have an immediate answer to her question. He had studiously avoided thinking about that door since the night he had somehow destroyed it.

"If those are indeed the points where the door broke, Professor, we need to consider the amount of force that each failed piece of equipment was designed to withstand. This means we need to consider the yield strength and possibly the tensile strength of the materials themselves. These can be inferred from tables but might also require laboratory tests. Hinges rarely fail, and doors rarely fail at the hinges, so this is an unusual case. We should avoid making assumptions and examine *how* they failed. How the bar failed also requires a physical examination..."

As he continued, Endicott found that he enjoyed discussing the strategy of solving a problem just as much as he liked to work out the tally of equations and numbers associated with a specific example. His time with Annabelle Currik flew by.

Keith Euyn was another matter. The great man was apparently feeling well enough to take part in the punishing test. Apart from the promised derivation on the Lessingham transformation, the older man's questions were not exactly complex. However he required that Endicott solve them in his head and out loud. He was unconcerned with how long this might take or how hungry his pupil might be getting.

Mentioning that he was hungry and needed to use the privy proved to be a mistake.

"The Book of Nature does not care that you are hungry, Mr. Endicott," Keith Euyn announced. "No one cares how you feel or whether you need to urinate. Mathematics, physics, and dynamics are not subject to your whims and make no allowance for your human weaknesses. The answers do not change, and the complexity is not altered. The reality is immutable to your moods or emotional reactions. How you feel is irrelevant to the nature of the world. You must toughen up."

There was a knock on the door. Keith Euyn opened it, allowing Bat Merrett to enter. Merrett scowled at Endicott as usual and then turned to the great man.

"Are you certain about this, Professor?" he asked in his deep voice.

"Let us proceed with my next question as discussed, Mr. Merrett."

"What is the Lessingham transform of a random and ergodic, infinitely long series of spikes, Mr. Endicott?" Keith Euyn asked the question in a monotone.

Endicott was about to answer when Merrett suddenly shouted. "Your mother makes stupid blouses!"

He looked at the soldier quizzically. "Do you mean my aunt? And her bl—"

Keith Euyn's monotone overrode him. "Answer the question, Mr. Endicott."

Endicott was about to return to the task when Merrett shouted at him again. "You're an attention whore, and you aren't well liked!"

Endicott started laughing. "Is this a joke?"

"It's the test, Mr. Endicott. Answer the question."

Endicott answered the question even while Merrett continued shouting random, mostly inaccurate, insults at him.

"I find you awkward and silly."

"You have emotional diarrhea!"

"You keep getting beaten up by a girl in the fence!"

Endicott had little trouble ignoring the comments, which were mostly ridiculous, but at a look from the great man, Merrett's comments turned darker—and more accurate.

"You can't save everyone, Robert!"

Endicott turned to the two of them and spoke coolly. "I find this to be silly and pathetic. What do you think you're proving?"

"Answer the question, Mr. Endicott," was all that Keith Euyn would say. "Mr. Merrett, if you would."

Merrett looked embarrassed, but he did as the professor required.

"Your father died because he was careless."

What do you know of my father?

Endicott's heart pounded a protest but the question, not the comment, needed an answer. He struggled to suppress his feelings and focus on Keith Euyn's question.

"There will be another girl just like Syriol, and you won't be there to save her."

There will not, there will not, there will not.

Endicott's hands shook, but he answered the question.

If they think they can make me fail over something like this, they are mistaken. Koria's warning did not hurt either. Still, his confidence did not prevent him from feeling angry.

What he says is irrelevant. The question, the question, not *the insult.*

He kept answering the questions.

"Not ready to give up, Mr. Endicott?" Keith Euyn glared at him. "Good." The great man said nothing more; he simply left the room.

At least Merrett had a red face to show for his efforts. "Blouse," he said, looking away as he went out through the door.

Lunch break at the Commons was cruelly brief. Endicott's stomach was knotted with stress from the test, from his need to pass it, and from the more accurate of the comments that Merrett had made. He had to take several deep, slow breaths before he was able to put any food into his mouth. Koria put her arm around his shoulders. "There is a reason, Robert."

"Really?" he said, calming a little. "Isn't there a verse that sounds something like that? Something about reason? Oh yes—

"Rage against the demon,

Enemy of reason."

Koria nodded, eyebrows raised. "Yes, but you neglected the first stanza."

He smiled at her. "Doesn't matter, I know the reason I'm here."

"How would I know the probability of a small clasp failing?" complained Heylor orthogonally.

Endicott only grunted. He guessed that everyone had probably had to endure questions tailored specifically for them and their individual weaknesses. He kissed Koria and diverted his thoughts from himself to Eloise. "Did you get a question from Annabelle about the strength of a bottle?"

"I haven't seen her yet, stupe," answered Eloise with a smirk. She still wore the deeply satisfied expression she had displayed first thing in the morning when she had congratulated Endicott as he exited Koria's room. Bethyn looked pleased as well, though in a similarly patronizing way, as if Endicott had finally passed a test of an altogether different nature.

"Anyway," Eloise added, "I already know the answer. The bottle is strong enough."

ENDICOTT'S NEXT EXAMINER WAS MEREDETH CALLUM. SHE LED HIM THROUGH AN IMBRO-glio of inverse estimates and thermal equations, of problems of probability and stories involving statistics. After two hours of such conundrums, even she began to look exhausted. With an almost desperate look, she left him with a page of problems to work on and went off somewhere for a prolonged period. When she came back, she had recovered her energy and seemed pleased that he had finished the page of problems already. Endicott, on the other hand, was now growing tired and irritable.

"Come, come, Mr. Endicott, we are barely twelve hours into the test. Have a drink of water and let us look at this problem utilizing the thermal equation and the Lessingham transformation." Her open smile seemed, for the first time to Endicott, cruel.

"How about dinner, Professor?"

She laughed richly. "Dinner is for those who finish the test. Your classmates are quite a bit further along than you."

I doubt that.

Meredeth continued smiling, clearly unconcerned by Endicott's openly skeptical expression. "Let us pick up the pace, shall we?" He nodded wearily, and she nodded back, satisfied. "Let us decide that the next one hundred questions will be addressed without paper—and timed."

By the time the hundred questions were done with, Endicott's voice was hoarse. The door opened, and Gerveault took Meredeth Callum's place. Gerveault also wanted his questions answered orally and quickly. Endicott started making mistakes.

"Ready to give up, Mr. Endicott?" Gerveault asked tonelessly.

"Were you ever a knight, Professor?" Endicott returned, thinking about the Lonely Wizard.

The old man laughed in what Endicott thought was a crochety fashion and launched into the next ten questions.

"That was incorrect, Mr. Endicott. You dropped the two on the left side of the equation." Gerveault's tones were pedantic and bored. "Now you have made the element too hot. Are you ready to give up *now?*"

What does a factor of two matter, you old coot? I still understood the concept.

Endicott's patience had almost reached its breaking point, but he hung on, surly and stale on the inside but cool on the outside. "Nope. How about you, Professor Gerveault?"

Apparently Gerveault was also not ready to give up, as he gave Endicott twenty more questions, supposedly for his impertinence. Endicott rushed two of the questions and made trivial errors. He went slow on the next three and made errors anyway.

"You lost a slice there. It is over, Mr. Endicott," Gerveault pronounced after Endicott misplaced pi on one side of an equation. Then he stiffly led the exhausted Endicott out of the hateful room.

Nothing about the test truly surprised Endicott until he switched rooms with Gregory and found himself face to face with a very old, very large knight he had never seen before. An unusually long, massive sword leaned against the wall near the man. Its scabbard was of faded and worn leather. The man's face was more beat up and creased than the scabbard. It was crisscrossed with scars, but framed by neatly trimmed white-gray hair, except where the scars ran into his scalp. He was dressed tip to toe in worn, dented plate armor, completely unlike the new, shiny suit of Sir Christensen, more like the dull sheen of old rocks. He looked tougher than an old rock himself. This imposing figure introduced himself as Sir Hemdale, the legendary Deladieyr Knight. The defector from Armadale. And the owner of another rare Finlay Endicott sword, this one even bigger than Gregory's.

Eloise's uncle.

Why is he wearing his plate armor to a mathematics test?

Endicott wondered if a true believer like Sir Hemdale never took his armor off. The rough-faced old man had the bulge-eyed, brow-furled, insane look of the true fanatic. He crackled with a ferocious certainty. Perhaps nothing could move such a person to take his dilapidated, smelly armor off.

Why is there a potted plant on the table?

"Why aren't you wearing a wizard sword?" The big man's voice came like a harshly accented punch in the face. If Eloise had an accent, it was a faded thing compared to Hemdale's. Accents can be funny. They can be disarming. Some can be irritating. Some make others think the speaker is stupid, others that the speaker is intelligent. Hemdale's accent did none of these things. Instead it seemed to make his words more demanding than they should have been, less reasonable. He sounded a lot like the two bald protestors.

Uh.

After a moment's hesitation Endicott guessed he meant a sword like Gregory's or Eloise's. He spread his hands; he had only brought a feather pen and ink. "*This* is my sword, sir."

"You gave one to my niece."

Uh oh. Here come the cousin-brothers-uncles.

Sir Hemdale was still talking, and Endicott realized he might have missed a sentence or two. "… sword is better than a ring. You marry her."

No no no no. No.

Endicott was not sure if it was a question or an order. "I love her, sir. Like a *sister*." Maybe that answer was not completely true, since no blood relation had ever made Endicott's blood boil like Eloise had, but it was mostly true.

I always try *to think of her as a sister.*

The big knight stared at him intensely.

Endicott resisted the urge to say more.

"Do you love everyone?" Hemdale's question sounded more like an accusation. It reminded Endicott of Eloise's constant admonitions about the profligate nature of his feelings.

"No."

A strange expression passed swiftly over the ancient Knight's craggy face. *Disappointment?*

"We shall see. I will treat you like my nephew."

Given the number and nature of the uncles he already had, Endicott was unsure if this was a stroke of good or bad fortune, but he nodded politely.

Hemdale grunted, possibly satisfied. "How often are you strong?"

"Excuse me?"

Hemdale made two fists and held them up and away from himself. "You tore the door. I *saw* it. How often are you strong like that?"

This again? The big man was staring at him intently, and Endicott thought back, trying to remember. "Maybe five or six times in my life, but never like that, Sir Hemdale."

"Not often." He frowned. "Ever in the sand?"

"Never within the fences of the practice ring."

"Look at that plant."

What?

"Look at it until I tell you to stop looking."

There was only one plant in the room. Endicott suppressed his astonishment at the request and sat down facing the small plant. It was a beautifully trimmed, diminutive, tree-like specimen similar to the miniature of a tree from South Harkness he had seen pictured in books: an acacia. He gently touched its elongate, almost needle-like leaves. *Can't be an acacia.* Then he sat back and simply observed the thing. As time went on, he realized that the exercise had some hidden meaning and that the period of observation would be enduring. Perhaps it would not end until he figured out what that meaning was.

He slowed his breathing and gazed upon the tree, letting his mind drift where it would. Finally Hemdale ordered him to stop. "Time grows short. Tell me what you thought."

Endicott told him, recalling what he had seen, felt, and thought, filtering nothing.

"I saw the tree first. It was green, orderly, alive. I felt that it was good. Looking at it gave me a feeling of . . . unpresuming happiness. I was content with it. Then, strangely, a memory surfaced of a slough—an old pond in a pasture—with a tree beside it that had a similar shape. That image confused me, so I returned to the plant. I wondered what other shapes it could take on, where it came from, and who had trimmed it so carefully. I wondered if that was you, Sir Hemdale. I wondered what you felt for the little tree and whether you loved it. I wondered about your relationship with Eloise and hoped she would be happy."

"I knew I should not be thinking so much about Eloise. Then a breeze seemed to stir, and I returned to the tree. Again I felt content with it. More time passed, and then something odd happened. I achieved the lesser breakdown unconsciously, without willing it, and I saw the history of the tree. I saw that you had trimmed it this morning, but I saw this as a single line of fact rather than a morphing cone of probability. I came back to the present and flowed forward into the future, but instead of the future of the tree, I saw you. You stood with a long stone wall behind you. In place of the tree I saw rows of planted wheat and a line of what I assume to be skolves running towards you through the rows. There was a smell of . . . rotting meat. And then I heard your voice saying that our time was about to end."

Sir Hemdale's brows were furled like twin caterpillars scrunched up and ready to crawl. Endicott wished they would crawl away. "What is this pond you mentioned?"

It was not the question he expected; most people would have asked about themselves, they would have wanted to delve the apparent danger the vision portended for them. Hemdale appeared to be immune to such concerns, so the young man could only shrug. "I don't know about the pond. It comes to mind from time to time. A memory of childhood perhaps."

"That is unsatisfactory." Hemdale leaned forward, his big, scarred, scary head extending a few extra inches towards Endicott, who tried not to lean back. "You are close, Sir Endicott, *close*." His eyes seemed to bulge out of their sockets. "But you are too complex in your mind." He pulled back and sat straighter.

Sir Endicott.

Recovering from his surprise over the generous honorific from a *real* knight, Endicott asked a question. "Too complex for what?"

"Come with me, nephew." Sir Hemdale shot to his feet, strapped on his incredibly large sword, clanked quickly to the door and passed through it. Endicott followed him with as much alacrity as he could muster this deep into the test. They marched rapidly down the hallway and through an antechamber where

Eleanor, Gerveault, and every one of his classmates sat or stood. Gregory leaned in exhaustion against an archway, Eloise was scowling at the ceiling, Koria was smiling wearily, Heylor had his face in his hands, and Bethyn's eyes were closed, her head lolling. Davyn and Deleske were in there somewhere. He saw them at the edge of his vision but never had a chance to register what they were doing.

"Finished at last, Sir Hemdale?" Eleanor asked, half rising from her seat chair.

"No," Hemdale replied curtly, not even slowing. "There is something I need to know."

"Where is he taking Robert?" Heylor said.

Endicott never heard the answer, if any came. He almost had to run to keep up with the knight in his dented armor. He wanted to ask Koria how her test went, even though he was certain about her mastery of the materials. They had already rounded a turn and it was too late even to yell a question back in the direction they had come from. Not that Endicott had any idea where they were now and what the consequences of this headlong rush might be.

What new test is this?

The big iron doors they finally passed through led to a colossal indoor training yard. Endicott had never seen it before. It dwarfed the hall that he and his classmates had been training in. This yard held eight distinct sandpits, each bordered by fences and separated by equipment racks and warmup areas. Except for the two of them, it was empty.

"What are your intentions, Sir Hemdale?" Gerveault's voice echoed from behind them. Endicott turned and saw Eleanor, Koria, and Eloise beside the old professor. Then the big iron doors were opened again as the other students jammed their way in.

Hemdale made no answer. He unbuckled his sword belt, leaned it carefully against the closest fence, and selected a longsword from a rack on the nearest wall. It looked puny—like a toy—in comparison to the one Finlay Endicott had crafted. "Pick one, Sir Robert."

Endicott approached the rack. All the swords were made of sharp steel rather than the dense wood he normally practiced with. They did *not* look like toys once the Endicott-sword was out of mind and the sharp end was considered. "I don't want to accidentally hurt you, Sir."

"Well, isn't that the point?" Hemdale looked at Gerveault. "You said you didn't want another Lonely Wizard, professor." He swung his longsword experimentally. "Let us find out."

"I said I didn't want any more dead students!" Veins stood out on the side of Gerveault's head. His face, neck and scalp had turned a dark red.

Sir Hemdale pointed his sword at the other students. "They need to leave. Might *cloud* the results."

Gerveault ushered a protesting Koria and the rest through the door. Endicott managed to catch her eyes fleetingly as she was pushed out of the hall. She mouthed a warning.

Be slow. Be calm.

Eleanor crossed her arms. "I am trusting you, Sir Hemdale," she uttered in her rough but fragile voice.

"*That* is *also* the point," Sir Hemdale pronounced. "Come, Sir Robert. Take the center and raise your sword." Seeing Endicott's hesitation, he added, "Do you really think you might *accidentally* hurt me? I assure you, Robert, that I will not *accidentally* hurt you. I only kill those I mean to, when I mean to, and how I mean to. I feel no remorse, for *before* I do a thing I make sure it is the *right* thing. *I* can be trusted to act so. Can you say the same? Or is most of what you do an accident?"

Eleanor sighed, releasing some internal tension. "Listen to Sir Hemdale, Robert. You need to understand this."

Gerveault walked up to stand beside her, adding, "We only do what we mean to do, done in the way we mean it to be done. Through calculation and rational decision-making." He was still so red that Endicott could see it through his hair.

For people that don't want another Lonely Wizard, they sure enjoy talking like him.

And now am I about to have this lesson beaten into me, or am I about to be murdered on purpose, according to some plan, in some precisely calculated way, and without remorse? Endicott tried to still his shaking hands and raise his sword.

Calm. Be calm. Remember Koria.

Hemdale came on like an avalanche.

Clang clang clang-clang-clang.

"I saw the empyreal sky jump when you watched the plant, Sir Robert."

Clang.

Endicott caught the last blow—barely, instinctively—and held Hemdale's sword still for a moment. "So?"

"You had power then," declared the big man in his harsh accent. "The temperature in the room dropped. Something moved you."

Endicott pushed back against the knight's immovable sword and found *himself* moving backwards. "I don't know what I was thinking when you saw . . . what you saw."

"It was when you remembered the slough."

Endicott attempted a counterattack of his own, but the big man anticipated him easily. "I honestly don't know, Sir Hemdale." He circled the knight, trying to keep from getting pinned against the fence. "I don't know what the story is with the damned pond."

"Memory!" shouted Hemdale. "It defies logic. You cannot remember what you want to, cannot forget what you need to." He raised his sword high. "Perhaps you don't know what you should remember and what you should forget."

Clang-clang-clang-clang-clang. Clang.

Endicott's sword went flying, then *he* went flying, cuffed by the gauntlet of the knight, and tumbled across the sand. He did not know if the gasps he heard were his or Eleanor's. He had a brief glimpse of her horrified face as she watched from beside Gerveault. She looked appalled.

He ran stumbling to his sword, picking it up just in time to parry Sir Hemdale's next blow. The old knight was not discouraged by this. He came on again, and he did not look like he was stoppable this time.

I can't fail! If I fail I won't be able to save Koria.

It was as much a feeling as a thought. But it did not seem to help him in any way against his aged opponent. Hemdale nearly had him backed up to the fence with nowhere to go. The knight lunged, thrusting a blow that Endicott knew he could not avoid.

He cracked the sky instinctively and imagined Hemdale stumbling.

"Gah!" Hemdale did stumble, somehow, in the sand. His blow went wide, and Endicott shot by him, placing his back to the center of the open ring.

That worked!

Endicott's sword crackled weirdly, frosting over. A wave of cold shot through the young man, chilling the sweat on his brow, on his whole body. His clothes went stiff they were so cold.

Oh, dammit, no, I wasn't supposed to do that!

"Dear Knights," gasped Eleanor, seeing the frost on Endicott's sword.

Gerveault was more angry than surprised. "I told you not to attempt any dynamics until we taught you, Robert!"

Hemdale picked himself up, brushing the sand off his greaves. "Couldn't help yourself, could you?"

"I-I thought I could change." Endicott trembled. He was cold, but he had been working hard, was still working hard, and his core kept him from freezing. He tasted blood in his mouth, felt it rolling down from his hairline, making a red slush of the rapidly melting frost on his face. "I know I need to. I need to slow down."

"Hmmf," Gerveault grunted.

Sir Hemdale laughed. "Change? You don't need to change; you need to allow yourself to become the *real* you. You need to become authentic. Who told you that you should change?"

"I certainly did," Gerveault answered, glowering.

Endicott waved him down. "Everyone says so. *I* say so. I need to . . . be better."

"Skolve shite," declared Hemdale. "You *can't* change, nephew. No one changes. Not much. If anything, what you need is to *speed up*." He lunged forward, sword swinging towards the younger man.

Clang, clang, clang-clang.

Endicott danced backwards under the new onslaught, trying to roll his wrists and use footwork, shoulder rotation, angles, anything to reduce the awful impact of each blow as it came.

Why does it seem like there are two contradictory lessons here? Koria, Gerveault, Eleanor, and all the other professors seemed to want to deliver a message of caution and care. They wanted him to go slowly. But Sir Hemdale was telling him something very different. There was no way to survive the big knight's assault, *except* quickly, *except* thoughtlessly, *except* through instinct. One group wanted him to change, while the other wanted him to stay the same. *How does this make sense?* No answers came, only more sword blows.

▽

ENDICOTT PICKED HIMSELF UP FROM THE SAND WHERE HE HAD LANDED YET AGAIN, FOUND his sword, and came to guard one more time. He was bruised and beaten but not yet finished.

I can't give up. I must stay here, stay the course. I must pass this test.

"Lady Koria dies in your heraldic dream, doesn't she? And my niece?" Hemdale paused to see Endicott's nod. "And you want to save them? You want to save everyone from what I hear."

"I *will* save them."

"Sir Robert, from what I can see, you aren't going to be able to save *anyone*, let alone *everyone*."

"I have to."

"Why?"

"I just do."

"What do you see, boy?" Hemdale turned his sword to reflect the lantern light in Endicott's eyes. "What happened at that pond? I saw the sky jump again when you mentioned it. You shone. What happens *after* the pond?"

"I don't know."

"If you want to change, you *need* to know."

To change, I need to know.

What? Endicott stopped, trying to remember.

But he could *not* remember. He *saw* the pond but could not place it in any context. It just was.

"I can't remember!" Endicott cried.

Sir Hemdale frowned again and thrust his sword at the younger man. Endicott barely caught enough of it to keep from having his floating rib sliced off. Hemdale roared and brought his sword around for an overhand strike. "If you can't remember, you will fail, and the girls will die."

His sword came down so fast and hard that it whistled.

The slough was quiet in the late afternoon, only a few insects and birds making sounds and rustlings that were not really noise. Those sounds were part of what it was to be at the slough. The three-year-old boy stood motionless, quiet, one hand raised up to rest on the back of his dog. The boy was part of the slough too, at peace, quiet in his mind. It was an unusual state for him, one that he only seemed able to find beside the still waters. It was a state of being that he needed. Instinct had brought him here, where he could see the purple crocus in bloom, the late pink rays of the spring sun on quiet water, and the small splashes of returning ducks. He had been here before, and it seemed necessary to be here now.

"Robert!" The voice came from very far away. Very far and a long way for short three-year-old legs. "Come on, boy. You need to hurry!"

They had covered her face by the time he got back.

His mom had finally passed away, and he had not been there.

Clang.

Endicott caught Hemdale's ferocious stroke on his sword and stopped it dead.

Clang-clang-clang.

He returned three rapid strokes, one on Hemdale's dented breastplate. He pulled his sword back to strike again, but the broken tip of it flew off across the sand on his backswing.

Whup whup whup.

"I wasn't there!" Endicott roared, brandishing the remaining half of his sword at the big knight. He lunged forward again, pointing the broken end at the old man. Hemdale did not move or flinch. A slow smile spread across the rough man's face, rolling across the scars and through the gray whiskers. "I was in the field and I missed it!"

"Robert!" It was Eleanor, running to put herself between the weirdly grinning knight and the distraught young man. "Stop!"

Endicott threw the sword aside, "I wasn't there, I wasn't there, I wasn't there! She died, and I was out looking at a slough. I can't even remember what she looks like!"

Eleanor wrapped him in a hug as he sank to his knees. Hot tears flowed down his face. "I couldn't sit still. I had to go out. *I wasn't there.*"

"It's okay, Robert," Eleanor soothed. "You were just a boy."

"But I—"

"No." Eleanor pulled him in tighter. "There was nothing you could do. Nothing." Eleanor held him tight again before turning her head and hissing at Sir Hemdale, "And just what was the point of this? You are out *way* past the line on this one, Hemdale."

Hemdale racked the sword he had borrowed with the other weapons. "He was out at that same pond again when I came by a few weeks later to talk to his pa and grandpa. I never got to know him then. I have now." With a great creaking sound, he knelt beside the massive scabbarded sword he had left leaning against the fence. The beatific smile that came over his scarred face was ghastly. "It was the least I could do."

"Did I fail?" Endicott asked Eleanor, somehow missing the reverential tone in Hemdale's voice, forgetting the old knight entirely for the moment. "I failed."

What am I going to do now?

"No, my boy," Eleanor said. "You were never going to fail."

"But Koria said—"

"Never." One of Eleanor's skeletal fingers dabbed a cloth to his face. "Koria misunderstood our intent. We just didn't want to *force* you to keep going this year. It would have been inhumane."

Oh.

"Come on, Robert, your classmates will be anxious to know what happened to you. One of them in particular."

Endicott managed to struggle to his feet only by leaning on Eleanor. He saw that Gerveault was still standing near the rail, eyes unreadable, silent. The dynamicist seemed to have nothing to say for once. Perhaps there was no mathematics to describe what had happened inside the fence, nothing objective to be said, and so, for him, nothing to say at all.

Still leaning on Eleanor, the young man turned to Sir Hemdale, who was back on his feet, sheathed sword in hand. "So is that it, then, Sir Hemdale? What was *truly* the point of this? Because I don't believe you came here just to say hello and make up for missing me fifteen years ago. I've been wrong about quite a lot, but not, I think, about this." He smiled wryly, taking a breath to raise his voice to a more commanding level. "Everyone tells me I *must* change, but you come along and tell me I *can't* change, even that I *shouldn't*. What am I supposed to have learned?"

Hemdale's eyes narrowed. "You don't know?" He shrugged, apparently relaxing. "You can't change if you don't know first who you are."

"Hemdale," Eleanor growled. It was almost a whisper. Endicott almost missed it.

"You're wrong about one other thing, Sir Robert," Sir Hemdale said as he walked away. "It's a good thing you can't remember your mother's face. You don't want to see what you love dead. If you had that in your head, you would never forget it. Never. Better you don't know exactly what she looked like. *All* women can be your mother."

Chapter Twenty-five

The Lonely Wizard

When most people step across the Line and enter the Ardgour Wilderness, they feel fear. I do not.

Most would say that the wilderness, any wilderness, has only two things in it: gods and monsters. It is an old idea from the long dark age before the Methueyn War. The notion has, in its venerability, grown strong roots in the human psyche. Given that the Methueyn War started precisely *because* Nehring Ardgour brought gods and monsters into his domain, and this decision created the wilderness named after him, the fear of gods and monsters might have seemed more rational at this one place on earth.

Seemed indeed. Human beings have an ample collection of ubiquitous weaknesses in their use of logic, one of them being too heavy a reliance on personal experience, recent anecdote, or stories about terrible events. If something stands out, it seems to count for several times its rational worth as a data point. One horrible death is treated like five when safety is considered. Two gods and a few thousand skolves in the Ardgour Wilderness are enough to cause the old county of Novgoreyl to be treated as if the Wilderness can only ever have gods and skolves within it.

I am neither god nor monster, and I *am* stepping across the Line. I do not care if all the feeble minds in existence think this will, by some foul means, make me demon or skolve. I cannot be responsible for Feydleyn's moral terror that crossing the Line will transform me. A place does not determine identity. My authenticity will not be transformed by one simple step. Only a child could think so.

Only I may choose my identity.

I stepped off the wall of the Castlereagh Line, falling through fifteen feet of air until my feet hit the ground again. Nothing happened, only the inevitability of physics.

I was bundled tight to move quickly, water skin strapped tight to one hip, and Expectation sheathed across my back. Feydleyn watched me from the far side of the Line, I knew, but I did not look back. Feeding his emotional fire would do him no good. I strode forward with the abruptness and speed of my fall from the wall and was gone into the night without comment, sound, or warning.

The dark ground rose sharply as I approached the mountains at a fast jog. I was open to the empyreal sky and could see in the dark like an Angel of Elysium would: with any wavelength of light or ray of probability. I did not stumble; I moved quietly with the perfect alacrity of Empyreal millisecond certainty. Nevertheless black night robbed even the wide spectrum of my vision of some of the nuances of these, the last old, wild fields of Ardgour before the mountains. The feral fields were not in the homogeneous order that a living farmer would work to achieve. Here and now, wild oats, barley, and wheat mixed with other plants that many would call weeds. I held one ear in my hand and felt the fragile rachis. These wild grains could spread randomly without the anti-entropic intervention of a farmer. But someone or something had been at the harvest. Many of the stalks had been trampled or torn.

Skolves.

Skolve spoor was abundant. Half-digested seeds peeped out of the scat, in some places germinating within it. I had not realized they could eat these grains, but it was clear that they did. I might be standing in a skolve feeding hall.

I saw them before they sprang out of the bushes. I observed the skolves before their infrared and ultraviolent forms came crashing towards me. I had Expectation at the ready.

The first skolve was fast. It tried to duck under the sweep of Expectation, but the maneuver did not work out for it. Instead of taking the creature's wolf-like head off at the neck, Expectation sheared through its face, splitting nostrils, flinging teeth, jawbone, and brain stem in a spray that blinded the skolve that followed. A normal sword would have broken at the force of the blow or stuck in bone, but Expectation was a probability blade that I had personally made. In our enlightened age, only one or two others might, at their peril, attempt to do as well. Instead of breaking or getting stuck, Expectation sliced through. Then it whistled as I turned its path to shear down through the head of the momentarily blinded second skolve. The sword stopped at his breastbone, and I stepped forward, arm extended nearly straight in a slight C shape, to kick the beast off my blade. Expectation loosed, I spun low on my feet to avoid the teeth chomping at me from the side and cut another lunging beast in half. Its chest and head flew past me, and the teeth clamped uselessly on the branches of a tree, still attempting to follow the lagging orders of a dying brain.

Skolves do not normally hesitate. They attack relentlessly until they or their prey are dead, never giving up an inch of territory they consider theirs. But *these* skolves did hesitate, and I did not waste the quantitative moment. They hesitated just long enough for me to break through and reach for the energies of heaven. I calculated a half space and cut a line of plasma through one hundred and eighty degrees and forty feet of radius that burned through everything at hip height in front of me. Frost shot out behind me and into Elysium. Eight skolves had been burned into two parts, neither alive. I missed the one skolve that had been attempting to circle me. Against nature, it felt sufficient fear to flee.

I remembered then that Nehring Ardgour, through miscalculation or misplaced greed, had pulled not a quantum of energy from Elysium but two demons whole from Hell. It was a feat that could not be reproduced or undone today. When Nehring reached again, whether to return the demons or for another chance at power, the skolves came instead. They followed their gods Skoll and Hati across empyreal space to the here and now. But I had forgotten that they still recognized the authority of their gods. Perhaps to this one surviving skolve, I had become one.

I left the fields moments later, jogging steadily up the incline, looking for the road I had seen on the maps. It did not take long to identify a cold, linear feature cross-cutting the slopes above me. I *guessed* that the feature was cold because of the reduced vegetation but *knew* that the artificial linearity could only be the work of man.

Once on the road I increased my pace, rounding each switchback and passing into the mountains proper. There was little skolve spoor here, and I saw no movement on the road. Feydleyn could never have kept up if he had accompanied me, and he might have died in the encounter with the skolves. It was better to be alone, where my actions could be unconstrained from any concern for his fragility and his doubts. When daylight came, I increased my pace yet again, relaxing my hold on the empyreal sky and running along the road. Once within the mountain fastness, the road alternated between the temporary, open saddle of a col and the shadowy confines of a canyon, or the narrow half-space defined by the side of a cliff. I dodged around boulders and leaped small chasms, running faster on the solitary stone path.

By midday I had surmounted a pass to find a dark, abandoned castle crouched beside the spillway of a turbid river. There was a resonance coming from the decayed fortress, and I was curious what could be found beyond the wrecked gate and tumbling tower. I opened myself to the empyreal sky and saw that my attempt at heraldry was irradiated by a locus. I guessed by the nature of the interference that its cause might be very old, though I had never encountered such a puissant locus before. I knew that if I went into the castle, I would find something momentous. I passed it by. Time was also passing.

An old wooden suspension bridge spanned the river not far from the old keep. The iron cables showed some rust and the wooden boards, once thick, were showing rot. Nevertheless it was surprisingly sound in appearance given that it could have had no maintenance in over two centuries. All the maintainers had fled or died those two centuries before. I reached for heraldry, trying to determine whether the bridge might fail me, but the locus still ruled. The future was unknowable.

It was enough that I knew what *I* would do. I set out to cross the rickety construction. I did not fear plunging into the turbid waters so far below. Fear is only an effective deterrent for those whose paths are negotiable by anxiety. I knew where I was going, and even if no further intelligence was available to me, this was my path.

The road narrowed into a rocky canyon shortly after the bridge. A wind came up and blew dust along the rough chute. I rounded a corner and saw, down the gully, in the distance, an armored form. It was a knight, turned away from me and facing further down the ravine. I slowed, advancing at a gentle jog. Coming closer, I saw it was a curiously wrecked and ruined knight, held up by what I did not know. I slowed to a walk and crossed the last distance between us.

If the devastated castle had been a melancholy sight, the knight was a harrowing one. He had been very large—almost certainly male—and he had been killed by a spear driven through his skull vertically. The haft of the spear was of some black metal, and it had been driven into the rock to hold the Knight up by his skull in an obscene and everlasting parody of life. Was this staging meant as a Methueyn scarecrow? Was it a mockery or warning?

Perhaps neither. Colored beads and rock surrounded the knight in a smoothed circular depression. Some of the rocks had dark, coarse hairs on them. Skolves again. They had likely gathered here on many occasions, given the number of beads and the wear on the rock surrounding the knight. They had either carried out or participated in some ritual around him. I did not know if the knight was a scarecrow or a god to the skolves, but I leaned towards god.

I opened myself to the empyreal sky. I still could not herald. It would have been fascinating to have heralded retrograde and seen what happened here, but even if the medium had not been irradiated by the locus, not even the furthest herald could have seen that far back. In any case this was not my purpose; the medium revealed other things to me. I could see that the spear was made of a cold-forged alloy. Some titanium was scattered in the matrix. I had seen a true spear of Nimrheal on the wall of the duke's castle in Vercors and another in the broken throne room of Old Engevelen City. This bore strong similarities to both. Another shattered weapon, an axe, also made of cold-forged alloy, lay nearby. The scarecrow could be the Methueyn Knight Volsang.

I played this out in my mind. The Methueyn Knight travels here on his way to the castle I had just passed. His mission carries great import or would have led to an important discovery or both, and that near future event was detected by Nimrheal, who came and killed him. It was very rare for Nimrheal to arrive *before* the event, but there was some historical evidence that it could indeed happen. My hypothesis went against the popular notion that death at the hands of Nimrheal was the result of a deal between inventor and demon, that death was the price of creation.

Many people believe this, but I do not. I have no doubt that a causal relationship drives the appearance of Nimrheal, but I am very skeptical that it is moral in nature. The demon is not called by some miracle of morbid justice. Creation is not a thing to be punished. True invention, true creativity is a powerful thing. I have seen it. A true act of creation sends a shock wave of surpassing strength through the empyreal medium. It is unique and transcendent; it can pass from our world to the worlds of Elysium and of Hell. But while I have seen the power of creation, I have never thought that the moral cost lies with the act, it lies with what follows.

But why does Nimrheal come if not to balance some cosmic purpose? A childish question. Morality is the responsibility of man, not some transcendental outsider. To look for an external adjudicator is to give up our own responsibility. Authenticity cannot be ceded to anyone else, not demon and not angel. I give the keys to my moral palace to neither camp.

If the Methueyn Bridge could be recovered and crossed now, I would not look for my soul mate on the other side. There is no perfectly compatible, spiritually congruous angel waiting to join with *me*. I will not be god, monster, or angel. I am my *own* man, and I respect the Deladieyr

Knight more for standing on her own than the Methueyn Knight's conjoining.

But I digress. Nimrheal *must* respond to something physical. If the incomparable, euphonic sound of creation is indeed a physical phenomenon, then perhaps the demon is merely reacting to stimulus. The riposte is not moral; Nimrheal simply responds as a demon does to all things that disturb its rest.

With death.

Nimrheal seeks not to balance the scales but to destroy the beautiful, creative mind of poet, scientist, or philosopher. This relationship has dominated our history and kept us in a dark age where the development of any new thought has been stunted by death. I do not believe these killings to be any kind of justice or any law of divine physics. These killings simply represent the murder of ingenuity and the retarding of hope for better days. They were causal, not moral.

The Methueyn Knighthood can be blamed obliquely for our long-standing and deep-seated acceptance of Nimrheal. After all, if a small group of men and women could bring the word of Elysium directly to earth, might not Nimrheal do the same? That is rather a stretch, though, and assumes that the agent of hell acts with the good faith of an angel of heaven.

But it is easier for people to imagine that there must be a moral reason for everything, and the reason must be good. The reason here was *not* moral and the actor was not reasonable. Given that the knight was killed in the Methueyn War, possibly late in the war, it could even be that this murder was the last act of Nimrheal before the medium changed.

I looked again on the tableau of the dead knight, ghoulishly hung on the spear like some martial scarecrow. It was wrong. No prayers or words had been spoken by peer or loved one. Of all things, only the skolves had come to pay homage with beads and songs from other worlds. I could not say why the skolves had such a reaction to the ruin of this knight, but it moved me. Yet despite this swell of feeling, I chose not to bury the remains. I left the morbid scarecrow to continue its standing watch.

It was a harbinger of some fell warning, a herald of nothing good, but I knew not what that terrible warning was. Perhaps that ignorance was reason enough to do nothing with the corpse.

But nothing was not enough. This dead Knight must not lie here without some human recognition.

Poetry is a gift of man alone. Its lyricism puts words to music, and I imagine love, if it exists, would be a similar orchestral fusion. *This*, skolves do not do, and so this is why I composed a eulogy there and then, and with Expectation carved it into the long-dead knight's breastplate. A Methueyn Knight would want it written in steel. My eulogy said:

> "Alone on the dark road, shadow of dead,
> Herald of ruined hope, and angel's dread,
> Held tall by spear, lieth the fallen knight,
> The man and dreams crushed by Nimrheal's might.
>
> This cannot truly be all that is left,
> A lonely grave and a forgotten quest!
>
> Raise voice and shout: Redoubt Empyrean!
> I know it's echoed in Elysium!
> For even here skolves show that they revere,
> Your strength, your cause, your soul surely endures."

I carved the words as a sign of respect to the man or woman, not the angel, and walked away.

Chapter Twenty-Six

Shorts

"**F**INALLY!" HEYLOR EXCLAIMED. "WE'VE BEEN WAITING FOREVER. HEY, DO YOU KNOW you're bleeding?"

The jittery young man had an extensive list of additional questions. Why did Hemdale fight with him? How was it to fight the old knight? Did he really break a sword on him? And more in the same vein.

Endicott had no answers, none at least that he could give yet. He was exhausted, face in Koria's lap, eyes closed. But he could see Heylor and imagine him. Heylor had all the energy and restlessness that the three-year-old Robert Endicott had brimmed with. Perhaps without the death of his parents, Endicott mused, he would have grown up to be indistinguishable from the other young man.

He did not mean the comparison as an insult. Endicott loved Heylor. He loved all his classmates. He loved Bethyn, even her truculence. He loved fierce Eloise, sharp Davyn, loyal Gregory, and the defensive Deleske. Most of all, he loved Koria, his secret stalker, his protector; a woman who carried her own painful knowledge, her own terrifying memory of a future they both needed to change. But he would become a dynamicist, and no cloaked man was ever going to touch them.

▽

"CONGRATULATIONS. YOU HAVE ALL PASSED THE TEST," SAID GERVEAULT WITH THE TINIEST of smiles.

Endicott pulled himself off Koria and painfully rose to his feet. All the professors were there in the anteroom except Keith Euyn. They were all smiling. Gerveault seemed to direct his little smile straight at Endicott. "Now forget the test. Go have a very late dinner at the Lords' Commons and get some rest. Tomorrow we will show you something new."

"Bring your shorts to breakfast. Someone will meet you there," added Eleanor.

Shorts?

WHO CANNOT CHANGE THEIR MINDS CANNOT CHANGE ANYTHING

People and Places

In the story of the Lonely Wizard

The Lonely Wizard, a Deladieyr Knight and wizard of immense power

Sir Ameleyn Forteys, a Deladieyr Knight

Aungr, marshal of the army of Engevelen

Feydleyn, squire to the Lonely Wizard

Bron, a small farming town within the Duchy of Vercors

Lord Latimer, agent of the Duchess of Vercors

Robert Endicott, a young man

Meycal Endicott, Robert's father, dead

Finlay Endicott, Robert's grandfather

Grandma, Robert's grandmother

Arrayn Endicott, one of Robert's many uncles

Deryn Endicott, another of Robert's many uncles

Aunt Ellys, one of Robert's many aunts.

Ernie, an old man who works at the Bron elevator

Paul, young man who works at the Bron elevator

Mair, a young woman who works at the Bron elevator

Glynis, a young woman who works at the Bron elevator

Nyhmes, a small city in the Duchy of Vercors

Laurent, a farmer

Aeres Angelicus, owner of the Nyhmes Registered Seed Office.

Terwynn, agent of Lord Glynnis

Conor Karryk, an old bum

Vercors, the capitol city of the Duchy of Vercors

The Duke of Vercors

The Duchess of Vercors

Lord Kennyth Brice, the heir apparent to the Duchy of Vercors

Eryka Lyon, chief constable

Vard, a young man

Lynal, a young man

Syriol Lindseth, a young woman, cousin to Jeyn Lindseth

Lord Arthur Wolverton, commander of the Military School

Deladieyr Knights

Sir Hemdale, formerly a citizen of Armadale

Sir Christensen

AT THE NEW SCHOOL

Eleanor, associate professor in the Duchess's Program

Lady Gwenyfer, administrator of the Duchess's Program

Gerveault Heys, senior professor of dynamics

Keith Euyn, professor emeritus

Meredeth Callum, senior professor of mathematics

Annabelle Currik, senior professor of physics

Koria Valcourt, a student

Eloise Kyre, a student

Davyn Daly, a student

Heylor Style, a student

Lord Gregory Justice, a student

Bethyn Trail, a student

Deleske Lachlan, a student

Jeyn Lindseth, a senior student in the Military School, cousin to Syriol Lindseth

Bat Merrett, a senior student in the Military School

Eoyan March, a senior student in the Military School

Lord Jon Indulf, a student

Lord Quincy Leighton, a student

Steyphan Kenelm, a student

Jennyfer Gray, an arts student

Elyze Astarte, a dynamics researcher

Vyrnus Hedt, a dynamics researcher

METHUEYN KNIGHTS. ABSENT SINCE THE END OF THE METHUEYN WAR

Urieyn, Angel of Music. Symbol, a blazing sun. First day of the week, Ursday.

Sendeyl, Angel of Endurance. Symbol, a broken sandal. Second day of the week, Senday.

Michael, Angel of War, usually but not always male. Symbol, a great sword. Third day of the week, Michsday.

Heydron, Angel of Protection, usually but not always female. Symbol, a shield. Fourth day of the week, Heyday.

Darday'l, Angel of Knowledge. Symbol, a scroll hung on a maul. Fifth day of the week, Darday.

Volsang, Angel of Righteous Vengeance. Symbol, an axe. Sixth day of the week, Volsday.

Hervor, Angel of Warning. Symbol, a bursting horn. Seventh day of the week, Hersday.

Leylah, Angel of Night, usually female. Symbol, a crescent moon. Eighth day of the week, Leyday.

SECULAR ORDERS OF KNIGHTS

Knight of Vercors

Royal Knight of Armadale

TRANSCENDENTAL BEINGS

Nimrheal, a demon who punishes creativity. Absent since the end of the Methueyn War

Skoll, a demon who appeared in the Methueyn War

Hati, a demon who appeared in the Methueyn War

Acknowledgements

Thank you to my test readers George Fairs, Dr. Greg Arkos, Serena Provincial, Cheryl Kendall, Graham Hack, Eric Street, Julie Rowe and Wendy Ross. My wife, Lori Hunt, was a test reader as well. You might think that being my wife she would automatically give my work a glowing review, but wives are not mothers, Lori calls it as she sees it, and she dislikes the fantasy genre. I will leave what Lori had to say as a mystery. No, actually, I won't. She liked it. Shawn Crawford, psychology professor at Mount Royal University was a very helpful resource; thankfully he never seemed to tire of my questions regarding trauma. John McAllister, my editor, also showed great patience and editorial acumen. He never tired of talking about commas, proper nouns and capitalization. Not many are willing to do that, especially for fantasy novels where the author can arbitrarily and perniciously decide what noun is proper and what is not. Jared Shapiro is the person responsible for the creative typesetting of the novel and Jeff Brown designed the equally interesting and unique cover. Nimrheal would surely slay both Jared and Jeff. The last person I must thank is Lyda Mclallen. She is my marketing advisor and, beyond being quite good at her job, was fun to work with.

And thank you, reader. I am selfishly glad you took the time to read my book. Having no one read your book is like having no one to tell a joke to. It is like talking to yourself. It's okay with me if some part of the book turned out to be upsetting for you to read because some parts were upsetting to me to write. If you want to argue about something in the book, so much the better. Reading, having some contrary thought, getting into a civilized argument, those are all good things. All those things get us out of the echo-chambers of our minds.